A Jennifer Malone Mystery

Best Wishes!

John [signature]

ALSO BY JOHN SCHLARBAUM

Barry Jones' Cold Dinner – A Steve Cassidy Mystery

When Angels Fail To Fly – A Steve Cassidy Mystery

Off The Beaten Path – A Steve Cassidy Mystery

A Memorable Murder – A Jennifer Malone Mystery

Lasting Impressions

Aging Gracefully Together – A Story of Love & Marriage

The Doctor's Bag – A Sentimental Journey

ABANDONED

A Jennifer Malone Mystery

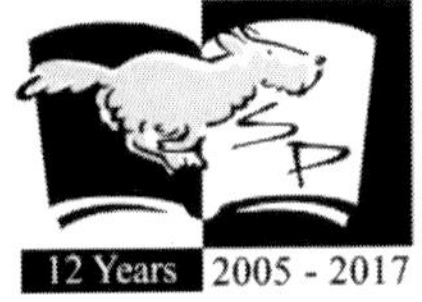

SCANNER PUBLISHING
Windsor, Ontario, Canada

ISBN: 978-0-9738498-8-2

Cover photo credit:

"Chair With Three Legs" by Miguel Ángel Avi García

See more stunning photos at:
www.flickr.com/photos/miguelangelavi/

Graphic cover formatting: Jennifer Hawksworth

Printed in Canada

Acknowledgements

Finding the right balance in a novel's storyline and its characters is a defining moment for any author. As I write the first draft my main goal is to find out how it ends. That may sound odd, but even though I have a vague idea how I'd like the story to conclude, the characters often have their own ideas. Once I'm satisfied with the second draft, it's time to give it to a trusted group of readers with no qualms about giving me the good, the bad, and the ugly on every word, page, chapter and character.

Special thanks to these friends who read each chapter as it was written. This isn't as exciting as it would seem, when you realize it might be a week, or two, or six before I sent out another 4-5 pages! It was a long process and I truly value your patience with me: Jessica Jarvis, Jennifer Laugher, Lori Wightman and Lori Farmer.

To Dorothy Schlarbaum, Jennifer Thorne, Tina Medford, Kevin Jarvis, Cathy Brooker, Priscilla Bernauer, Mary Stafford-Bocian, Irene Carson and Rebecca Bornai – I am eternally grateful for your opinions and suggestions.

For allowing me to create wonderful new characters with distinct personal traits and backgrounds, I want to thank Jennifer Grant and Beth Grant. It was a pleasure to dig a little deeper into your lives and bring your characters to life!

Also, thanks to the devoted readers who pledged their support during the Kickstarter campaign to make this book a reality!

Last, but never least, my heartfelt gratitude to Lori Huver, whose unwavering support keeps me smiling each and every day!

John Schlarbaum
November 2017

Dedication

To Hudson, Owen, Kara and Luke

The next great generation of readers!

ONE

PART I

SUNDAY

"Don't let them kill me."

It took a moment for Luke to understand what the woman had said. "No one is going to kill you, Helga, I promise," he replied with a genuine smile and short laugh, helping her onto the stretcher.

Once on her back, another concerned look came over Helga's face, as if a jolt of pain had flashed through her clouded mind. "You promise?"

As a patient transporter Luke had seen this expression countless times, not only on the anxious faces of the elderly like Helga, but also children taking the ride from the hospital's paediatric floor to the O.R. At least with the kids their equally terrified parents were present in the crammed elevator, trying to appear upbeat, although they weren't always successful in this regard. Patients above the age of thirty and more so senior citizens, were typically by themselves when Luke arrived at their room to whisk them away, often for tests they weren't aware had been scheduled. Most knew a surgical procedure was to be done, if for no other reason than their food and drink consumption had been cut off at midnight. The majority of the older transfers went down without any relatives or friends present, which Luke hated to see. It added pressure on him, as it meant he'd be the last non-surgical employee the patient would interact with before going under the knife.

"Yes, I promise," Luke said as he wheeled the stretcher to the nurse's station to pick up Helga's medical chart.

"Helga, you'll be back in no time with a brand new hip. How exciting," Stephanie, the daytime nurse for room 8103, said cheerfully, bringing a mild smirk to Helga's face. "Good luck."

"At this stage, it's not about luck, is it, Helga?" Luke broke in with a huge smile as he placed the chart beneath the edge of the mattress. "It's about skill!" Before stepping to the rear of the stretcher out of her view, he briefly rested his hand on Helga's arm and added, "We got this, right?"

Helga finally grinned widely, allowing the tension in her facial expressions to dissipate, if only for a second. "Yes. No luck is required today. We got this."

The old woman's use of modern terminology brought laughter to two nurses sitting at a nearby desk. "She's such a sweetheart," one of them said.

Luke inserted his key in a wall lock and hit the down button. "A special elevator for a special lady."

The elevator door opened and Luke pushed the stretcher into the small space, then hit "G" on the keypad. Once they were moving, he stepped to the side wall in order to speak with Helga face to face. "I noticed on your wristband that you were born in 1928. That's quite a while ago. Have you lived around here all this time?"

Luke had learned that during these short trips to the hospital's various departments and wings, this question was a good one, as it immediately focused the patient on a topic they loved to talk about: themselves.

The unexpected inquiry had its desired effect.

"Oh no, I was sent to this country when I was ten," Helga replied in a nostalgic tone. "I was born in Berlin, Germany."

"Wow, ten years old leading up to World War II. Those must have been some crazy times," Luke said. "I wasn't a big history fan in school, but I'm sure your stories would give me a new appreciation of what was really going on." The elevator came to a smooth stop as Luke inquired, "Did your family get out of Germany prior to the war?"

The lines on Helga's weary face again hardened. "Just my brother and me."

The elevator door opened, abruptly ending the conversation, as Luke still had a job to do and Helga had a surgery appointment.

"From the penthouse to the ground floor," Luke chirped as he guided Helga's stretcher down the O.R. corridor. "You know ... if you're feeling up to it, I can pop in to talk with you later. Would that be all right?"

Helga had zoned Luke out, as she stared at the cold and heartless hallway before them. This wasn't her first rodeo, as her young nurse had commented, but it was very different. The card attached to the flowers in her room made certain of that. The same message had been sent with another bouquet to her house the previous year, on the morning of a traumatic and life changing meeting. Its meaning wasn't intended to bring a smile to her face then, or now.

All the best, Helga! See you soon!

As Luke tried to keep her mind off the surgery, when she'd be unconscious and defenceless against a perceived attack, Helga scanned the faces of the people in the various waiting rooms they passed, as well as anyone in scrubs.

She knew they were here.

"I present to you: Ms. Helga," Luke announced to two nurses, as he positioned the stretcher against the wall and applied the brake. "She's all yours."

"Thanks, Luke," one of the nurses said as she took the medical chart from him. "We'll take good care of her."

"Excellent," he replied, stepping to the foot of the stretcher. "Now just relax. I hope I'll be the one dispatched to take you back to your room."

Helga held Luke's warm gaze, ignoring the nurses as they

began to fuss with her in preparation for her surgery.

"Remember what I said, Luke," Helga whispered, "because you're the only one who'll know later on."

Luke gave Helga a quizzical look, the way you respond to a child learning how to talk, or in this case, a crazy elderly patient hopped up on drugs to combat the pain of a broken hip. "I will, don't worry. You'll be fine."

Luke walked out of the room and called the Admitting department on his radio. "Luke here. That patient from eight is down in O.R."

"Okay, thanks," came the bored reply of the female clerk. "There's nothing on the board."

Luke put the radio in the front pocket of his scrub top and simultaneously pulled out his cell phone to check his email. As he passed the O.R. Family Waiting Room, he heard a man with a thick accent say, "She just went in. What do you want me to do?" Luke slowed to see who was talking, thinking one of Helga's relatives or friends had shown up in her time of need. Unfortunately, his eyes were greeted with the backs of three men, one at the payphone and the others on their cell phones in conversation. He would occasionally stop and say a few words to reassure the waiting party, but not knowing which of the men he'd overheard, or if they were even discussing Helga, Luke returned his attention to a new message from his girlfriend with the subject line: You!

"Hi, Luke?" his work radio squawked. "Can you get some labs on 4 West and then you can go on break?"

"I can, thanks."

Making his way to the elevator he again wandered by the waiting room and noticed that two of the men he'd seen previously were watching the television hanging on the wall. The third man, an older grey-haired gentleman wearing an overcoat, was no longer present.

Probably went for a coffee, he assumed.

Luke unlocked the express elevator and the door opened obediently. Inside, he pressed the "4" button.

"And here we go," he said to the walls, "another action filled adventure starts now."

As if on cue, the elevator doors closed and sent the happy-go-lucky employee on his way, unaware that within the hour Helga would be dead.

TWO

"Malone!" Mitch Carson called out into the newsroom bullpen. "When you're done gossiping about the new Liam Neeson movie with Cassie, can you give me an update on the Mayville story?"

Jennifer Malone gave a dismissive wave of her hand in the direction of her boss. "Give me a minute, Dad. This is like very important girl talk time," she said, continuing her discussion with the paper's Lifestyle section editor, who doubled as the relationship columnist under the penname Ms. Love.

Also ignoring Carson's intrusion, Cassie Hendricks leaned forward and asked Jennifer in a low tone, "So that was the end of the date?"

"Not exactly," Jennifer smiled. "A girl's gotta eat, right?"

"You let him buy you dinner, knowing he wasn't the one?"

"He was the one, just not the long-term one." Jennifer gave Cassie a little wink and grabbed a manila folder off the desk marked *Mayville*. "It was fun while it lasted, trust me."

Cassie laughed. "When you do find true love you won't know what to do with yourself – let alone him."

"I'll know what to do. He'll be the one needing to catch up."

Jennifer stood and made her way into Carson's office. He was giving her a strange look as she entered.

"Boy trouble again, Malone?"

Jennifer took a seat across from the desk, crossed her legs and folded her hands over the file folder. "What do you mean by 'again'?"

"Oh sorry – I meant *still*."

"That's more like it," Jennifer said. "There are simply no quality men in this city for me."

Carson relaxed back in his chair and put both hands behind his head. "What was this last sap's fatal flaw? Wasn't he a stock broker – someone smart?"

"He was, although I don't know how he achieved such a brainy position with his limited musical background."

There was a pause as Carson shifted and began to shake his head, closing his eyes as in disbelief. "Are you for real?"

"Seriously, who doesn't like The Beatles?" Jennifer replied, exasperated.

Carson opened his eyes. "Did he come out and say, 'I hate The Beatles' or was it along the lines of, 'I'm a Rolling Stones fan'?"

"Had he said *that*, he wouldn't have got to first base."

Carson cracked a smile. "Why are the Fab Four your litmus test for finding Mr. Perfect? Their final album was released in 1970 – a full decade and a half before you were born. Shouldn't you be asking if he likes Def Leppard or Nirvana instead? Pearl Jam, maybe? What about Phil Collins?"

Jennifer gave her superior a withering look. "It's a sign of respect to be familiar with such things, Mitch. You should know – you lived through that era ... cause, well ... you're old."

"No comment."

"You need further proof? This guy thought Eleanor Rigby was Jude's mother."

Carson burst out laughing. "Enough said. He's not a good fit for anyone."

"Thank you. I knew you'd eventually see it my way."

Carson sat straight and shuffled through papers on top of his desk. "Returning to planet Earth ... what's happening with the Honey Mayville story? Have you tracked her down?"

Jennifer opened the folder on her lap and reviewed its contents. Twenty-three-year-old Becky Mayville, aka Honey, aka Hot Beckster, aka Councilman Roger Tilley's whore mistress, was on the lam from the media and Mrs. Tilley. "I've got a few feelers out on the street that I hope will pan out. When the price is right, she won't stop talking, even if you want her to. Word is a 'classy dame' she's not, though the term 'gold digger' comes up a lot."

Carson looked disappointed. "Splendid." He handed Jennifer a piece of paper. "Until she surfaces, I want you to go to Met Hospital and speak with the coroner about that body they fished out of the river a couple days ago. They haven't identified the guy, but if you can get some newsworthy tidbits for tomorrow's Metro section, that would be great."

Jennifer glanced at the facts Carson had provided: Caucasian male, mid-twenties, fully clothed, no wallet, foul play? "Who found him?"

"Couple of joggers out for a run. The coroner might have their names, if you're eager to find them for a statement."

"Did any of the Metro hacks take a shot at this?" Jennifer asked as she stood to leave.

"Shields was going to, then his mother got sick and he didn't come in today," Carson replied.

"Figures. He's such a momma's boy." Jennifer stepped out into the bullpen. "I'm on it."

"Oh, while we're on the topic of mothers," Carson interjected. "Jude's mother – wasn't that Lady Madonna?"

Jennifer stopped and turned to face Carson, who was wearing a huge grin. "That is why you and I don't date. And believe me, you're missing out on something special."

"If you do say so yourself," Carson countered, jotting down a note on his assignment sheet.

"Oh, I do."

***

Jennifer never tired of she and Carson's platonic flirtations and entertaining tête-à-têtes. In another time and place, maybe they would have gone out for drinks. As it was, the seventeen-year age gap was a tad too wide. She could wait a few years to become the trophy wife of a distinguished pre-senior citizen. At thirty-three she still enjoyed enticing males her own age – or better yet, younger ones, but not too much younger. Her current cut-off age was twenty-eight. At this stage in her potential husband's life, his education was finished, student loans were paid off, a clear career path was established, and he'd be dying to shower a girl of her stature with all the attention she deserved, and often craved. Cassie was always warning her that being a serial dater would lead to a houseful of neutered and spayed cats and no gentleman callers.

Jennifer had no response to this scenario and continued to hope for the best, enjoying her single status as long as possible.

"One day," she kept telling herself.

On this particular day, Jennifer hadn't accomplished a lot. She attributed this to working a Sunday against her will, due to the new owner's edict that reporters be scheduled one weekend a month to *keep things fresh*. "There's news happening, or there isn't, no matter who's available to write it," argued the crotchety old scribes accustomed to their regular Monday-Friday gigs.

Jennifer stopped at her desk to get her reporter's notebook and walked two blocks (instead of the normal ten on weekdays) to her car for the short trip to Metropolitan Hospital. The early evening mugginess that had blanketed the city for days was keeping people indoors, including the petty street criminals, or so said the Police Chief. For Jennifer this news didn't hold much sway, as she'd always felt comfortable when walking alone and travelling by herself on the subway. Part of her strength was her intimidating glare, even when wearing her usual short, fashionable business dresses and low-heeled shoes. These clothes represented her outer armour, regardless of the flimsy material they were made of, but it was her steely, no-nonsense, 'Don't you dare think of approaching me, punk,' stance that sealed the deal. Years earlier, after her roommate was assaulted while on a pub crawl, Jennifer attended a free self-defence class the college offered and took the instructor's words to heart: "Keep your head up and eyes forward," he'd advised. "Look like you belong."

Although this wisdom had no doubt kept her safe on the mean streets, Jennifer often wondered if it had also deterred prospective suitors from approaching her for a date. *Maybe I should tone down my attitude when out socially. Otherwise, I'll soon be assembling carpet covered scratching posts throughout the apartment,* she thought, as she parked in front of the hospital, and then walked into the lobby to the security desk.

"Can I help you?" the petite female officer in her early twenties asked, looking up from her smartphone where her Twitter feed was displayed.

"Hi, my name is Jennifer Malone from *The Daily Telegraph* newspaper. I'm here to speak with the coroner. I believe his last name is Richmond or possibly Singh."

"Oh, hi," the guard replied, brightening up. "Can I just say that I love your work? I'm a journalism student – second year." She looked to her left and then her right. "I'm only doing this job for the money until I graduate. I'm Maryanne, by the way," she said, eagerly extending her hand for Jennifer to shake.

"Ah, a fan," Jennifer said, giving her admirer a quick handshake.

Maryanne removed her hand and stood, pointing to a nearby corridor by the Admitting area. "The Coroner's office is next to the morgue, down this hall to your left. As for who is in, it could be either Martin Richmond or Alpa Singh."

"I was close," Jennifer said with a smile, acknowledging her mistake. "Always double check your information before asking a question. I hope they still teach that old gem. I might have skipped that class."

"It's not your fault," Maryanne offered. "Generally, hospitals have one coroner, but we currently have two as Dr. Richmond is retiring this week. Dr. Singh is his replacement."

"Oh. I suppose one can only take seeing so many dead people before wanting to hit the beach to watch a bunch of live bodies parade by."

"Precisely," Maryanne concurred.

Jennifer took a step away from the desk. "Thanks for the information, Maryanne. Maybe I'll see you at the paper in the future."

"Do you think so? Next semester is my co-op and I was going to apply to *The Telegraph*."

Jennifer looked into the wide eyes of her fan. "Tell you what – send me your school's required paperwork and I'll deliver it to my editor."

"Mitch Carson?"

"Wow, you are a true *Telegraph* believer. But yes, I'll forward your application to Mr. Carson."

"I don't know what to say."

"Say you won't make me look bad."

"I won't!"

"With that settled, I'm off to see a dead guy and his keeper," Jennifer said as she walked toward the hallway. "Take care, Maryanne – and follow me on Twitter."

Maryanne was astonished as she realized that during their short conversation Jennifer Malone – THE Jennifer Malone – had noted her social media activity. "I hope I'm that observant when I'm a reporter," she said, as she again sat at her desk to search for Jennifer's page.

From previous visits, Jennifer knew the hospital's ground floor was a labyrinth designed to test the best maze runners. The wall signage listed too many departments, followed by small arrows pointing in every direction. The coloured lines on the floors and walls were equally useless to the majority of patients and their caregivers. By sheer will of perseverance, Jennifer navigated through the bland painted hallways, past the E.R. entrance, to a non-descript area by the rear loading docks. Although she was in the right corridor, she decided to ask a male in his early twenties wearing blue scrubs walking in her direction.

"Where are you headed?" he asked with a knowing grin before Jennifer could form her words into a question.

Cute smile. Nice hair. Hot body in scrubs.

"Am I that obviously lost?" she said returning his smile. "Luke, is it?" she added reading his nametag.

"It is," he said, now standing in front of the attractive blonde. He could smell her perfume and was curious. "Your perfume."

Someone as on the ball as me – check.

"Oh, is there a problem with it?"

"No," Luke stammered slightly. "It's just ...."

"That it's a man's cologne?"

"Yes. Fahrenheit, right?"

"Now it's my turn to say, 'it is'," Jennifer replied. "The hospital didn't go all scent-free since the last time I was here, did it?"

"When was that?"

"Two months ago."

"The bad news is the policy is two *years* old," Luke said. "The good news is that it's more of a suggestion than an enforceable rule."

"So I'm safe?"

"I'm not going to say anything."

"I thought maybe I was sentenced to walk these hallways until the scent was sufficiently undetectable. Only then could I speak with the coroner."

"Richmond or Singh?"

"I don't know. My editor was heavy on assigning me this mission, yet light on actual details."

"No worries. Let's find out who's in."

Luke stepped away from Jennifer and peered into an office window partially obstructed by a vertical blind. Pressing his hands together and leaning against the glass, Luke said, "Looks like ... Alpa is on duty today."

Luke's work radio crackled to life.

"Hey, Luke, Rob will meet you upstairs for that back door call."

"I'm getting the cart now." He placed the radio back in his pocket.

"Back door? What's that?" Jennifer inquired, unfamiliar with the term. "For your sake, I hope it doesn't involve going to the proctologist's exam room."

Luke laughed. "Ah, no ... kind of the opposite. Back door means the morgue, which is where I was headed to get the body cart to transfer a patient."

"Oh my god," Jennifer said flustered. "I didn't mean to hold you up."

"Trust me, there's no real rush for this call."

Luke let the implication hang in the air.

It doesn't even faze him anymore. Jennifer knew cops and paramedics who had the same attitude toward the deceased. She now regretted her earlier snide remark to Maryanne. "Of course not," she managed to say.

"So ... I think Dr. Singh is performing an autopsy," Luke began, trying nonchalantly to change the subject, "which is in the same section as the morgue. It's down here by the linen carts."

"Okay," Jennifer said, following Luke. "Besides being the Cart Pusher of Death, what's your job title?"

"Patient Transporter, or porter for short."

"It must be awesome to wear scrubs every shift."

"Yeah, it's kind of like wearing pyjamas to work." Luke took out a key ring to unlock a door marked G1098. "Come on in."

On the right was a large table top attached to one wall, while the other wall consisted of four stainless steel, ground-to-ceiling doors. Next to them was a dry erase board listing shelf numbers and the corresponding names of the recently departed.

"It's smaller than I thought it would be," Jennifer stated.

"With five hospitals within an eight block radius, each with their own morgue, this one seems about right size-wise," Luke said, as he pressed an intercom button on the wall. "Dr. Singh, are you in? It's Luke. There's a visitor out here for you."

A couple seconds later, Dr. Singh replied, "Who is it?"

Luke held down the button again and said, "I don't really know."

"It's Jennifer Malone, Dr. Singh. I'm a reporter with *The Telegraph,* here about the John Doe."

Luke let go of the button. "Do you have a card? One of the guards here wants to be a reporter–"

"And you'd rack up some goodwill points, right?"

"Something like that," Luke smiled, taking Jennifer's card from her.

"Here's a second one for your goodwill collection," Jennifer said, offering another card. In similar situations she'd have written her cell number on it and suggested the recipient call to discuss how the world worked over drinks, but she didn't get the vibe Luke was interested.

He's doing his job, leave him be, she chastised herself.

"I'll be out in a minute," Dr. Singh reported back.

Jennifer surveyed her sterile surroundings. "I'm going to wait in the hallway. I saw a chair against the wall."

"That's your best bet." Luke opened the door and let Jennifer out, deciding not to go into the rules against civilians being alone in the morgue. "It smells nicer out there too, if only marginally," he said re-entering the room.

Several moments later, Luke propped the door open and pushed the body cart into the hall, locking the door behind him.

"That's a fancy cart," Jennifer said, noting the elevated canvas cover top featuring butterflies painted on it.

"It's not much, but most of the patients and visitors who see it don't realize what it contains, which is a good thing. They might freak out otherwise." Luke stepped on the stretcher's steer lever and continued toward a service elevator. "If Rob and I don't get back here before you leave, it was nice meeting you."

"It was nice meeting you too, Luke."

Jennifer took her seat and watched as a cleaning lady up the hallway wiped down a stretcher, and then put on a bottom sheet, blanket and pillow for use in the E.R. Even though she tried to give off a devil-may-care attitude, in this environment Jennifer saw how fragile life could be and she didn't like it.

An ambulance being backed into the nearby E.R. bay was not helping. Soon, paramedics removed a patient wearing an oxygen mask laying on an industrial-sized stretcher that was swiftly pushed through the hospital doors.

"Jennifer Malone?"

Startled, Jennifer jumped from her chair and glared at Dr. Singh, an East Indian female who might stand four foot ten ... if barely.

"Is that what passes as morgue humour?" Jennifer cried out, clutching her chest. "You almost gave me a heart attack!"

Without missing a beat, Dr. Singh replied, "If that were the case, I'd call for Luke to take you to the cardiac wing. They are top notch up there."

Jennifer stared at the tiny woman in the bright white smock and took a deep breath to calm her nerves. "I got so involved in the drama outside – a paramedic jumped on top of the patient's chest and rode them into the E.R. on a stretcher. It was like a rodeo tryout. I didn't hear you come out."

"It's okay, dear. I sneak up on a lot of people. What can I do – it's genetics."

The tension broken, both laughed.

"I feel so stupid," Jennifer admitted. "I'm usually not this jittery, Dr. Singh."

"This isn't a good place to relax. The only perks are high-grade prescription drugs and warm blankets. At least that's what I've heard Luke tell the patients he transports from room to room."

"That doesn't include the dead ones, right?"

Dr. Singh looked back at the spot in the morgue where the body cart was regularly parked. "I don't think so, but you never know with part-timers. Please, let's go to my office where it's less stressful."

"Deal."

THREE

PART II

GENIFER

As she hung up the phone, Genifer felt sick. The fact that her two children were running in the living room acting out an imaginary scene for the next *Iron Man* movie didn't help.

"Tony Stark would be nothing without me, Miss Everhart, and you can quote me on that for your *Vanity Fair* article," 11-year-old Zoe declared loudly, stomping her left foot on the floor and placing her hands on her hips for emphasis.

Her younger sister of two years, Aleena, looked incredulous, not believing, or more likely understanding, the implication of such a bold statement. "I'll ... ah ... *quote* whoever I feel like *quoting*, Pepper Potts! You don't own me and ... and ... for your information, Tony only has eyes for me – not some silly girl who just hangs around his cool apartment!" Mimicking Zoe's stance, Aleena raised her right hand and proclaimed, "One day I'll be Mrs. Tony Stark and you're only going to have a dog to keep you company!"

Zoe was unimpressed and turned to her father to be the tie-breaking opinion. "What do you think, Dad?"

Seated in his recliner a few feet away, Stan was oblivious to any activity, as his eyes were fixated on the television mounted on the far wall. His beloved Minnesota Vikings were on the verge of beating the loathed Detroit Lions with one second left on the clock. "Kick the damn ball already!" he implored, as the placekicker paced off distance from where the ball should land *if* the ball holder actually caught it from the snap – an action he'd failed to do on two earlier field goal attempts.

The Grant living room went silent as all eyes tilted upward when the football was sent into the hands of the placeholder, who mishandled it, then stood upright and began to run toward the goal line seven yards away ... only to trip over his feet, stumble onto the back of one of his blockers and fumble the football.

"ARE YOU KIDDING ME?" Stan called out, exploding out of his chair, as a sure-handed Lions' defender scooped the ball off the ground and started running in the opposite direction. "Why? Why? Why?"

"With no time left on the clock, 335-pound Malcolm Harris will win this game if he can survive the 93-yard sprint laid out in front of him," the play-by-play announcer said excitedly. "If he does, this will be another heartbreaking loss for the Vikings."

The screen went black as Stan hit the OFF button on the remote and walked out of the room, his face fire engine red with the added bonus of engorged blood vessels protruding from his temples.

"Is the game over, Dad? Did we win?" Aleena asked innocently, more a soccer fan than a football one, to her father's chagrin. "Did that man score a touchdown?"

"Aleena!" Zoe snapped at her. "Don't you know anything?"

Stan gave a grunt and was out the back door, stomping his way across the lawn to their detached garage, where his beer fridge was waiting to offer him sanctuary from a world gone mad.

"Will Dad be okay, Mom?" Zoe asked.

Genifer sighed, "In time."

"Will you be okay?" Zoe followed up.

Genifer gave her an odd look before feeling faint and blacking out.

"Mom?" Aleena asked as she watched her collapse, knocking over the nearby table and sending the phone crashing to the floor. "MOM!"

Zoe was by her mother's side, lifting her head off the hardwood floor. "Go get Dad," she said in a calm voice to her frightened sister. "Mom'll be fine. Go, Aleena. Dad will know what to do."

Aleena looked into her sister's reassuring eyes, and like all younger siblings trusted that what she said was true. "Okay," she replied and ran through the kitchen and outside. "Dad, come back inside! Mom's hurt!"

Zoe could tell that her mother was alive by the rise and fall of her chest. "I'm here, Mom. I won't leave you, even in the ambulance."

At these words, Genifer began to shift slightly. "Ambulance?" she muttered, incoherently.

"The paramedics will help you get better on the way to the hospital, the way they do on the *Emergency Now* show."

"Hospital?"

Stan burst into the room to see his wife splayed across the floor and his daughter placing a throw pillow under Genifer's head. "Is she breathing, Zoe?"

"Yes and talking a bit, but she's really out of it."

"She seemed fine after you turned off the TV, then I saw her face go white and she ...." Aleena couldn't continue and started to cry. "She isn't going to die, is she?"

"No, Bean," Stan said. "She's just tired and couldn't stand anymore. Do me a favour and go to the washroom for a facecloth please. Run some cold water over it first. Can you do that for me, kiddo?"

With superhero-like speed, Aleena sprang into action and bolted down the hallway.

"You're doing good, Zoe," Stan said to his daughter who was fighting back her own tears. She gave him a frail, yet appreciative smile as he grabbed the phone.

"911. What is your emergency?"

"My wife collapsed and is going in and out of consciousness. We need to get her to the hospital."

For the second time, Genifer seemed to rouse from her semi-coma state. "No hospital," she mumbled weakly. "I can't go there. They're going to kill that lady."

"What did she say?" Stan asked Zoe, as Genifer slipped back into unconsciousness.

"It had to do with the hospital. Like, 'I can't go there. They're going to fill that baby.' What does that mean?"

"I don't know, sweetie. She's hallucinating," Stan said, shaking his head as he refocused his thoughts to the 911 operator. "How long before the ambulance arrives?"

"I've dispatched the first responders. They should be there shortly," came the reply.

"Thank you," Stan said, terminating the call. Looking at Zoe, he said, "Can you see what happened to Aleena? Then go into our bedroom for some overnight clothes for your mother – her pyjamas, housecoat and slippers."

"Will her Minions pyjamas be okay for the hospital?" Zoe asked, thinking of her mom's favourite gift from the previous Christmas.

Stan smiled. "She'd like those a lot."

Zoe scampered out of the room, calling Aleena's name.

Stan sat beside Genifer and stroked her hair, hoping his recent outburst hadn't played any role in her collapse.

"My dad told me that being a Vikings' fan would be the death of me, Genifer, not you," he said half-jokingly, terrified of losing his wife. "Can you hear me?" There was no visible reaction on her face. "Hold on, babe. We'll be at the hospital real soon."

With the sound of sirens getting louder outside, Stan stepped away and opened the front door. "They're here, Genifer. Hold on a little longer."

Genifer stirred, as sunlight from the open door stretched across the floor and into her eyes. Hearing a stretcher being unloaded from the ambulance, she made a feeble request that no one would ever hear: "No ... hospital."

***

It had been a long afternoon and evening for Genifer, as hospital staff endlessly poked, prodded and measured her every vital sign, plus a CAT scan. Through it all Genifer didn't complain, answering every question regarding her diet, sleep habits, headache issues or other health irregularities.

"We may need to call Dr. House in for a consultation," Maggie, the E.R. nurse, said, referencing the popular television character who specialized in tricky cases. "All your tests were negative."

Genifer knew they would be, and could have saved the health system a lot of time and money. She was fully aware of what had triggered her fainting spell, but didn't dare divulge the information to anyone.

If only I had fallen without an audience present, she thought.

Thankful that her children were in the care of her mom and her friend Lisa, and with Stan getting a coffee, Genifer lay listlessly on the E.R. stretcher, jumping whenever she heard an urgent-sounding announcement on the hospital speakers.

"What's a Code white?" she anxiously asked Maggie, who was examining the heart monitor attached to the wall.

"An unruly patient is causing trouble," Maggie said.

"And Code pink?"

"That's a medical emergency dealing with an infant."

"What if an adult – say, an elderly adult - needs help?"

Maggie adjusted the oxygen mask level and began, "We don't have different codes for different age groups. An adult is anyone over 18. And if they stop breathing, it's a Code blue."

"I heard a Code blue announcement a minute ago," Genifer said alarmed.

"Oh yes, I heard that too," the nurse replied calmly, "but it was cancelled."

"Meaning what?"

Maggie noted that her patient's heart rate and blood pressure were rising with each question. "Genifer, is there anything wrong? You seem very stressed."

Genifer took a deep breath. "I have an elderly friend who came into the hospital with a broken hip and I wanted to find out how she's doing."

"Let me check. What's her name?"

"It's Helga ... Klemens," Genifer said, not totally certain. If the woman's house was a regular delivery stop, Genifer would have probably been able to supply more personal information than Helga's family. Genifer loved the people on her postal route and they loved her. Fun and bubbly, Genifer was often the best part of some homeowners' day, especially senior citizens who enjoyed engaging in any topic in the short time it took to hand them their mail. Fate had Helga living two blocks north of Genifer's route, making her a complete stranger until her fall.

Maggie handed Genifer a foam cup. "Drink some of this and relax. I'll find out what's going on with your friend."

Genifer took a sip of ice water, watching as Maggie sat in front of a desk computer and began to tap keys. She saw the nurse's brow furrow before walking back to the examination room with a smile on her face.

"The computer shows that Helga is in surgery. She could already be out. Sometimes the status isn't quite up to date."

"That's a relief," Genifer said, relaxing her body into the stretcher. "I was worried something might have happened to her."

Maggie gave Genifer a questioning look. "Broken hips and the elderly don't make good dance partners. Plus, she lives alone and will need a lot of help in the coming weeks."

Genifer had no idea if Helga lived alone, or if the old man she saw running away from the house at the time was Helga's husband, brother or friend. The minutes between Genifer hearing Helga screaming through an open window and when the ambulance arrived were confusing at best. She was enjoying a leisurely mid-morning walk one minute, and the next she was entering a house to find an elderly woman with a broken hip at the bottom of a flight of stairs.

With the adrenaline rush she'd been experiencing, there wasn't time to process who the mystery man was and his possible role in Helga's fall. Helga certainly hadn't mentioned him to Genifer, the paramedics or the nice police officer.

Although Genifer had barely glimpsed the grey-haired gentleman, who was inexplicably wearing a tan overcoat, she believed she could identify him again if their paths crossed.

Clearly, and frighteningly, the man believed the same thing. Why else would he call Genifer at home a few hours later?

"You did not see me today, Mrs. Grant," the thick accented voice had warned.

Staring at the big screen television as her Detroit Lions were lining up against her hubby's Minnesota Vikings, Genifer had been distracted and said, "What did you say? Who is this? I think you have the wrong number."

Undeterred, the man had gone on. "This is the right number. What we're going to do to Helga is the same thing we'll do to your lovely girls, Zoe and Aleena, if you breathe a word of seeing me earlier. One dead old woman isn't worth risking your precious babies' lives, is it?" The caller had paused, then added, "Are we clear, Genifer?"

Genifer had immediately hung up the phone and tried to process what the man had said. She had watched in silence as her girls role-played characters from the *Iron Man* movies and her husband bit a fingernail as the Vikings attempted a field goal.

The family life she knew and loved had continued to swirl around her body, yet her mind was in a suspended state of shock. It was only when Stan had walked out of the house, breaking the tension in the room, that Genifer had felt sick.

"Will Dad be okay, Mom?" Zoe had asked.

"In time," she had managed to answer.

The last words Genifer had remembered before hitting the floor were, "Will you be okay?" and "Mom?"

In the ambulance, she had recalled a garbled conversation with Zoe about wanting to avoid the hospital. Something about 'filling a baby'.

It had been too much for her.

Stan had followed the ambulance in his car and was with Genifer as they wheeled her into the Metropolitan Hospital E.R. department.

"Where are Zoe and Aleena? Did they come with you? Don't let them out of your sight, Stan."

Stan could see the panic on Genifer's face and figured it was a by-product of her fainting spell, as well as being disoriented. "Your mom and Lisa rushed over and are going to take them to a matinee, then dinner at the mall," Stan reassured her. "I'll call them once we find out what's wrong with you."

There's nothing wrong with me! Genifer had fumed internally. "Good," she had said instead. "They'll be safe at the mall with all those shoppers."

As the admitting nurse had begun to pepper her and Stan with medical history questions, Genifer, in the same way Helga had, appraised her surroundings looking for anyone who seemed out of place. Regrettably, every race, sex and age group was represented in the nearby waiting area.

Is overcoat man already here?

A cold spike of fear ran up Genifer's spine.

It wouldn't take long for her to find out.

FOUR

TRILLIA

Trillia Johnston had struggled all her adult life to come to terms with the choices she'd made since high school. Never the classic beauty by definition, she'd been a popular student, particularly with the boys who liked tall, lanky and well-endowed dirty blondes. Her string of boyfriends during her teen years and one semester at university should have, but hadn't, prepared her for the following two decades of romances found and lost, then found and lost again. Her love life had turned out to be an unmitigated failure: married to a struggling musician; divorced; engaged to an equally inept novelist who left her at the altar in a wedding dress that couldn't conceal her pregnancy; and finally, being widowed when her absent-minded husband mechanic didn't lock off a lift being used to remove a beater's engine, which promptly landed on his chest as he was outstretched on the shop's floor.

Despite these crushing heartbreaks, Trillia had survived and thrived in the areas that would define her as a good mother, a respected career woman and a loyal friend. Her daughter, Harmony Jane, had finished a two-year business administration course and was seeking marketing opportunities with local radio and television stations in Lunsden, a mid-sized city five hours away.

At *The Buckster Stops Here* liquidation store where she'd worked for nine years, Trillia had recently been promoted to Assistant Junior Manager. The new title required her to carry out additional duties, like staff scheduling, which added 3-4 hours to her own work week. At first she was upset, until she figured out as a salaried employee she could streamline the store's operation and work fewer hours for more money. However, two pays into this lofty position had revealed the complete opposite. When she considered returning to her old position, she was told she'd be forced to leave the *Buckster* family. "We don't employ quitters here," the Junior Manager had replied in a harsh tone.

"Is that legal? Can they do that? I heard a radio commercial where a woman was in the same situation and she hired this law office to fight for her." Elaine Stanton drank a mouthful of her tepid green tea, as Trillia joined her at the kitchen table. "I don't remember the firm's name, but I'm certain any lawyer could help you out, Trill. Maybe they would do it *pro bono*."

"I doubt any lawyer truly works for free, unless I killed the store owner, then maybe," Trillia said with a sigh, as she lifted her cup to her lips, inhaling the birthday cake flavoured coffee before taking a sip. "This is tasty. I might buy another box tomorrow, *'cause once they're gone, they're gone forever*," she laughed, having repeated the store's signature slogan.

"That's the problem with liquidation places. The shelves are jammed with items the public has already deemed not good. It's like buying last year's unfashionable clothes at the close-out stores at the mall. Every month there's a new pile of jeans and tops at half price," Elaine said. "I don't know how they can do that."

Trillia smiled. "Two words: tax breaks. I've learned all about them since getting my promotion." She pushed her mug toward Elaine. "Take this coffee, for instance. The company that makes it decides it's not going to be a money maker and stops production. Unfortunately, they have 100,000 single-serve cups collecting dust in the warehouse. They then write off the inventory as an expense and sell it to stores like *Bucky's* for ten cents a cup. *Bucky's* then turns around and sells it at sixty cents a cup!"

"What? That's like a 40% profit," Elaine said shaking her head. "I wish I owned a *Bucky's* store, instead of working in the hospital kitchen. I'd be rich."

"You would if you got your employees to work extra hours for free, like me." Trillia stood and walked to her purse on the counter, where she retrieved two $20 bills, which she handed to Elaine. "Here's the money for the flowers. Are you positive they got to Jake's aunt's room?"

Elaine shoved the bills into her pocket. "I delivered them on my break. A dozen yellow carnations. She was asleep when I came in the room and I left them on the window sill."

"Thank you. I'll let Jake know," Trillia said, relieved. "Did you remember to make out the card? Jake was adamant the message be word for word."

"'All the best, Helga! See you soon!' as requested. I wrote it myself so there weren't any mistakes. I don't get why Jake didn't want his name on it."

"He said she would know who they were from," Trillia said.

"So," Elaine began, "when am I going to meet this new mystery man? Are you hiding him for some reason? I swear I'll be nice."

Trillia took a final mouthful of coffee and put the empty cup in the sink. "You will," she lied. "He's got a lot of meetings all over the country in the next few weeks and can't drop them to see little ol' me."

Taking the cue that their coffee visit was coming to a close, Elaine finished her tea and placed her mug by Trillia's. "But he hasn't seen you in person. What if he's a she? You've watched *Catfish*. It happens all the time on that show with internet hook-ups."

"The difference is that I've talked to Jake using video messaging, unlike the idiots on *Catfish* who only text or chat online."

"Sure you've talked, but haven't *felt* him yet," Elaine said playfully.

"I will in the near future," Trillia replied. "Love and travel schedules take time to work out, that's all."

Elaine gave Trillia a hug and they walked to the back door. "Have a great day. I need to get ready for my afternoon shift."

Trillia held open the door as Elaine stepped off the porch. "Can you check on Jake's aunt with her nurse and give me a call later?"

"I'll give you a shout after my rounds. I'm on dinner tray delivery duties, so I'll be on the eighth floor anyway."

"Perfect. We're doing inventory tonight, so leave a message on my cell phone if I don't answer."

Trillia waved to Elaine as she walked across their shared driveway and into her house. Trillia was glad she had such a good neighbour to talk with on a daily basis, even if their one common thread was bad luck with men. Elaine kept saying she was in a loveless marriage, but never made plans to leave her husband Bruce, despite the fact they had no children or substantial wealth to divide. Elaine was now living vicariously through Trillia's life in the dating world. From the moment Jake's name was spoken, Elaine's interest hit an all-time high.

"You better not be holding back any juicy details, girlfriend," she'd warned one morning.

"I'm not," came Trillia's modest protest.

Of course her on-going affair with Jake was a big lie, at least in the conventional sense. He did exist and over the past year had professed his undying love for her in emails, letters and cards. And Trillia had heard his voice, knew his speech patterns and what he looked like. She even had an opinion of how long his sandy brown hair should be for optimal hotness.

By the end of his televised murder trial with its guilty verdict, she was convinced that she'd found her soul mate.

The hard part was finding a way to make this relationship last.

FIVE

HENRIK

Henrik Dekker replaced the payphone handset in its cradle and tried to figure out the fastest way to the front parking lot from the O.R. Family Waiting Room.

He was tired and needed to go home to rest.

His job was done.

Helga was in surgery and it would now be someone else's responsibility to get her to the morgue. How this would happen wasn't his problem. His boss hadn't been pleased with the botched confrontation, but how was he to know she'd slip free from his grip, trip over a cat and then tumble to the first floor, breaking her hip on the way down.

If only she'd hit her head and hadn't started to scream before I could get to her, he'd thought.

The appearance of a woman through the unlocked front door had been the second unlucky incident, forcing him to run out the back door, where he found the fences were too high to jump. "It's impossible for an 80-year-old man to climb a six-foot wooden fence," he'd advised his boss as they drove out of the area.

Henrik was dropped off at a diner and told to stay put. "I'm heading back to the house. Hopefully there's still a way we can get this done."

But there wasn't.

The paramedics and police were at the King Street address in minutes, both responding to Genifer's 911 call.

"I sit and wait," Clive Hill said aloud, parking the stolen Alero up the street. He hoped that Henrik's account of what happened was wrong; that the target would be treated for a strained muscle and then left alone. If that was the case, he was ready to act brazenly to complete the deadly task today. "'She's an old lady,' he says. 'How much trouble could she be?' he says," Clive recalled in disgust.

Within twenty minutes, Helga was in the ambulance on a stretcher and driven away.

Unreal, Clive thought, hitting the steering wheel with his right palm.

On the front porch a police officer spoke with the good Samaritan who had crashed Henrik and Helga's party for two.

"Let's find out who you are, my pretty lady," Clive said, putting the car in gear as he watched Genifer walk out of the neighbourhood.

He followed her at a safe distance and was rewarded when Genifer entered her house several minutes later. Clive scribbled down the Whelan Drive address and the license plate of the grey Volvo C30 parked in the driveway.

Pulling to the side of the street, Clive retrieved his cell phone and placed a call. "I need information on everyone who lives at a house I'm watching. I see two girls' bicycles in the backyard. I want their names too." He repeated the house and car plate numbers to ensure there'd be no mistakes. "Call me as soon as you have anything!"

A few minutes later, his phone rang.

"Give me what you've got," he demanded.

"The house is owned by Stan and Genifer Grant. They have two girls: Zoe is 11 and Aleena is 9. The car comes back to that address. Stan is a CMM operator – you know, writes programs for die cuts in the tool and die industry – and Genifer has worked at the post office for twenty-three years. I think she's a carrier." The female caller paused as she scrolled through Genifer's Facebook page. "It appears she's very active at work. The vice-president of the local union, the Health and Safety Committee co-chair, a shop steward, a Human Rights Master Trainer, whatever *that* is."

"In other words," Clive broke in, bored already, "this woman doesn't take shit from many people and may be trouble."

After writing the Grants' home phone number, Clive disconnected the call and drove to the diner where Henrik was seated at a window table.

"Call this Grant woman and scare the living daylights out of her," Clive said, ripping the information from a pad and handing it to Henrik. "She cannot meddle in this job again. Do you understand me?" Clive's voice had risen in pitch and nearby customers had heard him.

Henrik took the page and read the chicken scratch on it. "I understand," he acknowledged slowly. "I'll do it after I'm done my coffee."

"You'd better," Clive said, giving an apologetic gesture to the patrons around them, before returning his attention to Henrik. "I have to fix your mistake. You need to get to the hospital as soon as you can. Take a cab," Clive said in a threatening whisper. "Keep an eye on that old woman and update me on what's happening."

"How am I going to do that?" Henrik asked with an air of defeat.

Clive put his hand on the man's shoulder, squeezing as he did so. "Like the commercial says, 'Just do it.'"

After Clive had left Henrik took his time sipping his coffee and ordered a piece of peach pie as he formulated a plan.

A half hour later he stepped out of a cab and entered the Metropolitan Hospital lobby.

"Can you assist me?" he requested of the female security officer.

"Of course," Maryanne replied cheerfully. "Are you here to visit someone?"

"A friend. Helga Klemens. She was brought in by ambulance."

Maryanne consulted her computer. "She's currently in the E.R. department."

Henrik noticed the security cameras that covered the lobby and lowered his head. "Thank you. I'll find her," he said, shuffling away from the desk.

"Just take this hallway and ..." Maryanne began as she stood from her chair.

"I know where I'm going," Henrik said with a wave and stepped out of Maryanne's view.

"Alrighty then," Maryanne said as she sat down and sent her transporter boyfriend, Luke, an email about meeting for lunch.

Although hopelessly lost in the basement corridors, Henrik didn't care as long as he wasn't near the guard desk. He kept his chin close to his chest so his face couldn't be seen by other security cameras. The fact he was wearing a very noticeable tan overcoat didn't cross his mind as he approached a kind of crossroads near the bank of visitor elevators.

"Can I help you?" asked a young woman in a smock pushing a cart with blood vials on it.

"E.R.?" Henrik said, exaggerating his already thick accent and appearing confused.

"You're close," the woman said, outstretching her arm. "Down this hallway and turn right, then left through the second door. Someone will be able to direct you from there."

Henrik mumbled, "Thank you," and proceeded to the E.R. department. Inside he noticed a large television monitor hanging above the front reception area and found Helga's name typed in the examination room 11 box. As no hospital employee was approaching him, he walked to a telephone designated for patients and their families across from Helga's room where the curtains were drawn. He placed the receiver to his right ear, while listening to a nurse speak to Helga with his left ear.

"We're going to transfer you to the 8th floor. The O.R. had a couple of emergency surgeries due to a multi-car accident that's backed up the entire schedule," the nurse stated apologetically.

"Will I still be operated on today?" Helga asked in a frail voice.

"Yes, I believe that's the plan. This way you can rest a while and when the surgery is done they'll bring you back to the same room." The nurse partly opened the room's curtain to exit, causing Henrik to step behind a partition, before walking back to the main desk.

"Excuse me," he said to the first person he saw wearing scrubs. "Where can I wait for a friend who's having surgery today?"

"I'm heading there now, if you want to follow me," the E.R. aide said.

Henrik was shown to the O.R. Family Waiting Room, where he learned from a volunteer that patients were taken into the surgery department through an adjacent set of doors. "You'll be able to wish your friend well when they're brought down," the sunny girl said with a wide grin.

Henrik found a seat in the crowded room with a view of the hallway where Helga would be appearing. He positioned his overcoat on a chair and walked to the nearby payphone to call Clive.

"Let me know when she goes in," Clive said. "And don't forget to call that nosy postie. She can't tell anyone about seeing you."

"I will," Henrik said, reaching into his pocket to retrieve Genifer's information.

To Henrik, Genifer's initial response was abnormal, only wanting to know who he was and suggesting he had the wrong number. Believing he wasn't being taken seriously enough, he dropped the hammer all the way.

"This is the right number. What we're going to do to Helga is the same thing we'll do to your lovely girls, if you breathe a word of seeing me earlier. One dead old woman isn't worth risking your precious babies' lives, is it?" He paused for effect. "Are we clear, Genifer?"

He then gently placed the receiver in its cradle, put on his overcoat and took his seat.

Three hours went by before a chatty porter pushed Helga's stretcher down the O.R. corridor. Henrik heard him saying, "You know ... if you're feeling up to it, I can pop in to talk with you later. Would that be all right?"

Henrik waited a few minutes, seeing as how Helga seemed to be glancing in every direction. "Goodnight, Helga," he said as he went to the payphone to call Clive a final time.

"She just went in. What do you want me to do?"

"Get out of there," came the reply.

"Gladly."

Henrik exited the waiting room and saw the elevators to his right. Immediately he felt lost and decided to go back to the E.R. where he could catch a cab outdoors. Remembering the blood vial lady's directions, Henrik entered the first door he saw, not the second door he'd entered earlier, which deposited him at the opposite end of the department. As he briefly observed each open-curtained room he was taken aback by all the patients who were in such pain or trauma, their last hope for a cure being a trip to the hospital. "Sad, sad, sad," he muttered, seeing the exit he needed.

With only a few steps to freedom from this horrible place, he thought he heard a familiar voice coming from a room where the curtain was closed.

"What if an adult – say, an elderly adult – needs help?"

As he'd done earlier, Henrik checked the monitor hanging above the reception area and discovered a miracle in the making: Genifer Grant was in the room he'd just passed. He scurried into a waiting area and watched for any activity. When the nurse exited, pulling the curtain shut, he knew he had a short window of opportunity to confirm his phone message had been received.

"We meet again, Mrs. Grant," he said in a stern tone, putting an index finger to his lips as Genifer gasped in horror. "Not a word or I'll kill both your children while they sleep." Genifer's face went slack. "I'll make this short: keep your mouth shut about seeing me and no harm will come to Zoe and Aleena." Henrik knew that saying the girls' names added another level of terror.

"Please don't hurt my children," she pleaded. "I ... I ... didn't tell anyone I saw you."

"What about the police officer when Helga was being carted away in the ambulance?" Henrik asked coldly.

He was watching me! Genifer's mind screamed.

"He didn't ask. Please believe me." Genifer tried to catch her breath. "Helga didn't say a word about you either."

That's interesting, Henrik mused.

"I don't know your relationship with Helga," Genifer said slowly. "I was just walking by and wanted to help. That's all. So please leave me and my family alone. I'll never say a word about what I saw ... because I didn't see anything."

Henrik had often encountered this act of desperation and promise-making in harder humans than Genifer could ever be.

He believed her.

"Do you swear on the lives of your girls and your husband Stan?"

He knows everything about us!

"I do."

"That's good," Henrik said, giving Genifer a sinister wink before walking out of the room and making a hasty retreat for the exit. He heard a bedside call bell begin to ring, but didn't hear Genifer screaming or see her room curtain move.

She's smarter than she looks, he said, stepping outside and walking away from the hospital with a satisfied smile on his face.

SIX

GENIFER

During her four-hour stay, Genifer couldn't help but empathize with the E.R. team who had valiantly tried to diagnosis her "fainting spell" (as Stan annoyingly kept insisting it was to anyone within earshot). The nurses, doctors, transporters, blood and CT techs couldn't have been more professional, making Genifer feel extremely guilty. She regretted lying to Stan and the girls and couldn't wait to crawl into bed to pull the covers over her head.

The frightening visit from the old man in the overcoat had put the fear of God in her. She was thankful the nurse had removed the heart monitor, otherwise numerous bells and whistles would've been set off, causing additional stress for all involved.

Maybe not everyone.

Throughout his in-person warning, Genifer took stock of the man in the same way she sized up opponents during union contract negotiations. She prided herself at identifying a person's strengths and weaknesses, sometimes even their facial twitches that indicated which way they were leaning on contentious issues. When tensions started to run high and the make-or-break deadline loomed, Genifer would use her mental abilities to shape her arguments to move forward toward an agreeable resolution.

Stunned silent by her tormentor's appearance, her usually reliable instincts froze until the man walked out, pulling the curtain closed. It was only then Genifer dared to show any emotion and broke into tears. When Stan threw the curtain open, the look of terror in Genifer's wet eyes troubled him.

"Babe, it's okay," he said walking to the bed. "They'll find out what's going on."

"I want to go home," Genifer sobbed. "I miss the girls and I feel better."

Dr. Cantelon stepped into the room and said, "I'm glad to hear you're doing better and promise there will be no further tests today." He picked up a box of tissues off a supply cart and handed it to Genifer. "I'm going to discharge you, but want you back for a follow-up exam next Wednesday."

Genifer blew her nose in a tissue and continued to cry.

"I'll get her here, Doctor," Stan replied. "Thank you for everything."

After a teary-eyed goodbye to the staff, Genifer pushed the final giant silver button on the wall to open the waiting room door, then walked in silence with Stan through the sliding doors and to their vehicle.

Free at last, she thought, entering the Volvo's passenger seat.

"Are you hungry?" Stan asked as he pulled out of the lot. "Restaurant row beckons," he said, as numerous fast food joints appeared in front of them.

"No, unless you're hungry," Genifer answered, unable to look him in the eye.

Zoe and Aleena were already asleep in bed when Genifer climbed the stairs to the second floor. She was exhausted. She'd thanked her mom and Lisa for taking care of the girls and left Stan to fill them in on their hospital trip. After brushing her teeth and putting on her favourite pjs, she almost felt normal again, although she knew this was an illusion.

On her back in bed, staring at the ceiling fan as it lazily spun round, Genifer tried to take in the first quiet moment she'd had since deciding to go for a walk before the football game. This serenity didn't last long, as the fear that her family was in danger invaded her thoughts. *That man will harm Stan or the girls if I say anything! I can't let that happen. Without them, I don't know how I'd survive.* She broke out in a cold sweat and started to cry. Turning on her side into a fetal position, she buried her face in the pillow so no one could hear her torment. *I really wish I could tell my lifelong friend Lacie about this. I'll just have to keep my mouth closed for once,* she advised herself.

As the minutes wore on, like an ice cube left in an empty glass, the trauma of the day's events began to melt away, allowing her brain to return to its original state of being. The cool, calculated person she normally was started to push aside the troubling images she'd fixated on and focus on elements she couldn't process earlier: namely, the man who'd threatened not only her family, but also Helga.

Genifer reached for the phone to call the hospital, then decided it could wait until morning.

I'll talk to her tomorrow, she decided.

Closing her eyes to help with recall, Genifer pictured the man positioned a few feet away from her in the E.R. He was in his late seventies or early eighties, 5'9" with a wiry build and slight paunch, thinning grey hair and wearing thick-rimmed glasses – a look out of style for decades. His accent was European – German or Austrian perhaps – and he had a coldness about him that was his most upsetting trait. When he spoke to her, it was a slightly embellished, yet rote repeat of his phone threat hours earlier.

His talking points, Genifer deduced, familiar about such things after witnessing labour leaders and company spokespeople step before the microphones to get their spin out to the public. In this instance, Genifer had a gut feeling the old man hadn't written his own script. If so, who did? The longer she replayed their encounter in her head, the more convinced she became that he was a hired hand; his speech in concert with the tone soldiers in trouble for a mission gone wrong state, "I was following orders."

This brought Genifer back to the place where she first encountered the man: Helga's house. It was obvious now he wasn't there to scare her, but to kill her. Genifer doubted this was a lover's quarrel gone bad. Yet, what if they were related? A family argument that got out of hand – and down a flight of stairs?

If none of these scenarios were right, the question left unanswered was frightening and bizarre: Who would send a hired killer that old to murder another senior citizen?

None of this makes sense!

SEVEN

PART III

The pandemonium inside the O.R. began to subside when the two porters, the respiratory specialist and a nurse wheeled Helga's stretcher down the hall to the express elevator. Exiting onto the third floor, the foursome ran into the I.C.U. department and with the help of three waiting nurses, Helga was transferred onto a high-tech hospital bed in room 8. As the team hooked their unconscious patient up to various machines, the porters quietly pushed the stretcher out of the room to wipe it down with disinfectant cloths.

"What do you think happened, Rita?" asked Jeff, the younger porter. "Hip surgeries don't usually go wrong."

Rita, a grizzled decades-long hospital employee who had seen it all, shrugged. "The hip probably wasn't the only problem. She's pushing 90. It's a miracle they brought her back to life at all, if you call that living."

"I guess," Jeff said as they discarded their rubber gloves and used cloths into a garbage can. "Who's next?"

Rita unfolded her call sheet and crossed off the line listing

Helga's surgery. "Mr. Mason on the sixth floor. Gallbladder."

As they approached the exit, a nurse filling out paperwork at her desk commented, "Thanks for bringing us more work."

"She's not even your patient, Amanda. What do you care?" Rita asked in a sarcastic tone.

"I cover for Pam when she goes on break, so technically 8 will be my responsibility at some point. From what I've heard, that bed may be vacant soon." Amanda checked the row of rooms. "I don't know what's in the water, but this wing could be rechristened *Critical Alley*, because the majority of our current guests won't be leaving by wheelchair."

The outer hallway door opened.

"What a coincidence – here's Luke now with the morgue cart," Amanda said as they watched him enter the department. "Where's your partner?"

"Rob's going to meet me. Room 2, right?"

"To start," Rita cracked as she and Jeff went on their way.

Luke gave a courtesy smile and left the cart in the aisle. He wandered the horseshoe-shaped department peering into rooms, thinking Rob may be inside one helping to boost a patient in their bed. Retracing his steps, he slowed his pace when he overheard the charge nurse on the telephone say, "Yes, she's in room 8 ... Helga Klemens, spelled with a K, not C. ... She apparently died on the operating table and they somehow managed to bring her back from the other side."

Luke turned his head toward Helga's room where a doctor, four nurses and a respiratory tech were hovering next to the bed. Momentarily forgetting his search for Rob, he edged the door open and asked in a shaky voice, "Do you need any help?"

The nurses looked in his direction and simultaneously smiled. Luke was one of the good ones. "No, we're alright here, Luke," the head nurse answered. "Are you on the floor for turns?"

"Ah ... no, I'm here to pick up number two," Luke said, his eyes unable to break from the sight of Helga with an oxygen mask over her nose and mouth and numerous I.V. drip lines attached to both arms. Wanting to leave the professionals to do their work, he quietly stepped out and walked in a daze to the body cart.

"Where were you?" Rob inquired, sticking his head into room 2. "Not that we're in any hurry." Returning his attention to Luke he asked, "Are you okay, man? You're as white as a sheet."

Luke switched into auto-pilot mode, knowing he couldn't get out of this call. Afterwards he'd take his second break to settle his nerves. "Yeah – let's get this done," he replied as they lifted the butterfly-emblazoned cover to reveal a steel slab that resembled the cooler trays in the morgue.

A few minutes later, Luke and Rob were exiting the elevator on the ground floor when an announcement was made over the hospital's speaker system.

"All available porters – Code blue. I.C.U. room 8 stat. All available porters – Code blue. I.C.U. room 8 stat."

Luke reached for his radio and stepped away from the cart.

"We can't go, Luke!" Rob insisted. "I'm not leaving a dead body in the hallway."

Two porters rounded the corner, passing the body cart like they were lapping their coworkers at a track and field meet.

"Don't worry, boys. We're heading to I.C.U.," Noelle, the female porter advised, jogging to the still open elevator door.

"Thanks for coming to work today, fellas," Brad, the male porter added, pushing the floor and door buttons. "Have fun."

Watching the elevator door close seemed to stir something in Luke, loosening the logjam of conflicting thoughts he'd been having of Helga. *She'll be fine.*

"Let's get this call done, dude," Rob said impatiently. "I've got a coffee date with that hot volunteer from the Help Desk."

"Clearly, she's the one who needs help," Luke said with a smile, steering the body cart down the hall. "Let's get buddy here settled in and go on break."

In the midst of offloading the deceased onto a morgue tray,

another announcement came over the airwaves.

"I.C.U. Code blue – cancelled."

Luke knew of only two reasons to terminate the call: the patient had been successfully resuscitated or died.

"That was quick," Rob said, pushing the tray further into the cooler. "I hope they made it."

Don't let them kill me.

"Somehow I don't think she did," Luke said glumly, removing his gloves. "I suddenly have a splitting headache. I gotta find some aspirin. Can you fill out the paperwork?"

Rob noticed that his friend was off again. "No problem. Take a power nap in the locker room. I'll drop the keys and checklist to security."

"Thanks."

After getting permission to take his break, Luke found an empty waiting room and collapsed into a chair, where he contemplated whether to tell anyone about his conversation with Helga or let it go. "Maybe it was just her time," he told himself.

He checked his cell phone and saw an email from his girlfriend about having lunch together. He replied he'd meet her in two minutes. Before that however, he touched base with the female porter who had attended the I.C.U. call and she confirmed, "The old lady didn't make it."

Enroute to the front lobby, a crestfallen Luke caught a glimpse of Dr. Singh in her office with the newspaper reporter he'd talked with earlier.

Maybe Jennifer could help me, he thought, remembering her business card in his pocket. *I'll ask Maryanne first.* After all, she had access to the security camera footage that might be helpful, if there ever was an investigation of Helga's death.

***

Jennifer repositioned herself in an uncomfortable plastic chair across from Dr. Singh, who sat behind a desk that resembled a miniature army tank.

"If your office supplies budget ever runs too low, I know a scrapper who'd gladly take this 1960's monstrosity off your hands." Jennifer smoothed her hand over the dull metal finish. "Emile could probably get $200, minus his commission," she added with a wide smile.

Dr. Singh laughed. "I believe the basement in any building is where old furniture goes to die, which in our case seems appropriate."

"It does."

Dr. Singh folded her hands together and put them on top of the desk. "So how can I help you? On the intercom you mentioned our latest John Doe."

"Latest? Do you get a lot of them?" Jennifer asked.

"Maybe a dozen or so a year," Dr. Singh replied nonchalantly, "but they aren't classified as John or Jane Doe for very long. In the majority of the cases, a missing person report is the key to identifying a body found in a field or an alley or floating in the river."

Jennifer retrieved her notebook and flipped to the information Mitch had given her. "The most recent *find* ... can you confirm it's a Caucasian male in his mid-twenties?"

"Yes to both questions. He was approximately 5'9" with a slim build and in good physical shape at the time of his death."

"Was the cause drowning?" Jennifer asked as she wrote down the details.

"Without a full autopsy it's hard to know conclusively. Using a large syringe, I did extract water from his lungs. There were also numerous contusions around his face and head. However, those could have occurred while the body floated in the water, making contact with debris in the river."

"And he was fully clothed?"

"He was. Blue t-shirt, jeans, black socks and one Nike shoe –

basic items you can purchase at any department stores. No jewellery."

"Tattoos?"

"None. Also, his palms were smooth. I don't believe he worked in a factory or did manual labour."

"Hmmm ... this guy really is a mystery man," Jennifer said. "So what's next?"

"A police sketch artist is coming tomorrow to render a drawing to be released to the media," Dr. Singh replied.

"That'll work if he has family or friends in the area. But if he was a tourist and got rolled for his wallet, he might not be claimed for quite a while."

"That is a possibility, yes. We can only do so much."

"The irony is if this was a found puppy case, there could be a microchip imbedded under its skin for fast identification."

Dr. Singh weighed this theory in her mind. "In the future that may be the case. As it stands, our fingerprints are still the best bet, but the police didn't get a hit when they ran John Doe's. I did take some blood samples for future DNA testing as well."

Jennifer scanned her notes and then closed the pad. "I guess I'll hold off with what you've told me until the police sketch is ready tomorrow." Jennifer stood and extended her hand that contained her business card, which Dr. Singh took. "If there are any new developments, please give me a call."

Dr. Singh shook Jennifer's hand. "Of course." Jennifer opened the office door. "Can you find your way back to the front lobby, Miss Malone?"

Jennifer looked at the bland coloured surroundings. "I will somehow," she said, leaving the door partially open and making her way down the hallway she'd travelled earlier. "Where is Luke when you need him?" she muttered to herself, finally locating a main entrance wall sign with an arrow facing north.

Outside the air was warm and fresh, the opposite of the morgue setting Jennifer had left behind. In her car, she gave Mitch a phone call.

"I'll tell Metro to get that sketch," Mitch said. "Write up what you've got – a hundred words – and I'll pass it along. How does that sound?"

"Like fifty words too many," Jennifer said, noticing a small mark on her dress. *Did it fly off the undercarriage of Luke the Transporter's death wagon?*

"What are you going to work on now?"

"Getting this stain out of my dress," she responded absentmindedly.

"What stain?"

"It's a long story, Mitch, involving a dead body. You wouldn't understand or condone with your religious upbringing," Jennifer said. "The less you know, the better. Plausible deniability. Trust me."

There was a pause on the other end of the line until Mitch replied, "You're right, I don't want to know or understand! I just hope you wore gloves and will call your P.I. friend now about Councilman Tilley's missing plaything."

"I hope those two wore gloves," Jennifer replied. "And yes, Jeffrey Hamill is on my call list today."

"Does he still work for a box of donuts?"

"No, he's increased his price to a box of cronuts. Specifically the chocolate-champagne ganache, orange sugar and champagne-chocolate glaze ones."

"Each one has 600 calories and 80 grams of carbs!" Mitch said in disbelief. "I'll hang up so you can call him, before his heart gives out."

Their connection went dead.

"And ... bye-bye," Jennifer said as Mitch's image was swapped out with a Liam Neeson screen saver. "Oh, Liam," Jennifer sighed, "please find me like those bad men who abducted your daughter. I promise not to put up as much resistance."

Her cinematic hero only continued to smile as Jennifer placed him on the passenger seat and headed toward the lot's checkout booth. As she handed the attendant her parking ticket, she saw Luke and Maryanne exiting the front doors and walking to a bench. Neither were smiling, but Jennifer didn't sense they were having a fight.

With her ticket paid (ten dollars per hour!) and receipt in hand, she waited for the bar to rise and slowly pulled next to the bench, rolling down her window.

"Everything okay?" she inquired. The words, 'You look like someone died,' hung back in her throat as she remembered Luke's last call.

Luke and Maryanne looked over in astonishment. It was then that Jennifer noticed that they were holding the business cards she'd given Luke earlier.

"Tell her what you told me, Luke," Maryanne implored, putting a reassuring hand on her boyfriend's leg.

Simultaneously, Luke appeared to be terrified and embarrassed.

"Yeah, Luke, tell me," Jennifer said with a grin. "I don't bite, even though I say I'd consider it on my dating profile. But hey, everyone lies on those websites, right?"

"I guess," Luke said with a shrug of his shoulders. "You know what – I am being ridiculous. People die all the time. It's a hospital." He paused. "She was a drugged up old lady when I took her to the O.R. You can't take what she said seriously, can you?" He glanced at Maryanne and Jennifer. "Patients probably say that stuff to nurses every shift and it means nothing. They're nervous. I would be."

"What patient and what stuff?" Jennifer asked, completely intrigued by Luke's rambling soliloquy.

"Helga Klemens," Maryanne answered. "She was 88 years old and her heart stopped on the operating table during a hip surgery. They got her back, only she died later in I.C.U."

"That fills in half of my question. What did this woman say,

Luke, that's spooked you?" Jennifer held his attention with her eyes.

Luke gave Maryanne one final look and received a supportive head shake in response.

"When I walked in her room, the first thing she said was, 'Don't let them kill me,' and now she's dead."

Jennifer wasn't sure what she'd expected to hear, although a suspected elder murder storyline wasn't in her Top 100 possibilities.

"Okay ...." she said cautiously. "A question for you, Maryanne. As a security guard, can you validate parking? Because I'm going to be here quite a while longer."

***

Jennifer re-parked her car and met Luke and Maryanne at a picnic table on the edge of the hospital grounds. As both were on a break, time was of the essence and Jennifer wrote down their cell phone numbers first.

"How long were you with Helga when you transported her to the O.R.?" Jennifer asked Luke. "And why are you giving any credence to the theory she was murdered? Was there anything else she said that got your Spidey senses tingling?"

Again, Luke had a far-off expression as he considered his answers. "To be honest, I don't know why Helga has had such an effect on me. On midnight shifts I do three I.C.U. rounds, stopping in each room to help turn, boost, or change the bedding of patients holding onto life by a thread. When I come back a few days later, many times these same people are gone – most of them passed away – and I don't give it a second thought." Luke stopped, realizing how cold that sounded. "You know what I mean. For me it's a circle of life thing. I feel sad for the person's family, but their loved one is no longer in pain and suffering."

Maryanne looked affectionately at Luke and put her hand in

his. "I feel the same way when I release a body to the funeral home."

Watching the two lovebirds, Jennifer felt a twinge of jealousy. "So, Luke, why is Helga different, aside from her request not to be killed?"

"I guess it freaked me out. She reminded me of my grandmother and if she made the same statement at her nursing home, I'd be worried too."

"Then to have Helga die, you stop and wonder if she wasn't telling the truth," Maryanne chimed in. "As a security guard and fledgling journalist that's how I reacted."

Yes, Maryanne, I recall you're a budding reporter, Jennifer thought, annoyed by this declaration as she checked her watch. "Did Helga mention any family in the area or her address?"

"Only that when she was 10 years old her and her brother left Germany. I don't know if he's still alive," Luke said. "Her medical chart listed her home out in Greenheart Station. I don't recall the specific address."

Jennifer jotted down the information. "Do you remember what room she was in?"

"8103."

"When will that room be cleaned?"

"Fairly quickly," Luke replied. "The floor could already know that Helga was going straight to I.C.U. A housekeeper would then clean 8103 for a new patient."

"What about her belongings?"

"Normally, a porter would be dispatched to get the patient's belongings and take them to the new room."

Jennifer pondered this information. "Luke, without causing suspicion, could you go to 8103 and see if there's anything out of the ordinary? I don't want you to get in trouble."

Luke and Maryanne exchanged glances before he said, "I can do that. As a transporter I'm in and out of rooms all the time trying to find pillows, I.V. pumps or nurses." He stood, ready to begin his new assignment. "Even if the room has been cleaned, I know the housekeeper on duty and can ask if she bagged any belongings."

"Bagged?" Jennifer asked.

Maryanne got up and smiled. "That's where I might be helpful, as security is in charge of securing deceased patient's belongings, until they are claimed by the family."

"And if they aren't claimed?" Jennifer inquired.

"Clothing is donated to area thrift shops or possibly thrown out. I do know we hold onto it for thirty days."

After promising Luke and Maryanne that she'd be in touch, Jennifer remained at the table to add to her notes. She wasn't certain this was any kind of news story beyond the obligatory obituary notice. It was, however, a nice, albeit bizarre, distraction from the cheating councilman and his missing-in-action honey pot circus she'd been chasing the past two weeks.

On a whim, Jennifer called the hospital switchboard, asked for room 8103 and was put through. Two rings later, a familiar voice hesitantly answered the phone.

"Hello?"

"Luke?"

It took him a few beats to catch on. "Jennifer?"

"Yes, it's me. I'm still outside," she said. "You work fast, don't you?"

"Maryanne went on patrol and I headed here. I only see the clothes Helga came in with."

"Any cards or flowers?"

"No cards, probably because she came directly from E.R. and not too long after went down for surgery. There are some flowers though, which is interesting," Luke said, excitement in his voice. "A dozen yellow carnations and a card that reads, *All the best, Helga! See you soon!*"

"Somebody knew her," Jennifer said. "Is there a store name or phone number on the back of the card?"

Luke gently removed the card and flipped it over. "It's from the hospital gift shop."

"Luke, I have a call for you, if you're done with your break," a female voice said on his work phone.

"I have to go, Jennifer," he said. "Do you want me to take the card?"

"No, leave it. Good work though. You're all right, Luke," Jennifer said. "In the interim, if possible, see if you can find anything dealing with Helga's operation or what happened in I.C.U. I'll be in touch."

"I'll do my best," Luke replied.

While Luke and Maryanne did their respective insider's work on her behalf, Jennifer visited the gift shop. The selection of items for sale were of the generic something-for-everyone variety, from books and stuffed animals, to trinkets, cheap jewellery and greeting cards for any occasion. However, what really caught her eye was the flower cooler containing a bunch of yellow carnations.

"Excuse me," Jennifer said to a pink vested female volunteer named Mary. "Do you have any more yellow carnations, aside from the six here in the cooler?"

The woman looked surprised by the request. "We had over two dozen yesterday," she said as she walked past Jennifer. "They're very popular." She turned to Jennifer. "They certainly brighten up a room."

"They do," Jennifer agreed. "I'm just a day late."

The volunteer studied the remaining selection of flowers. "What if you bought the carnations and a couple roses? That combination would cheer me up."

Jennifer tried to give the outward expression of thinking about such a purchase. "My heart was set on a full dozen. Will there be a delivery in the morning?"

The volunteer returned to the counter, picked up a spiral-bound binder and leafed through the pages.

"Yes, a new shipment is coming tomorrow. Do you want me to

hold twelve for you?"

Jennifer hesitated as she examined the security camera facing down from the ceiling. "If it's no bother," she said.

"And your name?"

"It's Jennifer."

The volunteer wrote the name on a pad and taped it next to the cash register. "There – in case I can't make it in for the morning shift. Now, is there anything else, dear?"

"No, that's it. Thank you for your help." Jennifer prepared to exit the shop, but stopped. "This may sound like an unusual request ... Could you ask the other volunteers working earlier if they remember if the buyer was a male or female?" The volunteer was perplexed. "It's a long story that I don't want to bore you with – family issues, sibling rivalries – that type of thing. I just want to be sure no one from my clan bought those flowers."

An expression of empathy flashed over the volunteer's face. "Wasteful drama. The worst times for any family are when a parent is hospitalized or dies, or there's a wedding."

"That's true," Jennifer said with a smile. "Okay, that's it, again. I'll be back tomorrow morning. See you then."

The volunteer wrote a second note to be taped below the first: *Who bought a dozen yellow carnations? Important! ~ Mary.*

On her way toward the front lobby escalator, Jennifer saw a middle-aged man with a take-out bag in one hand, and a helium balloon that read: *Congratulations!*

If he can wander around the hospital unsupervised, why can't I? Jennifer followed the stranger to the bank of elevators, where they both entered the same car.

"Floor?" the man asked Jennifer.

She noted he'd already pushed "7" and said, "Eight, please. Thank you."

They rode in silence until he exited, saying, "Have a good night."

"You, too," Jennifer replied, inching forward to hold the door open. She saw the man stroll by the nurse's station without stopping and disappear down the far right hand corridor. She noted the wall signage indicating rooms 7101-7109 were to the left and 7110-7116 were to the right. Jennifer let go of the door, which closed in front of her. "Go left. Go left. Go left," she repeated to herself. "Third room – 8103."

She'd already decided there'd be no need to talk to the nurses, or anyone else for that matter. Her objective was only to get a feel for Helga's room and the surroundings. Were there surveillance cameras installed in the hallways? Could anyone get to Helga without a nurse becoming aware of their presence?

The elevator door opened and Jennifer stepped confidently out onto the 8th floor, turning left at the nurse's station. She noted three nurses, each busily filling out patient paperwork in green binders. None looked up as she passed 8101, then 8102 and 8103, where a housekeeper was running a mop across the floor. Jennifer didn't see any belongings or flowers on the housekeeper's cart. *These employees don't waste any time here.*

Jennifer walked through a short corridor to the right hand hallway and back to the elevators, pushing the down wall button. Stepping into the car upon its arrival, Jennifer heard one of the nurses say that yellow carnations were her favourite flowers.

Jennifer's immediate impulse was to investigate further, but reconsidered. Nothing useful could come from questioning staff who might not know Helga was dead yet.

Time to go home. I'm sick of this place already.

She smiled at the irony.

Back in her car, she paid another exorbitant parking fee (not wanting to bother Maryanne) and headed to her apartment.

"This dress stain isn't going to come out on its own," she said as she pulled into traffic.

EIGHT

In her converted loft apartment, Jennifer took off her dress and sprayed a copious amount of spot remover onto the offending area above the hemline. While it soaked she changed into a comfortable pair of jeans and casual collared top, hoping she wouldn't be rushing out again this late in the evening. Plus, she wanted to bang out the John Doe story that Mitch had requested for the Metro section.

Twenty minutes later, she emailed the piece with the instructions: MITCH: ONLY RUN WITH THE POLICE COMPOSITE DRAWING!

While not famished, Jennifer figured she should eat something and opened her fridge that showcased take-out boxes from three different restaurants. "Thai, Italian or Greek?" she said to herself, deciding the portion of eggplant parmigiana would tie her over nicely. Reaching for the container, her mind flashed back to when she'd dated a semi-famous chef. She had offended him on numerous occasions by eating cheap restaurant leftovers before the succulent personal-sized dinners he prepared for her. "It's force of habit. I see that food as a day closer to being thrown in the garbage and can't do it," she had explained. To smooth things out, as a joke she'd bought a dozen small cardboard boxes from the Chinese restaurant on her block and presented them to Oliver on their next date.

The playful idea had had a very surprising outcome.

Jennifer figured the gravy train, as tasty as it was, had left the station when Chef Loverboy started to rant about the integrity of his food and his craft, instead of smiling, kissing her and filling a box or two with his delicious food. The scene became more surreal when a tabloid newspaper quoted an unnamed source saying their budding relationship failed due to her insatiable appetite for fast food and "dirty, greasy cooks." Following its publication Jennifer received dozens of date offers from pizza makers to short order cooks to bakers, none of which appealed to her as did the new man-boy barista at the *Don't Be Latté!* coffee shop she regularly frequented. Sadly, he fell below her current off-limits age, although under the right circumstances he might be made the exception to the rule for a couple of nights.

With her food heated, Jennifer sat on her couch with the plate in one hand and the TV remote in the other. "Let's see what I've been missing out on," she said, tuning into the *What's Next?* show on the National Cable Network (NCN) channel.

As the weekend came to a close, the stories were a rehash of the week's main news events, and random speculation of how each storyline could develop in the days ahead. The talking heads consisted of three male and two female so-called journalists, sitting around a table that couldn't possibly fit in Jennifer's living room. They were in their early thirties and photogenic. None, however, had worked in the reporter trenches or had broken any significant news stories on their own. She'd once broached this subject to Mitch in the paper's bullpen and he had the nerve to suggest she was jealous.

"Twenty years ago I'd have given my left nut to be on that panel," he'd stated with a huge smile to the assembled crowd.

"As visually disturbing as that is, too bad your wife got them in the divorce," Jennifer said to a chorus of laughter. "I guess it'll remain a mystery if you truly had the balls to play with the big boys."

"Laugh all you want, Malone," Mitch countered. "While you're schlepping it here at *The Daily Telegraph,* your journalism classmate Susan Donallee has become a household name because of that show."

"Fame and fortune are overrated if you have to sleep your way to the top," Jennifer countered. "Although I wouldn't mind having a hairstylist and a fashion designer at my beck and call. Can you talk with the Old Man upstairs about that, or should I do it in person?"

"Definitely in person," Mitch answered, "and I want to be in the room. I promise to keep a straight face the whole time."

"You can't keep a straight face now as you're telling me that!"

Jennifer knew her editor had a point and was only half kidding about wanting to be pampered by her employer from time to time. That she'd been offered a guest spot on *What's Next*? but declined, wasn't a topic she'd discuss with her colleagues anyway, fearing she'd be dubbed a hypocrite.

After finishing the leftovers and bored with the idiotic topic "Should Pets Be Cloned?", Jennifer caught sight of an interesting line running in the news scroll at the bottom of the screen.

... Becky Mayville offers to sell her story to the highest bidder ...

"Bless her little cheating heart," Jennifer said, grabbing her cell phone.

The number she called rang fifteen times before being answered, which was always expected due to Jeffrey's profession.

"Hamill Investigations here. Whatcha need, Malone? I'm kind of busy."

"Busy eating or private investigating?"

"Both!"

"Shocker."

"It's easy to multi-task while on stationary surveillance. It's when the subject leaves that things get tricky."

"Where are you?"

"George and Pike. Three blocks south of City Hall."

"Until when?"

"Maybe midnight."

"Do you want some company?" Jennifer asked. "Also, something's happening with Hot Beckster."

"Her pitch letter to the media?"

Jennifer let out a moan. "You heard already and didn't tell me? Some partner you are."

"Don't get your thong twisted, Missy Malone," Jeffrey replied. "I heard about it a half hour ago from a contact who owns a video production outfit in the west end. I was going to call you, only right then my subject and his girlfriend left the strip club and I had to follow them."

"A likely story," Jennifer said. "Who's your client – his wife or her husband?"

There was noise on the line as Jeffrey apparently dropped the phone and began to curse, "Where's my damn camera? Stay on the line, Malone, I have to get a shot of them on the balcony. Start heading down and call me when you're in the vicinity. Man I hate working at night!"

The line went dead in Jennifer's hand.

"What to do, what to do?" she asked the walls, thinking a cat might not be a bad idea after all, as she'd have a constant companion to talk to.

Soon enough Jennifer located Jeffrey's green Windstar van parked in a lot across from an apartment building. Due to the darkness and the streetlight's glow reflecting off the front windshield, Jeffrey was invisible sitting in the driver's seat, binoculars in hand.

"Which unit are we surveilling tonight?" Jennifer asked as she climbed into the passenger seat. The interior lights didn't come on.

"304 – second in from the left," Jeffrey said, pointing upward. "The lobby board lists the girlfriend's name as the current tenant."

"And that's a problem?" Jennifer edged forward hoping to see the couple doing something wrong, illicit or both.

"It could be if the signature on the condo deed is my client's ex-husband's. A pre-divorce date would be best for us as it would prove he's hiding assets ... and I'm not referring to the lovely ones gracing his girlfriend's chest," Jeffrey said with a hearty laugh.

The P.I. set the binoculars on the dash and turned his bulky frame to face Jennifer. A former athlete in his youth, the decades hadn't been kind to Jeffrey Hamill. Pushing fifty-five, when he entered the private investigations field in the 1980s he'd figured on having a cushy corner office job in a big insurance company downtown. However, the path taken bypassed downtown, midtown and uptown, only to stop at every drive-thru fast food window along the route. After hitting the 250-pound mark, Jeffrey quit weighing himself and ordered his doctor not to reveal the number during his yearly physicals. Although far from the stereotypical jolly fat man, Jeffrey had retained his humour, which in the face of aneurism-inducing stress each day felt like a victory. Plus, he had more street connections than an agency that employed a hundred investigators.

Jennifer reached into her purse and produced a small paper bag. "A gift for you," she said handing Jeffrey the bag.

Jeffrey opened it but didn't peer inside, inhaling its aroma instead. "Boston cream."

"The cronut place was closed, so I went with the second best option," Jennifer replied. "Real friends know these things."

"That they do," Jeffrey said, taking a bite out of the doughy present and placing its remains back in the bag. "It could be a long night. I'm going to save it for a midnight snack."

"So ... with the pleasantries dispensed and in your case, ingested, what's the deal with Becky's blackmailing the press?"

"I'm not sure 'blackmail' is the correct term. Either a reporter pays for her titillating tale, or no one does and her sleazy story gets bigger with each passing week in seclusion," Jeffrey offered.

"Do you think she's still sitting pretty, hoping that her one big pay day won't pass her by?"

"Her day is coming, Jennifer. All she has to do is count the weeks until the election." Jeffrey raised his binoculars toward his subject's balcony after a light in a room came on. "Time for bed."

Jennifer glanced up. "I hope you're talking to yourself."

Jeffrey laughed. "Malone, you couldn't handle a man like me."

"Ha – I can't handle any man for more than a week!"

"Men scare easily, that's all."

Jennifer turned to Jeffrey. "I'm scary?"

"To a lot of men, yeah. You're beautiful, you're without a doubt smarter than most of us Neanderthals, and you're aggressive due to your profession," Jeffrey said.

"I intimidate guys, is that what you're implying?"

"Only the wrong guys," Jeffrey replied waving his finger at her. "You need to find a man who will push back when you push forward – psychologically, not physically, of course."

"And where are these men, wise one?"

"From what I hear, you could begin with the chamber where Councilman Tilley works. You might not agree, but you and the Hot Beckster have a few things in common."

"Such as?"

"You're both easy on the eyes, tenacious and know what you want. Becky set her sights on Tilley and wore him down. He told a mutual friend that every time he tried to end her advances, she countered with something new, and after a while he began to enjoy the game they were playing."

"And the next thing you know, he fell right into her vagina while vacationing with his family in Florida," Jennifer said with a wide grin.

"Getting back to my point about Neanderthals, some are further down the evolutionary line than others."

The light in the apartment bedroom went out.

"I'll keep that in mind when I cover a city vote," Jennifer said. "So ... Mitch was wondering if there's any word on the street where Becky is biding her time?"

"Speaking of cave men," Jeffrey chuckled, "tell him I appreciate the compliment, but my informants have come up empty-handed. My guess is she's sitting on a private beach at a resort her daddy owns. Now that's the kind of man to set your sights on, Jennifer. He recently cracked Forbes Top 100 list of wealthiest men in North America."

"I'll send him a Facebook friend request in the morning."

Jeffrey reached for a thermos and poured himself a cup of coffee the colour of tar. "Want some?" Jennifer shook her head side to side. "Are you working on any other stories?"

Jennifer reclined her seat to view the bedroom window, while wondering what had really happened at the hospital earlier. "Maybe."

"I'm all ears," Jeffrey said, attempting to recline his seat without much success.

"I went to Met Hospital to find out about that guy they dragged out of the river. Until further notice, John Doe will remain John Doe," Jennifer began. "Then I found myself in conversation with a young couple – he's a hospital transporter, she's a security guard – who believe an old lady was murdered while having hip surgery." Jeffrey gave her a questioning look. "Yes, it sounds farfetched, but the transporter swears that prior to the surgery the patient begged him not to let *them* kill her. He sloughed it off as jitters and pain meds until she died first on the operating table – they rescued her from *the light* – and then for the last time in I.C.U."

"How old?"

"Late 80s."

"Forgetting the kid's account, is there anything else that points to foul play?" Jeffrey asked. "Old people die in hospitals. It's not exactly breaking news."

"There were flowers in her room although she'd only been in for a short time," Jennifer answered. "Luke – he's the transporter – didn't believe the patient had any family with her. I'd need to find out who sent them."

"So you are working on it?"

"I'm undecided," Jennifer said noncommittally. "I'm hoping

the security guard girlfriend can get the camera footage from the 8th floor or gift shop where the flowers were purchased."

"Check the *Telegraph's* obituary section in a couple days too. There may be a full list of family members you can contact after the funeral."

"We'll see."

Jennifer's cell phone rang, startling both of them.

"Malone," she answered.

"Hi, Jennifer?" the male voice asked tentatively. "It's Luke from Met Hospital."

"Your ears must be burning," she said.

"What's burning?"

Too young to get the reference, Jennifer thought. *You're the old lady in this conversation.* "Hey, Luke, never mind. Nothing's burning. What's going on? Are you still at work?"

"I am and I found some information about Helga that may explain why she believed someone was out to kill her."

Jennifer brought her seat to an upright position and found a notepad in her purse. "Go on," she said.

There was a brief pause and Jennifer heard Maryanne in the background encouraging Luke on, as she had on the hospital bench. "Helga was the star witness at a murder trial. Her granddaughter was killed by her husband, who was convicted and sent to prison."

"That's good he was found guilty," Jennifer replied. "Why would Helga be in any danger now?"

"Because there might be an appeal, and in the article I read the lawyer claimed without Helga's testimony his client would be found not guilty."

Jennifer wrote down this information and mulled over its importance. "But why kill her in a public place like a hospital? Why not make an attempt when she's home alone?"

"That's the thing, Jennifer, I think they did," Luke said cautiously. "The surgery was scheduled *after* Helga arrived in the

E.R. I spoke with her nurse and she remembered that Helga was tight-lipped about her fall at home. But she thought that Helga had mumbled, 'I almost got away from him,' only to dismiss it, like I did, because Helga was high on painkillers."

Jennifer was alarmed by this news. "Did you tell the nurse what Helga had said to you?"

"No, I'm too scared to tell anyone anything, aside from you."

Jennifer was relieved that Luke had kept his mouth shut. "From now on, please stop discussing Helga with any hospital personnel, besides Maryanne. I need to do some research on this murder trial. Can you text me the story link?"

"I'll do it now."

A few seconds later, Jennifer's phone made a pinging sound. "Got it, thanks, Luke. Get to the end of your shift and go home. I'll contact you in the morning," Jennifer said. "Are you working the same shift tomorrow?"

"No, I generally only work weekends, unless someone is sick and I'm called in to cover their shift," Luke answered. "Maryanne will be at the hospital from noon until midnight though."

"Sounds good," Jennifer said. "And one more thing: remember that none of this information may be connected to Helga's death, okay?"

"I know," Luke said.

Jennifer set her cell phone on the dash and re-read her notes, as Jeffrey remained silent for several moments.

"What are the odds that you found your next story to investigate?" he asked.

"One hundred percent, my friend," Jennifer said with a sigh. "One hundred freakin' percent."

NINE

Luke put his cell phone in his pocket and cleared the website history from the computer in the O.R. staff lounge. He didn't dare print off the newspaper article he'd found online until he got home. He sent Maryanne the link, knowing she would read it while manning duties at the lobby security desk.

"Luke, are you there?" an Admitting Clerk asked. "Can you check the linen bags in I.C.U.?"

"I can," Luke replied unenthusiastically. "Thanks."

"Feel free to stretch it out until the end of your shift."

"Will do."

Luke exited the lounge and saw a housekeeper mopping the floor down the hallway. "Hey, James, keep up the great work!" he called out with a short wave, not waiting for a reply, as he continued walking out of the wing.

The housekeeper, who was also in his twenties, gave Luke a nod, accompanied with a half-hearted smile, before going back to cleaning the floors.

On the elevator ride to the 3rd floor, Luke could hear Jennifer warning him not to discuss Helga with anyone else, but this call seemed like providence to do just that.

"I'll be discreet," he told himself.

The Intensive Care Unit (I.C.U.) and Critical Care Unit (C.C.U.) made up the west wing of the floor with nineteen beds inside. To Luke, there was no real difference between the patients; each one unlikely to survive without 24 hour monitoring of their current physical state. When someone did recover enough to leave the floor, as he wheeled them out Luke would joke, "It's a better view going through these doors this way, isn't it?"

Luke walked into the wing and took note of who was working.

The staff who would've attended Helga were gone for the day, which worked out well for his plan to gather further intelligence. He changed a couple linen bags and made his way to a young nurse sitting behind the desk.

"Hi, Jess, I heard there was some excitement in here earlier," Luke said in a confident friendly tone that belied the butterflies in his stomach.

Jess glanced up from her paperwork and smiled. "Are you talking about the woman who died twice this afternoon?"

"That's the one," he replied. "What's that old line – if at first you don't succeed ...?"

"Try, try again."

"That's it," Luke said shaking his head. "I guess there were complications during her surgery. Do you know what happened?"

"I didn't hear much at shift change. Apparently the procedure was going along as planned and then her heart stopped," Jess said in a low tone. "They brought her back to life and sent her here, where she had another seizure. It's so sad."

"They always are," Luke said slowly, deciding against adding his involvement with Helga. "Did she have any family?"

Jess looked toward a pile of medical charts on a shelf. "Her chart is already gone, so I can't find out if she listed any family or a contact number."

"Where do her records go?" Luke asked. "When we transfer a body to the morgue we only take the new checklist. The rest of the patient's paperwork is taken out of the binder and held together with an elastic band."

"That's right. Now you've got me curious. Give me a sec." Jess stood and walked out of view.

While he waited, Luke restocked isolation gowns for rooms running low.

Jess returned carrying a thin package of papers to the desk. "This Helga was a tough old bird, if this is all the medical information we have on her," she said, removing the elastic band. "The chart starts from her admission in E.R. earlier today."

Luke went behind Jess and scanned the information he could decipher over her shoulder. "She arrived by EMS," he said, trying to remember the ambulance number and names of the two paramedics, "with a broken hip."

"Life is so nonsensical," Jess sighed as she flipped to another page. "I heard she tripped over her cat! Nothing like that should happen to an elderly person in their home on a Sunday afternoon."

At the mention of 'home' Luke memorized Helga's address. He then looked for a next of kin listing and found something strange. "Her emergency contact is a Genifer Grant, but there's no phone number. What's the use of that?"

Jess saw the empty box and shrugged her shoulders. "She might have been in shock and couldn't remember. It happens. I've seen people in the E.R. who can't remember the names of their children or their date of birth. The brain is on overload dealing with how to stay alive and it shuts down the pathways required to count to ten."

"I guess," Luke said. "What'll happen to the cat?"

"Oh – I didn't consider that," Jess said with a concerned look. "Pets are the last loved ones to be cared for when a person dies. They have feelings too."

"Except maybe fish," Luke said, trying to lighten the mood.

A warning bell began to ring, making Jess turn her attention to a set of monitors. "Room 14 has pulled off her oxygen mask again. I gotta get this."

"No worries. I'm heading out. My shift ends at 11:00."

"Lucky you," Jess said, stepping toward the room. "I'll see you next weekend."

"Let's hope so."

Luke briefly stared at Helga's scattered records and was tempted to take them.

Walk away. You got what you needed.

As he approached the hallway exit, Luke reached out to get a handful of sanitizer from a dispenser. Rubbing his hands together, he hit the large silver button on the wall with his elbow and exited the doors.

Yes, it is definitely better going through the doors this way, he thought.

***

"I read the article you sent," Maryanne said as Luke approached the security desk. "It's crazy, right?"

"Only if Helga didn't die of natural causes," Luke responded.

Maryanne could hear the genuine concern in Luke's voice and it didn't surprise her that he was calling the dead woman by her first name, as if she were a family member. Unlike her job as a guard, whose main responsibility was to give directions to visitors, and the occasional restraining of unruly patients to their bed, a transporter had to establish a friendly one-on-one relationship with an unfamiliar person from the get-go. She knew Luke preferred to use the patient's first name when entering their room to break the ice; he became an old friend dropping in for a visit. He would also use the occasional 'Sir' or 'Ma'am' with elderly patients as a sign of respect. From the way his peers spoke of him, Maryanne had heard how great Luke was before they'd started dating.

Luke filled Maryanne in on what he'd learned in I.C.U. "I'll tell Jennifer in the morning."

Maryanne heard a slight tone of resignation. "Is something wrong?"

"I worry that I'm making too much out of this," Luke admitted. "I've transported hundreds of patients and when they're safely back in bed I just go to my next call. Helga should be no different."

"But she is and that's okay," Maryanne said reassuringly. "The odds are still high that Helga died of natural causes due to the stress of the surgery."

"If that's the case, I'm wasting Jennifer's time."

Maryanne disagreed. "As an investigative reporter that's 90% of her job, Luke. She doesn't have to look any further into Helga's death, and if she does and finds nothing, she'll be off on another story. I bet she's trying to find the tramp who slept with that councilman. Now there's a story to pursue."

"I suppose. I bumped into Dr. Singh awhile ago and she said she'd given Jennifer new information about that John Doe in the morgue."

"See, she's already got a lot on her investigative plate," Maryanne smiled widely, hoping one day she'd be doing the same thing. "You look tired, Luke. Go home and get some sleep."

Maryanne got up and walked into a nearby hallway, discreetly followed by Luke. With no cameras present, Luke gave Maryanne a kiss.

"Meet me for a late breakfast?" Luke asked.

"You know it," Maryanne replied.

Luke headed to the Admitting area to return his radio, as Maryanne sat back down in her desk chair.

A minute later, as Luke entered the lobby's revolving doors, Maryanne waved and warned him, "Don't watch any *Forensic Files* shows before bed!"

"I hear ya," he said with a grin.

TEN

MONDAY

After placing her overnight bag on the Jeep's passenger seat, Trillia felt the strong urge to pee. *Damn you, nerves!* she thought, deciding a fifth trip to the washroom was out of the question and backed out of her driveway. Atop the bag were printed pages of map directions to the Westhorn Penitentiary, some three hours away. She'd already texted Elaine that she was going out of town to visit a sick niece, but would be back the following day for her closing shift at *The Buckster Stops Here*. Even if she were delayed, Trillia knew one of the part-timers would gladly cover for her.

Trillia felt fortunate to have a day off, allowing her to make this trip to meet the love of her life in person, albeit through a thick pane of glass.

"My lawyer is working on the paperwork for conjugal visits," Jake had told her an hour earlier on the telephone. "He was confident he could get you in for a quickie visit today. What do you say, my little *Thrillia*?" he'd cooed, repeating the nickname every man in her life had used at one time or another.

"I can be there by two," she'd replied eagerly. "Where do I meet Vinny – in the main lobby?" she asked, as if high-profile attorney Vincent Palanovich was a childhood friend.

There was a noticeable pause before Jake said, "No, Vinny is working on my appeal and handed over the everyday duties to his associate, Carl Numan."

This explanation sounded plausible to Trillia. "Oh, okay," she said, already opening her closet door to pull out a small travel bag. "So Carl will meet me in the main lobby then?"

"He'll have a pass for you," Jake lied. "I can't wait to see you."

"Me, too, Jake. It's hard to believe this day has come," Trillia said, sounding like her former excitable self when asked to the prom by her school's older star quarterback.

"My time is almost up," Jake said. "One last thing: did you get those flowers to my aunt in the hospital with that message on the card?"

"I did," Trillia answered, not mentioning it was actually Elaine who delivered them, fearing this might cause trouble. "They were very pretty. I hope she liked them."

"I'm sure she did," Jake said, trying to dampen the delight in his voice, as a roguish smile spread across his face.

The line went dead.

"Jake? Are you still there? Jake!" Trillia pleaded, unsatisfied with how their conversation had ended. "Stupid prison phones!" she said as she hung up the receiver.

Now isn't the time to be angry, you have packing to do!

Within thirty minutes she was driving east with Tim McGraw blaring out of the speakers. She was on a mission, yet didn't go too far above the speed limit in case she got pulled over by a cop. Her disappointment in not being able to say, "Love you, Jake," diminished with every road sign that indicated the distance to Westhorn.

Although she'd never admit it, she was terrified how her first face-to-face encounter with Jake would go. She was shocked how fast he had responded to her pen pal request after he was convicted of killing his wife, Kaye. Trillia felt he was innocent and said so in the note she composed while in a state of disbelief, as well as loneliness. The words were meant to be encouraging, not as flirty. She wasn't expecting anything to come of it, but then her home phone rang one afternoon and a robotic-like voice informed her that a Westhorn Penitentiary inmate wanted to talk.

"Press 1 to decline this call. Press 2 to accept this call. Press 3 to report this call to the Warden."

Trillia had pressed 2 and the man she'd been fantasizing about during his trial said in a low, sexy tone, "Trillia? Is that you?"

With those four words, her life turned upside down.

***

For Jake Wagner, in a world that consisted of sitting alone in his cell reading, talking for short periods on the phone or using a computer was a cause to celebrate. With help from a few of his criminal connections both inside and outside of the penitentiary, he was afforded privileges other inmates couldn't afford. A meeting with his defence team had felt like Christmas morning, but the days of consulting with his big shot lawyer were over. The guilty verdict had abruptly ended those get-togethers. Vincent Palanovich's firm was still involved with the obligatory appeal, but Vinny had washed his hands of the loser case. Carl Numan, an underling, had been assigned the case and was doing an adequate job, not that Jake cared. He had no expectations that the verdict would be overturned in the foreseeable future. Having spent half of his life behind bars, prison was already Jake's second home. A string of poorly planned heists, countless bar room brawls, coupled with routinely assaulting police officers while carrying out their duties, resulted in a misspent youth, and a wasted adulthood. At thirty-four he should have known better, as his brother Benny had always told him.

Notwithstanding the length of his sentence, the biggest difference this time was the sheer number of crazy women contacting him. Each day dozens of letters arrived, were read by some official, and then forwarded to him on his lunch tray. Each writer desperately requesting to visit him, comfort him, do a research paper based on his feelings before, during and after the trial, or simply marry him. The first televised trial on the fledgling *Justice For All* cable channel had made him a celebrity. The letters were his fan mail created by inmate groupies, none of whom Jake ever planned to meet. To combat his own boredom, for amusement he'd decided to string them along for as long as he could – a letter here, a quick phone call there – keeping them entranced in the twisted notion they could change him somehow. For the cute gullible ones, he invited them up to see him, only to discover no guest pass was waiting for them at the guard house. Confused and unable to contact Jake, they'd go back home. A few days later, Jake would call to apologize for the mix-up, blaming the guards for not doing their jobs.

"I *felt* you outside, but couldn't get word to you," he'd claim innocently – and they'd buy it.

Every time.

The media saturated trial had encouraged savvy attorney Vincent Palanovich to take the case *pro bono*. "You can't buy this type of publicity," he'd told the reporters' scrum, all the while strenuously trying to convince the public Jake had been set up to take the fall for his wife's untimely death.

The gambit worked on many of the female viewers, hence the love letters to a convicted murderer, but wasn't believed by the eight women and four men on the jury. They returned a guilty verdict in less than two hours, even though the initial vote was unanimous soon after they began deliberations. "We didn't want to look like we rushed to judgement," the foreperson admitted later, "but the evidence was so overwhelming, there wasn't anything to debate. We got it right and justice was served."

At the end of each day of testimony, the media continuously rehashed the evidence against Jake Wagner:

- From the master bedroom thirty-year-old waitress Kaye Wagner had called 911 to report that a masked man had broken into her house and she was alone.
- During the call the unidentified man could be heard kicking at the locked bedroom door until it flew open.
- Moments before the man gained entry, Kaye pushed the cordless phone under a bed sheet and sobbed, "Don't

say another word. Please get the police over here. I'll be okay."

- Those were Kaye's final words as three bullets from a Smith & Wesson revolver entered her chest.
- The masked man had remained silent and was seen running out into the backyard, hopping a chain-link fence and getting into a waiting silver Chevrolet Malibu on a parallel side street.
- Police would converge on the Wagner house within minutes only to find Kaye dead.
- A half hour later, Jake Wagner arrived in his rusted truck and ran frantically to the officer stationed at the front door. "Did something happen to my wife?" he asked. "Was she shot?" That bewildering question would be the cornerstone of the prosecutor's case against Jake. The fact his fingerprints were found on the driver's door handle of the abandoned Malibu also assisted in obtaining a guilty verdict.
- The masked man was subsequently found dead with a single bullet to the back of his head in an abandoned amusement park. Identified as Freddy "Fingers" Colman, he was a known associate of Jake's and member of The Men – a small-time criminal gang, headed by career lowlife Clive Hill.

Regardless of such compelling evidence, at the onset the case against Jake was a circumstantial one. The gun was never found and presumed to be lost forever at the bottom of a nearby river. Jake admitted recently driving Freddy's car when they went shopping for new cell phones. Plus, there was his alibi: when Kaye was killed, he was helping a family friend do yard work at the man's house miles away from the Wagner crime scene. "It's basic physics: the defendant could not be in two places at the same time," Vincent Palanovich cautioned the jurists.

Unfortunately, Henrik Dekker faltered badly during an aggressive cross-examination. His pitiful performance, and the absence of grass clippings or garden dirt on the pants Jake was wearing when he arrived home, was another major factor in the jury's ultimate decision.

The final nail in Jake's trial coffin was a leather bound journal. Its pages were filled with Kaye's hopes for a life without Jake, and more importantly, detailed descriptions of the numerous beatings and injuries she'd suffered at his hands over a twelve-month period.

The diary's entries were significant as they provided a motive for killing his wife by documenting Jake's history of jealousy and violence. Shockingly, it wasn't written by Kaye Wagner, but by the one person she trusted with her secrets. A woman who loved her unconditionally from the first day they'd met in a hospital nursery three decades earlier. A grandmother who painstakingly transcribed her troubling conversations with Kaye after each heartbreaking visit, in the hopes it could one day help her escape a life no woman deserves.

Waiting to be called to testify, the old woman had sat silently on a bench holding her favourite picture of Kaye and vowing to be strong on the stand.

"I'm sorry I couldn't stop him before, Kaye. I promise I'm going to put him away today." Tears had begun to well in her eyes. "The prosecutor said without me that monster might go free. I swear, my angel, that isn't going to happen."

The courtroom door had opened and a bailiff stepped into the hallway. "Are you Helga Klemens?"

"I am," she'd replied.

"They're ready for you inside."

As she had entered, Helga had instantly seen the smiling face of Jake Wagner. *You don't scare me,* she thought. *And you wasted your money sending flowers to my house this morning with that card reading,* All the best, Helga! See you soon! *Such a fool.*

Jake had watched her walk into the witness box, where she placed her hand on a Bible.

"Do you swear to tell the whole truth and nothing but the truth?" the bailiff had asked her.

Helga glared at Jake before announcing in a strong, defiant voice, "I do."

ELEVEN

On November 27, 1919, *The Standard Gazette* began printing neighbourhood stories once a week, a mixture of local politics, gossip and recipes that ran ten pages. Throughout the city there were dozens of these publications, each claiming its own territory depending on which side of the street you lived. The handshake arrangement among the publishers not to cross established boundaries was generally respected and 'paper wars' didn't occur. Then on February 16, 1935, Morgan Telly, a West Coast media mogul, arrived and simultaneously bought all the newspapers at double their market value. Two weeks later, *The Daily Telegraph* hit the streets, covering news of the entire city, as well as national and international news. "West meets East. *The Telly* is the best thing that's ever happened to this place," Morgan was often quoted as saying. This kind of boast only encouraged recently laid off reporters and typesetters to incorporate their own venture, which they dubbed *The Star*.

With that, a fierce rivalry was born with both headquarters now housed across the street from one another.

"Do you think that hack Orr is having any luck locating the councilman's plaything?" Jennifer asked Mitch, staring across the busy thoroughfare below to where *The Star's* bullpen was located.

"He'd have a difficult time finding an actual plaything for a baby in a Toys R Us," Mitch laughed. "Don't worry, he's as clueless as you and your P.I. boyfriend."

Jennifer gave Mitch a puzzled look. "To clarify ... was that a dig at Orr or a shot at me and Jeffery?"

Mitch looked up from his papers. "Yes."

"Typical," Jennifer said, taking a seat on the couch. "When was the last time you tried to find someone who didn't want to be found?"

"Let me see," Mitch said, striking a 'thinking' pose. "After my divorce I tried reconnecting with my university girlfriend to meet for coffee. Does that count?"

"No," Jennifer stated. "I think she didn't want to be found by you. That's different."

"She really was a smart girl," Mitch replied.

"Smarter by the minute, if you ask me."

"Anyway ... thanks for the John Doe write-up. The composite drawing is being released at 2:00 and we'll run both tomorrow." Mitch marked the story off his To Do list. "While you were skulking about the hospital, did you peek into the Emergency waiting room to see if there were any stories floating around? A suspicious gunshot wound victim, a woman claiming to be pregnant with an alien baby – that kind of thing?"

"Do you honestly believe I'd be here if I could be interviewing people that were inappropriately probed by extraterrestrials?"

"So that's a no then?"

"Yes and no," Jennifer hedged.

Mitch leaned back in his chair. "Continue."

Jennifer went to her desk to retrieve the newspaper article she'd printed off. As she handed it to Mitch she asked, "What do you know about this case?"

Mitch read the first few paragraphs. "A little more than nothing now. You should talk with Simpson – he watches a lot of televised trials."

"To clarify ... you meant Rich Simpson down the hall, not O.J., correct?"

"At this point, either would be more helpful than me."

"Gotcha."

"Why am I reading this?"

"The short version is the witness the lawyer was talking about died while having a routine surgery yesterday."

"And?" Mitch skimmed the article. "The woman was a very senior senior citizen, Malone. At her age death isn't unexpected."

"I'd usually agree with that hypothesis, as it's a sound argument based on mortality statistics."

"But?"

"Not when poor Helga's last words were, 'Don't let them kill me,' – I'm paraphrasing Luke, the patient transporter – he took her by stretcher to the O.R."

"Could he have been just pulling your leg to scare you down in the basement?"

"One, I don't scare that easily, and two, he was cute. I would've let him pull my leg or any other body part," Jennifer said with a sly smirk. "He already has a girlfriend, who will be contacting you about an intern job with my wholehearted recommendation."

Mitch felt a headache coming on. "Her name wouldn't be Maryanne something, would it?"

"I didn't catch her surname. Maybe she's going the full Cher route – one name fits all."

Mitch opened his email and moved Maryanne's message from the Trash folder back into the inbox. "Did she hear this Helga begging for her life, or only second-hand from her boyfriend?"

"Technically, it's hearsay in her case, but we both believe Luke isn't making this up. There's something about him that's refreshing."

"If you say so," Mitch said. "So the question remains: was the old woman murdered?"

Jennifer got off the couch, stretched a little and retrieved the newspaper article. "Hard to say. I'm calling Luke now to go over some things."

"Keep me in the loop. This is the kind of story we should be investigating, instead of a tawdry affair of a married man and a bored rich girl with time on her hands."

"You know what they say about idle hands, don't you?" Jennifer asked walking out of the office.

"They're the Devil's playthings?"

"Right. And another item Orr across the street would have trouble locating in the toy department."

***

Jennifer spoke with an energized Luke on the phone for a few minutes. As he was at a diner having breakfast with Maryanne, Jennifer told him to call when he had more privacy.

"Maryanne says hi," Luke said.

"Tell her hi back. Talk to you soon."

Jennifer peered down the office hallway and sighted her next target.

"Jake Wagner. What do I need to know about him?" Jennifer asked, placing the newspaper article on Rich Simpson's desk.

Simpson was a throwback to the old-time reporters seen in classic movies. In his late fifties, tall with a distinguished greying beard, he resembled a history professor, which he was in his own way. The veteran who had seen it all.

He acknowledged Jennifer's presence with a nod. "And a good morning to you also," he said, picking up the piece of paper. "The first thing you need to know is that beauty is skin deep. A handsome, articulate man like Jake Wagner should be CFO material at a big corporation, not a convicted killer. What a waste."

"Wow – I didn't realize you two were so close," Jennifer said. "Do you want a minute to dab the tears from your eyes? I won't blab to anyone. I'm very discreet."

"I was only stating facts," Rich replied calmly. "Plus, he isn't my type. Men that good-looking are high maintenance. Nothing but trouble."

"Thanks for that dating tip. I'll remember it when Bradley Cooper calls."

"He has mommy issues," Rich stated. "I read it in *The Enquirer*."

"Take it from a woman – all men have mommy issues," Jennifer said. "Did it come out in trial Mr. Wagner had any such problems, or did killing his wife solve them?"

"You're not aware of this case at all?" Rich proceeded to open the *Justice For All* homepage and clicked on the 'People vs. Jake Wagner' link. "For starters, this was the station's flagship program, but even I'm offended there's a photo gallery to show all of this creep's emotions during the trial."

Jennifer viewed the pictures. "It's definitely tacky and you're right – Jake is one attractive man."

"I think Vincent Palanovich's law firm must run this website. There are far too many flattering shots of him and let me tell you, he isn't *that* handsome in person." Rich shook his head.

"You would know."

"Why the interest in this case?" Rich asked. "It's done. The jury got it right. Mr. Wagner is locked away and his wife is still dead."

Jennifer turned around an empty chair at a desk across the aisle and sat down. "What's happening with the appeal and how does the testimony of the victim's grandmother play into it?"

Without unearthing any notes he might have taken during the trial coverage, or referring to the website's 'Appeal – Update!' link, Rich relaxed in his chair.

"Like the lawyer said in this article, without Helga Klemens' diary Jake Wagner could be a free man," Rich said casually.

"She was that crucial to the case?"

"Yes, because she provided a detailed report of Jake's abuse and the marital troubles with Kaye that spanned a full year."

"Didn't Jake's defence team challenge her?" Jennifer asked. "She was obviously biased toward her granddaughter."

Rich pointed a finger at Jennifer. "Oh, they tried. There was a closed session to determine if the diary entries should be deemed hearsay."

"And they lost."

"Big time," Rich replied eagerly. "You see, Helga wrote the incidents in a way that there was rarely any emotion in them. They came across as if a robot translated the abuses after watching a closed-circuit feed of each fight."

"You do know robots can't do that?" Jennifer stated, interrupting Rich's account of what went down.

"Yet," he said smiling. "Even on the stand she was unshakeable during her testimony and the brutal cross-examination. She was the perfect witness and the jury believed what she said and wrote in that book."

"And that tilted a wonky circumstantial case in favour of the prosecution," Jennifer theorized, better understanding Helga's role in Jake's conviction. "So what would happen if a star witness couldn't make an appearance at a second trial?"

Rich glanced over at the Jake Wagner page on his computer screen. "If a second trial were granted and Helga couldn't attend, say for health reasons, it's likely this scumbag would go free."

"Her diary couldn't be entered into evidence again?"

"Nope," Rich answered, "because no lawyer has figured out a way to cross examine an inanimate object."

Jennifer stood and replaced the chair at the empty desk. "Yet," she said. "Thanks for the info, Rich."

"Anytime."

As she made her way up the aisle, Jennifer felt a fleeting pang of regret for keeping Helga's death a secret from Rich. *An exclusive is still an exclusive in this business.*

At her desk Jennifer leisurely browsed the *Justice For All* website. The pictures of Jake were fascinating and disturbing, as he looked like a man she would talk to at a bar or social gathering. "This is why I don't date," she said aloud.

"You don't date 'cause you're afraid of commitment," came a female voice from behind Jennifer, who didn't look to see who it was.

"Did I use my outside voice, Cassie?"

"You did," the Lifestyle editor said, propping herself on the corner of the desk. "Oh – who is this fantastic piece of male art? I'd take him into my bedroom."

"To be shot dead like his wife?" Jennifer replied, clicking on a crime scene photo of Kaye Wagner slumped against her bed. "Do you want to hear what your night of passion might sound like with this hunk?" Jennifer held the cursor over the '911 Call' link.

"What? No!" Cassie said, jumping off the desk. "Why are you looking at that nasty stuff, instead of logging on to *lonelyreporters.com*?"

Jennifer looked at her. "There's such a thing?"

"If there isn't, there should be."

Jennifer closed the website. "I'm doing some research for a story. Don't worry, I'm not going to hook up with this Ted Bundy wannabee."

"I'd hope not."

"What are you working on?" Jennifer asked.

"A couple of things," Cassie said. "A health article dealing with the healing powers of broccoli and asparagus."

"I get them mixed up all the time. Which one is green and which one is white?

"They're both green!"

"Oh. What vegetable am I thinking of then?"

"Cauliflower?"

"That may be it," Jennifer agreed. "Any other ideas for the weekend edition?"

"Yes, a dating piece about meeting hotties in the supermarket produce department," Cassie said with a huge grin, "which might be out of your comfort zone."

"I want a man who knows his way around meat, not vegetables," Jennifer said. "A manly man who can cook a steak, not toss together a salad from rabbit food."

"When you find him, ask if he has a friend and we can double date."

Jennifer's cell phone rang and Luke's name popped up on the screen. "Cass, I have to take this."

"No worries, I have my own work to do," Cassie said. "Want to do lunch at noon?"

"It's a date."

Before answering Jennifer grabbed a pen from her top desk drawer and opened her notepad. "Hey, Luke, how was breakfast?"

***

Despite the fact she was mildly perturbed that he'd disobeyed her request to stop discussing Helga at the hospital, Luke's information was gold.

"That's some solid investigative work, Luke," Jennifer complimented him, unaware he'd forgotten to mention Helga's listed next of kin on her hospital paperwork. "I bet Maryanne is jealous."

"A bit," Luke chuckled. "I saw the opportunity and took it. She'll do the same for me if she can."

"I have no doubt. She seems like the persistent type," Jennifer said, remembering that only hours, minutes perhaps, after they'd met, Maryanne had sent a message to Mitch about an internship. "What are your plans for the rest of the day?"

"I have a bunch of errands to run," Luke said. "Working different shifts every weekend throws your life off. Monday is the day I clean my apartment and chill, but I could get called in at any minute. What about you?"

"I'll do a drive-by of Helga's house and get the lay of the land. It's doubtful her neighbours know she passed away and I don't want to be the bearer of sad news."

"No good conversations happen when one person is crying," Luke commented. "I see it every shift in the waiting rooms or the cancer ward and I.C.U. wing. It's terrible to watch someone suffer and not be able to help them in some meaningful way."

"I'm sure you do what you can to comfort them," Jennifer replied. "Your job can't be easy, particularly when you have back door calls."

"It isn't," Luke agreed without expanding on the topic.

"I'm going to leave the office after lunch and will keep you informed about what I find or don't find," Jennifer said. "If Maryanne learns anything new today have her call my cell."

"I'll tell her." Luke hesitated before saying, "Thanks for doing this. I hope I'm not wasting your time."

Oh, Luke.

"It's no trouble," Jennifer said in an encouraging tone. "I also want to know what happened to Helga. Together we'll learn the answers and then move forward."

TWELVE

After splitting a pizza with Cassie from *Papa J's Buy The Slice,* Jennifer relocated her car and began to navigate the busy city streets. Unlike many of her colleagues, she enjoyed driving, although taking the subway wasn't terrible, especially when she had to pay high garage or lot fees – *Hello, Met Hospital!* Fortunately, Helga had lived in an older area named Greenheart

Station, where street parking was ample and best of all, free. By the time Jennifer pulled onto King Street, the imposing glass and metallic skyscrapers of downtown were in her rear view mirror. The air smelled cleaner and there were only three cars waiting for the traffic lights on the main drag to turn green. Citizens were walking unleashed dogs and stopping to talk to their neighbours on the sidewalk.

This is like a TV soundstage for a Twilight Zone episode, Jennifer thought. She was a city girl, born and raised, but believed she could trade in the asphalt jungle for the picket fenced house she'd just passed without any anxiety. What unnerved her more than the move was the idea that once settled she would have to find a husband, give birth to 2.3 kids and buy a sturdy Honda Civic or a minivan.

Jennifer Malone – Soccer mom!

Does Honda make a minivan?

The electronic female voice on the GPS said, "You have arrived at your destination," breaking Jennifer's concentration of the Norman Rockwell-themed neighbourhood.

The blocks surrounding Helga's charming two-storey dwelling consisted of houses built by different contractors at different times for wildly different budgets. The lots were a decent size, each with a big backyard and driveways covered in stones, instead of cement or decorative bricks. There was a portable basketball net positioned by the curb of one dwelling.

"Anywhere else and that would be stolen the minute it was left unattended," Jennifer said to herself as she parked on the street.

Studying Helga's former residence, Jennifer could envision where the ambulance and police cruiser had been parked, and how the paramedics would've had to carefully walk their stretcher up and down the three porch steps; once when it was empty, once with a passenger aboard. Jennifer's mind flashed back to the chaotic scene at the hospital the previous evening as a patient was rushed into the E.R. There were no vehicles in the driveway, perhaps indicating that Helga's driving days were over. Jennifer made a note to look into any community-based shuttle services Helga might have used to get groceries and go to medical appointments.

Jennifer got out of her car and walked to the edge of Helga's property. Only one thing appeared out of place: a wooden gate leading to the backyard had its base stuck on a clump of overgrown grass against the adjoining high fence. It was possible the first responders initially went to the rear door and propped the gate open. Yet it was feasible that someone quickly exited the backyard and pushed the gate hard enough for it to get stuck. Jennifer made a second note to speak with the EMS personnel about their movements upon arrival.

"Are you looking for Helga?" a man from across the street asked. "She's not home."

Jennifer turned to see an elderly gentleman who resembled a dapper garden gnome with a white beard and moustache inching toward her with the help of a cane. *Man, I love old people,* Jennifer said to herself, checking out his rumpled baseball cap with its classic Pepsi logo. "Oh," she said with a friendly smile, "do you know when she'll be back?" Guilt racked her again for not being forthcoming with the truth.

"No," came the response. "She fell down her stairs yesterday and broke her hip. They took her to Metropolitan Hospital by ambulance."

"That's terrible," Jennifer said. "I take it the two of you have known each other for a few years."

The man grinned. "If you think over 75 years is a few, then, yes, we've known each other a spell."

"Wow."

"Helga was my first love," the man admitted proudly, "and I was the first boy she ever kissed. We were only in Grade 5 at the time, but that still counts, doesn't it?"

"Absolutely," Jennifer agreed. "I thought I was hot stuff when

Harry Lancer kissed me at a Grade 8 dance, but that doesn't compare to you two lovebirds."

"It was a short romance, lasting until the end of recess, if I'm going to be honest."

"Yeah, Harry and me – he apparently goes by Harold today – went our separate ways after I discovered high school boys were more mature."

"Love's like that." The old man shuffled his feet a bit and introduced himself. "I'm Glenn. I live over there," he said, pointing to a small corner house two doors down. "I've been Helga's neighbour for four decades."

"I'm Jennifer. It's nice to meet you, Glenn," she said, getting a welcoming nod from her new friend. "Did Helga live alone?" Jennifer asked, knowing nothing about Helga's personal life.

"Yes, since her husband Herman passed away in 2001. Helga was always independent and didn't have any problems afterwards." They both looked toward her house. "Until this fall, she was as fit as a fiddle, as my wife Cathy would have said."

Jennifer noted the "would have said" reference and decided to veer away from areas of elder health and focus on the here and now, at least the present that Glenn was aware of. "Were you at home when the ambulance arrived?"

"And the police," Glenn answered. "I was watching TV in the front room and saw them pull up. I was hoping it wasn't anything too serious. At our age anything is possible."

"Where did they park?" Jennifer pointed toward the driveway, then silently berated herself for sounding like a reporter. "I mean, did they have to go through the back door to get to Helga?"

"Nope, they parked at the end of the driveway here." Glenn walked a short distance to a spot parallel to the front door. "Took out the stretcher and went right in."

"Did Helga call 911?" Jennifer couldn't imagine dragging herself across the floor with a broken hip to get to a phone. *Could she have been wearing one of those emergency call buttons?*

"No, a passerby heard Helga yelling for help and found her in the foyer at the bottom of the stairs."

Passerby?

"And the door was unlocked?"

"I guess," Glenn said, glancing toward the door in question. "Helga sometimes drinks her morning coffee on the wicker patio loveseat. Maybe she forgot to lock the door when she went back in. Her back door is usually unlocked, so no one would have had to break in and damage it."

"That was a lucky break for Helga – no pun intended," Jennifer said, deciding to drop the lock conundrum for now. "What about this good Samaritan?"

The question seemed to catch Glenn off guard. "Oh, yeah ... the woman from the post office."

Mental note #3.

"Her last name is Grant." Glenn paused and added, "How do you spell your name?"

It was Jennifer's turn to be caught by surprise. "The usual way? J-e-n-n-i-f-e-r."

Glenn began to chuckle. "I guess that makes our mail lady unusual, because she spells her first name G-e-n-i-f-e-r."

Mental note #3 – check.

"And no doubt she's loathed her parents ever since," Jennifer said as she shared a laugh with Glenn.

"I'm sure their intention was to make her feel special, like that 'A Boy Named Sue' song by Johnny Cash," Glenn said. "To each their own, I guess. Me and my siblings were named after famous celebrities from my parents' day. I was named after Glenn Miller, my sister after Barbara Stanwyck, and our brother after Henry Fonda, but we called him Hank."

"And what about your children? Any interesting names?"

"My wife was quite religious and settled on two good solid Bible names – David and Ruth."

Jennifer smiled. "With both easy to spell. That was smart."

"We thought so," Glenn said, his voice trailing off, looking up the driveway. "Was there something you were getting from Helga or just stopping in for a visit?"

"Ah ... a drop-in visit," Jennifer mumbled, unprepared to provide a reason to this adorable senior citizen.

"I don't know what the hospital visiting hours are these days," Glenn said. "I was going to see Helga tonight and tell her that Logan's okay."

"Logan?"

"Her cat," Glenn answered. "I have a key to the house and take care of Logan when Helga is away. I was coming over to feed him when I saw you."

The urge to find an excuse to enter the house with Glenn was overwhelming and it took all of Jennifer's considerable willpower to quash the idea.

Not now.

"I won't hold you up any longer, Glenn, as Logan is waiting for you." Jennifer made her way to her car. "It was a pleasure to meet you."

"I agree," Glenn replied with a lovable smile. "I'll let Helga know you dropped by."

Jennifer was unable to come clean to Helga's dear friend, and got into her car. She watched Glenn check the porch mailbox and then walk to the backyard, closing the easy-swinging gate behind him.

The front door lock and that gate bothered Jennifer, although she didn't know why. She hoped that the paramedics and Genifer with a "G" could answer these and many more questions.

***

The joint Greenheart Station EMS station and police department were located three blocks from Helga's house, ensuring a quick reaction time by all responders. As the ambulance had arrived first, Jennifer entered the station's lobby and approached the receptionist, who looked to be a summer student.

"Hi, my name is Jennifer Malone from *The Daily Telegraph*. I was hoping to speak to someone about a call your crew attended yesterday." Jennifer handed the girl a business card. Her response was nowhere near as enthusiastic as Maryanne's had been at the hospital security desk.

"Which one?" the girl with the nametag 'Gayle' asked in a slightly bitchy tone. "We had fourteen of them."

Annoyed, for effect Jennifer leisurely retrieved her notebook from her purse and began to flip pages. "I wrote the information down here somewhere." Jennifer stopped and scanned the area. "It's a good thing you're not busy," she said with a fake smile, "otherwise I'd be wasting your time." One more flip to a blank page and Jennifer declared, "Here it is – Helga Klemens on King Street around noon." Jennifer intentionally leaned forward across the counter. "Do you have that in your system, or do I need to speak to Philip – I mean, Captain Baker?" she asked, noting a wall plaque listing the station's higher ups.

The girl's aloof expression vanished as she typed in Helga's name on her computer. "Yes, we attended a residence on King Street yesterday. It says here that it was a fall."

"Could I talk with the paramedics who went there? I have a few questions I hope they can answer for me."

A superior attitude returned to the girl's face. "Due to patient confidentiality restrictions, the paramedics can't give out any information. Sorry," she said, not sorry in the least.

You little witch. Two can play this game.

"Oh. So, what, I have to get a court order?" Jennifer tried to appear flustered at her professional gaffe. "I can do that." She flipped to a new page in her notebook and grabbed a pen off the counter. "For the court papers I'll require who went to the call – not their phone numbers and home addresses. Their names will do. I'll include the station's address for the legal eagles to cross-reference. The wheels of justice move kinda slow when you don't check every box and fill in each line. Working here you must know that."

With each sentence Jennifer sped up her delivery and enjoyed the information overload in the girl's eyes.

"Ah ... I ... I can give you those," the girl said, out of sync with her own thoughts, much to Jennifer's delight. "Patrick Gesuale and Kristen Key."

Jennifer wrote down the names and stashed her notebook into her purse. "Thank you, Gayle, you were very helpful. Next time I go out to dinner with Phil and his better half – he's still married, right? – I'll put in a good word for you. How does that sound?"

Gayle's brain was spinning out of control and only managed to say, "I ... was ... ah ... glad I could help," before Jennifer was out the door, making a beeline to the two open garage bay doors where ambulances were parked unattended.

***

"Hey, guys," Jennifer said as she approached two paramedics restocking medical supplies in the back of an ambulance. "Are either of you Patrick?"

The brown haired, thirty-something paramedic turned in Jennifer's direction, a smile coming over his face. "I am."

Jennifer had a thing for men in uniform or authority-type figures. Police, military and healthcare workers had a warm place in her heart. She was also a sucker for men in suits. Somehow the EMS ensemble combined all her favourite personnel. Seeing Patrick's close cropped beard and moustache simply enhanced today's interview experience.

"Patrick, it's nice to meet you," Jennifer said, extending her hand to shake and to give him a business card. "Jennifer Malone. *The Daily Telegraph* newspaper. I was hoping we could talk for a few minutes." Jennifer assessed the clean-shaven, but equally fine-looking other paramedic. "I take it you are not Kristen."

The comment made the younger man blush. "Not today," he laughed. "I'm Owen," he said, also shaking Jennifer's hand and taking her card. "If you need her, Kristen will be back soon. It was her turn to make a coffee run."

"Don't you have your own kitchen here?" Jennifer asked, pointing toward the back rooms.

"That's firefighters," Patrick clarified. "They basically live at the station. Our break room consists of a mini fridge, a microwave and a coffee maker – all purchased at a Salvation Army store."

"We work eight hours like normal people and go home at the end of every shift," Owen added.

"I'd like your schedule over the fire department's," Jennifer said, "even though I haven't had a scheduled job in my life. The news never sleeps."

A blue Chrysler Neon with EMS logos plastered on its doors was driven onto the lot by a pretty female with streaked blonde hair, also in uniform. After parking the car, she exited it carrying a tray of Styrofoam coffee cups and a takeout bag. "Lunch is served," she said, handing her coworkers their beverages. "Baked goods roulette time," she said, holding the bag above her head.

Owen stepped forward and dipped his hand into the bag, retrieving a blueberry muffin. "Thanks, Kristen."

Next, Patrick put his hand in the bag and pulled out a giant chocolate chip cookie. "Thanks, Kristen."

"You're welcome," Kristen said, lowering the bag, claiming a jelly-filled pastry for herself. "Sorry, that was the last one," she said to Jennifer.

"No worries."

After one bite of his muffin, Owen excused himself from the group. "I've got paperwork to do. Something you would know all about," he said to Jennifer.

"It was good meeting you, Owen," Jennifer said, turning her

attention to the dynamic duo in front of her. "Kristen, I'm Jennifer Malone from *The Daily Telegraph*. I was hoping the two of you could help me."

Patrick and Kristen exchanged a look. "If we can," Patrick said.

"It's about a call you attended yesterday." As she had done with Gayle, Jennifer took out her notebook and started flipping pages. This time it wasn't to annoy the paramedics, only a subtle indication that if a reporter wrote a fact down, it must be important. "A Helga Klemens, down a few blocks on King Street."

"Tripped over her cat and broke a hip, right?" Kristen said before taking a sip from her cup.

"That's the one," Jennifer confirmed.

"Are you writing a story on her life?" Patrick asked. "It's a shame. She seemed to be doing fine when we left her at the hospital."

Jennifer stopped flipping pages. "I might be doing a story on Helga, but not the kind you're thinking of." Jennifer didn't feel the urge to elaborate more. "How did you find out about her death?"

"I got a text from another paramedic, who heard it from an E.R. nurse at Met," Kristen answered.

"I got the same text," Patrick admitted.

"It was a real shocker," Jennifer said, glad she didn't have to lie about Helga's current state of being. "I wanted to ask you what happened when you arrived at her house – off the record. I'm guessing there are paramedic-patient confidentiality rules ... though I'm not positive they apply when the person has died. Are you cool with that?"

The pair looked at each other. "Sure," Patrick said.

"Perfect." Jennifer made a line across her notebook page and dated the entry. "Can you give me a breakdown of what you saw and what Helga said to you?"

Patrick took a bite of his cookie, leaving the onus on Kristen to relate their experience.

"Well ... when we drove up the front door was open and then a woman came out to meet us. She was pretty shaken. My first guess was she was the patient's daughter, but apparently she was out for a walk and heard Helga screaming."

Genifer.

"This may sound like a strange question," Jennifer interrupted, "but did you notice if the back gate was closed?"

"I don't remember," Kristen said. "As soon as we were stopped I jumped out and walked to the rear of the ambulance."

"It was open," Patrick said confidently. "I was the driver and remember thinking, 'Oh good, the gate isn't locked and we can get into the backyard.' It was only when I got out of the ambulance I saw the front door open and knew that it would be our entry point."

Jennifer noted the information. "And there were no vehicles in the driveway?"

"No," Kristen replied. "That's usually a red flag, wondering if we need to break down a door to get in."

"We don't break the doors, that would be Randy's call," Patrick interjected. "Officer Randy Patterson. He showed up a minute after us."

"I'll talk to him next," Jennifer said. "So, once inside you find Helga at the bottom of the stairs in agony, I would expect, correct?"

"Actually, she was doing well, as long as we didn't move her too much."

"Did she tell you how she fell?" Jennifer inquired. "Did she actually trip over her cat?" The two paramedics exchanged a glance.

"What?"

Again, it was Kristen who took the lead. "No, there was a black cat named Lobo or Lucky or something."

"But?" Jennifer prodded.

"Helga had red marks on her lower arms, like she'd been grabbed."

"Hand prints?" Jennifer's reporter instincts were now on high.

"Maybe," Patrick said dismissively. "It wasn't until we were at the hospital that we noticed them. Helga was adamant they were bruises from the edge of the stairs as she fell down them, and they might have been."

"Interesting," was all Jennifer said. "Did Helga say anything else? What about the woman who found her?"

"Helga was fairly tight-lipped. She was in a lot of pain and a mild state of shock. Old people and broken hips are not a good combination," Kristen said. "The woman who found her was also a bit dazed, stumbling upon this the way she did."

"She didn't say a whole lot," Patrick chipped in. "Randy spoke with her on the porch as we dealt with Helga inside. He's on duty until 7:00 tonight. That's his car, the black Ford."

They looked across the parking lot to a new Fusion.

Jennifer pondered her next move. The back gate mystery was partially solved, but it was still unclear a crime had taken place within Helga's house.

"That's all the questions I have," Jennifer said, closing her notebook. "Thanks for your help."

"No problem," Patrick said.

As they parted ways, Kristen called out, "When you talk with the woman who found Helga, tell her we hope she's feeling better."

"Excuse me?" Jennifer came to a full stop in the parking lot.

"The woman – her name was the same as yours – had some kind of fainting episode after she went home," Kristen began. "She was the call right after we dropped Helga off at the hospital. I doubt they kept her overnight."

"We're talking about Genifer Grant, right?" Jennifer asked.

"Yes – spelled with a 'G,'" Patrick responded with a smile. "That's her. Small world, huh?"

***

Jennifer spent another ten minutes interviewing Patrick and Kristen about their call starring Genifer Grant.

"We figured it was a delayed response to the earlier incident at Helga's," Patrick said.

Kristen looked up the address for the Grant residence, while Jennifer was hoping Miss Snooty Gayle would pop her head in at that moment, but it wasn't to be.

Jennifer said her goodbyes and was heading toward the adjacent police department entrance when her cell phone rang.

"Hello, is this Jennifer?" an elderly woman asked, her voice crackling with age.

"It is," Jennifer replied cautiously, unable to place the caller.

"It's Sandy from the Metropolitan Hospital Gift Shop calling. You stopped in yesterday asking about our flower selection," the woman stated. "I found a sticky note on the cash register this morning when I opened."

"Yes, that was me," Jennifer said quickly. "Thank you for calling me back."

"It's my pleasure, dear. We have a flower shipment coming in and can deliver them to your friend at no extra charge."

"That's very kind of you, but she was sent home late last night," Jennifer replied.

"That's always good to hear."

Jennifer recalled the video camera above the gift shop cash register. "Was the volunteer I dealt with yesterday able to find out who purchased those lovely carnations before I had a chance to?"

"I sold them."

"Oh. I hope the buyer's loved one enjoyed them," Jennifer said, trying to keep the conversation going.

"I'll ask her next time she comes in," came the reply. "She works here in the hospital."

Breathe.

"What a coincidence. I have a lot of friends who are nurses at the hospital," Jennifer lied, fishing for more details. "Do you remember her name?"

"Oh, I don't. She isn't a nurse though," the woman said apologetically.

"A patient transporter, perhaps?" Jennifer asked, envisioning Luke.

"No ... I think she works downstairs somewhere. She wears a red outfit."

Jennifer could tell the woman was getting flustered by these questions. The buyer worked in the hospital. Luke and Maryanne worked in the hospital.

I'll discover who this woman is eventually.

"That's okay. Thank you again for this information," Jennifer said cheerfully. "I hope you have a wonderful day."

"You, too, sweetie. Bye for now."

***

Officer Randy Patterson was in his early sixties and cut from the old school cloth of policing. He was tall, with a noticeable paunch, and striking salt and pepper hair. He walked to the front lobby with an aura that indicated he ran the place, even if the bars on his uniform shoulders said otherwise.

"Miss Malone?" he asked, greeting Jennifer in the station's foyer. "I read your work all the time. It's a pleasure to meet you."

Jennifer took his hand and was impressed by his strong grip, and friendly smile. "It's good meeting you. After a weekend of crime activity, Mondays must be really busy. I wish I were here under different circumstances."

A concerned expression came over Officer Patterson's face. "Why don't we head to the conference room and talk in private."

They walked into a large room and sat on either side of a mammoth table surrounded by plush office chairs.

"How can I help you today? I hope none of my officers have done something outside of their duties to warrant a story."

"Not that I'm aware of," Jennifer reassured him. "It's regarding a call you attended yesterday at the home of Helga Klemens – an elderly woman who fell at her house. I've already spoken off the record with the two paramedics and they said you interviewed the passerby who helped Mrs. Klemens."

"Oh, that. The woman was beside herself," Officer Patterson began. "She was out for a leisurely walk and heard screaming coming from inside the house. Luckily, the front door was open and she found the old girl at the bottom of the steps. She called 911 and we were there in a couple minutes."

"The ... ah ... witness, Genifer Grant ... did she know Mrs. Klemens prior to finding her?"

"Apparently not, which is kind of ironic because she delivers mail door-to-door in the same area."

Jennifer wrote these details in her notebook. "A real life good Samaritan."

"Exactly."

"Did she say anything that struck you as out of place? Or did Mrs. Klemens?"

Officer Patterson set his hands on the table. "I have no issue answering your questions, Miss Malone, but can you give me an indication why you're so interested in a senior citizen's broken hip and the woman who found her?"

Jennifer was done lying for one day. "The truth is that the fall victim died last night and I'm looking into what transpired at her house prior to the 911 call – on behalf of some friends. So there is nothing sinister going on."

One white lie is allowed.

Officer Patterson looked relieved. "That's good to hear – the no sinister part, not the news about Mrs. Klemens." He leaned back in his chair. "My mother lives on her own and I worry a fall like this might happen to her. As for Mrs. Klemens, I only spoke with her to get the details of what happened and then let the paramedics do their job."

"And Genifer?"

"Like I said, she was upset. I see it with people who witness a car accident or are involved in a fender bender. The experience is so foreign to their everyday lives, they can't process the information fast enough to make sense of it later on."

"I get that."

"She said the old woman told her she'd tripped over her cat on the stairs. From my standpoint it was a reasonable explanation."

Jennifer debated bringing up the 'Don't let them kill me' declaration, ultimately deciding it would only muddle an already helpful conversation.

Maybe next time.

Jennifer packed her notebook away and stood.

"I hope your friends value the time you're taking to look into this for them."

"I'm sure they do," Jennifer replied, as they walked to the front lobby.

"After this conversation, I'm calling my mother to see how her weekend went," Officer Patterson said with a grin. "And discuss the advantages of giving up her cat."

"Good luck with that," Jennifer said as she walked out the door, heading across the parking lot.

As she unlocked her car door, Jennifer's cell phone rang with the caller display reading Greenheart Station EMS. Worried that it might be Gayle about to yell at her for talking with the paramedics without a court order, Jennifer carefully answered, "Hello."

"Hey ... hi ... Jennifer?"

"It is," she replied, recognizing the male voice. "Did you remember a detail you wanted to share, Patrick?"

In the background Jennifer heard both Kristen and Owen egging Patrick on. "Go on, stop being an idiot," Owen said.

"Yeah, Patrick, stop being an idiot," Jennifer said a little louder when she looked toward the ambulance bay where Patrick was holding the wall phone to his ear. "You should hang up and meet me in the parking lot, if you have something to tell me in confidence."

Patrick turned slowly and saw Jennifer staring at him. While replacing the receiver, she heard him say, "You guys are the idiots," to his coworkers in a room out of view. He stood still for a moment, brought his hands together to the centre of his chest as if to pray, and briefly closed his eyes.

Damn it, he's one of those 'I have to realign my spiritual chakras types.' I see a few yoga class dates in my near future. She watched as Patrick inhaled deeply and strode to her in a purposeful manner.

"Hello, again," Jennifer said, trying unsuccessfully to hide her enjoyment of his awkwardness.

"Hi ... again," Patrick said, now standing in front of her, taking out his wallet from a pant's side pocket.

Jennifer almost said, 'The interview was free of charge,' but didn't want to embarrass Patrick further. When he presented a business card she took it. "Patrick Gesuale – Author. Who knew?" she said astonished. "Is saving people's lives a hobby or is writing novels the sideline?"

"So far, writing is the hobby," he said more self-assuredly, the blush in his cheeks having subsided. "I used to work as a private investigator and write mysteries."

"Based on stories you heard on the job or purely fiction?" Jennifer flipped the card over to view the covers of four books. "They look interesting."

"The stories are fictional, but I do use aspects of my former life to bring some authenticity to my main character."

Jennifer scrutinized the tiny pictures. "'A Jet Talbot Mystery'. I like the name."

"A former rogue cop, turned flawed private investigator."

"He's not 300 pounds and likes cronuts, is he?"

"Nah," Patrick replied with a smile. "Jet is essentially my alter-ego, except he has more fun than I ever did as a P.I., but gets in more trouble than I'd ever want to."

"Sounds like the kind of book I could curl up with at night," Jennifer joked. "Question: would your boy Jet ask a strange woman he's only known for fifteen minutes on a date or would he wait to get to know her a bit first?"

"I don't think you're strange," Patrick said.

Jennifer smiled. "Nicely played."

"So ... would you like to get to know me a bit more this weekend?"

"What if I'm already dating an author who writes mysteries on a full-time basis?" Jennifer asked.

"It wouldn't be the ending I had in mind, but I'd respect my fellow writer's exceptional taste in women," Patrick stated in a gentlemanly tone. "That being said, I'd also hope he does something dumb for you to give me a call."

"How about Saturday night? I don't have assignment desk duties this weekend," Jennifer said, putting the business card in her purse.

"Sounds great," Patrick said, a happy grin stretching across his face.

"Give me a call later in the week and we'll figure out the time and place, okay?" Jennifer instructed as she got into the driver's seat of her car, Patrick helping to close the door.

"I look forward to it."

"Me too," Jennifer said as she drove off the lot.

THIRTEEN

The Grant household felt more animated than usual for a Monday morning. Genifer chalked it up to her family's relief that she was still alive to cook them eggs, bacon, hash browns and mini pancakes for breakfast.

"Thanks, Mom," Zoe and Aleena said as they ran out the door to catch the school bus.

"Love you!" Genifer called out.

"Yeah, Mom, thanks," Stan said grinning as he gave Genifer a kiss on the lips and took both of her hands in his. "Will you be all right? I can work from home today."

Stan had been the perfect husband throughout this ordeal. He said all the right things because he truly loved her, not for any marital brownie points.

"You go to work," Genifer said with a sigh, lifting their hands to her chest. "I promise I won't over exert myself. I'll clean the girls' rooms and do some laundry. Teena was happy to take my route after finding out what happened."

"I'll call every two hours," Stan said, leaning forward to kiss her forehead. "You gave us quite the scare."

Genifer could feel tears forming in her eyes. "You're going to make me cry, Stan. Get out of here already, so I can enjoy my day off." She gently pushed him away and led him to the back door. "Have fun at work, sucker," she said with a laugh, regaining her composure. As Stan made his way to the car, Genifer couldn't help but add, "How about my Lions kicking your Vikings' ass with no time remaining? Whoo-hoo, Lions!"

Stan smiled. "I guess I really am a sucker," he said, entering the car and then pulling out of the driveway.

Genifer waved goodbye and re-entered the messy kitchen. "The things we do for love, Harley," she said to the cat rubbing against her leg as she cleared the table. "Where's Princess, your partner in crime? Watching birds from the window sill?"

By 10:00 Genifer had cleared the floors in the girls' rooms, thrown in a load of laundry and had the kitchen gleaming. She sat on the living room couch to take a break. She hadn't slept great and knew that resting her eyes might result in a nap, which she didn't want to happen. Figuring Helga would be awake, Genifer phoned the hospital's number listed on a sheet she'd received in the E.R.

"Metropolitan Hospital, how can I direct your call?" the female operator asked.

"A friend of mine, Helga Klemens, had hip surgery yesterday," Genifer said.

There was a tapping of keys. "You said you were a friend of this patient – not a relative?"

"Yes, a recent friend," Genifer replied, smiling to herself. "I don't know if she has any relatives in the area."

There was an extended pause on the line.

"Is there any way you can find out if she has family in the area?"

"I could try," Genifer responded haltingly, not liking the tone of this conversation. "Is Helga okay? Can I speak with her?"

"Please hold and I'll transfer you to the 8th floor. The charge nurse up there can help you. Thank you."

The line went silent before generic elevator music came on. It didn't soothe Genifer's racing mind.

"Eighth floor. How can I help you?" a woman's stern voice inquired, as if she'd been interrupted.

"I'm calling to speak with a friend of mine – Helga Klemens. The switchboard transferred me to you."

"Oh," the woman said in a noticeably softer tone. "You did say you're a friend, right, not a relative?"

"What does it matter?" Genifer asked getting annoyed. "Is Helga on your floor or not? She had hip surgery yesterday." Panic set in as flashes of the man in the overcoat flooded her mind.

Please be all right. Please, please, please!

"We're supposed to wait until family members have been notified ...."

During the following moments, Genifer found herself unable to speak and fought through the urge to faint.

"No, no, no," Genifer cried softly as the nurse broke the news that Helga had died.

"I'm very sorry for your loss," the nurse said. "We were quite shocked as well." She gave Genifer a few seconds before saying, "Would you happen to know if Mrs. Klemens had any family?"

"I don't," Genifer said bravely. "She did live close to me. I can walk over there and ask her neighbours. They'll be as stunned as I am."

"If you could, that would be great," the nurse said, giving Genifer the direct number to the 8th floor desk. "Any information would help ... and sorry again."

"Thank you," Genifer said. "I'll be in touch." She was going to hang up when she remembered her recent hospital visit. "Excuse me – are you still there?"

"Yes, what is it?"

"I was in the E.R. last night and my husband was listed on the paperwork as my next of kin. Didn't Helga have anyone listed to contact in case of an emergency?"

"I believe she did," the nurse began, "but there was no telephone number and the person's last name is pretty common. If you think it might help, let me call I.C.U. and see if they have it down there."

The elevator music returned for a second time.

"Hello? They did have the name. Maybe Mrs. Klemens' neighbours will recognize it. Do you have a pen?"

"I do," Genifer said, reaching for a marker Aleena was using to colour a picture from her *Frozen* movie book. "Go ahead."

"The name Mrs. Klemens listed was Genifer Grant. Have you ever heard that name before?"

***

In the days ahead, Genifer would say she had no recollection of how the call with the 8th floor nurse ended or how she got to

Helga's house. It was all one horrific, frightening, and soul crushing blur. Helga was dead, as the old man in the overcoat had promised.

What do I do now?

"She's not home," a man said behind Genifer. "It's Genifer, right?"

Genifer spun around ready for a fight, only to be disarmed by the elderly man in overalls and a Pepsi ball cap. "How do you know my name?"

"You deliver mail to my cousin J.R. on Dalhousie Street. He lives above the Page 233 Bookstore. Plus, I've seen you walking your route in the area."

The tumblers fell into place. "You must be Glenn – he talks about you all the time." Genifer looked toward the intersection. "I guess I did know that you lived on King Street, but not at this end."

"I've been in this area forever," Glenn said proudly. "As a boy I helped my dad build a few houses on this street during one of the hottest summers on record. I was always glad when the roof was finally on and we got some shade, not that it helped a whole lot."

"Working for the post office, I've experienced my fair share of hot days as well," Genifer said with a small smile, relaxing as the apparent threat had vanished. "Were you and Helga good friends?"

Glenn put a bit more weight on his cane. "You said 'were'. Do you know something I don't?" Glenn could tell by Genifer's blank expression that his first love was gone. Taking a handkerchief from his pocket, he dabbed his eyes. "I hope she didn't suffer."

Genifer remained dumbfounded. "I'm so sorry for your loss, Glenn," she said stepping forward and enveloping him in a hug. "I only met her yesterday ... and now this. It isn't fair."

Their embrace lasted for close to half a minute, each consoling the other, neither saying a word. When they stood apart Glenn broke the silence by saying, "J.R. said you're a hugger when delivering the mail."

This made Genifer laugh even as she wiped tears from her eyes with her shirt sleeve. "What can I say – I'm generally a happy person."

***

The two continued to commiserate on Glenn's porch, sipping cold lemonade from Mason jars. Genifer still couldn't bring herself to mention the man in the overcoat, as he'd been very persuasive that doing so would put her family in harm's way.

"Did Helga have any family, Glenn?"

"No," Glenn answered. "Her parents and a brother are deceased, as well as her husband. They had one daughter who died at a fairly young age – in her early forties – from cancer. Helga had a granddaughter, Kaye," Glenn paused and looked at Helga's house. "A while back, there was the bad business with Kaye being murdered by her husband. When that happened ... Helga changed for the worse. It became harder to talk to her about anything except the weather. It was as if that monster murdered both of them."

Genifer put her drink down. "That's terrible. I had no idea."

"I take it you don't watch court trials?"

"I don't have much free time to watch adult shows like that, not that I would, mind you," Genifer said. "Was the granddaughter's killer's trial televised?"

"For three weeks, minus the weekends, on the *Justice For All* cable channel," Glenn said, taking a sip of lemonade. "I only watched because of Helga's connection. I don't go for that kind of gore. *Matlock, The Rockford Files* and the occasional *Murder She Wrote* are my speed."

Genifer shook her head. "I had no idea."

"Helga was the star witness."

"I didn't know that."

Before Glenn could fill her in on the details, Genifer was already thinking that Helga's encounter with the overcoat man was linked to this trial. To distract herself, she took a large gulp of her drink. The idea that Helga's death was the result of her testimony sent a shiver down her spine, a twitch that Glenn associated with his homemade drink.

"It does have a bit of a kick, doesn't it?" he said with pride, raising his lemonade in a mock toast.

"It does," Genifer agreed, placing the jar onto the table. "So ... I take it the killer was found guilty?"

"Jake Wagner won't be seeing the outside of his prison cell for decades, although I did hear he was planning an appeal."

To tell or not to tell? Would Glenn know the man from the driveway?

The safety of her family won over Genifer's mind. Standing, she said, "I should be leaving. Are you going to be okay?"

"I'll be fine," Glenn stated, "once I can make arrangements for Helga's cat, Logan."

"Maybe with you out here, where he can watch the birds in the trees? My cats love doing that."

Glenn thought for a moment. "I'll try that tonight and we'll see how it works out." He stood and braced himself against the porch railing as Genifer took out her phone case to get a business card.

"Here's my phone number if you need something. I'm only a few blocks away," Genifer said.

"I feel privileged." Glenn examined the card. "Two women with the same name – except the spelling – giving me their phone numbers today."

Genifer smiled at the line. "Who else gave you her number?"

Glenn reached into a pocket and handed over the card. "A newspaper reporter from *The Daily Telegraph*."

"Jennifer Malone. I've read her articles. She's good," Genifer said, returning the card. "Why was she slumming out here?"

"Helga," Glenn replied. "But I don't think she knew Helga had died."

"Interesting," Genifer said taking the porch steps to the pathway. "Okay, I have to get back home. Thanks for the lemonade and the company."

"You're welcome," Glenn stated. As the sun caught Genifer's profile, an idea came to Glenn's mind. "Are you Danny Grant's daughter? He was a tool and die operator at the Ford plant for years."

"I am," Genifer stated proudly. "He passed away in 2000."

For the second time that afternoon, Glenn choked up with emotion. "I'm sorry to hear that. He was a great man."

"He was the best," Genifer said with a smile as she turned to walk away. "Now don't forget to tell J.R. what an awesome hugger I am when you see him."

Glenn sat back down in his porch chair. "I'll do that, Genifer. And you have a great day."

FOURTEEN

Jennifer arrived at her desk to find a copy of the John Doe police composite drawing taped to her phone. In Mitch's handwriting were the words, *Didn't know Paul McCartney was in a band before Wings!* referencing their earlier Beatles talk and her questioning of interested suitors.

"Very funny," she called out toward her editor's open door. "When it comes to dating, you either have standards or ... you have you."

"Preach it, girlfriend!" Cassie shouted across the row of desks in the bullpen.

Mitch appeared in the doorway. "I have standards, only I keep them low. That way everyone's expectations are met and you can enjoy the date without feeling pressure to conform."

"Oh – I like that," Cassie said, writing down Mitch's statement. "I might use that in this week's column."

"Whose side are you on, Cassie?" Jennifer asked. "Team Girlfriend or Team Whoever Is Still Available At Closing Time?"

"You make it sound like I'm not a romantic at heart," Mitch said, walking to Jennifer's desk.

Jennifer sat and crossed her arms against her chest. "Tell me one unselfish act you've done to make your significant other happy."

"Hmmm ...." Mitch began, perching himself against the desk. "Okay, here's but one of many selfless acts. In high school I was dating this cute Ukrainian girl – Tori something – and I made her a mixed tape."

"In Grade 8 my 45-year-old Science teacher made me a mixed tape," Jennifer scoffed. "I found it creepy, not endearing."

"Let me finish," Mitch demanded. "That wasn't the romantic part."

"You can say that again," Cassie chimed in.

"The romantic part was that on Side A I only had Eagles songs sung by Glen Frey – her favourite singer – and on Side B I only had Fleetwood Mac songs sung by Christine McVie or Lindsey Buckingham, because she reviled Stevie Nicks' voice."

"Wow, what a sacrifice," Jennifer deadpanned. "I hope she was impressed."

"Oh, she was impressed ... in the back seat of my Chevy Nova," Mitch said with a wide smile. "But it was torture."

"The heavy petting?" Cassie asked. "You must have been doing it wrong."

"Not that – the mixed tape!" Mitch exclaimed. "How can you have the greatest hits of those bands without including *Life In The Fast Lane* and *Rhiannon*?"

"A question for the ages. You truly were in love," Jennifer laughed. "I take back my previous sarcastic comments."

"As if," Mitch said.

"So what happened to Tori? A girl like that you can't just let go," Cassie said.

Mitch released a long sigh. "After graduation we were going to backpack across Europe, then attend journalism school together in the fall. We were set to go when the school administrator called my house and told my mom there was one opening for the summer session, if I wanted it. Of course I didn't, but as an 18-year-old I had little bargaining power and started school early."

"Come September, was Tori in class," Jennifer asked, "or did she *take it to the limit* one more time?" Jennifer looked over at Cassie who had joined them. "Randy Meisner sang that one, meaning it was allowed on the mixed tape."

"If you say so," Cassie replied, either baffled or uninterested by the musical subplot of Mitch's story.

"The last time I saw her was at the airport," Mitch began. "She said she'd come back in three months, but never did."

"Whoa, whoa, whoa!" Jennifer exclaimed. "What the hell did you say to her? I hope it wasn't a mushy, 'I love you,' because she might have ditched you before the plane took off, only you didn't know it."

"No postcards or letters?" Cassie asked.

"Nope. I heard she was running a bed and breakfast in Tuscany."

"Talk about burying the lead! You should've stated that off the top, Mitch," Jennifer said. "As soon as those hot Italian stallions were involved you had no chance."

"None," Cassie agreed.

"Thanks for the support," Mitch said, walking into his office.

"On the bright side," Jennifer called out, "she'll never know the joy of checking into the *Hotel California*. The girl was a moron, I say!"

"Poor Mitch," Cassie said. "Maybe we can find her online."

"Or maybe we can find out everything there is to know about a hot paramedic who asked me out on a date today."

Cassie looked toward Mitch's door. "He can find his own lost love," she said, repositioning a chair from an adjoining desk. "Tell me about this medicine man. I hope he's a hands-on practitioner."

"So do I," Jennifer said.

***

Maryanne arrived at the hospital in her street clothes and went to the women's locker room to change into her security uniform. Her customary Monday Meal Madness breakfast with Luke was always a good way to start a new week. They only briefly discussed Helga's death. Instead, they talked about the upcoming double-bill concert featuring their two favourite bands – Sex At Seven and Unfinished Tattoos – and whether they should drive or subway it to the venue Saturday night. The subway was cheaper but limited their post-concert options with other hospital staff who were planning to attend. "Let's wait to see who is going, okay?" Luke had suggested, picking a piece of crispy bacon off his plate. "Car-pooling might benefit everyone."

Maryanne agreed, as she seemed to do a lot these days. This was a huge adjustment from her previous relationship with an overbearing auxiliary police officer who tried to make all their social plans. She fought him a majority of the time, yet ultimately settled with what he proposed. It wasn't until they split that she realized how much of herself she'd given up to be with this man, and vowed never to do that again. Luke was the antidote she needed to get back on her feet. When they randomly passed in the corridors he'd ask how her day was going, or if she'd attended any interesting Code white calls dealing with violent persons. The non-flirty chit-chats would last less than a minute, but each brief encounter made her feel lighter and happier. A few weeks after she started on the job, there had been a turning point in their work relationship.

"What shift are you working today, Luke?" Maryanne had asked, taking out her earbuds as she approached the locker room door.

"Eight to four," he said with his usual smile, stopping in front of her and pointing to the MP3 player in her hand. "Whatcha listening to?"

"A new band. They only have one album out so far. You probably haven't heard of them," she'd answered, almost apologetically. "They're called Unfinished Tattoos."

Luke's smile had widened as he took a step backwards. "Pick a track number and I'll give you the song's name."

"Get out of here," Maryanne had said with a laugh. Realizing Luke wasn't kidding, she'd scrolled down the screen and said, "Number 6."

"*When Angels Fail To Fly,*" Luke had replied, "and for bonus points, it runs four minutes and eight seconds."

In the days that followed, it was revealed they had a lot in common, besides the hospital and their musical tastes.

Now six months later, once in full uniform Maryanne made her way to the basement security office to sign out her portable radio.

"Anything I should be aware of today, Ken?" she asked her supervisor. He was sitting in front of a bank of security monitors, randomly scanning the one hundred and three camera feeds from throughout the hospital.

"Oh, hey, Maryanne," Ken replied, swivelling in his chair to face her. "We had one Code white in the E.R. – that guy's strapped down tight in AC 5. Same with an old timer in 7110D – he's more confused than angry. When his family visits he's pretty calm."

Maryanne wrote down the two rooms in her official log book and then watched the screens. She knew that only four security personnel were authorized to access the video in case of an emergency, like a patient wandering away from their room; or something serious, such as a deranged person in the hospital for reasons other than medical treatment. "How long is the video from these cameras stored on the server?"

Ken looked at the live images. "Two weeks. The millisecond Day 15 starts, the first day of the cycle is technically overwritten." Ken turned back to Maryanne. "Why – is pretty boy Luke being unfaithful and you want me to track his whereabouts? I would do that for you. Do you have a specific day within the last fourteen?"

"Ha – Luke has difficulty keeping our time together straight in his mind. He's not the organized type who could juggle more than one woman."

"That's what he wants you to believe."

"Trust me, I'm all the woman he can handle," Maryanne said, adding with a grin, "plus, he isn't *that* smart."

They talked for two more minutes and then Maryanne began her first duty of the day: a foot patrol of each floor to confirm all was safe from a security standpoint. The ward floors were the easiest as the nurses had the patients comfortable by this time of day. The tiresome component of the patrol was making sure specific doors were locked, keeping the public away from sensitive areas. Within a half hour Maryanne was done and headed to the front lobby desk so Austin could take his lunch break. As she neared the top of the escalator her cell phone vibrated. Taking a detour into an empty conference room, she took out the phone and looked at the text:

> Hey, Maryanne – Jennifer Malone from the Telegraph here. I was hoping you can follow up on some new information I received this morning. Call me when you can. Thanks.

Maryanne immediately tapped the phone number on the display and tried to steady her nerves. "Keep calm," she said to herself. "This might be your big break."

"That was fast, Maryanne," Jennifer said as a form of salutation. "Slow day at the hospital?"

"Slow is a relative term here," Maryanne replied, trying to sound professional.

"Same here. One minute you think you can take a powernap in an interview room and the next you're running out of the building chasing a hot lead," Jennifer said.

"Was your text part of a hot lead?" Maryanne asked.

"Not a hot-hot lead, but definitely a good one."

Maryanne pulled a flyer off a bulletin board and flipped it over, pen at the ready. "Any lead is good, right?"

"If it pans out."

Jennifer passed on the flower buyer information she'd received from the gift shop volunteer. "Do you know which hospital employees wear red uniforms?"

"Anyone working in the kitchen. Although ... aside from employees in the O.R. and related departments who only wear green scrubs, there isn't really a colour dress code for porters, nurses or housekeepers. As long as they're some type of scrubs, I guess so patients can differentiate staff from visitors, any colour combination goes." Maryanne stopped for a moment. "That doesn't help a whole lot, does it?"

"It eliminates the O.R. staff ... at least regarding buying Helga flowers," Jennifer replied. "There's still their involvement in her dying on the operating table. Now, Maryanne, when I visited the gift shop, I saw a security camera above the cash register. Is there a way to view the footage?"

Maryanne took her time answering. "Yes and no," she began tentatively. "The footage is saved for fourteen days, but unless there's some sort of emergency, I don't believe it's ever reviewed. There may be some kind of paperwork you'd have to submit. I can ask." Maryanne felt a pressure building in her chest, knowing she could easily manipulate Ken to review the gift shop video under the guise of tracking Luke's movements. However, she didn't know if Ken would then tell everyone else and embarrass Luke.

Thankfully, Jennifer let her off the guilt hook.

"At this stage I'm not going to get a court order to learn who bought Helga's flowers. Could you visit the gift shop and poke around some? Talk to the actual volunteer who sold them to our mystery buyer? Her name was Sandy."

"I can do that," Maryanne said relieved. "No use overplaying our hand about the video. Maybe we'll need the court order later for something else."

"I like the way your mind works, Maryanne."

"Thanks."

"Call me if you find out any more information. I have other leads to work on today. Have a good shift and we'll talk soon."

Maryanne said, "Okay, Jennifer, will do," and ended the call. As she made her way to the front desk she felt like she was walking on air and couldn't wait to visit the gift shop.

FIFTEEN

Genifer found Jennifer's business card stuck inside the frame of the front screen door, and a message on her machine. *She works fast,* Genifer thought, disappointed she wasn't home, although her time with Glenn on his porch had been extraordinary.

The desk phone rang three times before it was answered.

"Jennifer Malone here."

"Hi, Jennifer, this is Genifer Grant returning your call."

"Ah ... the infamous Genifer with a 'G'," Jennifer said jokingly, reaching for her notebook and a pen. "Your name came up a few times this morning. Thanks for getting back to me."

"I doubt I'm infamous in Greenheart Station. That makes it sound like I've done something wrong."

"Oh, not to worry, the paramedics, police and a kindly old man all had positive things to say about you."

"You talked to Glenn about me? Is that why you visited him today?"

Jennifer sensed that her counterpart was beginning to overact. "Please don't panic, Genifer. I was looking into Helga Klemens' fall and your interaction with her. Everyone said that it was very fortunate you were walking by at that moment."

Genifer took a deep breath, trying to figure out why this big city news reporter was checking up on Helga in the first place. "I was just in the right place at the right time," she finally said. "It was fortunate Helga's windows were open, otherwise no one would have heard her calling out for help."

"So when you arrived both the windows and front door were open?" Jennifer asked, slyly trying to confirm information she'd already gathered.

"I didn't say the front door was open," Genifer replied uneasily.

"I believe one of the paramedics mentioned you had gone through the front door," Jennifer said in a calming voice, unclear who had told her this fact, but still needing the answer. "Glenn figured Helga had her morning coffee on the porch and forgot to relock the door afterwards."

Genifer hadn't entertained such a scenario, although it was quite plausible. Her thinking was that Helga had opened the front door for the man in the tan overcoat and he bullied his way in on some false pretence, only to leave by the back door later. Or that after Helga fell, he had unlocked the front door to escape, but saw her coming and hightailed it out the back door. Finding no exit through the yard, he reluctantly walked up the driveway where their eyes had met.

"I don't know why the door was unlocked," Genifer answered

in a less than steady voice, "but, yes, it was."

Unlocked door mystery partially solved?

Jennifer felt something was amiss and returned to a non-threatening line of questioning. "Is it true you hadn't met Helga before this incident?"

"No, never," Genifer answered. "I was out for a walk, knowing I'd be watching football with my husband in the afternoon."

"Who's your team?" Having zero interest in football, Jennifer brought up the *Telegraph's* sports section on her computer.

"The Detroit Lions."

"Yeah ..." Jennifer began, stalling as she read the game recap, "I saw the end of that one. What a crazy finish, huh? No time left on the clock, a fumble and a long run for a touchdown, right?"

"Ninety-three yards," Genifer said, recalling the play that unfolded as she listened to the man on the phone threaten the lives of her family. "The Vikings are my husband's team, so it was that much sweeter."

"Apparently the celebration was short-lived?"

"Excuse me?"

"The paramedics said you were hospitalized in the afternoon. I trust it wasn't from an accident during your victory lap."

Genifer had to hold the phone away from her face in order for Jennifer not to hear the quick intake of air, as the memories leading to her hospitalization flooded back. The light-headedness. The panic. The fear for her husband and girls. The fall. The lies. The shame afterwards. "I fainted and everyone overreacted," she managed to say. "I'm still recovering and took today off work."

"I hope I didn't disturb your rest when I stopped by earlier," Jennifer said apologetically. She then remembered a point Genifer had stated earlier. "But you weren't home. You were with Glenn, Helga's neighbour."

"I went for a walk to get some fresh air and bumped into Glenn," Genifer admitted haltingly. "He was worried about Helga and ..." her voice stuttered as she recalled their teary embrace. "I broke the news to him Helga had passed away."

Jennifer's pen hovered above her notebook as she tried to decide how to proceed. Genifer's tone sounded troubling, as if she was holding back information, but why? She'd been out for a walk, heard a cry for help, became the hero and then suffered the consequences afterward. Jennifer had toyed with the idea of doing an inspirational story about neighbours helping neighbours, despite the fact that it was outside the usual scope of her articles.

"I'm sure he was devastated," she said, returning to common ground. "He told me the hospital said only family members were privy to Helga's condition ... nevertheless, you found out, Genifer."

"I ... ah ... was advised the same thing," Genifer replied, stumbling over her words. "I told the nurse who I was and she broke the rules. I guess she felt sorry about the whole sad situation."

Jennifer decided to circle her prey one last time before going in for the kill. "You didn't happen to send Helga flowers yesterday, did you?"

"No."

"Because I have information that the person who did was aware Helga was in peril," Jennifer revealed. "I'm trying to figure out if they acted on the info or passed it along to the powers that be, who ignored it. Either way, the truth won't bring Helga back."

Genifer wondered if Jennifer already knew Helga's next of kin contact information.

"I don't know anything about flowers sent to Helga."

Jennifer remained silent, waiting her out, then said, "But you do know something."

"I ...."

"Listen, Genifer, like you, I didn't know Helga. If I owned one, I'd bet the farm she was a sweet person and loved by everyone," Jennifer said soothingly. "That's why her untimely death is so tragic. My interest is what happened during Helga's surgery and later in I.C.U."

"She was an old woman," Genifer said, wanting to regain her standing in this conversation. "Maybe her heart gave out due to the stress."

"That's still a distinct possibility."

"Well ... I don't know how I can help you," Genifer said, desperately needing to end the call. "Please let me know if you find out anything concrete. I have to go. My girls will be home for lunch soon," she lied.

Jennifer felt she was losing Genifer and that wasn't good.

"I won't keep you from your children. I went to school in the city and never came home for lunch. It must be nice seeing them during the day. Another advantage to living in a small town. How old are they?"

"Zoe is 11 and Aleena is 9."

"I bet they are the sun and moon to you and your husband, am I right?" Jennifer tried to sound upbeat. "I don't have any children and my girlfriends insist I'm missing out."

"Maybe you will one day," Genifer said.

"Maybe." Jennifer rustled some papers on her desk wanting Genifer to stay focused on the topic of children. "I have one more question."

"I have to go."

The paper rustling stopped abruptly and Jennifer threw out her final question – a Hail Mary, one of the few football terms of which she knew the meaning.

"One of the paramedics believed there were bruises on Helga's arms that looked like handprints, which Helga claimed were from the stairs. My question is, did you see anyone else at the house while you were there? Someone you haven't told anyone, including your husband, about? Someone who went out the back gate, pushing it so hard it stayed open, stuck in the grass at the base of the fence?" Getting no reply, Jennifer said, "I apologize. That was three questions, not the one I promised. You see,

Genifer, I have other information of Helga's death that doesn't quite fit the 'old lady, broken hip, weak heart' scenario and I think you might have a missing piece to this puzzle."

Genifer began to cry. "I can't help you."

"I can help you though," Jennifer replied.

"How?"

"By carrying some of the load you've been dealing with the past two days and in the strictest of confidence."

"I don't know."

"I'm not rushing you," Jennifer said reassuringly. "You have my number. Call me when you want to talk."

"Okay," Genifer said. "I just need some time."

Their call ended with both women unsatisfied at its conclusion.

Genifer sat at the kitchen table wishing that her girls were coming home for lunch, as Jennifer made new notations in her notebook. The final entry was a question she underlined and added a star in the margin: Who was with Helga when she fell?

SIXTEEN

"I'm too old for this racket," Henrik Dekker muttered to himself as he spread strawberry jam on a slice of cold toast. "It's a young man's game today. Clive shouldn't have ordered me to kill that woman yesterday!"

He slammed his fist down in anger, startling the three cats at his feet, each waiting for a crumb to fall. Watching them scatter in different directions, Henrik called out, "A bunch of scaredy-cats! You'd better toughen up, because when I'm dead and gone the landlord will throw you out into the real world." He grabbed the plate off the counter and shuffled to his ancient recliner, plopping himself down to watch the morning news. "And the way I feel this morning, Felix," he said to the Siamese cat perched on the back of the couch, "it won't be long now."

Henrik didn't get much rest overnight, as his mind raced through the details of the task he'd failed to carry out. His left elbow and shoulder were also too tender to put weight on, the result of Helga pulling her way free from his grip trying to escape. The final struggle at the top of her stairs would be one he'd never forget, as she'd stumbled over a black cat and tumbled like a rag doll to the first floor. As he had watched, Henrik secretly wished for Helga to break her neck and he'd leave her for someone else to find.

That hadn't happened.

Worse yet, a nosy passerby had heard Helga's cries for help and blocked his exit via the front door, where he'd posed as a lawyer with news about Jake Wagner's appeal. He'd introduced himself as a new attorney on the case, there to advise her of a legal action to take place the following day. "I came out because I didn't want you to hear about this on the news tomorrow." As she was still in her nightgown, Helga had led him to the living room and excused herself to go change upstairs. He'd given her a minute of privacy before climbing the stairs and confronting her. They'd struggled on top of her bed, where he'd straddled her with the goal of strangling her to death. When she'd begun to flail her body to the left, then the right, he'd lost his balance and fell awkwardly on the floor. From the other side of the bed, Helga started down the hallway and was about to descend the first step when Henrik had pulled her by the arm. Their forward momentum had caused them to crash against the wall, at which time Helga had pushed herself away from her attacker, only to stumble over her frightened cat, sending her into a free fall to the main floor foyer.

With Henrik barrelling down the stairs in pursuit, she'd let out three loud cries of, "Help me!" praying someone outside would hear her. As he'd approached the house earlier, Henrik had noted that the front room windows were open and once on top of Helga again, he'd clamped his hand across her mouth and waited. When he'd heard a woman on the lawn say, "Hello, is everything okay?" Henrik had lifted Helga's head a few inches and then smashed it against the hardwood flooring, temporarily dazing her. With the unidentified woman now climbing the porch steps, Henrik had run to the back door, exiting into the yard. Peering around the gate, he heard the woman entering the house and telling Helga, "I'll call 911." Hoping she'd be further into the house looking for a phone, Henrik had made his move, pushing the fence gate open hard and walking briskly up the driveway ... to see the woman standing on the porch with a cell phone in her hand.

Having met her gaze, he'd begun to run down the street, hoping that his boss would pick him up.

Clive Hill hadn't been pleased, but Henrik felt he'd sufficiently carried out his follow-up duties at the hospital to make up for the failure at Helga's house. The unlikely appearance of Genifer Grant in the E.R. had only solidified Henrik's feeling of a job well done. After their talk, he knew she wouldn't say a word about him to anyone.

Finishing his meagre breakfast, Henrik took two painkillers he had left over from an ankle injury and stretched out on the couch, hoping the pills would take effect quicker in that position. Two hours later, he was awakened by loud knocking on the side door and yelling.

"Henrik – answer the door! It's Jimmy. C'mon already!"

What is he doing here? Henrik thought, trying to get his bearings. "I think I took one too many pills, Dixie," he said to the Persian cat on the loveseat. "I'm coming!" he yelled down the hall.

When he opened the door Jimmy Hughes, a lowlife 22-year-old gopher for The Men, stood in the door with an agitated expression on his face.

"Don't you answer your phone no more, old man? The boss has been calling all morning."

Henrik glanced at his watch. "I fell asleep on the couch. What does Clive want and why did he send you?"

"He wants you, that's what he wants, and he sent me to get you. Any more questions?" Jimmy asked. "So get some shoes on and let's ship out. I ain't got all day, grandpa."

Henrik didn't twitch at this verbal assault, pissing the kid off. "I'll meet you in the car," he said and slammed the door shut.

***

As he climbed the steps to the second floor office, Henrik maintained his distance from Jimmy. He didn't trust him and would've rather talked with Clive on the phone, but that was no longer an option. During their ride Jimmy had refused to turn down the obnoxious metal-rap music he claimed motivated him to stay alive each day. "Frank Sinatra does that for me and he's quieter than those vile punks," Henrik had replied, as he watched the world he'd created for himself unwind behind the car. Over the years he'd been the driver of similar journeys and now knew how his frightened passengers had felt, never knowing whether it would be a one-way ride until it was too late to buy a return fare.

Clive hasn't heard about my talk with that Grant lady. That'll show him I'm still valuable to the organization.

Jimmy and Henrik walked to a large room in which there was a desk and the chair Clive was sitting on. Upon their entrance, Clive stood and greeted Henrik warmly.

"My friend, I tried calling you this morning with some good news." Before Henrik could explain the unplanned nap, Clive waved off Jimmy and said, "Shut the door on your way out."

A disgruntled Jimmy did as he was told, leaving the two men alone.

Clive sat back down, forcing Henrik to remain standing.

"You said something about good news," Henrik said slowly.

"That old lady – the thorn in Jake's side – is resting in the hospital morgue. Isn't that fantastic?" Clive asked, his hands clasped together in the centre of the desktop; staring at Henrik as a smile crept across his lips. "We had to call in a favour or two, but we already had a few contingency plans in place. And do you know why that was?"

Henrik shook his head and kept his mouth shut.

"I'll tell you why," Clive began. "Because I don't have faith in you, Henrik. You're old and forgetful and incapable of carrying out my plans. Yesterday you had one job: go to that old lady's house and kill her. Did you do that? No."

Clive stopped talking, as if to let Henrik make a counter argument, only to be met again with silence.

"What I'm about to say," Clive continued, "breaks my heart. You and Pops were two of the tightest people I've ever seen who weren't blood. I'm glad he isn't alive to see how far you've fallen."

"I loved Nicky. We were blood brothers and I miss him every day," Henrik offered sincerely.

"We all do," Clive agreed, making his way to where Henrik was standing. "We've got a lot of history and that's why I hate saying that you're done with The Men."

Henrik didn't know quite how to react to this statement. "Done, how?"

"It's like a divorce – or forced retirement in your case."

"I'm a liability to you?"

Clive put his hand on Henrik's shoulder. "No, because you need a rest. You started at – what 13 years old? – running numbers for my Grandpop's club? Sixty-seven years is long enough, don't you think? It's time to relax." Clive administered some pressure to the shoulder, guiding Henrik toward the door. "Go out and have some fun. Get away and don't worry about money. As a thank you for your years of loyal service, you'll remain on the payroll. How does that sound?"

Henrik was genuinely overtaken with emotion. *I would like a vacation. I can't compete with the Jimmies of the world like I used to.*

Clive opened the door and turned to Henrik, who had his hand outstretched.

"How can I thank you, Clive? It's been an honour working with your family for all these years," Henrik said.

Clive looked at the hand and pushed it away in order to give Henrik a bear hug. "We're going to miss you," he whispered in Henrik's ear, his voice cracking.

The men broke their embrace and stepped out into the hallway.

"Hey, Jimmy," Clive called to the lackey. "Get Mr. Dekker here home safe and sound. Or drop him off at a travel agency, am I right?" he said to a beaming Henrik.

"Home will be fine," Henrik laughed. "Starting tomorrow I can sleep in."

Clive reached out to touch the sleeve of Henrik's trademark overcoat. "And then maybe spring for a new coat from this century. The ladies love new threads."

"I might do that," Henrik said as he began to descend the stairs, this time with Jimmy below him. "I feel like I can do anything from this day forward! Thank you, Clive."

"It's well deserved," Clive said loud enough for Henrik to hear, then adding under his breath, "You worthless senile old prick. My Pops couldn't get rid of you, but I sure as hell can."

SEVENTEEN

Delivering dinner trays to the 8th floor, Elaine was surprised to see that Helga's room was unoccupied and the hospital bed was made, ready for the next patient.

"What happened to the lady in 8103?" she asked the desk clerk on duty.

The clerk barely acknowledged her. "She died on the operating table."

"What?"

"They brought her back to life, only to have her heart stop for good in I.C.U." The clerk glanced up at Elaine's shocked face. "It's very sad. She seemed like such a nice woman. Did you know her?"

"Ah ... no," Elaine replied.

Elaine darted into the vacant room to call Trillia. She then delivered the remaining room trays on the floor and after returning her cart to the kitchen took a scheduled break.

Cigarette breaks outside in the designated smoking area generally consisted of employees bitching about their shifts or a supervisor. However, today Elaine's mind had drifted to Trillia's love life. *That girl has no luck.* She couldn't stop worrying how Trillia would take the news of Jake's aunt dying. The phone call had gone to voicemail and she hadn't heard back from her yet.

The two had been neighbours for five years and had become instant friends. Even their spouses got along. When Trillia's mechanic husband had died on the job, it was equally devastating for the three of them, though it was Trillia who had been the glue that kept everyone together, and who had remained the strongest. She hadn't considered dating for a full a year – "That's how long grieving books suggest, so you get all 'the firsts without', you know, first Christmas, first birthday, first anniversary – out of the way," she'd said. The timing had also coincided with Trillia's daughter, Harmony Jane, moving out to find a job in a city five hours away. Now an empty-nester, Trillia had felt ready to seek some kind of relationship, although she wasn't keen on marrying again.

It was while having coffee in Elaine's backyard that Trillia had initially mentioned Jake.

"Dorothy at the store says I have a secret admirer. Apparently a guy named Jake was buying some pens for a meeting and saw me shelving in the candy aisle. He asked her my name and if I was single. My other coworker Kara had a field day giving this stranger my name and said I needed a boyfriend! She told him to contact me through my profile on that free dating site I'm on. The nerve of that woman! I could have killed her."

Evidently, Jake had taken Kara's advice and sent an introduction via the dating site. Over the next few weeks more details of this mystery man emerged: Jake's luxury car had been damaged when a dump truck driver blew through a stop sign; his busy travel schedule had kept him away; and he had offered to fly her to the coast to sightsee after a conference he'd be attending ended. Elaine had been overjoyed for her friend, as well as a bit jealous. The most intriguing part of this budding romance was when Elaine asked to see a picture of Jake. Trillia had deflected by saying she'd forgotten to get a screen shot when they were video chatting and that he wasn't on any social media sites. "When you see a dark blue Lexus GS Hybrid in my driveway, stop by and I'll introduce you to him," Trillia had promised.

Elaine was still waiting for the opportunity to present itself.

With five minutes left in her break, Elaine butted out her cigarette and re-entered the hospital to buy some gum in the gift shop. Fresh breath was mandatory for the kitchen staff. She selected a pack of spearmint and placed it on the checkout counter, holding out a five dollar bill.

"Thank you, dear," Sandy said. When handing change back to the customer, she recognized the woman. "How did your friend like the yellow carnations?"

Elaine acknowledged the volunteer who'd sold her the flowers and frowned. "Actually, she passed away. I don't know if she saw them before her surgery."

"That's terrible. Were you two close – family?"

"No, I bought the flowers for a friend. It was the aunt of her boyfriend who is out of town on business."

"That'll be quite the shock for him. I hope she had a

productive life."

"Me too," Elaine agreed.

Sandy remembered her conversation with that newspaper reporter and her attention went to her customer's scrubs. "Does everyone in your department have to wear red scrubs, honey, or do you simply like the colour? I see a lot of staff wearing them, both men and women."

The question was odd, but Elaine answered, "I work in the kitchen. We have to wear scrubs in some shade of red."

"Thank you for clearing that up for me ...," Sandy bent slightly forward to read the woman's hospital badge, "Elaine."

"No problem and thanks for the gum," Elaine said as she stepped out of the shop.

Once the woman was out of view, Sandy reached for the garbage can to retrieve a crumbled piece of paper. She called the number written on it and waited. Unfortunately, the call went to Jennifer Malone's voicemail.

"Oh ... hello again, dear. This is Sandy from the Metropolitan Hospital Gift Shop. I have some information on the person who bought the yellow carnations. Her name is Elaine 'S'-something, in her late thirties or early forties. She works here in the kitchen and said she bought the flowers for a friend. I hope this helps. Have a great day."

***

Trillia's drive home from the Westhorn Penitentiary was one of anger and heartbreak. She couldn't believe the callousness of the guards when she requested a visitor's pass to see Jake. "C'mon lady," one of them said as he examined her driver's licence. "You're old enough to know better." She demanded to see a supervisor, who strolled out of an adjacent room and escorted her outside.

"Ms. Johnston, I'm betting you're a very smart woman, and I

won't pretend to know how you and a killer like Jake Wagner got together," he'd said as they headed out of the building. "But if you believe you can save him or that you're the only girl he's ... ah ... dating ... you need to rethink your priorities, 'cause you'd be wrong on both counts."

Trillia had stopped walking and stood her ground. "I don't need advice from a man who has no qualms locking up an innocent man for a crime he didn't commit."

The supervisor had heard this argument from his first day at the penitentiary three decades earlier. As a younger man, he felt it was his duty as a loyal employee and upholder of the law to argue each point to its fullest, sometimes getting into physical confrontations. One day his training officer said, "These women are not worth it. The goal is to get them out of the building and to their car."

From that day forward that was what he did.

"I understand where you're coming from, Ms. Johnston, however a person's guilt or innocence isn't determined here. They are tried in a court of law without my input. I'm a lowly cog in the wheels of justice. Anyway, I hear Mr. Wagner is appealing his verdict. Maybe down the line I'll be escorting him to a car, like I'm doing with you now."

The man's calming demeanour was contrary to that of the animals' conduct she'd dealt with at the front desk. However, working in customer service herself, Trillia knew what was going on, even though she appreciated the man's professionalism.

"I just wanted to see him so badly," she said. "I drove over three hours to get here."

As they approached the final gate leading to the parking lot, Trillia noticed the supervisor's expression change from concern for her well-being to a grin, which he unsuccessfully tried to hide. She surveyed the area of the lot he was looking toward and saw a woman getting out of a taxi.

"Who is that?"

"I shouldn't say, Ms. Johnston," the supervisor replied, as he waved his hand at the guard in the kiosk to unlock the gate.

As the woman got closer, Trillia was struck by the physical similarities to herself: a tall, skinny blonde with large breasts. The woman even dressed like her with a tight top and short jean skirt. What really caught Trillia's eye was the overnight suitcase.

"Tell me who that woman is coming to see."

The supervisor wished he'd retained his composure a few more moments to get this woman to the other side of the fence. "Inmate #28904." Before Trillia could respond, he gently pushed her through the now open gate and stepped back. "Lock it down!" he instructed the guard, who obeyed the command and hit a large red button on the wall. "Trillia, meet Anna," he called out through the fence as the second woman came within earshot. "Anna, meet Trillia. You two have something in common."

"And what's that?" Anna asked as she first glared daggers at the supervisor and then at Trillia.

"Jake Wagner loves you both, but not enough to request day passes for either of you." His voice tapered off as another taxi arrived and a third hard-luck, white trash female exited the rear passenger seat. "Wow – three at the same time. Jake's outdone himself today." The supervisor shared a knowing smile with the guard and said, "Make sure the audio and video are recording. This will be primetime viewing tonight in the lounge."

"Yes, sir," the guard replied with a laugh, as the supervisor began to walk back to the main building.

"Have a great day, ladies," he said. "See you on *Jerry Springer* next week!"

***

Twenty minutes later, a battered and bruised Trillia was gunning her Jeep out of the parking lot. In her rear-view mirror she saw the other two women rolling on the grass, hair extensions and high heels flying everywhere, as two officers in a patrol car watched in amusement.

Let them fight to the death.

Pulling into highway traffic, Trillia cranked the CD player's volume full blast when Tim McGraw's *Set This Circus Down* came on. She pictured her and Jake as the couple in the song, waiting for the opportunity to start anew on the outskirts of a small town. Now as she felt her aching left cheek where Anna had punched her, she knew that dream was over. Jake was like all the cheating men in her life, except for the mechanic, rest his soul beneath that black 1975 Monte Carlo.

As the hours ticked away under her wheels, Trillia considered that her life was a circus – out of control and with too much insanity going on. She needed to focus on the things in life that were concrete, like her career, her daughter, and her circle of friends. As she was coming to this conclusion, as if an omen, Elaine called her cell phone. Unable to safely pull off to the side of the road, she let the call go to voicemail and stopped at the next rest area to retrieve the message.

"Hey, Trillia – it's Elaine. I'm sure you're helping your niece, but I thought you should know about something I heard regarding Jake's aunt."

At the mere mention of Jake's name, Trillia ended the call, not wanting to hear anything about him or his relatives. "I wish they were dead," she said, throwing the phone down. "It's me time now! No one will ever get in the way of my happiness. Screw you, Jake Wagner! I hope you rot in that cell."

***

Entering her house, Trillia's frame of mind shifted from empowerment to isolation. Today's trip was supposed to signal a new phase in her life. She'd known it wouldn't be easy, but had truly believed Jake would win his appeal and they'd start a real relationship. She hadn't figured out the details, only trusting her gut instincts that this crazy dream could come to fruition.

She dumped the contents of her overnight bag on the bed and held back tears when the celebratory bottle of wine she'd taken fell to the floor. It was followed by a heart-shaped box of chocolates. Trillia grabbed both items and marched into the kitchen. She had no plans for the evening, after cancelling her motel room near the penitentiary. She didn't have to work and no one knew she was back in town.

"This is my free night! Let's get the party started!"

Trillia poured herself a large glass of wine before randomly sampling the chocolates. "Alcohol and chocolate is all a woman needs to survive," she cried out, toasting her reflection in the hallway mirror as she made her way to the computer desk. "One last email to Jake and I can begin moving forward."

> Dear Jake,
>
> When you said I was one in a million, I believed you. After meeting tramp Anna and that other slut today, I have no doubt you have 999,997 easy to dupe women still out there. Good luck replacing me. I can't understand why you would do this to me. I wanted to help you in any way I could and you betrayed me. I'm not only out gas money for today's trip, I'll never see that $40 I spent on those flowers for your sick aunt, will I? It's ironic she had the same first name as that old woman who put you away! Ha! I'm sure both of them knew what a loser you are.
>
> I'm done. Don't contact me. I hate you.
>
> The Thrillia is gone!!!!!

Trillia finished off the wine as she reread the message. It

sounded good and felt exhilarating. "The end!" she yelled as she hit the SEND button, wanting nothing to do with Jake Wagner again. "Now I can move forward," she told herself as she walked to the kitchen to refill her wine glass. "What was I thinking?"

EIGHTEEN

As Jennifer finished writing notes on her call with Genifer Grant, the desk phone rang.

"Jennifer Malone speaking."

"I heard you're looking for Becky Mayville," a husky, Demi Moore *circa St. Elmo's Fire,* female voice inquired.

"You heard right. What's in it for you?" Jennifer shot back.

Not expecting such bluntness, the caller answered, "I ... don't know."

"Call me when you do," Jennifer said, deliberately hitting a number button to emit a noise to scare the listener.

"No, wait!" the caller insisted. "Hear me out."

Jennifer didn't disconnect the call, remaining silent, waiting for additional information to come her way.

"I know a guy who says that she's hanging out on the top floor of a high-end hotel in Chester Hills."

"A guy? Could you be more vague?"

"He's a friend of mine, who works for a catering company that deals with this hotel."

"The exclusive one ... out in Chester Hills, right? The east end, near the park."

"Yeah."

"Does your guy friend have a name?" Jennifer asked, her pen poised to jot it down.

"I don't think he'd want me to give it to you."

"Not until we make a deal concerning your valuable information, correct?"

There was a pause before the caller replied uneasily, "I guess."

"Well," Jennifer said agreeably, "as I'm unaware how it works at *The Star* or *TMZ* or any of the news stations you've already contacted, here are the journalism rules I live by: Number one – never believe anything anyone tells you until the information can be independently verified, preferably by two sources. Number two – journalists don't pay for stories. And number three … well, there isn't a number three."

"What?"

"Was I going too fast? Let me condense it for you: I don't pay for information, and won't believe your information until I verify it."

"How is that fair?"

"Fair? What are you, twelve?" Jennifer turned to her computer and typed: *Chester Hills upscale boutique hotels*. As she browsed the search engine's results she said, "If you didn't already know, I'm a big time reporter employed at a big time newspaper. I have a lot of power to make and break people, but in general I don't. It's too time consuming. What I do, though, is give credit where credit is due, and as long as you don't want to remain anonymous, your name and possibly face could become famous overnight. I can see the caption: Inna Kelly helps find Councilman Tilley's infamous playmate!"

"How do you know my name?"

"Call display. You're not as bright as you think. Fortunately, I'm still interested, so give me your friend's info or call your next media prospect. We aren't calling her Hot Becky for nothin'. Some schmuck reporter will want to hear what you've got to say."

"What do I get in return? There must be some kind of reward."

"I'm guessing Mrs. Tilley would give you her left arm, including the giant rings she displays on her hand, for Becky's whereabouts. I'm not her." Jennifer let a few seconds tick off before saying, "What I can offer is to make you famous."

"How famous?"

Jennifer looked at the receiver in disbelief. She hit another button and said, "Hey, Inna, I have a call coming in from the Northwinds Plaza Hotel. I think that's in the Chester Hills area – near the Kigar Museum of Science. Can you give me a sec?" Jennifer pressed the HOLD button and continued to browse the luxury rooms for rent in one of the city's most desirable blocks of real estate. *How can these places go for $2000 a night? For that price it'd better include meals, limo and a driver who doubles as a gigolo.*

"Malone, you busy?" Mitch stood in his office doorway, a slip of paper in his hand.

Jennifer minimized the hotel listings and continued to ignore the flashing HOLD light. "I've got a minute."

"A second John Doe was found in the river. I want you to go back to Met and see if there's a connection to your other guy."

"Interesting," Jennifer said, picking up the receiver and punching the caller's line. "So, I'm swamped all of a sudden, Inna. Could you tell your information to our editor, Mitch Carson?" Mitch cocked his head at the mention of his name. "I'll transfer you to him now."

Jennifer put Inna on hold again and then retrieved the paper from Mitch's hand. "I'm all over this." Jennifer grabbed her notepad and purse. "Line two is for you. A possible break in the Tilley/Beckster story."

"And why aren't you talking to this person?"

Jennifer glanced at the paper in her hand, trying to decipher Mitch's handwriting. "Because I've got to investigate this mysterious elderly man who forgot how to swim. Don't worry, I'll keep you updated, Mitch."

"I suspect his overcoat slowed his progress in the water,"

Mitch replied, watching Jennifer walk away. "Check to see if there are any rocks in his pockets. That'll sink you every time."

***

Jennifer took the subway to within a block of Metropolitan Hospital, bypassing the hassle of paying the outrageous visitor's parking lot fees or a cab fare. Even though she'd be reimbursed for these expenditures, it was the principle of the thing. She wouldn't describe herself as a miser, as she loved spending money on clothes, and restaurants, drinks while out on the town and vacations. She simply wasn't in the habit of wasting money, no matter whose it was.

Another perk of walking to the station was the incredible atmosphere that presented itself. Unlike static Greenheart Station, the city streets and sidewalks were alive with eclectic activity. Between the buskers, the panhandlers, the homeless, the dropouts surfing the free café internet on their expensive phones and the business men and women of every age and ethnicity, the intermingling experience of humans (and the occasional pet dog, cat, rat or rooster) was never the same. The collective made the city great and why Jennifer wouldn't be leaving it anytime soon.

In the subway car, Jennifer texted Maryanne to say she'd be at the hospital in fifteen minutes and wanted to meet. Moments later, the reply stated to visit the security desk in the lobby.

"Okiedokie," Jennifer said.

As the other riders swayed with the motion of the train, Jennifer glanced at the newspapers some were reading: *The Star*, *The Orangemen Record* and the city's one tabloid, *The Watch*. *Not a Daily Telegraph in sight,* she smiled to herself. *I'm surrounded by heathens.* Nevertheless, she read the headlines facing her, paying close attention to any that alluded to the search for Becky Mayville or the scandal of which she was associated. The accompanying stories rehashed the councilman's transgressions, but none indicated that Chester Hills was part of the narrative, which calmed her nerves.

Jennifer dug out her phone and called Mitch.

"Which slacker have you dispatched to Chester Hills in search of Hot Becky?"

"No one, yet," Mitch replied. "Your caller Inna would only say her boyfriend worked at the Bella Vista late last week. She started babbling how once we confirmed that information she'd want something in return." Mitch laughed. "She's out of her mind on that score."

"When I'm done at the morgue, I'll check it out. Any hits on the police composite of John Doe #1 from online readers?"

"I don't know," Mitch said, writing a reminder to call the web editor. "We'll get all kinds of crazies calling when it runs in tomorrow's paper."

"Maybe Inna Bo-beena will be able to help," Jennifer said. "Okay, gotta go. I'm at my stop."

Jennifer disconnected the call before Mitch could wrap up the conversation.

"I hate when she does that," he said, putting down the receiver. Through his open door he called to his dutiful secretary, "Amy, can you get the dweeb who runs the website on the line for me? What's his name again?"

"Mitchell – like your name, but longer," came her caustic reply.

"Longer isn't necessarily better," Mitch said, knowing his secret girlfriend would crack a smile.

"That's what they all say," she said, beginning to laugh.

***

"Hey," Maryanne said cheerfully as she stood to greet Jennifer. "Are you here on official business?"

"Officially, yes," Jennifer replied, "but not on the story you're hoping I'm here for."

"Oh."

Jennifer noticed an older security guard watching them and asked Maryanne, "Miss, can you assist me in getting to the E.R.? I know it isn't far. The thing is I left my glasses at home and have a hard time making out wall signs."

"Sure thing," Maryanne said, turning to her coworker. "Norm, I'm going to assist this lady – she can't see without her glasses." On cue, Jennifer gave him a shrug of the shoulders and shook her head as if to apologize.

"Can't a volunteer do that?" Norm asked, sounding perturbed.

Maryanne ignored the comment and walked around the desk. "I was taking my break anyway," she said glancing to the wall clock. "I'll be back in fifteen minutes. Do you want a coffee or donut from the cafeteria?"

The prospect of free food lightened Norm's attitude. "A medium coffee with two creams and an apple fritter. Thanks." He returned to his book as Jennifer and Maryanne walked out of view.

"I don't want to get you into any trouble," Jennifer said as they passed the O.R. Family Waiting Room and public elevators.

"Norm's harmless and I am due for my break."

"Were you able to talk with Sandy at the gift shop about the flower buyer?"

"No. We've been quite busy today. Sorry."

"It's okay," Jennifer reassured her eager protégé. "What kind of calls have you had to attend?"

"Stupid stuff," Maryanne began. "Like the elderly man in a wheelchair who got into a fight with a teenager in a bathroom. He cornered the kid and wouldn't let him leave."

"Did the kid try to rob him?"

"If it were only that simple. He had the audacity to use the handicap stall because all the other ones were occupied. But by the time the guy in the chair wheeled in the stalls were empty ... except the one he needed to use."

"Did the kid apologize?" Jennifer wondered.

"No – that was the problem. He kept arguing, 'Hey, dude, the toilets are for everyone. The one I used is wheelchair *accessible*, not *reserved*. Like the ramp outside! Are you going to yell at people for walking on that too?'"

Jennifer laughed as she pictured the scene in her head. "He kind of has a point."

"He does, but we can't appear to take sides," Maryanne explained. "We told the teenager to leave and cautioned the old man against holding anyone hostage like that again."

"And how did that go over?"

"Quote, 'I have to crap and don't need an audience.' Unquote."

"A dignified response."

When they reached the E.R. entrance, Jennifer said she was going to visit Dr. Singh about the new John Doe. "It shouldn't take long. I'll stop by the front desk on my way out."

Maryanne looked toward the coroner's office and the morgue door. "I think Helga is still here. Do you want me to check?"

The uneasiness Jennifer felt during her last visit to this area returned. "No, I'll discreetly ask Dr. Singh myself."

"Will you let me know what she says?"

"Of course." Jennifer saw the tension in Maryanne's face fade.

The crackling of Maryanne's radio made both women jump. "Hey, Maryanne," Norm said, "can you get me chocolate milk instead of a coffee?"

"No problem, Norm," Maryanne replied.

"One crisis after another for you today, Maryanne," Jennifer said. "I'll talk to you in a bit, okay?"

"Text me and I'll make a different excuse to leave the front desk."

"You got it."

NINETEEN

As Jennifer passed the morgue the door swung open, giving her a sudden shock.

"Oh dear, I hope I didn't scare you," Dr. Singh apologized, exiting into the hallway. "That was not my intention. You arrived quicker than I expected." She touched Jennifer's forearm to calm her. "You look like you've seen a ghost."

"This place creeps me out, which surprises me," Jennifer said, shaking her arms as if to rid herself of the fear. "I'm usually good with scary movies or going to those haunted houses at Hallowe'en."

"The difference is you're cognizant they are phony. Actors in costume. Fake blood and all that." Jennifer followed Dr. Singh to her office. "But here is different. It's true life … and death, from which we can't escape the reality we have an expiration date." Dr. Singh gestured for Jennifer to sit in the chair in front of her desk. "And if that doesn't alarm you, nothing will."

"What about you – are you ever scared down here?" Jennifer asked as Dr. Singh took a seat.

"Only of the occasional spider," she said, pointing to a cobweb in a corner of the ceiling. "The truth is I made my peace with my role in this world a long time ago. My job is to deal with the dead on a daily basis, in the same way yours is to deal with newsmakers."

"Somebody's got to do it, is that what you're saying?"

"Most definitely."

Jennifer let Dr. Singh organize a few papers before saying, "There's a rumour that you found another body floating in the river."

"I didn't actually find it. It was delivered here by the police earlier today. I figured since you did such a first-rate job with the last John Doe, you might help us out again."

Jennifer opened her notebook. "I'd be happy to. So … what are the details of how this individual was brought here? I heard it was an elderly man, possibly wearing an overcoat of some sort."

Dr. Singh picked up a manila folder and opened it, turning over the photos she'd taken of the man, not knowing how squeamish Jennifer was about such things. "Caucasian male, late seventies, 5'8", thin build with a bit of a paunch, balding grey hair. At the time of death he had on a tan overcoat, white collared shirt, slacks, socks and loafers. He had no rings or jewelry. No watch. And from slight discoloration on the bridge of his nose, he probably wore glasses occasionally, but none were with the body."

"No wallet?"

"I shall address that shortly," Dr. Singh said. "The police are going to run his fingerprints through their system, but that could take a few days."

"If the body only just arrived, isn't there a real possibility his family will report him missing today or tomorrow? Why do a story on him so soon?"

Dr. Singh placed a hand on top of the photos. "Because this man's injuries are consistent with the other John Doe. With the first one, I couldn't decide if some of the marks on his body were from initial trauma before he died or after, as he was in the water for a long period of time."

Jennifer gave Dr. Singh her full attention. "I'm listening."

"There are actually two areas – one on each side of the head above the ear. They appear to be indentations caused by a small solid object. I noticed them on the first John Doe, but because his skin was waterlogged and stretched, I couldn't get an accurate measurement or see any detail to the affected region."

Jennifer tried to keep up with Dr. Singh's commentary. "But you could with this new John Doe?"

"The areas of impact were very clear and I think I know what caused them."

"Do tell," Jennifer said.

"A hard-leather billy club."

Although Jennifer knew what a billy club was she had trouble coming to terms with what Dr. Singh had said. "We're talking about that handheld thingy with lead inside of it, right? Looks like a beaver tail?"

"That's it!"

"Do they still make them? I'd have thought they were outlawed."

Dr. Singh tapped away on her computer keyboard and then angled the screen toward Jennifer. "I can buy one off the internet."

Surprisingly, at the click of a button you could own a personal knockout weapon as used by the police and shady detectives in films from the 1940s.

"Look at that," Jennifer said, genuinely amazed as she read the seller's description. "Available in many convenient sizes to fit your needs. Who knew?"

"I'm afraid the person who hit our John Does in the head before pushing them into the river to drown, that's who."

The magnitude of the situation began to settle in.

"Are you saying this is the work of a serial killer?"

Dr. Singh exited the website and closed the folder in front of her. "Officially, I cannot say anything of the sort. The police have to make that determination."

"Have you advised them of these similarities?"

"No, for the simple reason I need to confirm my hypothesis and thoroughly compare the marks. That's going to take a day or two. I have no interest in setting the city on edge with the news a killer is out there smacking unsuspecting folks in the head by the river."

"Have you told anyone else of this possibility or would I have an exclusive?"

"I have opened up about this to you only," Dr. Singh said firmly, "but you are to keep it out of the papers until the proper time."

"I can live with that," Jennifer replied respectfully. "To be clear, do you still want a blurb on the new John Doe, or for me to hold onto that information for the time being?"

"You can run a story about this new man, leaving out the medical aspects I've entrusted with you for now. I'm positive the police wouldn't mind some unsolicited help to lighten their work load."

Jennifer reviewed her notes. "You said there was a wallet. Clearly it didn't have any identification."

"Oh, yes," Dr. Singh said, reopening the folder to remove a plastic bag containing a small, faded, black and white photograph. "The wallet was emptied of identification, credit cards and such, but this was overlooked in one of the inside slots." She handed the picture to Jennifer. "It looks like the same man only thirty or forty years younger. You can see the mole at the corner of his left eye. The woman may be his wife or girlfriend."

Jennifer examined the image and saw the birthmark. The man was wearing a dark overcoat and a fedora on a city sidewalk outside a restaurant. He was either grimacing or smiling awkwardly when the photo was taken. The slim brunette next to him had a pleasant smile and they looked to be about the same age, late forties or early fifties. There were no legible street signs or landmarks to identify the location. Two letters at the end of an overhead logo could be read: EN.

"Do the police know about this?" Jennifer asked.

"I called after they left. I was the one who found it – they'd missed it in their original search."

"Are they picking it up to help with identification? You know, if someone calls looking for their grandfather who liked taking strolls by the river?"

"I scanned it and emailed them a copy. They told me to keep

it on file."

"While I'm here, can I take a shot of it with my phone?" Jennifer reached into her purse. "I won't run it in the newspaper until the police say it's okay."

"Why not?" Dr. Singh gently took the picture out of the bag for Jennifer to snap a picture.

"Thanks," Jennifer said as Dr. Singh replaced the picture in the bag, then the folder.

"Is there anything else you need from me for this short human interest story?"

Jennifer put her notepad and pen in her purse. "I do have one more line of questioning. I'm not sure you'll have the answers though."

A concerned look brushed across Dr. Singh's face. "I'll try my best," she said to the now distressed reporter.

"It's about another body in the morgue – at least I think she's still in there."

"Helga Klemens?"

Astonished, Jennifer said, "How did you know that?"

"Trust me, I'm not clairvoyant," Dr. Singh said with a quick laugh. "There is currently only one female in the cooler. It was simple deduction."

"Right," Jennifer said blushing, not considering the obvious.

"Was she a friend?"

"No. I've been asked to find out any information about her death by a couple very close to me." Jennifer hoped this explanation would suffice without going into the crazy-sounding theories she, Luke and Maryanne had already bandied about. "If there is something you can tell me off the record, I would appreciate it."

"From a cursory review of her chart yesterday," Dr. Singh began, "it appears an old heart failed to handle the stress of a major surgery. It happens all the time with the elderly." She tapped the side of her head. "The mind may be willing, but the heart sometimes can't cope."

"Is there any significance that she apparently died twice?"

Without hesitation, Dr. Singh replied, "Just that it's a medical marvel she was resuscitated at all. That's how incredible our medicines and surgical teams are these days. Sadly, her body couldn't sustain the miracle forever."

"What about an autopsy?" Jennifer asked.

"Martin – I mean Dr. Richmond – will be performing it tomorrow. It'll probably be his last before retiring."

Jennifer recalled this bit of information from her first encounter with Maryanne. "Retiring is a long way off for me."

"We thought the same about Dr. Richmond. He's in his early fifties and his resignation was a shock. He's been on the staff at Met since he was 19."

"Tired of the clientele?"

"A little of that ... and some personal issues, which may have played a role in his decision."

Dr. Singh's tone indicated sadness and Jennifer decided not to pursue any further inquiries. Maybe the good doctor was battling some disease. Whatever the reason for his departure, Jennifer knew Helga would be in trustworthy hands.

"I hope a golf course and sandy beach are in his future," Jennifer said, standing to leave. Dr. Singh didn't reply and stood. "Do you have a lot of work left to do today?"

Dr. Singh gathered a few folders and led Jennifer into the hallway. "A couple of tests and a meeting with a colleague from Cardio-Pulmonary. We try to get autopsies out of the way in the morning, so that we're then free to return calls, write notes and other follow-ups in the afternoon." They had reached the morgue door. Dr. Singh pulled up a key attached to a retractable cord clipped to her hospital badge and unlocked the door. "And what about yourself, Ms. Malone?" she asked, propping the door open with her shoe.

"Routine reporter stuff and things."

Jennifer's eyes drifted past Dr. Singh and into the morgue, settling on the status board Luke had shown her. It listed the names and cooler trays each body was assigned:

Tray #10: Helga Klemens

Tray #11: John Doe - 1

Tray #12: John Doe - 2

"Why are trays 10, 11 and 12 written in red marker, while the others on the board are in black?"

Dr. Singh studied the board. "Those trays are reserved for police usage – bodies involved in murder or associated with some criminal activity, as well as any John or Jane Does. There's a metal gate locked with a padlock across each shelf."

Police usage?

"Why would Helga's body be in that row?"

Dr. Singh looked at the listings. "I'm assuming due to space issues. You can see there are some available trays, as a few bodies were picked up by funeral homes earlier today."

Jennifer extended her hand, which Dr. Singh shook. "Thanks again. The John Doe #2 information will be on our website tonight and in the paper tomorrow."

"And I will update you on my findings regarding the billy club marks."

"Great."

Dr. Singh entered the morgue, leaving Jennifer alone in the hallway that gave her the heebie-jeebies. Unable to shake the feeling, she cut through the nearby E.R. waiting room and into the fresh afternoon air. It was the sight of Helga's name attached to the two John Doe bodies that disturbed her. They were literally locked up together, stacked one on top of the other. *Is it possible all three met their maker before their time?*

Jennifer sent Maryanne a text saying she couldn't visit the security desk due to another hot lead. "She'll buy that," Jennifer said to herself.

Back at her desk to type the John Doe #2 story, Jennifer sat contemplating Dr. Singh's opinion that Helga's death was likely caused by her aged heart. It made sense. As for the flowers, they could have been purchased by an employee who knew Helga. Maybe they were going to visit her after the hip surgery and didn't get the chance. The more she thought of Helga's passing, the more she considered maybe she'd got caught up in the hysteria of two excitable young people's conspiracy theory. Although there did appear to be some interesting clues supporting their claims – the bedside declaration, Genifer Grant's uneasiness to talk – none of them seemed to be completing the big picture.

Like any good detective story, Jennifer was aware it only took one small piece of the puzzle to fall into place to crystallize what you had and what you still needed. She made the executive decision to put Helga's story on the back burner until new and tangible information came to light. She had other interests to pursue.

Jennifer opened the image on her phone of the half-smiling man in an overcoat. "Aside from the fact you're dead, today's your lucky day, buddy, because Jennifer Malone is determined to find out who you are."

TWENTY

TUESDAY

Jennifer texted Maryanne to call and less than a minute later, her cell rang.

"Hi Jennifer – it's Maryanne. Is this about the lead you texted about yesterday?"

Jennifer tried to recall what message she'd sent after escaping the morgue hallway. "No, this is something else. Can you talk?"

"I'm on patrol. Hold on." Maryanne unlocked a conference room door and locked it behind her. "Okay, what's happening?"

"First off, I spoke with Dr. Singh and her opinion was that Helga died because her heart couldn't deal with the stress of the surgery. This was always a possibility, so we can't dismiss it."

"I've heard Dr. Singh is very good."

"That being the case ... the relevance of who bought Helga's flowers shouldn't matter anymore, but I found out who did."

"Oh," Maryanne said, her skin now tingling. "Was it a relative?"

"No, a woman named Elaine. Her last name starts with an 'S' – in her late thirties, early forties, who works in the kitchen. Does that name ring any bells with you, Maryanne?"

"No. We don't generally have much interaction with the kitchen staff."

"Could you find out her last name?"

As a journalism student Maryanne learned that a reporter working a story often needed trusted and confidential sources to assist them. She also knew Jennifer was fully aware that a security guard would have easy access to patient and employee records. *Is this a test?* she began to panic, trying to determine a way to justify supplying this woman's information. *Is there a way Jennifer could uncover the same surname without my help?* After witnessing the way she'd lied to Norm about forgetting her glasses, Maryanne envisioned Jennifer boldly walking into the kitchen and asking Elaine flat-out why she bought those flowers. *I'd love to see her do that.*

"I can," Maryanne replied, concluding this person's surname might be on her hospital badge for the public to see. An online 411 telephone search and a few cold calls would locate this woman sooner or later. Maryanne felt comfortable that she was simply saving Jennifer time, not divulging highly sensitive details like medical conditions or treatments.

"I don't want you to do anything illegal," Jennifer said. "I can find the information on my own," she added, as if reading Maryanne's mind.

"There's a way I can get that surname without going on the computer," Maryanne stated confidently. "There'll be no electronic paper trail, trust me. Give me ten minutes and I'll call you back."

Jennifer liked Maryanne's initiative and did trust her. "I'll be here."

Seven minutes passed until Jennifer's cell rang.

"It's Stanton. Elaine Stanton. She's worked at the hospital for fourteen years. Presently in the kitchen."

"Nice. Dare I ask how you got this information so fast?"

"It was pretty easy," Maryanne said, replacing the document in her hand under the magazines where she'd found it in a staff break room. "There's a union handout that lists the seniority level of every hospital employee. I went through the ten pages and found only one Elaine with a last name starting with 'S'."

Jennifer could feel the warmth of Maryanne's smile emitting through her cool, confident voice. "Nicely done, Maryanne."

Having already dipped her toe into the pool of employee misconduct, Maryanne had gone a step further, pulling up the hospital's personnel records that were listed in alphabetical order. She figured if questioned, she would say she was making sure her new address was correct. Had she typed in 'Elaine Stanton' and was caught … she'd probably be in deep trouble with administration.

"She lives at 162 Lemon Tree Street here in the city. Do you want her phone number? It's listed in the latest phone book."

"You are all sorts of revelations today. Go ahead, give it to me." Jennifer wrote the address and phone number down in her notepad, hoping this was the break she'd been waiting on. Then again, if Helga died of natural causes, Elaine's motive for buying the carnations would be moot.

"What's next?" Maryanne asked. "Are you coming back to the hospital to talk with her?"

Jennifer looked at her watch. "No, I have to get out to Chester Hills for another story. Plus, I'd rather speak with Elaine outside of the hospital. No use causing waves if you don't have to."

"Of course," Maryanne said, remembering that discretion was key to a good journalist's reporting. "Can I let Luke know what Dr. Singh said and about Elaine?"

"Sure, and feel free to go over the top about finding Elaine. He'll be awed by your superior girl mind."

"Luke's no slouch as an investigator either," Maryanne said.

"And that's why you click. Great minds think alike."

"That sounds about right."

"Okay, I have to hail a taxi. I'll keep you informed of any new developments."

"Good luck with that new lead," Maryanne said.

"Thanks, I'm going to need it."

TWENTY ONE

Jennifer's jaunt to Chester Hills wasn't a complete waste of time, as she learned how the other half truly lived while visiting the city. In doing so, she knew she'd never be financially stable enough to play the type of reindeer games required to shell out thousands of dollars a night for a hotel room with a spectacular vista view of the river, a bed the size of her apartment, a giant wall-mounted television and incredible shower stall for a group of ten, if you were into that sort of thing.

Not happening, Malone, she told herself.

The Bella Vista Hotel & Spa event planner was quite helpful when Jennifer approached her about writing a story on high-end parties and receptions. "I'm looking to branch out creatively for a piece in our Life section," she'd said, "and need some facts for my pitch. Could you assist me?"

Up to this point in their conversation, Wanda Collard had exuded the aura of an unflappable businesswoman who was at the top of her game. She oozed confidence and Jennifer liked her instantly. Unfortunately, when Jennifer floated the idea of an article, Wanda's ultra professional mask slipped, to reveal her inner teenage girl, giddy about seeing her name in print and a possible photo to accompany the article?

"I certainly can, Jennifer. Please take a seat. This is very exciting," Wanda gushed, picking up promotional folders from a counter before sitting at her desk. She carefully laid out each folder to face Jennifer, as if she were a prospective client. "You can take these home," Wanda instructed. "They show the different event levels the Bella Vista can coordinate for parties up to 500 guests." Wanda leaned forward and in a lower tone said, "Since I took over this position six years ago, we've ranked number one in every poll done by business and travel publications."

The woman isn't shy about tooting her own horn, Jennifer concluded, although whispering seemed out of place with just the two of them in the room. Playing along, Jennifer grabbed the folder marked "The Golden Tier." Flipping it open, the first thing she read was a banner indicating that the contents within were for the cost-conscious client planning to spend fifty to one hundred thousand dollars for their event. *Cost-conscious?* Jennifer glanced at the other two folders – "The Platinum Tier" and "The Titanium Tier" – and shuddered at their price ranges. "What about catering? Is it all in-house?"

"For the most part, yes," Wanda began, trying to hide her disappointment that Jennifer didn't acknowledge her stellar track record in the hospitality industry. "However, when there are multiple events that overlap, we hire one of only a few prestigious catering companies in the area." Wanting to bring the focus back to the Bella Vista she added, "But that's a rare occurrence since we upgraded and expanded our world class kitchen facilities a year ago."

"By chance did that rare occurrence occur late last week?"

The question struck Wanda like an accusation; her head swirling with negative scenarios. "What do you mean?"

Jennifer could see the panic on Wanda's face. *Sensitive and fragile – check.* "Let me explain. A friend attended an event here and said it was beyond phenomenal." The tension in Wanda's fake smile faded a bit. "Apparently one of the servers gave her the catering company's name, but she forgot it. I realize this is off topic. I didn't intend to throw you for a loop like that."

"Oh, you didn't," Wanda lied through her pearly white teeth. "I was concerned there'd been a problem and hoped to solve it as fast as possible. Our motto here at the Bella Vista is 'Guaranteed Elegance!' and we make every effort to live up to it for clients and attendees alike."

Jennifer looked down at the folder on her lap. "There it is on the cover in bold type. I like that. It's short and catchy. By any chance did you come up with it, Wanda?"

"I did," Wanda said beaming with pride.

Jennifer circled the phrase on the folder's cover with a dash, writing 'Wanda's idea', making sure she saw the notation. "Perfect. Now would you recall what event my friend might have been at and which outside company was used?"

"It was the Morris/Blick wedding," she stated confidently. "Very last minute. The bride was the goddaughter of a prominent member of government. We were glad to help the family out when a fire damaged their original reception hall. So it was a timing issue beyond our control that we had to outsource the catering to Excelsior Dining."

Jennifer wrote the name down and tried to figure out how to

leave without hurting Wanda's feelings. "Oh, my phone is ringing," she said, reaching into her purse. "I had it on vibrate. I'm sorry, but I have to take this. It'll only take a moment."

"Oh, yes, go ahead."

"Jennifer Malone … Another one? … Okay, I'll head to Met and speak with the coroner. I believe Dr. Singh is on duty today."

Jennifer ended the call and dropped the phone into her purse. "I can't believe the timing of this. I have to go get some details on a man found in the river. I hate to leave, as we were only getting started."

"When something unforeseen comes up, you have to deal with it right away," Wanda said. "That's exactly how I operate here at the Bella Vista."

Wow – what a great self-promoter!

Jennifer stood and took the folders from the desk. "I'll review these and get back to you if the article goes ahead. You may get a call from Cassie Hendricks, the Life section editor, to confirm a few details."

Relieved that the feature was still possible, Wanda shook Jennifer's hand and with her biggest smile yet said, "That would be wonderful. It was so nice to meet you." She walked Jennifer out of the office. "I look forward to talking more about the advantages your readers could experience by booking their events here at the Bella Vista."

Stop the insanity. She needs a man in her life, Jennifer surmised.

Before leaving, Jennifer made discreet inquiries with three cleaning staff employees if there had been any famous visitors staying in the hotel lately. Remarkably, each answered with the same line: "I can't give out that information." Jennifer respected their adhering to the rules of confidentiality. Being a housekeeper in a place like this generated larger tips than at lesser properties. Next, she spoke with the concierge, a bellhop and a desk clerk going on his break – each repeating the mantra from the hotel's employee handbook.

Stepping into the sun, Jennifer smiled at the older, distinguished doorman wearing the nametag 'Carlton' and asked, "Do you know if Becky Mayville has ever been a guest here?"

"I'm sorry, even if she had I can't give out–"

"That information," Jennifer cut him off, completing the party line. "But you do know who she is, right?"

"I believe she is a young lady who appears in the news quite often," the doorman said with a grin. "I've read a story or two on her."

"Then you know what she looks like?"

There was a mild nervousness in the man's voice when he replied, "I do."

Jennifer handed him a business card. "I can tell you've been doing your job for many years. You don't get a position like this by revealing the inner workings of your employer to reporters. I respect that."

"Thank you, Jennifer," he said, examining her card.

"I would be remiss," Jennifer began, "if I didn't ask that you call my number when a female resembling Miss Mayville happens to drop by the Bella Vista, even for a drink alone at the bar. Is it okay to request that?"

"You just did," was the amused reply. "May I get you a taxi?"

"You may."

The doorman waved a waiting driver to move ahead to allow Jennifer to get in. "Have a great day," Carlton said cheerfully as he closed her door.

"Where to?" the cabbie asked, starting the meter.

"*The Daily Telegraph* building."

On the ride back to the office, Jennifer used her phone to search for the Excelsior Dining catering company, and found the address and phone number. Nothing about Inna's phone tip seemed remotely credible, but other investigations had started with much less.

***

Carlton the doorman walked into the Bella Vista's private elevator and entered a code given to only a select few. The doors closed and he was whisked non-stop to the top floor. There were two private suites on this level: one with a city view and one with a river view. He pressed the PH1 wall bell and waited, looking directly at the small camera to the left of the door.

The door opened a crack and a woman in her early twenties with hair dyed a royal blue frowned at him. "What?"

Carlton handed over Jennifer's business card. "This reporter was asking around about you."

Becky Mayville stood dumbfounded. "What did you tell her? Should I start packing, Carlton?"

The doorman remained calm; grace under pressure, as always.

"From what I gather no employee said anything about you. They know that to do so would be cause for immediate termination. They might think this was a test by the owners and they passed with flying colours."

"Then how did this Malone reporter get so close?"

"I'll be investigating that further."

The two looked at each other with no words passing between them.

Carlton took a step back. "Have a pleasant evening, Miss Mayville. I'll contact your father and sort this out, as we've done in the past. Don't worry, you're safe."

Becky smiled politely as Carlton entered the elevator and keyed in his code. After the doors closed, Becky locked herself in the suite and collapsed on a spacious leather sectional. Turning over the business card in her hand she asked herself, "How did you get so smart, Jennifer Malone?"

TWENTY TWO

The number of staff working in *The Daily Telegraph's* Local section once topped fifty. Today there was one full-timer, four part-timers and numerous students (aka free labour). Technology had eliminated much of the tedious trench work, but like a public library, librarians by any other name were required to help clueless reporters find background details for stories from years gone by.

If Maryanne were accepted into the intern program, this crowded and cluttered area would likely be her home for the summer months.

"Hi, Jennifer. Are you lost?"

Jennifer grinned toward the mature man at an oversized desk in the far corner, sitting on a chair that dated back decades. Lovingly referred to as The Dean, Vic Durand was the longest serving employee at the paper, having been hired one day before his future wife, Julie, who got a job in the secretarial pool. That was 49 years ago.

"Are you still working here, Vic?" Jennifer quipped as she approached him. She moved a stack of papers off a visitor's chair and took a seat.

"Oh, they want both Julie and me gone, but we're adamant to make it to 50 years," Vic laughed. "Maybe by then I'll have mastered sending emails. I get these kids to run handwritten notes to the establishment upstairs."

"Don't feel bad. My computer login is 'changepassword'."

"I see my interns on their phones surfing the internet, texting their friends, watching videos, and it blows my mind. When I was hired, I was allotted five hundred sheets of lined paper and ten big red pencils. When they were gone I had to submit a supply requisition form to my boss for approval."

"Who was that – Fred Flintstone?" Jennifer asked. "Anyway, your age … and wisdom, of course … are the reasons I've dropped in today." Jennifer brought out her phone and opened her photo gallery. "Can you tell me what you see in this picture, Vic?" She knew he'd run the City section for years and had forgotten more knowledge than most current reporters or editors possessed.

"For starters … it's in black and white," he said with a smile, "so it must be old." He looked closer at the image. "From the cars in the background, I'd have to say this was taken in 1976 or 1977. It's a pity they don't build gas guzzlers like that anymore." Next, he examined the man's clothing. "The overcoat and fedora were a big deal then, although it wasn't my style. I look terrible in hats of any kind. Ask Julie when you see her."

Jennifer stood to point out the streetscape. "Do any of these buildings look familiar?"

Vic put on his glasses and noted that there weren't any high-rises in view, only a row of mid-sized brick buildings stretching the length of the street. "I'd say east end … where Erie Avenue intersects with Waterfront Road. A block from the shipping piers at the mouth of the river. Maybe the 200 block."

"I'm impressed," Jennifer said.

Vic handed back the phone. "In time you would have figured it out. You're a smart egg, Malone."

Jennifer studied the picture again. "I don't know how, apart from the time period because of the vehicles. I was going to stop by Napoleon's desk in the Auto section."

Vic pointed to the upper right hand corner of the picture. "EN," he said. "That's all you needed to focus on."

"Two letters isn't a lot to go on."

Vic walked to an overflowing shelf by the window and selected a hardcover book titled, *Our City – History In The Making*, which he began to leaf through. "This will help," he said, turning the book toward Jennifer.

Jennifer's eyes moved effortlessly from the EN in her picture to the final two letters of a sign ending in the same letters and font. "Davey's Den? How old is this place?"

"When did prohibition begin - 1920?" Vic answered. "It was a legitimate restaurant for a few years, then became a popular blind pig."

"Blind pig?"

"A speakeasy. Where you'd go to buy liquor when the country was dry."

"A bit before my time," Jennifer joked, "but I've seen documentaries. Weren't those establishments run by organized crime?"

"You betcha. They had the money to pay off the coppers and city officials to look for crime elsewhere," Vic answered with enthusiasm. "I wouldn't doubt some shady deals are still going on down there today."

"What – this place is still operating?"

"Weren't you listening to me? It's located in the 200 block of Erie Avenue by the river." Vic shook his head.

"Is there anything else I should know, my wise old – and I'm emphasizing 'old' in deference to your superior brain – friend?"

Vic settled comfortably into his chair. "Two things: one, if I'm not mistaken, the woman in the picture was the owner, at least on paper. Her name was Deangela Rossi. Her husband, Alberto, was a big shot for years, only to be rubbed out during some turf wars in the late 1960s."

"Is she alive?"

"Ask Rich Simpson. He used to cover the crime beat."

"I'll do that," Jennifer said. "And the second thing?"

"Davey's Den has the best arancini and meatballs this side of Rome."

"And here I thought you were going to tell me who Davey was."

"If memory serves it was an amalgamation of the 'David and Goliath' and 'Daniel in the Lion's Den' Bible stories," Vic replied, referring to the brief description in the history book.

"That's one less question I'll need to ask when I visit there," Jennifer said as she stood. "As always, Vic, you are the best resource this dump has to offer."

"I'll take that as a compliment," he said with a small laugh.

Jennifer began to walk down the aisle and turned to Vic. "Be sure to email me the date of your retirement party."

"I'll do my best, Jennifer."

***

"What now?" Rich Simpson asked as he saw Jennifer walking toward his desk. "I don't have Jake Wagner's cell number, if you're looking for a date."

Jennifer sat across from him. "Cell number. Cute. I see what you did there, even if you were commenting on my love life in a disparaging manner. Do you and Mitch get together over drinks to write these zingers?"

"I believe Mitch solicits responses from the daycare kids next door and we split the lines between us."

"I knew you weren't that clever on your own."

The two stared at each other until both broke into a smile.

"Jake Wagner is old news," Jennifer said, handing off her cell phone. "Today I want to know why that man has his arm around the waist of the owner of Davey's Den in the late 1970s. Any guesses?"

Rich glanced at the picture. "Where do you find this stuff?"

"The morgue," Jennifer stated proudly. "Do you recognize the fashion plate with Mrs. Rossi?"

"Should I?"

"Then that's a no?"

Rich used his fingers to expand the image, bringing the

unidentified man full screen. "Do you know how many 'made men' there were in those days in this city?"

"This guy was a gangster?"

Rich handed back the phone. "Let me put it this way: no one would dare to touch Alberto Rossi's wife unless he was *family*, if you get my drift."

After leaving Vic, the idea had occurred to Jennifer that John Doe #2 was mob-related. He had that look. Although Rich was implying this man was likely a member of Rossi's band of criminals, what if he were a blood relative? *Deangela's brother?*

"What if he was family-family?" Jennifer asked.

Rich took back the phone. "I don't see a family resemblance. Anything is possible, I guess." Rich pivoted to his desktop computer and searched Deangela's name, getting several hits, most associated with her husband's untimely death while supervising the filming of a porn movie. He entered the words 'siblings' and 'brother'. "Looks like a sister, no brothers." Rich then did the same for Alberto's name. "Only child," he said.

"I know the restaurant is still operating. Is Deangela alive?" Jennifer asked, knowing the woman would have to be in her eighties.

Rich skimmed the article he'd opened. "Alive, but not seen in public for years."

"I wonder if she's been kind of forgotten as the new crews have taken over. Young people aren't as respectful of their elders these days," Jennifer said.

"Personally, I don't think The Men and their ilk give the past a second thought."

"Wait ... what?"

"What?" Rich countered. "I thought we were joking around here. You bring me this picture saying it has nothing to do with Jake Wagner, knowing the gang of hoodlums he associated with call Davey's Den their headquarters." Rich tried to read Jennifer's stern expression. "We weren't playing a game?"

Jennifer grabbed her phone back. "We weren't, although I might have won something somehow. Tell me about Davey's Den and their questionable regular patrons of ill repute. I am all ears."

Rich's short history lesson covered the period after prohibition when the Rossi organization virtually ran every illegal operation in the city. They had been unstoppable and uncontested until Nicholas (Nicky) Hill had arrived one late summer day in 1967. Aggressive and fearless, he and his thugs had begun to challenge every enterprise that Alberto oversaw. The on-going war had paralyzed sections of the city, as drive-by shootings oftentimes had taken out more pedestrians with stray bullets than the intended targets. The battles had ended abruptly when Alberto was killed by Nicholas Hill on the set of *Her Lyin' Blue Eyes*. Hill had then dictated that his gang, and what was left of the defeated Rossi gang, would become one organization to be called The Men.

"So … who is Clive Hill – the guy who runs The Men today?" Jennifer inquired.

"Nicky's son. He was standing next to his daddy when Alberto was shot between the eyes."

"Was it 'take your kid to an execution' day?"

"Apparently," Rich said with a shrug of his shoulders.

"Whatever happened to the Father of the Year? Did his son shoot him at a parent-teacher meeting?"

"No, cancer got him a few years ago and Clive took over. From what I've heard, he'd been running the show for quite some time behind the scenes."

Jennifer sighed and looked at the picture on her phone again. *Late seventies, after Deangela's husband is dead, The Men enjoying Davey's meatballs, and this guy with the fedora is in the thick of things without a care in the world.*

Remembering she hadn't told Rich that Mr. Overcoat was cooling off in the morgue, Jennifer continued her questioning. "What are the chances this gentleman is alive? Should I go to

Davey's Den and ask some questions?"

"Why is this guy so important to you?" Rich asked.

"A long-lost love story. Cassie asked me to do a little legwork for a story she's writing."

"That's crap, Jennifer. This has to do with the Jake Wagner trial and appeal. You can tell me."

Jennifer started toward her desk.

"Okay, whatever, whatever," Rich said unhappily. "But if you decide to snoop, take someone with you – and I don't mean Cassie. Take a man."

"Thanks for the advice, Rich."

"By the way, I already have plans for dinner, Malone," Rich said, loud enough for the other reporters present to hear. "Please stop begging me to go out with you."

"Can one of you check on Simpson?" Jennifer called out in the same loud pitch to her coworkers. "He's rambling in his sleep at his desk! He's delirious if he thinks he can date me."

As she passed Cassie's desk the Life editor lifted her hand. "Preach it, girlfriend."

"Amen, sister," Jennifer said, high-fiving Cassie as she started to wonder who might accompany her to Davey's Den for a bit of skullduggery. "Who indeed," she said to herself, opening her phone's contact list.

TWENTY THREE

Preparing to leave the office, Jennifer's cell rang.

"Jennifer Malone here. How's it going, Patrick?"

"Better now that I'm talking with you," the handsome Greenheart Station paramedic replied. "So you want to move our date from this weekend to tonight?"

"That makes me sound desperate, but as I said in my voicemail, I need a man to go with me to some sketchy restaurant for a story." Jennifer hoped he'd heard more than 'desperate' and 'need a man'. *Why is my love life so complicated?*

"I'd only be protection then? Your bodyguard. All business, no play?"

Jennifer smiled. "Let's not get carried away. Of course, that'll depend on your bodyguarding skills during dinner. It's of the utmost importance you keep an eye on me at all times."

"That's what I plan to do on Saturday night," Patrick said, a hint of mischief in his voice. "Regrettably ... I can't go tonight. I have to teach a CPR class for a youth group at a community centre this evening. Can you wait until tomorrow night? I'm done work at seven."

If writing a different story, a one-day delay would be acceptable, but Jennifer didn't know when the coroner was going to release John Doe #2's photo to the public, thereby cancelling her exclusive.

All business, no play – check.

"You know those damn kids are going to slobber all over your life-size doll or, heaven forbid, each other like rabid dogs, right?" Jennifer speculated. "Plus, there won't be any alcohol to consume, like at Davey's Den."

"Trust me, if I could switch with Kristen or Owen, I would in a heartbeat."

"That old line might work on your other conquests," Jennifer lightly chided him. "Next thing coming out of your mouth is that you'll make it up to me Saturday night."

"Is that what you want me to say?"

"That isn't what you were going to say?"

"I was thinking about it ... but it seems it would be redundant and sound insincere."

"So you were going to say it?"

"If you hadn't interrupted me ... probably."

"Then I'll take back that dig about your other conquests, which now sounds kind of mean."

"If I had other conquests, Jennifer, would I have returned your call so quickly?"

"Touché," Jennifer replied. "For the record, you were my first call."

"It's nice to know that I'm on your brain. I initially worried you were going to bail on Saturday."

"And that would make you sad?"

"I'll tell you how much on Saturday."

"The one where you beg for forgiveness after ditching me to entertain a bunch of tweens and pubescent juveniles?"

"That's the one," Patrick said. "So who is the next lucky guy on *your* conquest list?"

Jennifer looked at the names she'd scratched on a piece of paper. It was a short list. "I could ask my editor, Mitch, but I think he has a not-so-secret rendezvous with his secretary. Then there are the usual suspects in the reporter pool, but they don't count, as they're married, divorced or plain creepy."

"What about your ex – the chef?" Patrick asked. "He would know his way around a restaurant, wouldn't he?"

Jennifer was happy Patrick had enough interest to learn more about her, but she didn't take the bait. "He knows his way around *his* restaurants. I don't believe he'd have much use visiting an establishment likely operated by a major criminal organization. It wouldn't surprise me if he has some outstanding gambling debts too – an extra incentive for him to lay low."

"The plot thickens. A major criminal organization?"

"Allegedly," Jennifer said, "but that's not why I'm going. I'll let hacks like Rich Simpson do that type of story. This is a more basic 'boy meets girl' plotline."

"So no editor. No creepy reporters. Who else is on your list?"

"I have a private investigator who owes me a favour."

"The one who likes cronuts?"

He is a good listener. "That's the one, although on short notice I doubt Jeffrey would break off surveillance for me, even if it's an Italian restaurant."

"What kind of loser wouldn't change plans to spend time with you," Patrick said, before adding, "Oh, wait."

"It really is your loss," Jennifer said playfully. "In your stead, it looks like I'll have to solicit another hot-looking male who works in the medical profession."

"Is he a doctor or a surgeon?" Patrick asked. "I could see you dating one of them."

"Nah. After a few weeks of yachting through the Caribbean, flying to Paris for lunch and hosting extravagant dinner parties for Fortune 500 CEOs and their trophy wives, I would get bored. I'm a simple girl at heart."

"Who likes simple things ... like paramedics."

"And patient transporters," Jennifer said. "Luke, however, is in love with his girlfriend, who happens to love me ... as a role model and reporter."

"Sounds like the three of you are a perfect match."

Their conversation was interrupted by the squawk of Patrick's work radio.

"Jennifer, I have to head out on a call. I'm sorry about tonight."

"No worries, Patrick," Jennifer replied in a softer tone. "We both live unscheduled lives. I'll call you tomorrow and talk about this evening's adventures, deal?"

"Okay and tell Luke he's a very lucky man."

"I will."

Jennifer terminated the call and was left staring at her sad list of go-to men. *If I had a little black book, the names would run from A to B!* She rolled up the paper, deposited it into her garbage can and began to scroll through her contacts to find Luke's number.

***

The late dinner crowd at Davey's Den was sparse, with a handful of patrons scattered between the tables and the bar. For Beth Jordan it was a typical weeknight, though to the public peering in the front window it might appear to be slow for such an iconic establishment. After 40 years of loyal service to the place, however, Beth knew differently. The big spenders were present, but out of sight in a back room where the real money flowed in day and night, every week of the year. There were no holiday hours posted. No dress code. No age, race or gender restrictions. And no limit to the amount of money to be won or lost on any given hand of blackjack or poker. The one simple rule: Cover your wager or pay the consequences.

Walking to the hostess stand, Beth briefly stopped to move a candle to the middle of a table. "Perfect," she said to herself, making a mental note to speak with the busboy about being more conscientious.

As Beth approached a couple in a side booth, the young woman said, "Excuse me, is this bread gluten-free?"

Though she was only asked this question occasionally, each time Beth had to force a sympathetic smile and say, "It is not, dear. The recipe is from the old country and any change to it would alter its unique taste." After this logical pronouncement Beth would steady herself for the diner's argument that the kitchen should prepare specific meals for specific customers, without considering the trouble or cost associated with doing so. *This is a restaurant, not a private spa. Do I tell you how to cook your meals at home?* Beth wanted to reply.

"No, I love your bread," the woman said enthusiastically. "Don't change a thing."

Beth smiled. "I'll pass your compliment along to the baker. Your appetizers will be right out."

Walking away from the booth, Beth lightly placed her hand on the man's shoulder, in the same way she'd do with a member of her own family. That's what Davey's Den was to Beth – family.

She could also relate to the young couple, who appeared to be on a first date. If there was any way to enhance their dining experience she would, in the same way the owner had treated a twenty-year-old Beth and her date years ago under similar conditions. The difference was that John had been familiar with the place, having worked in the kitchen for years to help pay for his schooling to become an accountant. For him, the great thing was he was guaranteed a job upon graduation. "He's going to balance all of our books," Deangela Rossi had said with a prideful smile. "Since my husband, Alberto, passed away, we've needed a good accountant."

"One more semester, Mrs. Rossi," John had replied with reverence and affection for his employer.

That evening had turned out magical and was the start of a short courtship. Their wedding had been a small joyful affair, but the reception saw Davey's Den packed to capacity. "Welcome to your new home away from home," Beth was told over and over by men in expensive suits and their wives. "John can't wait to have a family of his own." Beth was already very aware of this desire. However, she had insisted on first graduating with her university degree in Management, as well as finding a suitable replacement for her own accounting/payroll duties at her father's tool and die shop in the west end of the city. Children could be added once these two responsibilities were deducted from her life.

The transition to being a wife had come easily for Beth. She had loved John and wished only good things for him. Although she had believed his days at the diner would come to an end when he applied to one of the big accounting firms like Deloitte or Price Waterhouse, it hadn't happened. A year into their marriage, Beth wanted to know why John didn't feel compelled to send out resumes. With some trepidation he'd pulled back the curtain on his current job obligations to reveal how wealthy they were, and how powerfully he was regarded within important circles. "We're set for life, Beth," he'd said with a huge grin.

Beth had been astonished by John's admission that he was the accountant for The Men, a criminal organization implicated in the press for illegal gambling, loan sharking, and the protection racket. Davey's Den was a front and Beth had had no clue. "I don't want to live a lifestyle built on deceit," she'd stated clearly. "I want you to get a legitimate job!"

Her protests had fallen on deaf ears and a positive pregnancy test a few weeks later had sealed her fate. Being in the family way meant she was now a member of The Family, whether she liked it or not.

"Life is a blank canvas," Beth's art teaching mother told her. "You control every aspect of the picture you want to paint. Use the best brush, mix the right colours, make each stroke count and you'll create a masterpiece to be proud of."

That's exactly what Beth had vowed to do with her life for the sake of her unborn child, whom she regarded as her first priceless work of art.

***

"Good evening. For how many tonight?" Beth asked the man and woman who had walked in.

"Two," Jennifer replied, looking at Luke.

Beth grabbed two menus and said, "This way."

Unlike the couple on their first date, Beth couldn't figure out the relationship of these attractive diners. She was in her early thirties, while he was a decade younger. They didn't give the impression they were related; the visiting older sister taking her brother out for a special occasion. They also didn't give off a boyfriend-girlfriend vibe, though as they made their way down the aisle their banter indicated they were very at ease with each other.

Once they were comfortable in the booth, Beth asked Jennifer, "Can I get you started with drinks?"

"Do you have vanilla vodka?"

"We do."

"Okay, I'll have one of those with a splash of cola."

"And for you?" Beth asked Luke.

"Something diet, please."

Beth removed the unused drink menu. "I'll be right back. Thank you."

Jennifer and Luke took a minute to take in their surroundings. When they'd arrived in Jennifer's car, the familiar Davey's Den sign was lit by a row of fluorescent tubes – a marketing relic from days gone by. There was a non-descript door next to a large window that had lacy curtains outlining its edges. Inside, Jennifer counted fifteen tables and six booths, with a short bar where two world-weary men drank their whiskeys. Through a set of speakers on top of the bar, Tony Bennett could be heard crooning, *Fly Me To The Moon*.

"I don't know who warned you about this place," Luke said in a low whisper. "It looks harmless, if you ask me. Depending on the food, I might bring Maryanne here."

"I agree," Jennifer said as she began to look at the old black and white photos of local celebrities that adorned the walls. "Maybe we came on a quiet night and the real fun happens on the weekend."

As they perused their menus, Beth returned with their beverages.

"I love your short haircut," Jennifer told Beth as she placed the drinks on the tables. "It totally suits you."

"Oh, thank you," Beth replied, appreciating the flattering remark. Almost sixty, she thought it helped take a few years off her already older-than-you-think looks. "It's no fuss, no muss and easy to take care of. I'm not moving it out of my eyes, the way the younger waitresses have to."

Jennifer reached to her shoulder to examine a few strands of her hair. "I've had mine this length forever. What do you think,

Luke – would I look good with a shorter bob-type cut? Like … I'm sorry, I didn't catch your name," Jennifer said to the waitress.

"It's Beth."

"Like Beth's cut?" Jennifer asked Luke, who now appeared to be uncomfortable.

Luke glanced from Jennifer to Beth. "I'm the last person to ask. You'd look good in any hairstyle," he said to Jennifer.

Jennifer smiled and looked to Beth. "I do believe that was a compliment from the young gentleman across the table from me, don't you?"

"Definitely," Beth answered, as she saw Luke begin to blush. "Are you ready to order or do you need more time?"

"I don't know about him," Jennifer said, pointing to her menu, "but can we start with the arancini? And for my main, I'll have the eggplant parmesan."

"You won't regret that," Beth said, writing down the order. "And you, sir?"

"I'll try the meatball entrée with a Caesar salad to start, please," Luke said, handing his menu back.

"You will also not regret that choice," Beth replied with a smile. "I'll be right back with your appetizers."

Luke waited until the waitress was out of earshot, then asked, "Did I miss something?"

"You mean the haircut discussion?" Jennifer answered.

"Yes."

"First off, thank you for saying I'd look good in any hairstyle. I disagree, but appreciate your honest opinion," Jennifer laughed. "As for our waitress' haircut … it does look good on her, the way the hair frames her face."

"So?"

"So, tell me her name, Luke."

"It's Beth."

"We didn't know that before and now we do. As my editor is always saying, 'Knowledge is power', or something like that."

"Okay, I get what you did, but we don't know her last name, nor if she's related to anyone here."

"Yet," Jennifer said. "By knowing her first name, I can casually use it later. She already likes me – you, I don't know. Either way we aren't strangers anymore. That's why when I bring out John Doe #2's picture it won't be weird."

"You better hope so or you'll be swimming with the fishes or waking up with a severed horse's head in your bed."

"*The Godfather* movie marathon on channel 11, right?"

It was Luke's turn to laugh. "You're right, again."

"Always, not again. If you keep that in mind when talking with Maryanne, you two lovebirds will last a long time."

"Noted." Luke lifted his glass and proposed a toast. "To always!"

Jennifer clinked her glass with Luke's and echoed, "Always," even though she was still searching for that match who believed the same thing when it came to a relationship with her.

One day.

TWENTY FOUR

"Does anything funny ever happen at the hospital?" Jennifer asked Luke as they consumed their appetizers. "It must feel like you're staying in a bad hotel and every room is occupied by miserable people suffering in some way. No one wants to be there, no one gets any sleep, and the patients and staff get on each other's nerves."

"Yep. We're one big dysfunctional family, although most patients are grateful for any help they get from porters," Luke replied with a grin. "I try to be friendly and outgoing to boost their spirits, if only for a minute or two. Then I'm gone. The comedy part of the job usually comes from coworkers."

"Go on."

"This happened last weekend," Luke began, putting down his fork. "Me and another porter, Sue, are transferring a woman from her bed into a wheelchair, which is a typical call. So, we get the patient standing, pivot her to the left and sit her in the chair. No problem, right? I was thankful as this woman was a retired nurse with a reputation of being ornery and uncooperative."

"If you successfully got her into the chair, what was the hitch?"

Luke started to laugh. "Because Sue then bent down to help place the woman's feet in the wheelchair's foot rests and asked, 'Can you just lift your paw for me?'"

"Wow – what did the woman say?" Jennifer responded.

"At first she said nothing," Luke said. "I asked Sue, 'You meant *foot*, right?' She looked up at me in shock and then over to the old lady. I almost called a Code blue when she started to die of embarrassment. She apologized profusely, stuttering and stammering that she was thinking about her dogs – like that was helpful. Meanwhile, I'm thinking we were toast. Thankfully, the patient believed it was an honest mistake."

"I bet you got out of there as quickly as possible."

"Yep – we left once the patient was comfortable. I thought Sue was going to have a coronary out in the hall. She couldn't believe she'd said that ... at least not out loud."

"Every workplace has those moments," Jennifer said. "I remember telling my editor that his secretary was far too smart to sleep with a dolt like him, and she'd only do it on a dare in the final moments before a nuclear warhead hit our office building."

"And when did you find out they were a couple?" Luke asked.

"Two minutes later, after I'd bragged to the Lifestyle editor about my putdown."

"Awkward."

"I don't think Mitch ever told Amy of my faux pas. But is it a faux pas when everyone at the paper was kept in the dark?"

"I'd say you were right to make fun of your editor if he hadn't shared the information with anyone else."

"That is the correct answer, Luke," Jennifer replied. She took a mouthful of the delicious arancini rice ball and savoured its goodness. The taste sparked a memory of a late night meal with Oliver, her ex-chef boyfriend, that made her smile, yet also caused a pang of sadness and frustration within her. *Let's get back on track here,* she reprimanded herself. "Now, Luke, for all the circumstantial evidence we've dredged up, have you figured out how Helga could've been killed under the surgeon's nose? As much as I've enjoyed this investigative distraction, that's my biggest issue with this whole thing. What if her autopsy reveals she did die from a weak heart?"

Luke finished his salad and pushed his bowl away. "I hope you don't think I'm some bored hospital employee who sees conspiracy theories in every back door death call I attend."

"I don't," Jennifer answered. "As a reporter my job is to connect seemingly unrelated events and make sense of them. To uncover the truth, not someone's *version* of the truth. You must have some kind of theory."

Luke sat back, an unhappy expression on his face. "I hate to say this, but it would've been easier to figure out if Helga was killed with a knife or a gunshot. There'd be evidence that could be traced to one person. As it is, I think she was only frightened when I took her from the 8th floor to the O.R. She wasn't delusional – although I know, she sounded like it with her 'Don't let them kill me' line."

"You believe Helga was physically fine – aside from the broken hip – when you left her, right?"

"I do."

"That kind of eliminates the 'there must have been something in the flowers' idea," Jennifer said. "I'm still going to follow that lead. You never know. The hospital employee who bought them had some type of connection to Helga."

"Maryanne texted me the woman's name who works in the kitchen. It didn't look familiar. I might know her on sight, but that's it."

"I may pay her a visit tomorrow," Jennifer said as she forked the last bit of arancini. "So can you walk me through what could have happened to Helga after you left? Do you ever work strictly in the O.R.?"

"Maybe a few shifts a month. It's kind of a separate division from what I ordinarily do," Luke said, taking a sip of his drink. "They have a trio of full timers, each responsible for three or four operating rooms. Each has a list of the day's scheduled surgeries and get patients from the floors or the Day Surgery area, which most of the patients go back to before they leave the hospital."

"There's no difference then from patients already admitted to the hospital coming from a floor and the ones leaving at the end of the day?" Jennifer said.

"Generally not between 8:00 a.m. and 6:00 p.m., when most surgeries take place."

"I'm confused." Jennifer leaned forward. "Helga's surgery was after 6:00 p.m. What's the procedure then, if the full timers have already finished their shift?"

"I'd get called to bring the patient down," Luke said. "They do have evening surgeries – usually add-ons for emergency-type cases, like Helga's hip."

"She didn't schedule a hip surgery *per se*, but it had to be done fairly soon," Jennifer said.

"Yes. I've taken patients down at 10:00 at night or later when the surgeon could finally operate on them."

"Are there a lot of these done in the evening?"

"At night there could be two or three operating rooms going, compared to ten during the day. Why?"

Jennifer paused before saying, "I'm trying to imagine the O.R. waiting room in the daytime. From what you've said, I see it packed with patients on stretchers, porters pushing them from this room to that room, doctors and nurses all over the place, as well as clerical staff trying to keep everyone on schedule. Is that about right?"

"Pretty much," Luke answered. "It can be kind of a madhouse."

"And in the evening?"

"When I push a patient down the hallway it looks deserted, or closed, but it's not."

"But the waiting area where you leave patients is relatively empty?"

Luke saw where Jennifer was going. "Yes, during the day that area has four to nine people waiting for the surgeon to talk with them one last time."

"And once they go into surgery, a new set of patients are wheeled or walked in to wait?"

"Yes. When an operation is concluding, one of the surgeon's staff calls the porter and instructs them to go get the next patient for that room."

"Constant turnover, lots of moving patients and staff, in and out of that area during the day ... but at night it's a ghost town."

"Meaning there are fewer people who could've had contact with Helga," Luke surmised.

"Yes," Jennifer said. "If there is foul play involved, the list of suspects is a lot shorter than if Helga's surgery was between 8:00 and 6:00. This is a good thing, Luke."

"I guess. The fact that there's a list at all isn't a good thing though."

"True. Let's stop pondering the *why* and concentrate on the *how*, okay?" Jennifer asked. "If I wanted to get close to a patient in the O.R. waiting room, how would I do that? Aren't there security passes that need to be swiped? Couldn't Maryanne help find out who gained entry into that wing of the hospital?"

"She could, although that might get her fired," Luke replied.

"Only if she's caught," Jennifer said, before breaking out in a wide smile. "Forget I said that."

"Are you going to forget you said that?"

"No," Jennifer answered. "Let me worry about that another time. Right now, tell me how I get to frightened Helga without being noticed."

"Well," Luke began, "there are two corridors into the O.R.: one off the main hall by the elevators, which you need an employee badge to open. And one from the Day Surgery recovery wing that family members use when they take their loved ones home."

"There's no card swipe required?"

"In the evening, once the Day Surgery wing is closed," Luke said. "Until then, basically anyone can enter that area and walk into the O.R. waiting area by turning right instead of left."

"And if questioned, the person could say they got lost," Jennifer said, nodding her head.

"Like you did the first time we met by the morgue," Luke offered as an example.

Jennifer laughed. "I still get anxious down there," she admitted. Jennifer reached into her purse and retrieved her reporter's notepad and a pen, pushing them across the table. "Can you draw me that section of the hospital, marking which doors or hallways anyone can walk through and the ones you need an employee badge to access?"

"I can," Luke answered, taking the pen and pad. Numerous scraggly lines later, he'd replicated the basic blueprints of the O.R. and Day Surgery areas.

Jennifer examined it. "What's this room – PACU – in the middle of the two main areas?"

"It's the recovery room that patients go to after their surgery." Luke thought for a moment. "The letters stand for Post-Anesthesia Care Unit. Nurses monitor your vital signs to make sure there are no complications as the anesthesia wears off. Then, usually an hour later, they'll have a porter move you back to Day Surgery to get ready to leave the hospital, or to your room on a floor."

"Was Helga ever in that area?"

"No. They took her directly from the operating room to I.C.U. on the 3rd floor," Luke replied.

Jennifer noticed the mere thought haunted Luke and changed the subject. "What about housekeepers? When do they work back there?"

Luke didn't hesitate. "All the time. There are specific cleaners for the operating rooms and other general staff who primary work in the Day Surgery area, wiping down stretchers and making them up as patients come and go." Luke noticed a perplexed look come over Jennifer's face. "You don't think one of *us* killed Helga, do you? That's crazy."

"By 'us' you mean hospital staff as a complete entity, correct? Doctors, nurses, housekeepers, porters, clerical – the parking lot valet?"

"I can't believe you'd even entertain that idea," Luke said, avoiding answering her question.

Oh, geez – he's going to get up and leave!

Beth arrived to take their empty plates. "How were the appetizers?"

Not breaking their mutual glare, Jennifer and Luke mechanically said, "Very good," but otherwise ignored their waitress.

"I'll bring out your entrées shortly," Beth said, backing away from the table without interfering in the brewing domestic dispute. *That's what you get when you date younger men, honey.*

"I'm not implying *you* harmed Helga," Jennifer said, trying to reassure Luke, not expecting that he'd take the notion of a killer on the staff so personally.

"I can't see anyone I work with as a killer," Luke said.

"Look, there may be no connection at all," Jennifer responded. "Helga could have had a heart attack and boom – she's gone. No rhyme or reason in the big picture of life. We should hold off any further discussion about the hospital staff until Dr. Richmond completes Helga's autopsy."

"Martin is doing her autopsy?" Luke replied bewildered.

"That's what Dr. Singh said. Why – is he bad?"

"I don't think so, but after what happened ...."

"After what, Luke?" Jennifer was now concerned that Dr. Singh hadn't told her the truth the last time they spoke. "And you better not tell me he was harvesting organs and selling them on the black market. Because I'm looking forward to eating my eggplant parmesan and that kind of news will upset my stomach."

"It wasn't like that," Luke said, shaking his head. "The rumour was he was doing some unauthorized, after hours work in the morgue and was forced to stop."

"Did this involve repurposing spare body parts to create a monster with giant bolts on the side of its neck? I've read the book and seen the movie, Luke. I know what I'm talking about here."

"No one is positive."

"Meaning what?"

Beth arrived at the table with two hot plates and a pepper mill. "And here you are," she said proudly, placing one dish down at a time in front of Jennifer and Luke. "Pepper?" she inquired.

"I'm good," Jennifer said. "This smells amazing."

"None for me either," Luke replied, eyeing the two giant meatballs covered in steaming homemade marinara sauce.

"Can I get you a refill?" Beth asked, seeing both customers' glasses were empty.

"Yes, please," Jennifer said, handing her glass to the waitress.

"And I'll have a shot of Jack Daniels." Luke looked at Jennifer. "It's not like I'm driving tonight."

Beth took Luke's glass and walked to the bar, trying to figure out what the 'spare body parts' conversation was referencing. *They are an unusual couple.*

Sensing that Luke was going to speak, Jennifer raised her hand to stop him. "Let me enjoy a bite of this dish and then you can tell me the gory details of Dr. Frankenrichmond. Deal?"

"I can do that," Luke agreed amiably, deciding if a knife was needed to cut into the meatball.

It wasn't.

After a few minutes of small talk about how great their meals were and the arrival of their new drinks, Jennifer said, "Dr. Richmond. What's his deal?"

Luke had consumed one of the meatballs and was already full. He put down his fork and wiped his mouth with the cloth napkin. "A year ago, Martin – Dr. Richmond – appeared to be living the dream life. A beautiful wife, two adorable children, a great career. The complete package."

"I never trust those guys," Jennifer interjected. "If it seems too good to be true, it usually is. Carry on."

"Apparently, he got bored with his fairy tale existence and decided to experiment with a force that was too powerful even for him."

"Witchcraft? Using corpses in a forbidden manner?" Jennifer asked, captivated by the direction of this conversation.

"Worse – nursing students."

"And corpses?" Jennifer replied, truly appalled by the idea.

"Like I said, no one – at least in my department – knows, although a friend of a friend of a friend claims to have seen the soft core pictures Dr. Richmond allegedly took in the morgue – not with any dead bodies or anything – only of girls laying on a metal gurney, that type of thing."

"Wait a minute. Weren't you just aghast I would dare to consider a coworker might be involved in criminal activity, and all along you knew this? Hello, Kettle?" Jennifer said, forming her fingers to resemble a telephone receiver. "This is Luke the Pot."

"Honestly, I wasn't equating a cold blooded murderer to a hot-blooded married photographer," Luke said laughing.

"That kind of thing doesn't happen anymore, right?" Jennifer responded, thinking of Helga and the John Does in the morgue.

"Again, not that I'm aware of," Luke said. "Dr. Richmond hasn't done many autopsies since Dr. Singh was hired. I guess that's why I'm surprised he's scheduled to work on Helga."

"It's his final one, or so believes Dr. Singh," Jennifer advised. "You called him by his first name earlier. Do the two of you get along?"

"It's more of a professional relationship," Luke answered. "I've never seen him outside of the hospital and he has everyone call him Martin. It's his *thing*, so not to intimidate other staff. He seemed like a good guy, until I heard the whispers about the photo shoots. Then he announced he was retiring." Luke shook his head. "Honestly, I have no idea what to think of him now."

"The story sounds very strange, but as long as he takes care of Helga that's all that matters," Jennifer said.

"Hopefully his last autopsy for Met will be his best." Luke raised his shot glass. "To Dr. Martin Richmond – enjoy your retirement!" He didn't wait for Jennifer to lift her glass to complete the toast, downing the Jack Daniels in one fluid gulp.

Jennifer and Luke worked on their meals between more talk about how Jennifer became a reporter, how Luke and Maryanne met, and the musical merits of Sex At Seven and Unfinished Tattoos – bands Jennifer knew nothing about, compared to similar grown-up bands that she did, like Train and Maroon 5. They occasionally both glanced at the framed wall pictures in the vicinity of their booth. The images featured actors or celebrities, as well as plain old customers who had eaten at Davey's Den over the years. The majority of the pictures were taken inside, although several were shot on the sidewalk.

"Jennifer, do you think if we looked at all the walls your second John Doe would pop up a few times?"

"Possibly," Jennifer offered. Seeing Beth exiting the kitchen with two salads for a couple of businessmen on the opposite side of the dining room, Jennifer took out her cell phone and opened the mystery man's image. Glancing at Luke she said, "When the waitress comes back, follow my lead."

Before Luke could ask what Jennifer meant, he saw Beth walking toward their table. As if this were some stage cue in a play, Jennifer lifted her phone so the image of John Doe #2 and Deangela Rossi faced him.

"It must be fate that on the very day we were coming here, my friend found this picture of Davey's Den while going through her grandmother's old albums," Jennifer said with a big smile beaming across her face. "I was like, 'I'll try to find out who they are tonight.'"

Beth arrived at their table and saw the image on the cell's screen. "That's right out front," she said with enthusiasm.

Jennifer feigned surprise, turning her phone for the waitress to see the picture. "That's what I told my friend. You can tell from the EN on the sign." Jennifer let Beth take the phone in order to look more closely. "From the cars on the street, it looks like it was taken in the 1970s." Jennifer paused to let this information sink in. The waitress' expression was one of amazement and she wore a pleased grin on her lips. "You wouldn't know who they are, would you, Beth?" Jennifer again emphasizing her first name, as if they were old friends who had found buried treasure together.

"They were so young." Beth turned her attention back to Jennifer and Luke.

"So you do know them?" Luke inquired, playing along as instructed.

"Yes. The woman is the owner of Davey's Den, Deangela Rossi," Beth answered with a grin. "She no longer runs the daily operations, but usually comes in for lunch after Sunday Mass at St. John's. The gentleman is Henrik Dekker. You can tell by his overcoat. He might still have that old thing hanging in his closet."

Check and checkmate! "They're both alive?" Jennifer asked, trying to convey astonishment without overdoing it. "Does he come in here often?"

Beth gave Jennifer back her phone and replied, "Most weeks. I don't recall seeing him the last couple days. Maybe he is sick or something. Getting old sucks."

Oh, he's something and it does suck, Beth, Jennifer thought. "Would they like copies of the picture – maybe to put up on one of the walls? I could drop them off here or mail them. Do they live in the city?"

Beth considered the best options. "If you want, leave one picture here for the owner and mail the other one."

"Do you have the gentleman's address by chance?" Luke asked innocently.

"No, but he's in the telephone book," Beth said. "His last name is spelled D-E-K-K-E-R. Henrik Dekker."

"We'll absolutely do that," Jennifer promised. "Isn't this cool, Luke?"

It took a few seconds for Luke to answer, as he was staring at a framed magazine page on the wall behind Jennifer. "Yeah – cool," he said half-heartedly.

Beth followed Luke's gaze. "Ah, that. We are very proud of that article in *The Business Scorcher*. It's a restaurant publication and they voted us 'The Best Legacy Eatery' in the city, which is a big deal in our industry."

Jennifer craned her neck to look at the article that showed an older Deangela Rossi proudly standing behind the front hostess stand. *Good eye, Luke.*

Luke had no way of knowing Jennifer was proud of him for spotting the updated image of Mrs. Rossi, in the same way Jennifer had no idea that he hadn't noticed the owner at all. His focus was on the smaller picture in the right-hand corner, featuring customers eating merrily at the packed dining room tables. From his vantage point, Luke was certain one of the men lifting a drink in celebration was Dr. Martin Richmond, the soon-to-be-retiring coroner.

"Are you okay, Luke?" Jennifer could see that her dinner partner seemed lost in thought.

"I am, sorry," Luke lied, his heart beating like a jackhammer powered by rocket fuel. "I was straining to read the words below the headline and zoned out."

"That's kind of funny," Beth reassured him, "because when we got the call from the publisher we also zoned out for a while."

Jennifer, Luke and Beth laughed together, with only Luke faking his enjoyment of the moment.

As their collective laughter died down, Beth asked, "Would you like to see a dessert menu?"

Jennifer was about to say yes, wanting to celebrate her John Doe #2 identity scoop with a large piece of tiramisu and a couple zeppole balls thrown in for good measure.

"No," Luke answered, much to Jennifer's disappointment. Noting this, Luke added, "Sorry, if you want something, Jennifer, go ahead. I'm full of meatballs."

Jennifer looked at Beth. "Can I get the tiramisu to go?"

"You can," Beth replied, taking their plates off the table and walking into the kitchen.

"You could have eaten your dessert here," Luke said, feeling his temperature rise.

Jennifer waved a hand. "Trust me, I love food that comes in take-out containers. It's one of the bad habits that my last beau couldn't wrap his two-star Michelin winning chef head around."

"His loss," Luke said in a genuine tone that betrayed the internal conflict rampaging around in his head.

You have to tell her! She's an investigative reporter!

"In all seriousness, you're the smartest man I've been out with recently, Luke," Jennifer said as Beth carried a small box to the table, along with the bill.

"It's been a delight to serve you this evening," Beth said, before looking to a far wall. "I see exactly where that picture of Deangela and Henrik can hang." She then addressed Jennifer, "Do you know the name of your friend's grandmother? Maybe she was a patron here at one time also."

Jennifer had prepared for this question and said, "I'll find out for you, Beth, and write it on the envelope when I drop off the picture."

"That'll be wonderful. Thanks again."

Luke watched Beth walk away, as Jennifer set her wallet on the table. "What do I owe?"

"As if," Jennifer replied with a smile. "This meal – including my takeout dessert – will be expensed to the paper. The one thing truly owed here is my gratitude for coming out tonight. Mission accomplished, even though the threat level seems to have been exaggerated by my coworkers. Plus, I'm glad you explained how the O.R. and Day Surgery areas are connected, figuratively and literally." She picked up her notepad with the sketch of the hospital floor layout and put it back in her purse. Extracting several bills to leave for Beth, Jennifer said cheerfully, "Our work here is done."

Luke was the first to slide out of the booth and thought of running for the front door. He was overheating from a combination of anger, doubt, and confusion, only wanting to get outside into the fresh evening air.

"Are you sure you're okay, Luke?" Jennifer asked, noting the redness of his cheeks.

"Yeah – the marinara was a little too spicy for me," he lied again as he took a few steps away from Jennifer, who was now standing and examining the posted magazine article.

"*The Business Scorcher*. Never heard of it," she said jokingly, claiming her prized boxed tiramisu. "Let's get you home, or I can drop you off at Maryanne's."

"My apartment is good," Luke said as he pushed the front door open and stepped outside. "Maryanne has to study for a big exam tomorrow and I'm tired from all the food tonight."

Once in the car and heading across the city, Jennifer told Luke that she'd have to confirm Henrik's identity with his neighbours. "I'll wait until the morning. I already submitted my story for tomorrow's paper. Who knows – maybe the description that Dr. Singh gave me, in particular the detail about that overcoat, will spur someone's memory. I hope that isn't the case and I can get some mileage out of my exclusive identification of John Doe #2. We'll see."

Their time together was cut short when Luke pretended to answer a text from a friend who was free for the evening. With new plans made, Luke insisted that Jennifer drop him off at the next subway station and he'd take a train uptown to meet his buddy at a favourite pool hall.

Getting out of the passenger seat, Luke said, "I'm glad I was able to help you at the restaurant tonight."

"I enjoyed the company," Jennifer said warmly. "Maryanne's a lucky girl."

Luke wasn't so sure as he said goodbye and shut the car door. As Jennifer drove away he gave her a small wave and descended the subway stop stairs. Out of view, he counted to thirty, waiting for Jennifer to leave the area, before continuing his journey on foot to his apartment. He felt awful lying to his girlfriend's newest, bestest professional friend, but he was experiencing a shortness of breath, and had to clear his head.

Walking on the sidewalk in the opposite direction that Jennifer had driven, Luke began to process what he'd observed in the framed article: not only did the Met coroner appear to be quite comfortable at Davey's Den – a known criminal organization hangout – but next to him sat a younger man turned slightly from the camera, who also brought immediate recognition. There was something about his profile that was unique and had caused Luke's zoning out episode. Was it the nose? His chin? In any case, Luke was 90% convinced he'd met the man and that troubled him deeply. *I need to see that article up close.*

As he entered a convenience store to buy a bottle of water, Luke didn't notice Jennifer stopped at a traffic light watching him. She'd driven two blocks north, then made a U-turn after realizing there were lane restrictions ahead. "Interesting," she said. "What happened to you at the restaurant, Lukey boy?"

As a seasoned newspaper reporter Jennifer was well-versed in the art of deflection by her interviewees. Even when they didn't fully answer her questions, they'd make it appear like they were trying to help, without incriminating themselves in the meantime. Sometimes it was, 'An alien stole my wife,' whopper of a lie, while others were as simple as, 'Yeah – the marinara was a little too spicy for me.'

TWENTY FIVE

WEDNESDAY

The Daily Telegraph's decision to include the picture of the 1970's era mystery gentleman next to Jennifer's John Doe #2 story was made by a junior editor – one of Mitch Carson's loyal followers. Three hours before deadline, he'd seen a news release from the Metropolitan Hospital Coroner's Office seeking help identifying the man from a photo found in his wallet. The City Police had authorized its release, not wanting to send their sketch artist out again to draw a new corpse composite. "Our feeling is that this male is or was well-known in certain social circles in the city," a Detective Michael Speers was quoted as saying. What wasn't released was the left half of the picture showing a beaming Deangela Rossi with the man wearing a fedora and overcoat. Detective Speers had no intention of involving Mrs. Rossi or her illustrious *associates,* unless he had to. The pressing goal was to figure out who the man was and whether he had any connection to the first John Doe, also resting in a locked morgue cooler. Both males had been found floating face down in a stretch of river that ran through Speers' divisional boundaries, and he intended to end any talk of a serial killer in their midst. The picture had run in the Local section and the public's response was immediate, although not everyone was happy about its existence.

"Are you a moron? How did you miss that?" Beth heard her husband John screaming in the home office, moments after their telephone rang. "You were this close to being asked to join and you blew it!" There was a momentary halt to his tirade while the caller gave their side of the story. "But you didn't clean it out, did you?" John began yelling again, followed by another shorter pause. "Are you telling me this Dr. Singh is a liar? The fact is you had one job and you screwed it up, Jimmy. We'll deal with you in time, trust me on that. Put Clive back on the line."

Beth walked into the kitchen and found their *Daily Telegraph* newspaper was strewn across the counter and on the floor. "What in the world?" she said as she picked up the various pages and put them back in order, minus one section.

John stormed down the hallway and entered the kitchen with the missing newspaper pages in hand. He crumpled the pages into a ball and threw it against the wall in anger. "If you're searching for the Local section, there it is!"

After decades of married life, Beth knew not to antagonize or question John while in this frame of mind, which was rare. He was an accountant after all. *How stressful could it be counting other people's money?*

"I'm more of a Lifestyle section girl, John," she said, kissing him lightly on the lips. "Sit and I'll make you breakfast. From the sound of things, I'm guessing you're going to work earlier than usual today."

It was this kind of tact and thoughtfulness that John loved about Beth. Even though these days her primary job was as a server and the wise den mother to the younger female wait staff at Davey's Den, she was in no sense an unaccomplished woman.

Through the years she'd used her educational background and personal skills to gain experience as a bank teller, a pharmacy technician, and a gift shop clerk, all while helping to raise their six children. Her desire to remain somewhat independent went against the thinking of the other wives in their circle of friends – all of whom were tied to The Men in one way or another. Beth took full advantage of their relatives' desire to babysit, along with a nanny who came every day. "We have the money for domestic help," John had told Beth. "The kids will be fine. Plus, a happy wife is a happy life, right?" This belief matched her own mantra: *Find a job you love and your life will be much better*. Unfortunately, a botched surgery where the surgeon cut a spinal accessory nerve allowing her arm to move sidelined Beth from going back to work. The healing process that should have taken a few months never materialized, leaving Beth in constant agony. Between the good and bad pain days, she decided that working part-time at Davey's Den was a necessary distraction. She enjoyed the atmosphere and meeting new people every night. On weekends she worked strictly as the hostess, assigning the serving responsibilities to the starving artists and students the bar employed. During her recovery at home, Beth had found with their children now grown and gone that she craved company on a daily basis. Aware of this, John bought her two Dachshund puppies whom they named Jet and Sissy.

Their lives would be forever changed.

John dutifully sat down at the table, trying to miss stepping on the crazed wiener dogs running haphazardly around his feet. Purchased primarily to calm Beth's anxieties, he had learned to love their antics too. Watching them tear around the house like cartoon drawings come to life made him smile. "Clive and I have to deal with a pressing situation," he said, as the dogs began to rip apart the ball of newspaper that had bounced off the wall onto the floor.

Beth reached down and took the abused Local section from

them, tossing a squeaky toy from a pile near their beds into the living room to get their attention. She set the paper ball on the counter and poured a cup of coffee, which she placed in front of John. Walking to the fridge to get eggs, milk and ham, she said, "I hope it isn't serious." Having overhead John on the phone, however, she knew this wasn't the case. Although she only saw the young man occasionally, she'd heard he couldn't always pull off the outward tough guy persona he tried to convey.

"Serious enough. It'll be fixed, don't worry," John stated, not elaborating on the gruesome options running through his head. This Jimmy kid was no genius, yet he'd recently followed through on some very delicate jobs. Still ... he was now a liability to the organization. "What's that line about change you used to say all the time?"

Beth looked up from the egg yolks in the fry pan and answered, "Nothing changes if nothing changes."

"That's the one! Nothing changes if nothing changes," John repeated. Losing his appetite, he sipped some of the coffee and got up. "I'm sorry, but I have to go, my sweet Beth. Give my breakfast portion to the dogs. Don't they love eggs?"

"I'll ask them when they come back," Beth said. "These were going to be mine anyway, so no need to apologize."

John stepped behind Beth and kissed her neck. "You're the best," he whispered in her ear, meaning every word. Without her peaceful presence this morning, he knew that Jimmy would have already been in the trunk of a Lincoln Continental. As it was the idiot may be granted a reprieve, depending on how the story of Henrik's death played out.

Or not, John thought as he picked up his briefcase.

"I'll see you later at the bar," Beth said as John walked through the back door.

John waved goodbye without saying a word, another trait Beth had gotten used to over the years.

"Jet! Sissy!" Beth called out and immediately heard the staccato of eight short legs paddling furiously across the hardwood flooring in the hallway. In no time, the dogs were at her heels, eyes wide and barking in unison. Beth took out a small plate from the cupboard and transferred half of the eggs onto it, dividing the remaining portions evenly into the dogs' food bowls. "Bon appétit."

As was their morning custom, Beth walked to the front window to see John pulling out of the laneway. He turned in the driver's seat to wave at her and they both smiled.

"Good luck, Jimmy," Beth said, straightening the curtain. "You'll need it today."

By the time she returned to the kitchen the dogs had devoured their eggs and were looking for more. "No," Beth said firmly, taking her plate and the Local section ball to the kitchen table. "Let's see what got Daddy so upset, pups," she said as she unravelled and smoothed out the eight pages.

Scanning the headlines for a clue, Beth ate her eggs, not knowing what could have set John off. The section was a hodgepodge of stories that rarely amounted to anything newsworthy for the masses. Taking the last piece of egg in her mouth as she flipped to the back page, she almost choked when she saw the headline, "Police Seek Help" with the subtitle, "Do you know this man?"

Beth was so shocked at the sight of Henrik Dekker standing in front of Davey's Den, that it took a second to realize that Deangela Rossi had been cropped from the image. "Why would they do that?" she asked, although she soon knew from the article. "Our feeling is that this male is or was well-known in certain social circles in the city," she read.

Certain social circles.

In rapid succession Beth's thoughts fell in line: Henrik's dead. Jimmy killed him. John and Clive ordered the hit.

Her hands began to tremble, causing the newspaper to shake more violently. Letting go of it, she tried to remain grounded. *You know what John does. You know the people he deals with every day. You know that he and Clive run The Men. Why does this news shock you so?*

"Because I knew Henrik," she said, answering her inner voice and slamming down her fist.

Beth sobbed uncontrollably at the kitchen table. Seeing this, Jet and Sissy quietly went to their beds and watched their adoptive mother from across the room, not knowing how to make her smile.

Through her tears Beth gulped for air. "What am I going to do?" she cried out. She looked at the image and said, "Henrik, I wish I could've stopped this from happening."

It was then Beth read something that further shattered her world: the writer's byline.

Beth stood and pushed her chair backward, causing it to overturn, frightening the dogs in the process.

"Last night at the restaurant that fucking bitch knew Henrik was dead!"

Beth grabbed the cordless phone off the kitchen island and called John, who picked up on the first ring.

"Hello again," he answered amicably. "What's up?"

"What's up is that you have bigger problems than Jimmy. Her name is Jennifer Malone – a reporter for *The Daily Telegraph* – and her boyfriend Luke!"

TWENTY SIX

Deciding to stay home another day, Genifer Grant made chocolate chip pancakes for Zoe and Aleena, as well as oatmeal for Stan. Since he had an on-site mid-morning meeting, Stan offered to drive the girls to school, much to their delight. "It'll be faster, because my bus doesn't stop to let more passengers on," he joked. After checking the girls' homework and packing their lunches, Genifer lavished kisses on her brood and told them to have a great day.

"You too, Mom," Zoe replied.

"Don't work too hard today," Aleena chimed in, laughing.

"Oh – I guess you don't want me to clean your room, huh?"

Aleena thought it over. "Work a little, I guess."

"Don't do too much," Stan added, giving Genifer a second kiss.

Genifer looked out the window. "It's going to rain today. This could turn out to be a couch/bonbon eating kind of day."

"Don't forget to get the paper before it does," Stan suggested, as he and the girls walked out the back door.

"I'll get it now."

Genifer found *The Daily Telegraph* on the lawn near the front porch steps. "So close, paper guy," she said, removing the elastic band that held it together. "Any good news today?"

Stan pulled out of the driveway and the girls waved wildly at their mother like they were departing on a trans-Atlantic cruise.

"Love you!" they shrieked in unison.

"Love you too!" Genifer replied as the car was driven out of view. "Rain is a-comin'," she said to herself, eyeing a large patch of dark clouds heading in from the north. *I'm glad I'm not delivering mail today*, she thought, silently thanking her coworkers Teena and Sue for helping out. Genifer had planned on going to work, feeling guilty for taking time off, and missing the people on her route. Those plans had changed after her conversation with that reporter, who had known there was more to Helga's 911 house call than Genifer had told her.

Genifer knew she'd have to tell someone about the man in the tan overcoat, but his threats continued to resonate in her ears. If he were responsible for Helga's death, what would stop him from harming the girls, Stan or herself? The risk was too great for everyone involved, even though the others had no clue there was something wrong.

Inside Genifer put away the dishes and cleaned the kitchen counters, before making a cup of flavoured coffee and sitting at the table to read the newspaper, which she usually read after finishing her route. It was a way to unwind until the girls got home. Setting the News section aside, not wanting to see anything political that might upset her, she opened the Sports section. The Detroit Lions were still basking in the glory of their stunning win that would forever be linked to the simultaneous call from the man at Helga's house. She read a short story comparing the Lions' quarterback Matthew Stafford to the New England Patriot's superstar quarterback Tom Brady – the two going head to head on Sunday afternoon. *Go, Matthew, go!*

Finding nothing else of interest, Genifer next checked the Lifestyle pages for her horoscope: *You will find love with someone who shares your political and ethical values.* "Found him," Genifer said aloud. She also liked to read the Ms. Love relationship column that today began, *A coworker recently told me he keeps his dating standards low, so that everyone's expectations are met and you can enjoy the date without feeling pressure to conform. My first thought was, Brilliant!* As usual, the rest of the article was fun and informative, putting Genifer in a happy mood. She'd learned over the years to take any advice, no matter its origin, and evaluate its merits. "Knowing is better than not knowing," her parents used to say. Genifer modified that statement to, *When you know better, you do better*, and could honestly say this philosophy had enriched her life many times over.

Taking a sip of coffee, Genifer began to read the headlines of the fourth section – Local. As vice president of her postal carriers' union, she was drawn to two stories dealing with area strikes: a library board forcing librarians out on the picket lines – *That is beyond belief,* she thought; and a school board locking out its support staff of custodians, secretaries and maintenance workers – *Who do you think runs the schools? Hello?* she said, annoyed by both actions, and speculating how her union might lend a hand to these fellow brothers and sisters walking the line. Genifer sent a text to the president of the union: "`We need to talk!`"

With this new project circulating in her head, Genifer skimmed through the following pages, bypassing non-Greenheart Station stories. Flipping to the back page Genifer's attention was distracted by the vibrating of her phone and a text message reading, "`Talk about what?`" Reaching across the paper to send a reply, her eyes involuntarily followed her left hand as it passed above a picture of a man wearing a fedora and an overcoat.

Instantly frozen in fear, Genifer conjured up the man's voice and heard him clear as a bell whisper the article's second headline: "Do you know this man?"

Well – do you, Genifer?

TWENTY SEVEN

Jennifer wasn't happy when her cell phone started to ring incessantly on her night table. Seeing the call display didn't help her mood.

"What is wrong with you?" she lightly scolded her boss. "It's 7:52. I know the news cycle lasts 24/7, but I don't."

"Wow – are you always this miserable in the morning, Malone?" Mitch asked. "If so, it would explain your boyfriend problems," he joked.

"They have the intelligence to let me sleep in," Jennifer replied as she sat up in bed and stretched. "Are you at least calling with good news? Has Hot Beckster reappeared? Did the councilman's wife leave him for his more handsome brother? Was Liam Neeson in your office asking for me?"

"No, on all counts," Mitch answered, "but the police got a hit on your second John Doe. That's why I'm calling."

"That's good, I guess," Jennifer said, flipping to the photo of the man outside of Davey's Den. "I'm a better writer than I give myself credit for if a reader identified a person from my story's description."

"With all due respect, one, you're not *that* talented. And two, I think the picture of him wearing a fedora in front of an infamous city landmark was the clincher."

Jennifer stared at the image on her cell screen in disbelief. "What picture?"

There was a pause as Mitch gauged the slight level of hostility in Jennifer's voice. "Ah ... the one that ran next to your article. It's in the morning edition and online."

"I didn't submit a photo. Where did it come from?" Jennifer went to her computer and opened the *Telegraph's* website, searching her name.

The story she'd submitted remained intact, except to the left of it was an image that only showed her mystery man. The caption read, *City Police are asking for any information about this unidentified male from a photograph discovered in his wallet by Metropolitan Hospital Coroner Dr. Alpa Singh.*

"Huh," was all Jennifer could utter. *There goes my exclusive.*

"I guess Duncan on the afternoon shift inserted it," Mitch said, referring to the evening editor. "He's pretty smart."

"Smart isn't the word I'd use, but so be it," Jennifer said, stinging from her missed opportunity. *Or was it?* "Did that wunderkind of yours crop the image, or was it sent out that way?"

Mitch checked the coroner's press release sitting on his desk. "Sent out that way, why?"

Jennifer had been trying to decide when to bring Mitch up to speed on her investigation of Helga's death. That was one of two reasons she'd had a restless night. The other was her new suspicion that Luke wasn't the person he'd been portraying himself to be. His behaviour at Davey's Den was normal until he'd started to stare at the framed magazine picture on the wall. That, along with his fake friend texts charade and subway stairs reappearance, had left Jennifer unsettled. *Am I being played?* she'd asked herself on the drive home, unwilling to believe Luke had anything to do with Helga's sudden demise. Yet, she couldn't ignore he was with the old woman immediately before the surgery and had total access to the O.R. with his swipe card. With his looks and charm he would be the last person any staff member would suspect of being a criminal. He'd proven this time and again with Maryanne present and on the phone.

Maybe being charming is his thing, she'd thought, remembering Luke's phrase for why the retiring coroner wanted to be addressed by his first name. *Jeffrey Hamill Investigations will be getting a call and box of cronuts from me in the near future.*

"No reason," Jennifer lied.

"I don't believe that for a second," Mitch said.

"Moi – not telling you the whole truth? When has that ever happened?"

"You can make fun of me all you want," Mitch advised her in a parental tone. "But the fact you haven't asked me the John Doe's name tells me your kitten head is swirling with some pertinent information I'm not privy to."

Damn he's good.

"You know me too well," Jennifer confessed.

"And?"

"And I want to know the name of John Doe #2 now."

"His name is Henrik Dekker, age 80, with ties to organized crime that go back decades – if the callers to the newspaper and police are to be believed."

I believe it, Jennifer thought. "Kind of old to still be hanging out with gangsters. Isn't there a retirement age for these type of guy-guys?"

"Yeah – the day after they rat on their bosses or screw up a job," Mitch offered philosophically. "Mr. Dekker might have went against his associates' wishes and he was done."

"Is that what the police are saying?" Jennifer asked as she simultaneously searched *The Business Scorcher* website for the Davey's Den legacy award piece.

When it was finally on the screen she saved the article's photo and then opened it in an art program to be able to zoom in and out more easily. She was certain the image of a radiant older Deangela Rossi wasn't what had captivated Luke so thoroughly. *What then?* Nothing in the background seemed out of place. The photo could have been taken the previous night, as if the place were timeless. *If not the what, it must be the who,* she thought as she scrutinized the cheerful faces of the patrons. No matter how intense she looked, she didn't see Henrik Dekker amongst the diners. *Not a fedora or overcoat in sight*. Stymied to uncover Luke's fascination, Jennifer printed off a smaller version, which she slid into the back of her notepad.

"I haven't contacted the police," Mitch began, "because I'm an editor, not a reporter like yourself."

"Subtle, Mitch."

"I try," he replied. "The bonus is that Mr. Dekker floated into your buddy Detective Speers' neighbourhood. Give him a call and maybe we can get a scoop before those idiots across the street accidently dredge something up."

Jennifer checked her phone again to admire Deangela Rossi's smiling face. "Oh, I'll get you a scoop, don't you worry."

***

After a hot shower, Jennifer got dressed and had her usual breakfast of English muffin and jam with a coffee. She was trying to remain calm. Although she wanted to call Dr. Singh to voice her displeasure about not getting any warning about the photo's release, she knew she couldn't. *She was doing her job,* Jennifer kept telling herself. *Maybe the police told her to send it out.* The new topic of conversation would be who had decided to crop Mr. Dekker's wallet picture in half. In all probability, Dr. Singh would have no knowledge of the woman in the picture, nor the connection to Davey's Den. The police on the other hand ....

Jennifer called Detective Michael Speers, an old friend on the force who may have bent a few rules for her in the past.

"If it isn't my favourite newspaper reporter, Jennifer Malone," Speers said in his booming voice. "How are you this fine morning?"

Jennifer could hear the background police station hubbub and pictured Speers standing at the front desk, his imposing 6'4" muscular frame towering over the officers in the room; his brown eyes, crooked nose and scarred right cheek striking fear into everyone nearby. "I must say this morning started okay – I woke up, unlike our mutual acquaintance – or more accurately *associate* – Mr. Dekker in the Met morgue." Jennifer paused, then went on, "Has anyone from The Men or Davey's Den called to claim his body?"

Speers didn't answer immediately, trying to evaluate what Jennifer had said. He'd expected her to gloat that her article had helped identify the John Doe, but from her tone he knew she'd uncovered a lot of details about Mr. Dekker that hadn't been released. "Give me a second," he said, pressing the Hold button and walking to his office, where he closed the door. "I'm back."

"And not a moment too soon," Jennifer laughed. "Did you have to pay for the coffee and donut delivery?"

"I wish," Speers replied. "My wife is on a health kick and dragging me along with her. This morning I had a green tea and California avocado toast with a fried egg."

"I'm so sorry for your loss of manhood, Detective. If you like, I can pick up an order of greasy bacon and home fries and drop them off on my way to the office."

"Although tempting, Jennifer, that woman has spies in this building who'll rat me out in a heartbeat."

"So much for enjoying this lovely morning."

"It was until you called," Speers said with a laugh. "Can I assume that you and Mr. Dekker are buddies? Did you interview him for a crime investigation piece you're working on?"

"No, the closest I ever got to the man was his overcoat and wallet in the coroner's office at Met," Jennifer confessed. "Because I wrote an earlier John Doe article, Mitch saw fit to name me his go-to reporter for any similar themed stories."

"One down, one to go," Speers said optimistically. "You mentioned you were near Dekker's wallet. Aside from the hidden photo, did you find anything else of interest? Something triggered this phone call, and it wasn't to offer me a delicious breakfast."

"Can't a girl call a great guy to say, 'Hi,' anymore?"

"No."

"Alright, alright, I have a couple of questions – on the record – about the mysterious Henrik Dekker."

"Shoot."

"Did the police or the coroner crop out Deangela Rossi from the picture found in the wallet?"

"The coroner," Speers answered confidently.

"Did she know who the woman in the picture was at the time of said cropping?" Jennifer followed up.

There was a brief delay in Speers' response. "This is off the record, okay?"

"Off it is."

"Thank you," Speers said, appreciating Jennifer's lack of anger at being censored. "From what I've heard, Dr. Singh wasn't aware of the woman's identity, but the officer who authorized the photo's release did. He may have recommended that by cropping the picture to only show the man with the fedora, it would focus the public's attention."

"May have recommended?"

"Yes, may have."

"Are we back on the record?"

"It'll depend on the question, I guess. What's next?"

"Have the police confirmed whether Mr. Dekker was currently involved with The Men criminal organization that's reportedly run out of unseen rooms at Davey's Den bar and restaurant?"

"On the record, Mr. Dekker is known to the police and has had ties with criminal organizations in the city for many decades."

"Are the police now looking into Mr. Dekker's death differently due to his association with the criminal world?"

"As with any sudden death, the police will investigate Mr. Dekker's final days to determine whether there was any foul play before he entered the river."

"Check, check, check and … check," Jennifer said in a mocking tone. "I'm thinking I could've written those quotes myself, or with the help of a random sentence generator program on the internet."

"I hate to disappoint you, Jennifer," Speers said. "Off the record – Dekker was an old-timer who probably had some physical episode while out for a walk and stumbled into the river. It does happen to regular folk from time to time. In all likelihood, an actual blood relative will come forward, claim the body, have a simple service and bury Mr. Dekker in a few days."

Jennifer silently concurred with Speers' opinion. Even if the police did a cursory investigation, the end result would be that an old mobster was no longer on streets, which could only benefit the public good. "Still off the record – because honestly, it's a lot more interesting than your on the record drivel – is there any word on the street that this was a hit of some kind? Was Dekker high enough up that someone wanting to climb the company ladder might take him out to move up the food chain?"

"I pulled his rap sheet, Jennifer, and he was a small-time guy in 1960 and continued to be a small-time guy until his death," Speers answered. "If he's missed at all it'll be due to an outstanding tab at Davey's Den or another neighbourhood bar."

"So you're saying I'd be wasting my time examining Mr. Dekker's life any further?"

"I'm not telling you that," Speers said carefully, "but, yes. You must be working on other important stories unrelated to the untimely death of a senior citizen."

The phrase upset Jennifer as Helga popped into her mind. "You'd be surprised."

"Sounds interesting. If you need anything else, call me or type what you want me to say into your sentence generator. How does that sound?"

"Perfect," Jennifer replied, imagining his smiling face. "One last question: Does Met Hospital fall inside your jurisdiction?"

"Why yes it does, Miss Malone. Are you planning on breaking some laws during your next morgue visit?"

"Not that I'm aware of," Jennifer answered. "I owe you a breakfast."

"When my wife lets go of my food rations leash you'll be the first one I call!"

TWENTY EIGHT

With the folded Local section of *The Daily Telegraph* under her arm, an anxious Genifer walked to the house of Helga's neighbour and rang the doorbell.

Opening the front door, Glenn broke into a friendly grin. "Are you delivering mail on this street now, Genifer?" he asked. "I hope that isn't a demotion."

"It wouldn't be, but no, I'm here for a visit, if you have the time," she said apprehensively.

"At my age all I have is time! Come on in." He stepped out of the way for Genifer to enter the living room, then pointed to the adjacent kitchen. "We can sit at the table and have a drink. Are you thirsty?" As Genifer settled into a chair, Glenn opened the fridge door. "I have water, Pepsi, iced tea, orange juice and lemonade. I could also make a fresh pot of coffee."

"Orange juice will be fine. Thank you."

Glenn poured them both a glass and took a seat across from Genifer, who had placed the newspaper on top of the table.

Genifer sipped the juice and then asked, "Do you subscribe to the *Telegraph*?"

"I used to," Glenn said. "Too much crime, politics and bad news for me to handle these days. I watch the dinner hour newscast and read the *Greenheart Station Echo* once a week. That's all I need to stay sane. Why?"

Genifer set her glass on the table, her hand shaking a bit. "I read a story today in the Local section that upset me ... and was hoping you might help me with it."

"I'll do what I can."

Genifer unfolded the section to reveal the story of the John Doe found dead in the river. "Have you ever seen this man in the neighbourhood or near Helga's house before her fall?"

Glenn examined the black and white photo and read the short article written by Jennifer Malone, the reporter he'd met at Helga's house. "Should I have? He doesn't look familiar. Was he a door-to-door salesman or religion peddler?"

"Are you positive you haven't seen him, or someone like him wearing a tan overcoat?" Genifer asked, ignoring Glenn's questions. "This is very important."

"I can see it's very important to you, Genifer, but I don't know this man. What's his connection to Helga?"

Genifer remained silent for a few seconds. She had hoped as an independent collaborator of the John Doe's presence on King Street, Glenn could identify him to police. "I saw him in the area of Helga's house the day she broke her hip," Genifer replied slowly, not wanting to state that the man appeared to be exiting the backyard at the time of the sighting. "Well, I remember seeing a man that fit the dead man's description. I don't know. I was really frazzled, finding Helga and then talking to the paramedics and police afterward." Genifer took a gulp of her drink.

"I'm sorry I can't help," Glenn apologized. "The arrival of the ambulance and police cruiser has been the only excitement that's happened recently."

Genifer folded the newspaper back up. "No, don't apologize. I shouldn't have bothered you like this, dropping by without a warning."

"Oh, I was warned," Glenn smiled as he bent forward to lift a black cat off the floor. "This here is Logan, Helga's cat. He sits in the front window watching the world pass by, including people coming to the front door. When that happens he starts to meow."

Genifer reached across the table to pet the cat on the head. "I can't believe Helga isn't coming home to take care of him," she said in a low tone. "Have you been able to find any out of town relatives to break the news to them?"

"I did." Glenn put Logan down on the floor and walked to the microwave cart to retrieve two books. Passing the first one to Genifer he said, "This is Helga's personal phone book. I went through it until I found a woman who believes she's a third or fourth cousin. She thanked me for taking care of Logan and the house. She's supposed to call when she talks with some of her relatives."

"That's excellent," Genifer said, not disclosing that she was Helga's next of kin contact listed on the hospital admitting paperwork. "And what's the second book?"

"It's kind of a diary – more like a thought journal," Glenn said, placing the worn leather bound book between them. "I found it in the same drawer as the phone book. At first, I wondered if it was the diary she'd given to the prosecutor for her granddaughter's trial. The police may still have that one in storage. It could be in the house somewhere too. I didn't pry through everything."

"Of course you didn't," Genifer reassured him.

"Anyway, I don't understand what the stories mean. They aren't dated, so it's not a diary. From the pages I glanced at it reads like an autobiography – events Helga was trying to remember and then put pen to paper."

"That sounds interesting," Genifer replied, wondering if there were any references to the John Doe in it. "When she writes does she refer to anyone? Family, friends, people who have impacted her life?"

Glenn had absentmindedly been moving his index finger over the soft cover as Genifer spoke, as if caressing it in a loving manner. "I don't know. I read one passage and heard Helga's voice in my head. Has that ever happened to you? It was as if she were here at the kitchen table with me." Glenn stood and walked to the back door to open it, in an attempt to compose himself as tears welled up in his eyes. "I couldn't go on and put it away."

Glenn remained in the doorway with his back to Genifer, who gingerly opened the book to a random page. The handwritten sentences that flowed across the printed lines were eloquent and easy to read. The title of this section read, "An Island In Paradise," and began, *The dawn broke across the sandy white beach like the warmest widest smile possible.*

Genifer flipped to other pages. "Did Helga do a lot of travelling, Glenn?"

Glenn turned and replied, "She loved to travel."

Genifer pushed the book across the table. "This is a kind of travelogue, although some entries don't say where she was at the time."

Fascinated, Glenn sat down and opened the book for himself. "I only read one," he said, peeling back the cover to reveal an entry entitled, "Linares" that caught his eye. "Is that a city or a country?" he asked Genifer. "She writes about a woman who is separated from her family at a young age and how that shaped the rest of her life." Glenn looked from the page. "When I realized the writing was about her, I closed the book and haven't read anything else." He handed the book to Genifer. "Please take it."

"I can't," Genifer said, shocked by the suggestion. "These are Helga's private thoughts. Her family needs to have this."

Undeterred, Glenn said, "And they will. I just want you to know what kind of woman Helga was. You met her when she was in pain and scared – that wasn't her." He shook the book. "This is her. This is the woman I want you to remember. Take this home and read it, then return it to me. I'll put it back where I found it before her family arrives."

Seeing the determination in his tear-filled eyes, Genifer took the book and said, "Thank you for this, Glenn. I know I'll feel closer to Helga than I already do."

***

Getting up to leave, Genifer scratched behind Logan's ear and then gave Glenn an extended hug. "Let me know when you hear from any of Helga's relatives."

"I hope they call," Glenn said. "I can't stand that Helga is still in the hospital morgue. She needs a proper burial next to her husband. He's waited a long time to be reunited with her."

Glenn watched Genifer walk down the sidewalk, and stand briefly at the end of Helga's driveway, as if she were paying her respects. "She's a good woman that one, Logan," he said to the cat as he closed the door.

What Genifer was actually doing would have disappointed Glenn, as she'd never told him of the mystery man on Helga's property that fateful day. She was going to, but the timing wasn't right. The photo in the newspaper didn't have the same reaction from Glenn as it had for her. She was positive it was the same man she'd encountered at Helga's and in the hospital E.R. room.

Before departing the area, Genifer spoke with several other

individuals living in houses on the street, showing them the newspaper article and asking if they'd seen the man in the neighbourhood. When she was positive no one else had seen the John Doe, she decided to place the telephone call she'd been dreading to make all morning.

TWENTY NINE

After her telephone conversation with Detective Speers, Jennifer called Mitch to update him on the John Doe #2 situation.

"In short, Speers said Henrik Dekker was a lifelong, small-time mob member who died by drowning after a possible physical episode, I guess like a heart attack or something similar."

"So it isn't gang-related?" Mitch asked. "That would be a better story."

"Speers sounded like it would soon be a closed case," Jennifer replied. "It's definitely not a high priority for them."

"And the coroner? Have you talked to her again?"

Jennifer browsed through her bedroom closet trying to find an outfit to wear for the day, when a text from Maryanne arrived on her cell phone screen:

> Hi, Jennifer - Do you know why Luke is acting weird after your dinner at that restaurant?

Jennifer sighed and pulled a blue and white dress off its hanger. "I'll be heading to the hospital on my way in, Mitch."

"Try and find something new on this guy that no one else will have for tomorrow's paper. A morsel that wouldn't be found in his obituary."

"I already have something to blow the competition away," Jennifer said with pride, thinking about the photo of Henrik and Deangela Rossi together. "Have faith, Mr. Editor Man."

"I knew you were holding out on me, Malone. What is it?"

"In due course. Give me an hour and have the website guys on high alert for an exclusive."

"Damn it, why do you have to be so dramatic?"

Jennifer laughed. "I've learned from you, Mitch. Meaning I've learned from the best. All will be revealed. Gotta go."

In his office Mitch looked at the phone in his hand and pondered slamming it down into its cradle. "Stay calm," he told himself, recalling the time he injured his wrist when he attempted the same move a few months earlier. "She's not worth it."

***

Jennifer texted Maryanne that she'd be at Met in a half hour and that she too had some questions to ask.

During the drive Jennifer composed her story copy in her head. The other papers would be running *Man Identified* items naming Henrik and possibly his connection to the criminal world, but maybe not. He wasn't that important of a player in the big picture and the police didn't seem to care about his passing. However, the picture burning a hole on her cell phone would be a bombshell, or a small explosion that would keep the story going one more day. Jennifer only needed to confirm that Dr. Singh hadn't shown the whole two-person image to another reporter.

Jennifer lucked out and found a parking spot a block from the hospital. Entering the lobby she didn't see Maryanne at the security desk, and went to visit Dr. Singh. By now Jennifer knew how to get to the morgue. As she walked the corridors she was hoping that Luke had been called in and would appear, so they could talk. She wondered if he had arrived for work and that was when Maryanne noticed he was acting peculiar.

Walking past the Cat Scan waiting room on her left, Jennifer's attention shifted to the O.R. Family Waiting Room on her right. Next to it was a door with a sign reading "Swipe card access only". Sure enough, on the wall was a small box for employees to swipe their badges to gain entry. Jennifer stopped and took a position against the far wall to see what actually occurred at this entrance every day. She retrieved her notepad and squared up the blueprint Luke had drawn at the restaurant to fully understand the layout before her.

It didn't take long for staff dressed in solid green scrubs to enter the O.R. hallway, each using their cards to swipe the door open. The door stayed that way for several seconds and Jennifer concluded that anyone could simply walk into the secured area. Thinking of doing just that, Jennifer remained in place and maintained her surveillance position. As the minutes ticked by, it became apparent that other employees in various coloured scrub tops and bottoms had clearance to enter the O.R. hallway. Some were pushing patients on stretchers, as Luke had described he'd done with Helga, while others entered and exited alone or with steel carts containing surgical equipment. There were also staff members in suits and casual office attire who entered, as well as family members accompanying patients on stretchers. *This is crazy,* Jennifer thought, believing that only employees in distinctive green scrubs were allowed in the O.R. area.

Still tempted to walk in on someone else's swipe, Jennifer consulted Luke's map and looked to her left toward the elevators. On the side of a desk where an elderly volunteer sat was a sign that read "Day Surgery" with an arrow pointing to the right. Jennifer walked to the desk and checked out the hallway. At the end of it were two yellow doors.

"Is Day Surgery this way?" Jennifer asked the volunteer who was playing solitaire on an employee computer.

The woman turned her attention to Jennifer and then down the corridor. "Yes. Go through those doors and speak with the clerk at the reception desk."

Jennifer thanked the woman and proceeded down the hallway. Nearing the doors she saw a small swipe card box and a large silver button on the wall that she pressed, opening the doors to the Day Surgery reception and waiting room areas. Going through the doors, Jennifer consulted Luke's diagram and noted the two doors that led into PACU where Helga should have gone after her hip surgery. There was another silver button on the wall, although no security swipe box. Jennifer hit the button and the doors marked "Authorized Personnel Only" opened, allowing her to see through to the end of the room to the O.R. hallway she'd watched a few minutes earlier. *That corridor isn't secured at all, is it? Anyone from the public could easily walk into the area to harm someone without a staff member accompanying them.* In time, Jennifer was confident a hospital employee would stop a stranger meandering through the hallways.

Jennifer continued to the Day Surgery receptionist desk. From Luke's sketch she knew there was a large waiting room to her left, and then through another set of doors were the actual Day Surgery recovery rooms. Wanting to pay close attention to the security features of the doors leading into the O.R. waiting room where Luke had left Helga, Jennifer asked the clerk, "I'm here to pick up a friend who had surgery this morning. I got a text saying she was in room 2. Is it through there?" Jennifer indicated the two doors and prayed that the clerk wouldn't ask for her imaginary friend's name.

The clerk, swamped with paperwork, scarcely acknowledged Jennifer. "Push the silver button on the wall behind you and go through the door, turning left," she said before getting back to work.

Jennifer followed the instructions and found herself at an intersection. Go left, you end up in the recovery area. Go straight and you enter a sterile-looking wing marked Urology/Cysto

Clinic. Go right ... and you enter the O.R. area with a simple push of an unsecured silver button on the wall.

Jennifer stopped to allow an O.R. porter in green scrubs to push a male on a stretcher into the intersection. The patient was in his late thirties and Jennifer assumed it was his wife walking beside him.

"So ... we're going through those doors ahead into the O.R. now," the transporter said. "You can wait for the doctor in the O.R. Family Waiting Room next to the elevators." She pointed to a line on the floor. "Just follow the red tape."

"Okay," the woman answered, and then kissed her husband on the lips. "I'll see you after the surgery. Love you."

"Love you too," the man said, as the stretcher began to move forward.

Pushing the silver button on the far wall, the doors into the O.R. hallway opened up and the transporter pushed her patient inside.

The doors remained open a few more seconds and Jennifer stepped through them. At a discreet distance, she trailed the transporter and patient around the corner to a waiting room. Numbers were hung above spots separated by office cubicle walls. All but the first two had chairs, with the others designated for stretchers. Knowing her time was running out, Jennifer took in the entire area with a sweep of her eyes. She was standing at the end of the O.R. hallway she'd scouted earlier, that was also accessible through PACU. There didn't appear to be any other entrances into the waiting area, so it was highly doubtful someone could come in and out unnoticed, like a magician with a trap door trick. Behind her and to her left were doors that she knew led to the actual operating rooms. Again, as hospital staff members walked through this area, they entered these separate hallways with a push of a silver button on the wall.

"Can I help you?" the desk clerk asked Jennifer.

"I might have made a wrong turn. I was going to the Day

Surgery recovery area," Jennifer replied.

The transporter who had brought the patient into the waiting room smiled and said, "Happens all the time. I probably distracted you – I saw you standing there. Go back the way you came and head straight."

"Thank you," Jennifer responded with an embarrassed smile, leaving the O.R. wing by herself. Experiencing a bout of anxiety, she exited the Day Surgery wing altogether and walked down the hallway toward the elevators. Noticing an empty area with chairs and children's toys on a table, Jennifer sat to catch her breath.

Her first unsteady thought was how easy it was to gain entry into the O.R. and its waiting room, if only for a few moments before being detected. The second sobering thought was the realization she had stood in the room where Helga had experienced her last lucid moments of life.

I need this to end, Jennifer told herself. *Did Helga die of natural causes or was she killed? A coroner would know for sure.*

"Let's get this over with," she said to an inanimate plastic fire truck on the floor.

Turning the corner near the morgue, Jennifer was glad to see that the coroner's office door was open. Stepping inside she saw Dr. Singh behind her desk talking to a man sitting in a chair.

"Oh, I'm sorry, Dr. Singh," Jennifer apologized. "You're in a meeting. I can come back," she offered, figuring she could find Maryanne instead.

"No, Jennifer, we were finishing some shop talk, right?" she asked her guest who stood to face Jennifer.

"Yes," the man in a white smock replied.

Jennifer felt some connection to this person. He looked familiar, but she had no idea where they'd met.

The man stepped forward and held out his hand, which Jennifer shook.

"Jennifer Malone," she said. "I'm a reporter for *The Daily Telegraph.*"

"I know all about you from Alpa," the man said, looking to Dr. Singh. "I haven't had the opportunity to introduce myself. I'm Dr. Richmond. You can call me Martin – everyone else around here does."

THIRTY

Jennifer stood, momentarily dumbstruck. From Luke, she knew the retiring coroner's name and background, yet his words and face weren't properly computing in her mind. When he'd stood Jennifer had a guttural reaction she'd seen him somewhere recently, but where? As she'd attempted to figure that out he said his name, followed by the casual, 'You can call me Martin,' line, and the two facts threw Jennifer for a loop. She looked to Dr. Singh and tried to remember if she'd told her that Dr. Richmond would be performing Helga's autopsy. *She did because you spoke to Luke about it at dinner.* Jennifer continued trying to place his face.

"I hear from Dr. Singh that it's your last day," Jennifer said as a way to clear the fog from her brain. "Are there any white beaches calling your name?"

"One or two, at least," Dr. Richmond replied with a smile. "It'll be very different heading to the water with a tropical drink in one hand and a book in the other, instead of walking into this basement ... but I'll adjust."

"In two minutes," Dr. Singh offered.

"Probably."

"I give you credit for being here today," Jennifer told Dr. Richmond. "I'm calling in sick on my final work day to avoid my coworkers' tears and crying fits. I don't need that kind of negativity in my life."

"He was going to leave on Monday and come in to clean out

the office," Dr. Singh, "but then got sick as a dog – is that the proper expression? – and felt he owed us one more day."

"It's the least I could do," Dr. Richmond said.

Jennifer waited for, 'after all the trouble I caused with my unauthorized photo shoot in the morgue,' to come out of his mouth and was disappointed when he didn't comply. It was then she noticed the white board behind the coroners and had another troubling sensation flash through her body. Written in black marker were the words: Helga Klemens - Richmond. Although aware of this fact already, with everything else going on lately, the days of the week had warped into one blob of information overload. However, one piece of conversation by Luke at Davey's Den invaded her thoughts:

Dr. Richmond hasn't done many autopsies since Dr. Singh was hired. I guess that's why I'm surprised he's scheduled to work on Helga.

"I should get heading upstairs," Dr. Richmond said to the two women. "I have a final meeting with the CEO in his office. A final coffee and chocolate chip muffin in the cafeteria. Then I'll be back for my final autopsy. A lot of finals today."

"It was nice meeting you … Martin," Jennifer said, moving out of his way.

"Me too," he replied to her. "I won't be long, Alpa," he said to his colleague.

"Take your time. I can always do the Klemens autopsy. It would be no trouble," Dr. Singh responded with a smile. "It would be my departure present to you."

The line should have evoked an appreciative grin from Dr. Richmond.

It didn't.

It was a small thing, but Jennifer saw Martin's facial features bunch up for a millisecond, and he appeared to lose his footing and trip forward ever so slightly. "No, no, no," he responded to the offer. "I can do it."

To Jennifer's ears his tone was a combination of joking and

unnatural bravado. She looked to Dr. Singh, who didn't appear to have registered the answer in the same way.

Something is off, Jennifer thought. *Nothing should be off when it relates to Helga.*

Dr. Richmond stood unmoved.

"Have it your way," Dr. Singh agreed while examining a document in her hand. "As you're going upstairs already, can you drop this order at the lab for me?"

Dr. Richmond physically relaxed and took the sheet. "Anything for you," he said, raising his hand as if making a toast and then bowing at the waist. With this grand gesture made, he walked into the hallway.

Jennifer peered out to confirm Dr. Richmond wasn't doubling back, like Luke had on the subway steps. Finally putting his face to a place, Jennifer quietly closed the door and locked it, a move that surprised Dr. Singh.

"Is there something wrong?"

"I think so." Jennifer was jumpy and fidgeted to retrieve the ever present reporter's notepad from the inside of her purse. Taking the printout of the Davey's Den legacy award magazine picture out, she placed it on Dr. Singh's desk and smoothed it out. Taking a step back she asked, "The man in the foreground lifting his glass - is it or is it not Dr. Richmond?"

Dr. Singh was still staring at Jennifer, wondering if she was okay. "Let me look," she said, sitting down and pulling the picture toward her to examine. Without faltering she confirmed Jennifer's theory. "It is, but I've never seen it. I would have expected Martin to hang it here in the office. Where did you find this?" She read the cover headline. "Where's Davey's Den? Is it a nice restaurant to take my husband to for our anniversary this month?" Dr. Singh held out the page for Jennifer, who was still in a state of shock. "What is troubling you, Jennifer? First you lock the door and next you show me this picture, like I should have knowledge of it."

Jennifer replaced the picture in her notebook and sat across from Dr. Singh. "I didn't mean to frighten you. I only wanted to make sure Dr. Richmond wasn't coming back before you could see that picture." Jennifer stopped to slow her racing mind. "I know this will sound unrelated to what's happened in this room so far, but I need to ask you a few questions about Helga Klemens' autopsy." Jennifer pointed to the white board on the wall.

"Okay," Dr. Singh replied, her head nodding slightly and her shoulders rising as if to say, 'I have no idea what is going on here and see no way out, so go ahead with your questions, crazy woman.'

"Thank you. I hope I can clear everything up for you soon," Jennifer began. "First though, Helga Klemens came in here on Sunday afternoon and died later that night, right?"

"Yes."

"Why wasn't the autopsy performed the following day?"

"It hadn't yet been decided if one was required," Dr. Singh said in a composed voice. "Plus, in cases like this when an elderly person has died, we often wait to find out the family's wishes. In most instances the family doesn't want an autopsy."

"Why not?"

"It's respect for their loved one, especially for a woman Helga Klemens' age," Dr. Singh replied. "For the surviving children and grandchildren the idea of anyone cutting open their beloved is beyond intrusive and messy – it's barbaric – and in the majority of deaths like hers, unnecessary. A frail woman. Her body under stress from a fall. The pain of a broken hip. The uncertainty of the surgery. These things all factor into how the heart reacts when under anesthesia."

Jennifer fully understood the reasons Dr. Singh had stated for skipping an autopsy. "I guess what's confusing to me is why an autopsy is being done now? Has her family come forward and requested one? If she's in the morgue, I take it no one has claimed her body."

"Funny you said that, as the hospital did get a call from a woman late last night. She left a message and Martin called her before I got in," Dr. Singh replied.

"What?"

"A woman left a message at our extension and Martin called her back," Dr. Singh stated in a clear, cool tone. "A distant cousin, I believe."

"Do you know what he said to her?"

"You'll have to ask him," came the reply. "This isn't an uncommon thing, Jennifer. This morning I have to call two families about their loved ones as well."

"Let's forget this phone call business for a minute."

"Forgotten," Dr. Singh responded with a wave of her hand.

"You said a moment ago a decision hadn't been made to do an autopsy, yet, today there's one scheduled. Can you tell me who authorized Helga's autopsy and why?"

"Ultimately, it was Martin's call," Dr. Singh said, leaning against the back of her chair. "We have the authority to carry out a 'required autopsy' in deaths that may have medical and legal issue ramifications. In Helga Klemens' case an autopsy could confirm that her age, her fall and subsequent broken hip were the likely causes of her heart stopping on the operating table, and not due to a surgical team error."

Jennifer digested this new piece of legalese. "So … when did Dr. Richmond decide this? You said he's been sick all week."

"He was away for a few days, but could still examine our files from home, which he said he did," Dr. Singh explained. "He told me Helga's case puzzled him and that he would consult with members of the surgical team and in I.C.U."

Jennifer remained quiet. *How can I say that my reporter's gut is telling me her beach bound coworker made no such calls – to the hospital staff or to Helga's mystery relative?*

"Jennifer, I'm very worried about you," Dr. Singh said in a loud voice, seeing that her troubled guest was acting irrationally.

Jennifer snapped out of her daze. "I'm sorry for this," she said, standing quickly and walking to the door, which she unlocked. "What time is Helga's autopsy scheduled?"

Dr. Singh was now also on her feet. "Later this morning, I think." Seeing the crazed expression again cross Jennifer's face, she pleaded, "I'm unclear what is going on, but please calm yourself, my friend. I wouldn't want to next meet you in the room down the hall."

Jennifer stopped in the doorway. "I'll do my best," she said and began sprinting down the corridor and out of view.

THIRTY ONE

Jennifer was thankful that the Solitaire playing volunteer she'd spoken with earlier had departed, leaving the two employee computers unattended. Jennifer took the seat nearest the far purple-painted wall, so as not to be mistaken for a tour guide to the hopelessly lost in the maze of hallways. She texted Maryanne that it was urgent they meet at the desk near the Day Surgery entrance. Setting her phone down she clicked on the computer's internet browser icon and hoped she didn't need a staff login password. Able to surf immediately, in the search engine box she typed: "Dr. Martin Richmond Coroner Pathologist criminal charges The Men conduct jail prison trial" and waited 0.23 seconds for a long list of results to appear on the screen.

The first headline astounded her: *Coroner testifies at Jake Wagner's murder trial.*

"Damn," she said out loud, "this ends poorly for all of us." She clicked on the link that opened to the *Justice For All* website's 'People vs. Jake Wagner' page, which Rich Simpson had shown her at the office. "Wow - just wow," she muttered as she read the opening lines of the article:

Today at the Jake Wagner murder trial, Metropolitan Hospital Pathologist Dr. Martin Richmond testified that thirty-year-old Kaye Wagner died after being shot three times in the chest at close range. Dr. Richmond confirmed that the weapon was the Smith & Wesson revolver admitted into evidence as Exhibit #1.

Jennifer's phone vibrated with Maryanne's reply that she'd be there in three minutes. While she waited, Jennifer read the article that slipped into a dull overview of the trial's second day. With a definite connection to Helga now completed, Jennifer realized it was time to get Mitch involved.

"Where's your scoop, Malone?" Mitch asked before Jennifer could say a word. "The geek boys who run our overpriced, fancy dancy, Etch-a-sketch website are waiting for your big surprise. What's the hold up?"

Jennifer had forgotten about her photo of Deangela Rossi and ... "Henrik Dekker," she said, her thought process derailed at the sight of his name in another search result listing.

"Dekker?" Mitch replied. "That dead John Doe is holding up your story?"

Jennifer ignored Mitch's smart alecky comment and clicked on a headline that read: "Witness crumbles under cross."

Today at the Jake Wagner murder trial a witness called to provide an alibi for the accused found himself in a losing battle of wits with Prosecutor Gillian Bell. During a fierce cross examination Henrik Dekker couldn't describe in detail the yard work Mr. Wagner had done on his property, located several miles from the crime scene where Kaye Wagner was found shot to death. Earlier in the day, Mr. Wagner's lawyer, Vincent Palanovich, promised testimony that would blow the case wide open, stating for the jury, "There is no way the defendant could be in two places at the same time."

"How did I not see this before?" Jennifer chastised herself, as she saw Maryanne step out of one of the elevators.

"Saw what before?" Mitch yelled, exasperated by the call. "Malone? Are you still there?"

Yes and no, her mind screamed. "Maryanne, can you find us a room where we can talk in private?"

"Come this way."

"Who's Maryanne and why do you need a room? What's going on over there?"

"I'll call you right back, Mitch, I swear," Jennifer said ending the call, and following Maryanne to a door up the hall, which she unlocked with her set of security keys.

"For the love of St. Francis de Sales!" Mitch cried out, never shy to evoke the name of the Patron Saint of Journalists, even though he wasn't Catholic. "Give me strength, Father!"

Jennifer heard none of this angst, although she knew Mitch wasn't a fan of no "goodbye" goodbyes, as his mother had drilled it into him it was bad phone etiquette.

Maryanne pushed the door open to allow Jennifer inside and then locked the door. "Is Luke in some kind of trouble? Did something happen at that restaurant?"

Jennifer could see the fear on Maryanne's face and the apprehension in her voice. "I don't think he's in trouble," she replied, "but he may be hiding something from me ... and apparently you. Tell me what he said that got you worried, and I'll try to fill in any blanks." Jennifer sat in one of the comfy office chairs at the table and pointed to one for Maryanne to take. "Sit down."

Maryanne was a bundle of nerves. "He called me last night from somewhere downtown. He was rambling about a magazine article. I told him to take a subway to my place to talk and then stay the night."

Jennifer didn't ask Maryanne how her exam studying had gone, knowing it had been an excuse for Luke to go to his fictional friend's house. "What did he do?"

"He didn't come to my apartment."

"Have you talked to him since?" Jennifer asked, concerned for Luke's welfare.

"He sent me a picture from home an hour later with a message that he was tired," Maryanne replied, her pitch rising with every word. "He did the same thing this morning, so I know he's okay. I just don't understand why he won't talk to me."

"I have an idea that he recognized someone in a picture - a framed magazine page - we saw at Davey's Den and it spooked him." Jennifer opened her purse and extracted the folded printout from her notepad. Laying the article on top of the table in the same way she'd done with Dr. Singh, she said, "Tell me who you see behind the hostess in this photo."

Watching Maryanne lean forward, Jennifer felt claustrophobic and her head started to pound from within. *If you're going to have a coronary or stroke, you're in the right place, sister,* she told herself, nervously waiting for Maryanne to utter, 'Dr. Richmond' or 'Martin' or "the retiring coroner' or 'the morgue pornographer.'

When the first name Maryanne stated wasn't any of those, Jennifer felt overwhelmed, as a rush of blood coursed through her veins and invaded every pore of her face and any working cell in her brain. The psychological ship aboard which she'd been cruising since Dr. Richmond had walked out of the coroner's office crashed against the rocks and began to take on water at an alarming rate. "Can you please repeat that? Much slower this time," she managed to say.

Maryanne was baffled by the atmospheric change in the room and tone of this simple request. "It's James," she said again, "right here." She put her index finger on a young man whose face was partially turned away from the camera.

Jennifer hadn't noticed the man before. "Anyone else?" she asked as her eyes burned a hole in the forehead of Dr. 'But you can call me Martin' Richmond.

Maryanne moved her hand back a bit and answered, "Is that Dr. Richmond?"

Tired and woozy, Jennifer didn't experience any joy in Maryanne's identification; that fact had already been confirmed by Dr. Singh and the *Justice For All* website. *How is it only 9:31?* she thought glancing at the clock on the wall. She reached over and took Maryanne's hand with its outstretched finger and pushed it onto the face of her latest mystery man. "Who ... is ... James?"

Sensing that her reply was going to be a major deal for reasons she couldn't comprehend, Maryanne inhaled a short breath and said, "James Hughes. He works as a cleaner in the Housekeeping Department."

Amazed, disbelieving and catatonic all at once, Jennifer followed up with, "Anything else of interest?"

Without hesitation Maryanne answered, "He hates being called James."

"Let me guess - he likes to be called Jimmy," Jennifer said wearily.

Shocked, Maryanne asked, "How did you know that?"

Jennifer stood and walked to a phone in the corner, then positioned it on top of the conference table. "They won't teach you this in journalism school, Maryanne, but trust me on this one: in every piece you'll ever write there's always a *Jimmy*. He's the guy circling around the edges of a juicy story for no particular reason. You'll bump into him at peculiar times during an investigation. He's not smart enough to be a leader, yet can be a reliable follower. A 'what can I do?'-type, instead of a 'can do' guy. An individual hanging in the shadows awaiting his next orders." She looked over to make sure her student had got the point. "There's always a *Jimmy*. Never forget that and you'll go far."

Jennifer picked up the phone's receiver. "I want to keep my cell line free. How do I get an outside line?"

"Dial 9," Maryanne said, happy to help her mentor out, even if it was a small detail in the greater scheme of things.

"Of course."

The truth was that Jennifer was having difficulty keeping

anything straight. Nothing this morning had gone as planned and she knew the rest of the day would be a colossal cluster from the second Mitch answered the phone. *He'll be my second call.* Glancing up at Maryanne who wore a very eager expression, she said, "Watch and learn. Class is in session."

On the third ring, Jennifer's call was connected.

"Detective Speers. How can I help you?"

"Good morning to you, too. It's me - the lovely and vivacious Jennifer Malone again. Do you have a moment to chat about a possible homicide at Metropolitan Hospital?"

THIRTY TWO

PART IV

Trillia locked the store's front door and walked across the parking lot with her coworker. "See you in the morning, Polly."

"Unless I win tonight's lottery," the woman in her mid-fifties replied with a grin. "We have to hit it one of these days!"

Trillia opened her car door. "I'll get a ticket on my way home. The draw's at ten."

Polly entered the passenger seat of a waiting pickup truck, said, "Hey, baby," to her husband, then turned back to Trillia. "Call me afterwards and we'll go out drinking."

"Win or lose?" Trillia answered with a laugh.

"Hell ya. I'm in either way!"

Trillia got behind the wheel and waved to Polly and Wally, her ideal couple, as they drove off the lot. They were the inspiration for her tall tale about the salesman who fell in love with her at *The Buckster Stops Here.* Of course she had only told Elaine, who didn't shop at the store, so there was no fear her deception would be revealed. Now, after deciding to go the single route, the new lie would be short and simple: "I broke up with him because of his work schedule."

After buying a lottery ticket at a convenience store, driving through the nearly deserted streets, Trillia reflected on how well she was coping with her decision to end it with Jake. She felt the relationship slate was totally clean ... until the next time.

And there will be a next time, she mused, pulling into her driveway.

Trillia first checked the mailbox and took out a few flyers, which she tossed in the recycling box on the porch. From the corner of her eye she saw a blue sedan being parked in front of Elaine's house; its headlights quickly extinguished, although no one exited it right away. This didn't alarm Trillia, as the neighbourhood had a high turnover rate due to the rental properties in the area. People were dropped off all the time, often just talking in the vehicle before getting out. She turned and didn't recognize the vehicle that, unbeknownst to her, had been following her at a discreet distance since she left the store parking lot. Unfazed, Trillia inserted her key in the front door lock and opened it. As she did so, she heard one of the sedan's doors close and saw a man half-jogging toward her porch.

"Trillia Johnston?" he called out.

Frightened, Trillia stared at the unidentified twenty-something man wearing a dark suit and flashing a police badge. "Yes," she replied, "I'm Trillia Johnston. Is there anything wrong, officer?" Her panicked thoughts went to her daughter. "Is Harmony okay?"

The man had no clue who or what a Harmony was, nor did he care. He'd been tasked by Clive Hill to interrogate this woman and get answers by any means possible. "It's a matter of national security, Ms. Johnston," he stated. He looked at the nearby houses and saw a few lights on within. "Can we step inside?" he asked respectfully as he took another step toward her, before placing his right hand on her waist and guiding her inside.

A moment later, they were standing face to face in the dark living room, the only light coming from a vertical fish tank on a corner table.

"You scream and you'll regret it," the man instructed Trillia in a steady, practised tone. "Are we clear?"

"Yes." Trillia gripped the edges of her purse, putting it against her chest as a barrier. "Please don't rape me."

The request caught the man off guard and Trillia saw the confusion in his eyes. Having dealt with more than her share of abusive men, Trillia resolved long ago to never be the victim again. The self defence class at the YWCA had been only the beginning of a personal reawakening. It had been followed by attending free lectures at the community college and buying books on taking back one's self respect. All of these mind-expanding activities had delivered her to this very moment and she wasn't going to waste a second of it.

Now!

With lightning speed, she lowered her right shoulder and pushed herself into the man's chest, causing him to temporarily lose his balance. Continuing to move forward she wrapped her right hand around the man's waist, like he'd done to her on the porch, and pushed him to the base of the stairs, where he fell backwards unceremoniously, arms flailing to break his fall. On his back, with his legs spread, Trillia delivered a mighty kick to his groin – "the ball shot" her instructor called it – that forced the man to bend awkwardly forward, both hands trying to block a second blow to the family jewels. His head fully exposed, she balanced herself long enough to regain her footing, then delivered a second kick to the man's throat. Again his hands were on the move, this time to his neck, gasping for air. Although Trillia was ecstatic with her successful execution of her martial arts inspired moves, she knew this confrontation wasn't over. Forgetting her training, she all of a sudden remembered the hundreds of horror movies she'd watched as a terrified teenager. In every one there was a pivotal scene when the psychopath was laying unconscious and the heroine turned her back on him to run for help. Trillia and her girlfriends would scream at the TV or the movie screen, "Kill him! He's still alive!" to no avail. Unless there was only ten minutes left, the girl would eternally regret her decision not to finish the sick bastard off.

"Not today!" Trillia screamed, kicking the man precisely in the middle of his face, breaking his nose and causing him to stop moving.

***

Scared to her core, Trillia heaved the unconscious intruder's arms upward and used duct tape she'd found in a nearby kitchen drawer to bind his hands to the stair's sturdy banister. *There's no way he can break free without injuring himself more,* she thought. Fearing the man may have an accomplice, she locked the front door, and kept the lights off. Her only company was the ancient goldfish, appropriately named 'Fish', swimming in its tank. "Yes, I'm calling 911 now," she assured the wet pet. She gingerly peered through a curtain as a passing car's headlights hit the blue sedan. No one was visible in the front or back seats. Relieved, Trillia sat on the couch's armrest to go over the frenzied last few minutes of her life.

"What just happened?" she asked herself.

Trillia's voice caused the man to stir; his head moving in a groggy manner, his eyes flickering open and shut, as he tried to will himself awake. The realization that he was bound and would be unable to escape helped the process. "Do you know who you're messing with?" he asked, his speech muffled due to his broken nose.

Trillia walked to the phone on a side table. "I don't, but with the help of the police I'm going to find out."

Before she pressed any numbers, the man yelled, "You call the cops and we're dead, lady!" He shook his head, as if that would clear his mind. "Let me go and don't say a word about this to anyone."

Trillia couldn't believe the man's nerve. "Who do you think you are? Did your brain stop functioning when I kicked your face in? It's ironic that you're the one wanting to be let go. Maybe Alanis Morrisette could use this for an updated version of her song, don't you think?" Trillia laughed uneasily at her joke. After a busy shift she was ready for bed and didn't need this hassle.

Seeing no rational way out of this mess, the man blurted out, "I'm a cop. If you call 911 I can guarantee you any officers that arrive are my friends," he lied. "I'll tell them I was driving in the area and saw a man lurking in the shadows near your house when you arrived home. I'll say I chased him off and was making sure you were safe when you attacked me, believing I was his partner. You were frightened and surprised me with your karate skills."

"That isn't what happened!" Trillia said angrily. "You're the man lurking in the shadows. You attacked me. You're the one in trouble here, pal, not me!"

A noise caught Trillia's attention: a vibrating cell phone. She checked her purse only to find it wasn't her phone ringing. Her captive's anxious expression gave the game away.

"You should've set it to silent," Trillia said as she retrieved the phone from the man's pocket.

"Don't answer it!" the man protested as Trillia looked at the caller display.

Ignoring him, Trillia pressed 'Accept' and put the phone to her ear.

"Colin, what's going on?"

Trillia mouthed the words, "Hi, Colin," and continued to listen.

"Stop foolin' around. Clive wants an update and he's already called me three times!" The idea that Colin hadn't answered finally dawned on the caller. "Who is this?"

In her head Trillia counted to five, to make clear the caller knew his question had been heard before ending the call. She then noticed the police badge lying on the floor. Picking it up she realized from its weight that it was fake. "Let me guess, Colin – your real one is in your other coat at home." She threw it at him. "And your boss Clive is pissed that you haven't called in a status report." Trillia wasn't certain if the man flinched at the sight of the airborne badge or the name Clive. Either way he appeared resigned to his fate. "If you want, I can give him an update. I'm sure the police will want to talk to him and they can give him the 411 of what went down tonight."

Trillia reached for her cordless phone again.

"911 – what is your emergency?"

"An intruder pretending to be a cop attacked me in my home. My name is Trillia Johnson. Please send the police as fast as you can to 160 Lemon Tree Street. "

"Is the attacker gone?"

"Nope, we'll be right here waiting. I'm opening the front door now. Please hurry," Trillia said, concluding the call.

"Do you think this is over?"Colin asked with a twisted smile.

"Over?" Trillia yelled. "I get up, go to work, come home and go to bed. That's my life! That's it. I quit smoking, quit drinking and go to the gym every third day. YOU are what I need to be over!"

Unmoved by her speech, Colin said, "Aren't you as pure as the driven snow? The innocent damsel in distress who craves to bang a convicted murderer. What do you have to say for yourself, Trillia? Your parents must be so proud."

Trillia stood stunned. Outside she heard one, possibly two, police cruisers speeding into the area with their sirens blaring. "What did you say?"

"Don't play dumb – you know who I'm talking about."

"Jake sent you here?"

"Ding, ding, ding – winner, winner, chicken dinner!" Colin said in his best game show host impersonation.

A bolt of fear ran down Trillia's spine. "He wouldn't do that. And if he did, why?"

The sirens were getting closer.

"Remember the flowers you delivered to his aunt? He wanted you to forget about them."

Trillia thought of correcting the man, but why get Elaine involved? "That's what this is about? I did him a favour and he sends you to scare me to death?"

Two cruisers came to a screeching stop – one parking in Trillia's driveway, the other blocking the street to the north; the red, white and blue LED lights flashing across the row of houses. The slamming of car doors followed.

"They're here," Colin said as heavy footfalls were heard on the porch. "If it eases your mind any, he wasn't going to kill you like he did his wife and brother."

A male and a female officer burst into the house with their guns drawn. Seeing the intruder they instinctively aimed their weapons in his direction.

"Are you Trillia Johnston – the owner?" the female officer asked. "Are you hurt? Is there anyone else in the house?"

"Yes, no and no," Trillia replied, a wave of relief washing over her, causing her to feel faint. "I need to sit down," she commented to the officers, their full attention on the man tied up with bright red duct tape.

"Please, go ahead," the male officer said. "I admire your handiwork," he continued, tugging on the tape to ensure the attacker couldn't get free. "He's not going anywhere."

"Good job," the female officer said with a smile, as she holstered her weapon, feeling there was no threat to her or her partner.

Trillia sat on the couch silently watching the officers radio in details of the call and state that no other units were required. As her breathing returned to normal levels, Trillia's mind tried to recall what the man had told her. *The officers must have heard the claim that Jake had killed both his wife ... and brother?* She had no clue what he was referring to, as during Jake's trial there had been no mention of any siblings.

The sudden appearance of Elaine's husband in the doorway unsettled everyone. "How are you doing, Trillia?" he asked, waiting for an officer to give him permission to enter.

"This is my neighbour, Bruce," Trillia said as she walked to him. "Can I go outside to talk with him?"

"Sure," the female officer said. "We'll deal with this scumbag and untie him."

Trillia passed Bruce on the porch and ran to the middle of her front lawn, where she inhaled the fresh evening air. "He walked up behind me when I got home from work. That's the car he drove," she said, pointing to the unattended blue sedan.

Bruce went to the vehicle and noted the mud covered license plate numbers. "Did he say anything to you? Was he trying to rob you?"

Trillia recounted how the man had threatened her life and her swift reaction. "I was praying that bargain duct tape we sell for a buck would hold him until the cops arrived." Not wanting to add any more confusion to her story, she conveniently left out the cryptic phone call and the real explanation for the man's visit.

A third cruiser with the word 'Supervisor' painted on the front panel arrived on scene and an older officer got out. "Is everyone okay here?" he asked Trillia and Bruce.

"Yes, thanks," Bruce replied. "Your officers are in there with her attacker."

The three of them looked toward the front door as the female officer inside cried out, "He bit me! You son of a bitch! Watch his right hand, Chris!"

The supervisor was instantly on high alert and unholstered his Sig Sauer handgun. "Get out of here!" he instructed Trillia and Bruce, who ran down the sidewalk, then across the street.

Seeing unaware neighbours standing on porches, Bruce started to yell, "Get inside! He has a gun!"

Trillia turned to see her attacker exiting the house with the officers scrambling after him. Colin was waving a dark object in his right hand, which he pointed at the supervisor coming toward him. With a deranged smile on his face, Colin yelled, "I'll kill you, you mother–"

Two shots from the supervisor's gun easily found their marks – one to the heart, the other through a lung. Colin was dead before he tumbled off the porch and landed on the grass.

"Nooooooooo!" Trillia cried out, knowing any secrets Colin could've shared about his relationship with Jake were probably gone forever. "Why did they have to shoot him?"

Bruce held Trillia as she began to sob. "He had a gun and could have killed you."

"He didn't have a gun, Bruce. He had a cell phone."

Bruce focused on the three officers standing over the attacker's lifeless body and saw each holding a gun in their hand.

He was going to kill someone with a phone? That's crazy.

***

By the time the coroner's hearse arrived, Trillia had answered as many of the officers' questions as she could and only wanted to take a calm tab to steady her nerves.

"Do you have somewhere else to stay tonight?" the female officer asked.

"She'll be staying with us for as long as she wants," Bruce spoke up without conferring with Elaine, who arrived home from the hospital moments after the fatal shots had been fired.

"And I've left a message with her daughter," Elaine added.

Bruce stayed behind to secure Trillia's house for her.

"Is she okay?" the male officer inquired as he prepared to leave.

"As well as could be expected, I guess. The whole thing is so surreal."

The officer left for a long night of interviews with the service's Special Investigations Unit, followed by paperwork, paperwork and more paperwork.

Inside her house, Elaine got Trillia settled in the guest bedroom and asked if she wanted to talk.

"I can't," Trillia said, on the verge of crying. "I need this night to be done."

"I understand, Trill." Elaine walked into the hallway, leaving the bedroom door ajar. "Bruce called in sick for his midnight shift, so both of us are here for you."

Shutting off the night stand lamp, Trillia reflected on what Elaine had said. The phrase, 'here for you' reminded her of the ordeal with the dead attacker, Colin.

He was there for you too, she thought, *and on Jake's orders. What did I get myself into?*

The melatonin pill Elaine had given her began to take effect, and Trillia found herself drifting asleep in defiance of the jumbled thoughts colliding in her mind:

Who is Clive?

Helga's flowers?

Winner, winner, chicken dinner?

Jake's brother?

What did it all mean?

THIRTY THREE

The decision to send Colin to Trillia's house hadn't sat well with Jimmy. "Don't take this personally," Clive had told him.

"You have to work – that can't change – and this needs to be done tonight." Jimmy hadn't been so sure, although he was happy Clive was talking to him after failing to remove that photo from Henrik's wallet before pushing him into the river. He could have sworn it was empty. The idea was to make it look like a robbery gone bad. In retrospect, he should have taken the wallet, but he'd been following orders to prove to The Men what a good candidate he was for inclusion into their organization. He understood this screw-up had set him back a few jobs, like the one taking place at the house of Jake Wagner's pen pal girlfriend.

Jimmy knew Colin wasn't the right guy. *He's too pushy.*

His instincts proved to be correct when Clive called asking if he'd talked with Colin. "Yesterday," Jimmy had answered.

Clive wasn't pleased. "If he calls you, call me. Got that?"

Not true friends, there was a bond between Jimmy and Colin: they had come from the same neighbourhood, raised by single mothers. It wasn't that they'd disliked each other, it was that they'd had the same goal in life.

After the third call from Clive in ten minutes, Jimmy wheeled his cleaning cart into an office and called Colin's number. Several rings later, it was picked up. "Colin, what's going on?" Getting no reply, he said, "Stop fooling around. Clive wants an update and he's already called me three times!" Still no response. "Who is this?" he demanded. The answer came five seconds later when the call was terminated. He immediately called Clive to say, "I think something's wrong," and filled him in on the details of the call.

"Are you shitting me with this? What is wrong with you fucking idiots?" Clive barked into the phone. "Do I have to do everything myself?"

I could help, Jimmy almost said before the call was abruptly terminated. Now angrier than before, Jimmy pushed his cart back into the hallway and called his supervisor. "Conference rooms one and two are done. I'm going to start the west wing admin offices."

"Thanks," was a man's short response.

As he made his way down the corridor, Jimmy checked the Job Postings board outside of the HR office. There were no listings that only required a high school diploma, regardless of his employment experience. The three years doing this job had moved him up the seniority list on page ten – the last page of the document. The one benefit was knowing his schedule a month in advance, to plan when he could assist The Men in any "projects" they needed completed in a timely fashion. Growing up poor in rundown, subsidized housing while his mother worked two jobs hadn't been easy. He was always getting into fights on the playground, then in pool halls and dive bars. He shoplifted items from stores in the neighbourhood, and regularly missed classes at school. By fourteen he'd been on the verge of being sent to a home for troubled youth. Then at a sentencing hearing for his involvement in a stolen car joyride, a man he'd never met had stood before the judge and said, "I take responsible for this young man, Your Honour. You'll never see him in this court again."

The judge had readily agreed and Jimmy had found himself leaving the courthouse accompanied by his sobbing mother and the sharply dressed stranger.

"My name is Joseph Monteleone. You can call me Mr. Monteleone," he'd told Jimmy in the parking lot, offering his right hand, which the teenager shook. When he had tried to pull his hand away, the man held it tightly. "Did you hear what I said to the judge in there?" Jimmy silently nodded that he had. "Good, because my word is gold and if you tarnish it – even a little bit – you'll find yourself in the worst juvie facility I can find later that same day. Do we have an understanding?"

Jimmy had looked to his mom, who was crying tears of joy or fear, he couldn't tell. "We do," she'd promised the man, who gave her a searing look.

"I didn't ask you, baby," the man had said, turning his full attention to Jimmy.

"We do," Jimmy had vowed.

"Oh, I know we do," the man had said, sliding his arm around the waist of Jimmy's mom. "Let's go and get some food. Then afterwards Jimmy can clean our plates in the kitchen as practise for his new job as a dishwasher."

On the drive to the restaurant Jimmy sat in the back seat of Mr. Monteleone's Cadillac and listened to the conversation up front. Soon all the pieces of the day's events began to fall into place. He knew his mother worked as a waitress at Davey's Den, but wasn't aware she had a boyfriend. That term was a bit of a stretch as Mr. Monteleone was married with three children. *Lover? Sugar Daddy?* Within a week, Jimmy and his mother's crammed living arrangements had changed to an apartment building complete with an outdoor swimming pool and free cable TV. "He's going to leave his wife," Jimmy had often heard his mom brag to her girlfriends on the phone. After three weeks toiling as a dishwasher, Jimmy was aware how delusional this idea was, even if his mother hadn't at the time. Mr. Monteleone turned out to be a bigwig in The Men organization, who had women stashed in apartments all over the city. Knowing this, Jimmy still never pitied his mother, who was doing what she needed to survive and take care of her only child. Jimmy would arrive at work as scheduled, do his job without complaint, keep his grades up and graduate high school against all expectations. When offered an "apprenticeship" opportunity by Mr. Monteleone and Mr. Hill, Jimmy had taken it. His dishwasher days were complete, although his days and nights as a janitor had continued. "The best money is made the hard way. Trust me, your time is coming, Jimmy," Henrik Dekker had told him. "Follow the rules and Clive will reward you."

For Jimmy, there was no joy in killing the old man. Most days Henrik treated Jimmy with respect, but orders were orders and Henrik had failed to kill that Helga woman. She'd been someone who required special attention because of her importance to Jake Wagner's appeal. Still, Jimmy wished he'd been tapped on the shoulder to finish her off. He was positive the drama in the hospital later wouldn't have occurred. Plus, he'd already carried out one high level hit for The Men.

After leaving Clive's office, Jimmy had detoured to the riverfront, where he and Henrik walked into a secluded section by the river's edge. Jimmy had asked Henrik if he had any plans now that he was retired. "No," he'd answered. "I guess I'll have to find a hobby." As he looked out onto the murky water below, Henrik had appeared to be at peace with the world, which Jimmy took as a sign. Seeing no witnesses nearby, he'd withdrawn the small leather billy club from his jacket pocket and hit Henrik on the left side of his head, followed by another one to the right temple. The old man's features had cringed in pain and then had gone slack. On the ground, Jimmy had emptied Henrik's wallet and then heaved the body over the waist-high guardrail into the swift running water below.

The adrenaline Jimmy had felt wasn't as intense as it had been a week earlier. He doubted anything would match the excitement of killing someone for the very first time. The fact Clive was there to distract the man as Jimmy crept up from behind a bush, the billy club in hand, was an honour, or so he'd thought. The day before, Clive had told Jimmy the man was spying for the Fed's anti-crime unit. "He's got to be dealt with and that's all there is to it."

Jimmy was flattered Clive trusted him to share in this task and only later discovered the man was Jake Wagner's younger brother, Benny. That had been the first blow. The second came when Jimmy overheard two members discussing how smart Clive had been to be at the river to witness the offing, so he'd have leverage with the prosecutor's office if he found himself in trouble with the law. "Jimmy will be thrown over the edge faster than Benny was!" one of the men had commented with a laugh.

Jimmy had tried to put the idea out of his mind. *I followed orders and will be rewarded,* he kept telling himself.

Completing his work in the admin offices, Jimmy updated his supervisor and was told, "Can you do a check of the waiting rooms on the ground floor? Mary-Lou was feeling sick and left. I'd ask Rebecca, but she is already busy up on six and I need you to cover those areas. Okay?"

It wasn't a question.

"Yeah, Manny," Jimmy replied unenthusiastically.

"Thank you very much, James," came the reply, the supervisor's attempt at being humourous by using Jimmy's given name.

Jimmy despised when anyone called him James. *Why is Jimmy so hard to say?* In school the teachers used his formal name, but that was kind of their job. At Davey's Den members generally called him James out of respect. During his shifts in here though, it was simply dickish behavior when uttered by coworkers who believed it was a harmless joke.

Jimmy knew he was biding his time in this thankless position for only a few more months. He could take the childish verbal abuse without losing his temper for a little longer. However, once free of the place, he dreamed of applying his new billy club skills to exact revenge on at least two bothersome individuals: Manny, the housekeeping supervisor, and Luke, the patient transporter.

We'll see who's laughing then, Jimmy thought as he swiped his employee card across a wall sensor and entered the hospital's O.R. wing to check on Mary-Lou's rooms.

THIRTY FOUR

Clive Hill was not in a good place. Scratch that: he was on the verge of an all-encompassing meltdown and had only himself to blame. "Amateurs!" he'd screamed at the top of his lungs when turning onto Lemon Tree Street. "If Colin isn't dead, he will be soon enough."

It had been *déjà vu* all over again, as he'd parked a few houses from Trillia Johnson's house to see how badly one of his men had failed at a simple mission. Sad sack Henrik Dekker somehow couldn't kill an old lady home alone on a Sunday afternoon and now this. The fact three police cruisers and an ambulance were on the scene with their lights flashing hadn't been an encouraging sign. The arrival of two news crew vans had been even more unnerving.

Unable to see the front steps, Clive had put on a ball cap and gotten out of his car. Noticing a man on his porch, Clive had asked, "Do you know what happened?"

"Police shot a guy running out of the house," the man had said nonchalantly, as if updating a friend who went to get a beer during an episode of *Cops*. "He's covered with a sheet on the lawn."

"You don't say," Clive had replied. "Was anyone in the house hurt or killed?" He half-hoped Jake Wagner's pen pal girlfriend would be a second fatality.

"Nope," the man said.

"That would be too easy," Clive had said to himself, heading back to his car knowing he'd see Colin's corpse on every late newscast.

The news that evening had been worse than he'd imagined. Not only had Colin fought with officers inside the house, he was shot dead charging a third officer outside. All that after being overtaken by Trillia Johnson, who tied him to a banister. "Pathetic," Clive said as he'd sat by himself in the second floor office at Davey's Den, drinking whiskey on the rocks.

"The police say the unidentified man ran out of the house with what looked to be a gun in his hand," the blonde newscaster had reported, "and yelled, 'I'm going to kill you.' A police supervisor arriving at the scene saw the man escaping from custody and fired two shots, killing him instantly. The police later confirmed the man had been brandishing a cell phone, not a gun at the time."

Cell phone? Clive had thought, his head spinning with the possibilities of how the police would track his unanswered calls to his cell phone. Even with his number permanently blocked, he knew they'd find a way to connect other contacts in Colin's phone back to The Men.

"IDIOTS!"

Clive's outburst had made people playing a high-stakes poker game next door pause and listen for further bizarre behaviour. When none was heard the group returned to playing cards, oblivious to the fact their favourite gambling hall's days were numbered.

***

Clive's well-oiled world encountered another squeaky wheel needing attention when a desperate Jimmy showed him a *Daily Telegraph* article with the heading: "Do you know this man?"

"I could have sworn it was totally cleaned out!" Jimmy had cried. "It won't happen again, Clive."

Clive had no patience for whiners or apologists. He did give the kid credit for admitting his mistake in person. There were a few young associates who'd have bought one-way tickets to Mexico and vanished. "Get John on the phone and tell him what you've done," Clive yelled. "Maybe he can fix this without you joining Henrik and Benny in the river!"

The call had ended with Clive and his right-hand man delaying Jimmy's punishment until all three were in the same room. That plan changed when John called to say a reporter had been flashing a photo of Henrik and Deangela Rossi in the restaurant the previous evening. Clive looked at Jimmy and said, "Get outta my sight, as fast as you can go! I'll deal with you later!"

Left alone, Clive tried to re-evaluate where he'd gone wrong. "I trust too much," he said to his reflection in a mirror, "that's the problem." He could pinpoint the moment his world had began to spin out of control: the day Jake Wagner had arranged to have his wife shot dead by Freddy "Fingers" Colman. Clive had offered Jake advice on how to handle Kaye, a waitress who loved bad boys, but to no avail. Their wedding had been a bona fide 'feel good' event. Unfortunately, Jake's eyes wandered as often as Kaye's once had and fights became routine. When he'd heard a rumour that Kaye was sleeping with one of her regular customers, Jake had lost his mind and envisioned committing the perfect murder. However, to do so would require the perfect killer and the perfect accomplice, neither of which could ever be Jake and Fingers.

For as long as he lived, Clive would never forgive Jake for his selfish act that impacted The Men's organization in such a negative way – not that its members were perfect. Still, Clive had stood by Jake, supplying the money asked for by superstar defence lawyer Vincent Palanovich and his team of high-priced associates. Feeling pulled in two directions, Clive had found himself liking Jake's younger brother, Benny, and had taken him under his wing; a replacement for Jake, whom Clive knew would die for some infraction while incarcerated. Yet, like Jake, who let his heart rule his head, Clive had let a rumour that Benny was a rat solidify in his mind and he'd acted irrationally. Instead of killing Benny himself, Clive had brought along Jimmy. "Think of this as a rite of passage," he'd declared to the young punk. Jimmy had acted admirably, attacking an unsuspecting Benny and throwing his body in the river. Now that had been perfect planning: Jimmy had done the deed and would forever be loyal to Clive. Clive, on the other hand, could always throw Jimmy to the cops if he found himself in trouble.

Jake seemed unaffected by his brother's death, even when Clive had told him what happened in a note smuggled into the

Westhorn Penitentiary. Jake didn't mention Benny in a reply letter, although he had requested one favour to 'reset our ties' and proposed having Helga Klemens killed. "Vince says if there's no Helga, my appeal will go forward quicker," he'd written.

Clive wasn't convinced that Jake's appeal would ever be granted, regardless of Helga's health. It's why with his first choice, Benny, dead, and Jimmy unavailable due to his hospital shift, that Clive's judgement was too lax and he'd called on Henrik to kill the old woman. "You're practically the same age," he'd said. "She'll trust you at the front door and you'll be out in two minutes. I'll even drive, okay? What could go wrong?"

Everything.

The one saving grace was that Helga was taken to the medical facility closest to her Greenheart Station home. Anywhere else and Clive's work would have been a lot harder. Luckily, he had an ace up his sleeve at Metropolitan Hospital: Dr. Martin Richmond.

***

The pathologist's testimony at Jake Wagner's murder trial had been an insignificant blip for the *Justice For All* panel of legal experts. Dr. Richmond was called by the prosecutor to testify about Kaye's cause of death and the gun that had fired the three deadly bullets. Bored by the unnecessary waste of court time, the defence had asked no questions. However, several weeks after the trial, Dr. Richmond had been observed sitting in his car on consecutive days watching the comings and goings of people at Davey's Den. Dressed in casual clothes and wearing sunglasses, he'd believed he was doing a good job of being *incognito*. The street was constantly busy and there was no way he'd be found out. When two men exited the restaurant and pointed at him, he'd realized how much he'd misjudged this group. Of course they'd be carrying out counter surveillance, checking for new vehicles with tinted windows or suspicious behaviour by their rivals.

Hoping to get away without incident, Dr. Richmond had started the car's engine, only to have two other men in dark suits appear out of nowhere — one at the driver's side door, one with his hands on the hood.

"You need directions, pal?" the man at the side window had asked. "Because my friend here and I can tell you where to go."

Terrified, Dr. Richmond had rolled down the window and replied, "I was in the area looking for real estate for a new business."

"What kind of business?"

"A medical clinic." Dr. Richmond figured he should stick to a subject he knew something about.

"Can't property agents do that for you?" The man had slid his hand across the top of the driver's side door. "That way you don't have to bring your expensive car down here and get it dirty."

Dr. Richmond had looked up to see the second man coming around the front of the vehicle. "Hey, I know you," the man said enthusiastically. "You're on TV." The man had backhanded his partner's chest. "Louie, this is the coroner guy from Jake's trial. I'm right, right?" he'd asked Dr. Richmond.

"You are. I'm Dr. Martin Richmond." Then without thinking about where he was and what type of men he was dealing with, as was his habit, he added, "But you can call me Martin."

The men had given one another a curious look. "Louie, meet Martin — your new best buddy."

Louie had pulled on the door handle and found it locked. "Take the keys out of the ignition and place them on the dash, Martin. Then unlock the door and step out of the vehicle."

The way Louie spoke, Dr. Richmond had wondered if he'd ever been a cop. Following directions, he'd found himself standing on the street with the two men who were more intimidating than ever.

"Let's go have a coffee at Davey's. It's on us," the other man had offered with a smile. "We have some catching up to do."

Dr. Richmond had looked at the open car window and his key ring on the dash. "What about my car? Shouldn't I lock it first?"

Both men had laughed.

"Trust me, no one will be touching your pretentious car, my friend," Louie had said.

***

The tense coffee chat that had followed with Dr. Richmond, Louie and the other man, Danny, soon grew by one participant.

"Dr. Richmond, I hope the boys are treating you well." The man outstretched his hand. "My name is Clive Hill, but you probably already knew that from the trial or news reports."

Dr. Richmond shook Clive's hand. "I don't know a lot about you, Mr. Hill, but yes, some things I do come from the media and the trial, I suppose."

Clive had taken a seat in the booth. "I was told you were thinking of setting up a medical clinic on this street. Would it be a full service operation or specialize in gunshot wounds and broken bones, that kind of thing?"

Dr. Richmond hadn't been able to tell how much of what Clive was asking was serious. What he did know was that this meeting was more mesmerizing than anything he'd conjured up in his dreams. *I'm talking to the head of a crime family,* he'd thought, finding himself no longer nervous. *This is wild!*

"I'm considering opening a practice — that wasn't a lie," he'd said to Louie and Danny, "in a year or two."

"Do you think the locations you scouted yesterday and today will be available then?" Clive had asked. "Seems to me you were scouting something a little different, Doc. Why don't you just say what that is and maybe I can help you out."

Deciding to lay all his cards face up, Dr. Richmond had confessed to Clive and his men of a fascination with organized crime and mobsters since he was a youth. As he'd gone on, no one asked questions because they were either engrossed by his story, or felt that a dead man should say his last piece without interruption. No matter what the case, Dr. Richmond had finished with, "Since testifying at the trial, I've obsessed over coming to Davey's Den ... and possibly meeting a few members of your ... group."

"To what end?" Clive asked. "Are you going to write a book or do you need something?" Without admitting to it, Clive was equally spellbound by this successful pathologist. He'd decided the man's story was genuine, but he was still being cautious. "I have a lot of connections if you need to secure a building loan, or if you're in need of a new girlfriend. Tell me and I can see what I can do."

"I don't need any of those things," Dr. Richmond had responded.

"In case you're wondering, we don't blame you for Jake's murder conviction," Louie had chimed in. "You were doing your job." His two associates had turned to stare at him. "What — he should know, that's all."

"Perhaps you're a gambling man," Clive suggested, feeling more comfortable in the midst of this man. "Do you play cards?"

"I do," Dr. Richmond had replied. "Do you know a place where a game is happening? I brought some cash."

With the die cast, Clive, Dr. Richmond, Louie and Danny had walked to the rear of the bar and down a hallway next to the kitchen. Within the hour, Dr. Richmond was up several thousand dollars — like all marks at the start of this delicate courtship. Within five hours, he was several thousand dollars in debt to The Men around the card table and had eagerly entered into a high interest plan to repay his losses.

From a second-floor window, Clive watched the doctor return to his parked car and saw a smile cross the man's face as he retrieved the key ring off the dash. Starting the engine, Dr. Richmond had looked up at Clive and gave a brief wave, before departing the area.

It had been the launch of an unusual arrangement: Clive had obtained an intelligent inside man with medical supply connections to help furnish requests by particular clients of The Men; while Dr. Richmond had fulfilled his unique childhood fantasy. Even after the nursing students' photo shoot misadventure and tendering of his resignation, the doctor's loyal contacts had remained on Clive's payroll.

On the afternoon that Helga Klemens was taken to Met Hospital and Henrik was left at a diner, Clive telephoned Dr. Richmond.

"One of my guys royally messed up an assignment today and I'm handing it off to you, Doc. Can you handle it?"

Dr. Richmond had been at home watching a football game. "That depends, Clive."

"It's a job that will clear your outstanding debt with me and you can retire debt-free. How does that sound?"

Now fully awake and sitting on the edge of his couch, Dr. Richmond had answered with two words that would change his and Helga's lives forever.

"I'm listening."

THIRTY FIVE

PART V

As expected, Mitch wasn't pleased Jennifer had laid out her murder theory to Detective Speers prior to mentioning it to him.

"When were you going to enlighten me – at the book launch party?" Mitch yelled into his office phone. "Is this the big exclusive you've been hiding from me?"

"Technically, no," Jennifer replied. "Before I got sidelined with the coroner angle of Helga's death, I had a picture of John Doe #2."

"What picture? We've already run the photo the police sent out."

"Not the entire one." Jennifer accessed her phone photos and emailed the shot of Henrik Dekker with Deangela Rossi. "Check your email. This is the full photo found in John Doe #2's wallet."

"Hold on," Mitch said as he opened Jennifer's message. "In that phone of yours do you have a picture of Hitler sunning himself on a beach in Argentina in the 1960s?"

"I'm waiting for my friend Santiago at the *Buenos Aires Herald* to get back to me on that one, but the picture I sent is 100% legit," Jennifer confirmed.

"So let me get this straight," Mitch began consulting his hastily written notes. "John Doe #2 had a picture of Deangela Rossi in his wallet. Deangela oversees The Men crime organization which had a member Jake Wagner, who was convicted of killing his wife Kaye, whose grandmother Helga Klemens testified against him, sealing his fate."

"Ah ... yeah, correct on all counts," Jennifer said.

"And now you're telling me the coroner scheduled to do grandma's autopsy is associated with The Men, and may have had something to do with her death while she was a guest at Met Hospital, right?"

"Conceivably. Dr. Richmond is to do the autopsy today, although with Detective Speers heading here that'll be postponed," Jennifer replied. "As for Helga's death ... I'm still trying to figure that out."

"Can you tell me how you're going to find out?" Mitch asked as he took a seat at his desk, the potential storylines too numerous to figure out before his third cup of coffee.

"I have one last lead to follow up on, involving flowers

delivered to Helga's hospital room on the day she was admitted."

"Why is that important? Patients get flowers all the time."

"Because, Mitch, they were bought by a hospital employee who appears to have no connection to the old woman. A dozen yellow carnations with a card that read, *All the best, Helga! See you soon!*"

"Is there any hint the buyer is connected to The Men or Dr. Richmond or John Doe #2?"

"That's what I'm going to ask her," Jennifer answered. "I don't like the coincidences piling up or The Men's involvement at Met. But with no direct link between Helga's fall and subsequent hip surgery – which was the sole reason she was in the hospital – I can't confirm a thing."

"Do you have the address of the flower woman? I don't want you to make a cold phone call to her," Mitch said.

Jennifer flipped through her notepad pages. "162 Lemon Tree Street."

"C'mon – isn't that the street where the police shot a burglar dead last night?" Mitch went to the *Telegraph's* website on his computer. "What was her address again?"

"162. What shooting?"

"Suicide by cop incident at 160 Lemon Tree Street – the house next to your flower buyer's!" Mitch cried out. "Malone, I need you down there a.s.a.p. to get both stories from this lady."

Jennifer's pulse had also quickened, though the two stories were probably not connected. "That isn't possible. Speers ordered me to stay at the hospital. He will be here in a few minutes, then I'll head out to Lemon Tree Street."

"Okay," Mitch said grudgingly. "I guess a murder inside Met trumps some loser thief dying in a hail of bullets. Stay with Speers until he gets tired of you and then go out to Lemon Tree Street. Got that? Those are direct orders, Malone."

"I hear you," Jennifer answered.

"And keep me updated on what you find out, when you find it out. Not in a week from now!"

"Oh – an ambulance is rolling into the E.R. bay," Jennifer said looking at her apprentice who was entranced by Jennifer's performance at the conference table. "Gotta go, Mitch. Talkatcha later." Jennifer hung up the phone and said, "And that, Maryanne, is how it's done."

***

After Maryanne returned to the security desk to await Detective Speers' arrival, Jennifer remained in the conference room to make one final call.

"Hey, Luke, it's Jennifer."

"Maryanne texted me that you'd be calling," Luke said, his voice dejected. "I apologize about last night."

"Trust me," Jennifer said, cutting him off, "our business date was more enjoyable than most of my romantic ones lately. At least in your case, I know why you were acting strangely when I was driving you home."

Luke appreciated Jennifer's attempt at humour, but still felt bad. "I should have told you I recognized Martin – Dr. Richmond – and Jimmy."

"Don't you mean James?" Jennifer said.

"Yeah – James. If I knew what kind of people he hung out with outside of the hospital I'd have called him Mr. Hughes," Luke replied, relieved that Jennifer wasn't angry with him.

"So, to confirm, describe to me where your esteemed colleagues were situated in that magazine picture."

"Dr. Richmond was sitting with his glass raised and Jimmy – James – was on the right with his head slightly turned."

Jennifer had removed the printout and was looking at it. "That's all I needed," she said. "You didn't get called in for an extra shift?"

"Not yet," Luke said.

"Thanks for your help, Luke, and Maryanne's input."

"I can't believe how one short conversation with a patient has escalated into this nightmare."

"As my grandfather was fond of saying, 'From small acorns mighty oaks grow,'" Jennifer said. "And boy, was he right."

***

Jennifer returned to the coroner's office to speak with Dr. Singh, to confirm nobody else was given the photo found in Henrik Dekker's wallet. Not clear how close of a relationship the coroners had, Jennifer delicately brought up the identity of the woman in the picture.

"Does the name Deangela Rossi mean anything to you, Dr. Singh?"

"No."

"Or an organization that calls itself The Men?"

Confused by the question, Dr. Singh replied with a smile, "Again, no. Are they a sports team? I don't follow any sports. My husband watches the occasional cricket match."

Jennifer thought that The Men and a cricket team did have one thing in common: they both used bats to smash tiny balls, but that was neither here nor there. "I was just wondering."

"The woman in the picture – is she Deangela Rossi? Is she still alive?"

"Yes, as far as I know," Jennifer answered, as a text from Maryanne arrived stating Detective Speers was at the front desk. The plan was for Maryanne to take him to the conference room they'd used earlier. "I have to go, Dr. Singh. I really do appreciate the use of the wallet picture."

"It's a little thank you, that's all, Jennifer," Dr. Singh said as the reporter walked out of the room. "I see that you've calmed down a lot."

"I'm trying my best," Jennifer said before turning the corner.

Nearing the elevators she saw Maryanne and Detective Speers

coming toward her, followed by a tall, handsome security guard. At the volunteers' desk Maryanne introduced her supervisor, Ken, who was a bit perturbed.

"Can any of you please tell me what's going on?" he asked the group. "First Detective Speers arrives unannounced and next Maryanne is requesting an extended lunch break to confer with you, Miss Malone, about an urgent matter. As head of security at the hospital, I need to be consulted on any criminal activity that's taking place here."

"At this point, Ken, you're as informed as I am," Detective Speers said. "If the ladies don't object, I'd like for you to join us – even out the teams, so to speak."

"Sounds like a plan," Jennifer said. "Shall we, Maryanne?" she said, indicating the open conference room door. Moments later, all four were seated around the large table.

To everyone's surprise, it was Maryanne who began the meeting. "Ken, we've got a problem."

By the end of her presentation of the facts of Helga's suspicious death, Ken was in shock. "I can't believe you didn't bring this to me," he said to Maryanne. "Or Luke."

"We were going to ..." she said, but let the sentence fade.

"They're kids with wild imaginations, Ken," Jennifer jumped in. "I didn't believe them either. What mature adult, like myself, would with such flimsy information to go on? Old woman dies on the operating table. That isn't really news at any hospital, right?"

"No, but still— "

"Isn't there an autopsy that needs to be postponed?" Detective Speers asked, his firm voice clearly trying to diffuse the tension. "After hearing from Maryanne, Jennifer, and Luke in absentia, I believe sufficient circumstantial evidence exists to warrant a detailed investigation of Helga Klemens' death. Also, we'll have to take a closer look at the backgrounds of Dr. Richmond and James Hughes." He spoke directly to the security supervisor. "Can you assist me with that, Ken?"

"Whatever you need," Ken replied.

So as not to cause undue suspicion throughout the hospital, Maryanne returned to her security duties, while Jennifer remained in the conference room alone. As ordered, she called Mitch, who had a more exciting update of his own.

"The guys in the website unit told me your picture of the dead guy and the mob wife is breaking the internet. Is that good?"

"Yes, very," Jennifer confirmed. "I hope they have it fixed for this murder at the Met follow up."

"I like that. *Murder At The Met*. It's catchy. I'll have the art department work on a logo for it," Mitch said, thinking this could become a full week feature, like the serialization of a new story by a famous author. "When are you heading to Lemon Tree Street?"

"As soon as I get a status report of what Speers and the security boss have done, and plan to do. So far it's all off the record."

"You're embedded like those journalists who ride with military convoys on Top Secret missions," Mitch said. "I get it. Don't leave until it's safe to do so. You know, storywise."

"Ah ... and I thought you were worried I'd be accosted by The Men, Mitch."

"Not true. I fear for your life ... as a reporter who has an incredible story that needs to be sent to me a.s.a.p. I've got a paper here to run, Malone."

"That might be the most honest thing said during this conversation," Jennifer said, ending the call without saying goodbye.

***

The first order of business for Detective Speers and Security Ken was to change the padlock that held the metal gate across the morgue refrigerator trays that housed Henrik Dekker, Helga Klemens and John Doe #1. The shelves were now officially part of an active police investigation, with only the hospital security boss in possession of the new padlock key. They then spoke with Dr. Singh, providing few specifics.

"I find this highly irregular," she said.

"So do I," Detective Speers replied in a reassuring tone.

"I'll have to inform Dr. Richmond when he returns. He was scheduled to do an autopsy on the woman today."

"Don't worry," Ken said, "we'll tell him. Mark it as 'On Hold' for the time being."

The men left Dr. Singh with a mistrusting look on her face and proceeded to the CEO's office on the main floor.

"Gwen, is Michael in?" Ken asked Michael Browne's assistant, noting that his door was closed.

"He's in a meeting that should be over soon," she said. When she saw Detective Speers she added, "Unless there's an emergency."

"I wouldn't want to interrupt such an important man," Detective Speers said with a smile, knowing Dr. Richmond was likely the CEO's guest. "Would it be okay if we wait in the meeting room next door?"

"Go ahead. It's not booked for the rest of the day."

"Great," Detective Speers said, turning to walk out. "After you, Ken."

Ken and Gwen made eye contact, each conveying a 'do as the man says' expression. Once in the conference room, the perplexed security boss asked Detective Speers, "Why didn't you go into the office and confront Dr. Richmond while we had the CEO sitting right there? We could've killed two birds with one stone."

Speers sat in a comfortable chair at the head of the table. "Because our only goal is to speak with the CEO and no one else. We need to inform him of what we believe has happened and ask for his permission to proceed." The detective could sense this plan wasn't the way Ken usually ran hospital operations. "Is Mr. Browne as nice as he appears to be on TV?" Speers said, changing the subject.

"He's a good man," Ken said, taking his own seat and looking out the window onto one of the city's busiest streets. "I brief him on any security calls we've had and how they were dealt with. I also keep him abreast of staff problems, thefts and inappropriate behaviour with patients. The whole gamut."

Speers knew why the man was miserable. "If Jennifer's story is true, don't blame yourself for not seeing the coroner and cleaner for who they really are before today. It happens to the best of us. The thing to remember is that the people you think you know at work can be very different individuals when behind closed doors."

"I hear what you're saying, and I agree," Ken said. "My problem is that when Dr. Richmond admitted to taking photos in the morgue, he should have been fired outright."

"Let me guess – the union or his lawyer were involved in the negotiations?" Speers asked.

"Yep. And if he had any role in that woman's death because of some involvement with The Men ... they're going to have to deal with that too."

"I know all about office politics," Speers said, shaking his head. "The police let their own get away with things regular citizens would go to jail for. In my profession it's called the thin blue line. What would they call it here: the thin blood line?"

Both men began to laugh at the bad pun when they heard the voices of two men nearby.

"Send a postcard from Mexico, or wherever you're planning to land, Martin," CEO Browne said.

"I will. Thanks again for everything."

There was a short pause as the men presumably shook hands and then only one set of footsteps was heard going up the hallway.

Detective Speers positioned himself to see his man walking past. "Let's go talk with the CEO. The coroner will find out we've switched that padlock soon."

"What if he makes a run for it?" Ken asked, concerned that Dr. Richmond would get away.

"Not to worry," Speers said, "I already have a cruiser near the employee exit where Richmond's Jaguar is parked. We're good."

Amazed at the detective's forethought, Ken decided he was only along for the adventure and intended on enjoying every moment of it.

Inside the CEO's office, Ken made the introductions. "Michael Browne, this is Detective Speers."

"It's very nice to meet you, Detective," the CEO said amicably.

Taking the outstretched hand before him, Speers replied, "I'm glad you said that now. You might not be saying that when I tell you why I'm here."

THIRTY SIX

With a coffee and a chocolate chip muffin in hand, Dr. Martin Richmond took a back flight of stairs musing to himself, *One final piece of business and then I'm free!*

The meeting with the CEO had gone better than expected. They talked of their respective time at the hospital and the good times they'd had as friends outside of work, which would continue after today. "Pack your camera for the trip," the CEO had joked, "but leave the nursing students here, okay?"

Richmond's contact with any current students on hospital grounds was strictly forbidden as a condition of his "retirement" deal. The funny part was he'd moved onto the nursing students' instructor, a lovely woman who'd be going away with him starting tomorrow. As the hospital board had zero interest in the infamous morgue photo shoot(s) becoming public knowledge,

Richmond had the upper hand, even when he was in the wrong.

Dr. Singh wasn't in the office when he arrived and he sat at her desk to enjoy his lunch. Looking around, he knew he'd miss the old place, if only for a short while. Although he'd stated that a new life in an exotic country was on the horizon, those days would maybe last a month, as he had bigger plans in the works. Tanned and relaxed, he would return to open his dream practice within a new medical clinic near Davey's Den — his new adopted home.

Finished with his coffee and muffin, Dr. Richmond entered the morgue and unlocked the autopsy room with his set of keys. Setting out the surgical instruments he'd need, he felt this was a waste of time, as he already knew what Helga Klemens' autopsy would reveal. In fact, he'd typed up his findings two days ago. A little cut here, a little incision there, a small sample of the heart and the lungs over there. It was all very routine for a corpse of this age. The difference on this day was that the samples sent to the lab would inexplicably be contaminated; their secrets lost with his report left as the final verdict of death. He felt bad that he had to mutilate the old girl's body at all, however appearances were everything.

"Family or no family, the official record has to state 'natural causes,'" Clive Hill had demanded. "Had Henrik done his job it would've read 'brain injury due to fall' but that didn't happen. So it's up to you, Martin. Get this done."

And he had ... with the help of Jimmy who had been more adept at sleight of hand and acting than he could have hoped for. The prospect of Martin finding a way to apply the small Coniine soaked patch he'd prepared to Helga's skin was not an option, only a last resort. He'd told Clive it was too risky, as he rarely went into the O.R., and if he did it would draw attention.

"We can put it on her when she's back in her room and exhausted. Patients rarely remember the lab techs coming in to take blood late at night or in the early morning hours, because they're fast asleep and think they're dreaming," he'd said over the phone. "It's still an unpredictable situation, Clive."

"What about Jimmy? He can get into the O.R., right?"

"He can, but he also has access to her room after surgery."

Clive had considered each scenario. "Give Jimmy the patch and tell him where it goes. My first choice is to get it on her before surgery to make it look like a heart attack on the table. If he feels it can't be done without being caught, then he needs to do it before the end of his shift. Got it? I need this taken care of tonight. Do we understand each other?"

"Perfectly," the coroner had replied. "I'll text Jimmy now."

Dr. Richmond hadn't known why there was such urgency, as Jake Wagner's murder conviction appeal hadn't been filed, and from what he'd heard, wouldn't be for a few weeks. *We have plenty of time to knock the old lady off*, he'd thought. In any case, he set up a meeting during Jimmy's break at a diner a block away from the hospital.

"Here's the deal – don't touch this with your bare hands," Dr. Richmond had warned as he slid a sandwich bag containing the lethal patch across the table.

"What's on it?" Jimmy had asked turning the bag to examine its contents more closely.

"Coniine. Have you heard of hemlock? It's a by-product of that plant and starts to paralyze a person's muscles within thirty minutes. The beauty is that the central nervous system isn't impacted. The person remains conscious and aware until they begin having a hard time breathing."

"So she dies *before* the surgery?" Jimmy was worried he'd be the last person to see the patient alive.

"No, but timing is very important. The patch has to be on her skin before she goes under the anaesthesia for the Coniine to start working. When they take her into the operating room she should be starting to feel the effects. They are minor at first," Dr. Richmond had said, proud of his choice of toxin. "It's like a nicotine patch where tiny amounts of poison are released over time. The full effects will hit her after she's out. The real cause of death is lack of oxygen to the brain and heart because of respiratory paralysis. The surgical team won't figure that out in the heat of the action."

Jimmy had stared at the doctor. "Have you ever used this stuff?"

"Never. That's why it's so exciting," Dr. Richmond had responded. "I read about it and learned the lethal adult human dose is about 500 mg, so I figured in her age and weight to guesstimate the dosage."

"You didn't use the word 'guesstimate' when describing this plan to Clive, did you?"

"Ah ... no."

Jimmy had put the bag in his scrub pants' side pocket. "Any specific area of the body I need to attach this?" he'd questioned, anxious about the logistics.

"Somewhere out of sight – the base of the neck, mid-back, maybe? If it's found a nurse will probably rip it off and throw it in the garbage. If not, I'll dispose of it when I do the autopsy and *forget* to record it in my findings."

"I'll do my best," Jimmy had said with a shrug. "If not in the O.R., then later tonight."

"Remember, don't take the risk if there are doctors and nurses in the area," Dr. Richmond had advised. "It may be Clive's preference in order for the surgery to cover up any irregularities, but it isn't worth getting caught if we don't have to, all right?"

Jimmy had laughed as he got out of the booth. "Once I'm in the O.R. there's going to be no 'we' getting caught, only 'me' getting caught ... and yes, I have an idea how this will work. I've watched a lot of transporters dealing with patients who'll do anything they're asked."

"Okay, good luck."

Recalling what that annoying toolbag Luke was always saying,

Jimmy had replied, "It's not about luck, it's about skill," and had exited the diner alone.

***

With the tools of his trade laid neatly out next to the metal examination table, Dr. Richmond walked to the morgue's stainless steel, floor-to-ceiling doors and opened the third one. Switching keys, he reached to unlock the padlock to release the security gate over the tray where Helga Klemens was located.

"What the—" he said, as the key wouldn't fit into the base of the padlock. Thinking he had simply used the wrong key, with his hand now shaking, he tried another one with the same devastating result. He stepped back from the door. "No, no, no, no," he cried out. "Alpa! Why did you change the padlock?" He ran out of the morgue and back to the office, which remained empty. Picking up the desk phone he called the switchboard. "This is Dr. Richmond. Please page Dr. Singh to return to the morgue."

"Okay, Doctor, no problem," the operator replied.

"For you there's no problem," Dr. Richmond muttered.

Over the hospital wide speaker system came, "Dr. Singh. Please return to your department stat. Dr. Singh. Please return to your department stat."

***

In the CEO's office Detective Speers stood, followed by Security Ken and Michael Browne.

"We have to go, Mr. Browne," Speers said, his hand already on the door knob. "I promise our next encounter will be longer."

The CEO was speechless as the men ran out of his office.

"Is everything all right, Michael?" his assistant asked.

"For the sake of the hospital, I hope so. Please reschedule my meetings for the rest of today," he said. "And get Morton Dennison on the line for me."

"What if he's in court?"

"Tell him if he's not here within the hour his firm is going to lose a million dollars in billings. That'll get him moving."

Running down the hallway Detective Speers was on his cell phone with the officer in the cruiser outside. "It's go time. Don't let that Jaguar out of your sight."

"Ten-four."

"Do you think he'll run?" Security Ken asked, pushing open a door leading to a stairwell.

"I would," Speers said with a big smile.

Exiting into the middle of a long hallway, Speers reoriented himself. Seeing the elevators, he knew where he was and continued to follow the security boss. *His turf, his route.*

"Hey, wait!" Jennifer yelled, coming into view after hearing the overhead stat page. "What's happening?"

"Nothing yet," Speers replied, slowing his pace.

Approaching the final hall intersection connecting the main hospital with the adjacent Cancer Centre, Dr. Singh appeared, walking at a rapid pace. Seeing Jennifer with the others, she stopped and glared. "Jennifer, what did you do? Is this about that photo? If I'd have known there'd be all this trouble, I wouldn't have shown it to you."

"Dr. Singh, I swear this isn't about the photo," Jennifer said, catching up with the assembled group.

"Did you page me," Dr. Singh asked Detective Speers, "or was it you, Ken?"

Unaware of whom his colleague was talking to or why, Dr. Richmond ran out of the office and turned in the direction of the voices. "I paged you, Alpa!" he called out, causing the group of four to turn in his direction. For the first time he became aware that Dr. Singh was with the head of security, a large police officer and a female grasping a reporter's notebook. *Oh shit,* he thought, calculating the chances for escape by sprinting to his car parked outside an exit to his right.

"Don't even think about it!" Detective Speers' bold voice carried down the hallway, as he reached to unsnap his gun holster. "If you believe that because we're in a hospital I won't take this out and aim it at your heart ... well, you'd be wrong."

"I'm not going anywhere, Officer. I work here with Dr. Singh. She can vouch for me. My name is Dr. Martin Richmond," he said, moving his hands away from his body and not making any sudden moves. "But you can call me Martin."

Because everyone else around here does, Jennifer thought, disgusted by the events playing out in front of her.

"Because everyone else around here does," Dr. Richmond said casually. "Ken, did you know the padlock inside door number three was changed? That's why I paged Alpa."

The group began to make their way toward Dr. Richmond, each one wondering what could happen next. Only Dr. Singh was truly in the dark. "Can you tell me why that padlock was changed?"

"All in good time, Dr. Singh," Detective Speers said in a soothing tone, coming face to face with the man of the hour. "All in good time."

THIRTY SEVEN

Jennifer retreated to the conference room, as the "lawmen" questioned both coroners in their office. The Q&A didn't last long once Detective Speers told Dr. Richmond he wouldn't be arrested, but was a person of interest. Hearing this news, the coroner bolted out of his chair and left the hospital, squealing his car's tires as he exited the staff parking lot.

Re-entering the conference room, Jennifer asked Speers, "So, full confession? Or did you lock him in the fridge until he's ready to talk?"

Speers looked to Security Ken. "That was an option?"

Ken smiled, "I have other padlocks."

"Next time," Speers said. Turning to Jennifer, he added, "As for Dr. Richmond, he fled on foot, but my guy is on him. I didn't have anything solid to hold him on."

"What about suspicion of murder or accessory to murder?" Jennifer was now angry and perplexed. "Didn't anyone tell you that tomorrow he's starting a new life somewhere beyond this country's borders?"

"I believe you did, Jennifer," Speers answered, "and my people are calling the passport people as we speak."

"Did he deny everything?" Jennifer inquired, unhappy that the doctor was free to kill again.

"He confirmed that he was scheduled to do the Helga Klemens' autopsy — that's it," Ken replied.

"And Jimmy? Don't you think the good doctor is on the phone with him as we hang around here?" Jennifer asked.

"I doubt it," Detective Speers said confidently.

"Is that because you confiscated Richmond's cell phone?"

"That and I had Mr. Hughes picked up for questioning before I came here," Detective Speers advised with a wry smile. "As a precaution if the coroner wasn't cooperative."

Jennifer was amazed that Jimmy would go with the police anywhere. "He's in custody?"

"Custody is such a negative word," Detective Speers said. "I prefer to say he's a guest of his own free will, as he helps us with a non-existent theft ring here at Met."

"Tricky," Jennifer laughed.

"I thought so."

"What's next, Detective?" Ken asked.

"I heard Maryanne say there's a state of the art video system on the premises. I'd like to see it, if you've got the time."

Jennifer's cell phone rang, interrupting the flow of conversation in the room. "Jennifer Malone here. How can I help?"

"Hi, it's Genifer Grant calling. I was wondering if we could meet? I'm coming into the city, if that helps."

Jennifer sat up in her chair. "Sure. Are you okay?"

"It's about the day of Helga's fall," Genifer answered slowly, "but I want to talk to you in person, not over the phone."

"Pick a time and place. I'm at Met Hospital, if that helps with logistics."

"The hospital?" Fear crept into Genifer's voice.

"I was stopping by to visit a friend who works here," Jennifer lied, winking at the men in the room. "I can meet you anywhere." *As long as it's not Davey's Den or by the river.*

They settled on a popular outdoor café near the *Telegraph's* offices.

Jennifer gathered her purse and started for the door. "Gotta go, gents. Keep me informed on the video viewing," she said to both. Passing Detective Speers, she patted him on the back. "And see you at the station later."

"Thanks for the warning," Speers chuckled. Then to the hospital's head of security, he said, "Onward?"

"Right this way, sir."

***

Detective Speers took a chair next to Security Ken behind a large console. Before them was a wall of monitors.

"Where do you want to begin?" Ken asked, typing the date of Helga's surgery into the search engine.

"When did Luke bring Mrs. Klemens down from her room?" Detective Speers replied.

"Around 7:00. I checked with the O.R. clerk, who said two

members of the surgical team were ready to speak with her upon her arrival."

"Okay, do your thing," Speers said, motioning to the screens.

Ken punched in the time frame coordinates and pointed to a specific screen. "The footage will appear there. I can switch from camera to camera to follow the action."

"Impressive."

The first camera selected was one in the hallway near the O.R. Family Waiting Room. During the following few minutes, numerous staff in scrubs and other individuals were seen swiping their employee badges against a small box on the wall, activating the two doors leading into the O.R. corridor to open.

As a stretcher was pushed through a small door Ken said, "That's Luke with Mrs. Klemens."

Detective Speers looked closer at the screen. "She seems frightened already. Glancing all over the place."

"I've seen that expression on a lot of older patients," Ken said. "In her case, Mrs. Klemens might be worried if she'd be able to live independently after the surgery. It's a big deal for anyone who has survived alone for years and now find themselves needing help."

"True," Detective Speers said, watching as Luke manoeuvred the stretcher through the open doors and out of view.

A new camera from inside the O.R. corridor was switched on, showing Luke continuing down the hallway. He then entered the patient waiting area and positioned the stretcher against a wall. There were two female staff in green scrubs waiting for him and he handed one of them a green binder. There was some small talk with Luke and the women exchanging smiles. He next turned to Mrs. Klemens and said something to her with a smile on his face. However, the smile dipped slightly as the old woman replied to him. Luke's expression eventually changed back to its usual sunny disposition. At the same time, the two surgical team members were on either side of Luke, one reading the contents of the binder at the foot end of the stretcher, the other near Helga's head adjusting the pillow.

"Pause it there!" Detective Speers ordered. "Who's that at the top of the stretcher? She could be Dr. Richmond's accomplice."

Ken stopped the footage. "Dodi? She's been here forever and I've never heard an unkind word said about her." Ken hit a button that put the video into a slow-mo mode. "I think she's just fluffing the pillow a bit, Detective."

As the footage rolled, Speers agreed. "You're right."

Luke and the nurses left the waiting area, with Luke retracing his steps to the swinging doors, which he exited. The unblinking camera continued to monitor Helga's stretcher and the immediate surrounding hallways.

"Where did the nurses go?" Speers asked. "Can you bring up a new angle of this area?"

Ken tapped more keys on the keyboard until a wider angled camera filled the screen. Rewinding the footage, it showed both nurses entering through a set of doors.

"Where do those doors lead?"

"The operating rooms," Ken answered.

"Now Mrs. Klemens is all alone," Speers observed, pointing to the empty clerk desk. "Is that normal?"

"I can find out," Ken replied, reaching for the room phone and punching in an extension. "Hey, Chelsey, Ken here from Security. I have you on speaker. Can you answer a question for me?"

"What is it?" the O.R. clerk asked.

"Hypothetically, when a patient is brought down by stretcher as an evening add-on, is there ever a time when they're left alone, even for a little while?"

"Not for an hour or anything," came the reply. "Maybe a minute, as I get paperwork or am away from the desk for some other reason. Someone is always within hearing distance if the patient needs help. Plus, you said they were on a stretcher, so a call bell would be tied to the railing. Why, has some family member complained their dearest didn't get a warm blanket in a timely manner?"

"No, you're good," Ken replied. "Thanks for the info."

"Anytime," the clerk said.

Ken replaced the receiver. "There's your answer."

Before he could reply, Detective Speers was getting out of his chair, his focus on the O.R. footage. "What's that?"

At the bottom of the screen a cleaner's cart came into view, followed by its nervous pusher.

"James Hughes, also known as Jimmy," Ken said, now riveted to the silent movie being played out.

Detective Speers was immediately on his cell phone and ordering, "Don't let that Hughes kid out of your sight! I'll be there shortly to interrogate him. Got that?"

In silence, they watched as Jimmy checked out the numerous hallway corners and then positioned his cart next to Helga's stretcher. Jimmy looked like he was starting a conversation, all the while keeping his eyes peeled for staff to appear. He smiled and imitated Luke's cheerful behaviour as he put on a pair of plastic gloves. Turning away from Helga, he opened a plastic bag and took out a small item, placing it on the palm of his right hand. Turning to Helga, there was an exchange of words as he stepped forward and raised the back of the stretcher, allowing Helga to sit a bit more upright.

"What's in his hand?" Speers pondered under his breath. "She can't see it."

Now comfortable, Helga leaned forward and with his right hand Jimmy reached behind her to pull the pillow upward a few inches. After Helga returned a warm smile, Jimmy removed his gloves and threw them in the garbage bag on his cart. There was another friendly exchange of words before Jimmy hastily walked around the corner pushing the cart.

Soon, the O.R. clerk returned to her desk and sat down, oblivious to Jimmy's visit.

"It must have been a patch of some kind that he applied to her back," Speers said. "Can you call Dr. Singh to come in here?"

"I can."

A couple minutes later, Dr. Singh entered the room and was overwhelmed by all the monitors. "I hope your assurance to let me in on your secret *in good time* is now, Detective Speers, because I've had enough of these games for today."

Detective Speers offered his chair to the coroner. When seated, Speers said, "I promise, this is the final game, Dr. Singh. I call this one, 'How did the patient die?' Are you ready to play?"

THIRTY EIGHT

The first face-to-face meeting of Jennifer with a "J' and Genifer with a "G" took place at the *Lasting Impressions Café and Deli* — a city attraction since before either woman was born. Genifer was full of nervous energy with her fight-or-flight response on high alert when she saw the *Telegraph* reporter already seated at a patio table.

You can still walk past her, Genifer thought. *She doesn't know what you look like.*

Coincidentally, Jennifer was thinking the same thing as she watched for someone to make eye contact. *She could be any of these women.* Although primarily a newspaper reporter, Jennifer did appear regularly on TV news and interview shows, and was a recognizable semi-celebrity in the city (even if Beth the waitress didn't know her at Davey's Den). If that prominence reached the suburbs of Greenheart Station was yet to be confirmed.

"Hi, Jennifer?"

Jennifer looked up to see a woman in her forties with collar length, dirty blonde hair parted to one side. Her warm smile didn't quite hide the anxiety that covered the rest of her face. "Genifer?"

"Yes, Genifer Grant."

"Thanks for meeting me. Do you want a coffee or something a bit stronger?"

"No, thank you," Genifer replied, as she sat across from Jennifer. "I'm in the city for a meeting and don't have a lot of time."

Jennifer couldn't tell if this were the truth or an easy way out to end their conversation later. "I'm all yours until you have to leave."

Genifer didn't know where to start. From their previous telephone conversation, she knew the reporter had her own suspicions about the events surrounding Helga's fall. "Did you find the person who sent the flowers to Helga?" she asked, recalling that earlier line of questioning on the phone.

"Yes," Jennifer answered. "A woman who works at Met Hospital. She is next on my list of people to speak with today."

"Is she a relative or a friend?"

"I'm guessing a friend or a friend of the Klemens family. There aren't many of them around according to Glenn." The name produced an instant smile on Genifer's face. "He's one of the nicest men, don't you think?"

"He is. I visited him today and he's traumatized by Helga's death."

"He told me she was his first love and they'd stayed friends for 75 years, or some crazy number like that," Jennifer said. "In my line of work I can rarely retain friendships for 75 days."

That brought another grin to Genifer's lips. "Try being the vice-president for a postal workers union. Friendships can end in 7.5 minutes during contract negotiations."

"I've had some relationships go south in that time period with men who didn't understand me," Jennifer admitted. "Apparently

Glenn and Helga didn't have that problem."

"It would seem so," Genifer said, trying to determine a way to transition into the real purpose of this meeting. Thinking that a visual cue might help, from her purse she took out the *Telegraph's* Local section, laying it out on the table. Pointing to the only picture on the back page, Genifer stated, "This man was at Helga's house before I arrived and I believe he tried to kill her. I know he was also at the hospital ... because he found me in the E.R. and threatened my family if I told anyone."

Tears of relief began to stream down Genifer's cheeks, as Jennifer stared at the picture of Henrik Dekker.

"This man? Henrik Dekker?" Jennifer put her index finger over Dekker's grinning pose. "He was at Helga's at the time of her fall?"

Genifer wiped away her tears. "You know him?"

"Of him," Jennifer replied, her mind in full blender mode. "I know of him. Tell me what you saw at the house and the hospital, and what he said to you." Jennifer opened her notebook and was ready to write, not wanting to miss a word.

With adrenaline pulsating through her veins, Genifer recounted her story: seeing Henrik in Helga's driveway; getting his phone call at home; the fainting spell; and going to the hospital E.R. where he visited her while Stan was out of the room.

"His last question to me was, 'Do you swear on the lives of your girls and your husband Stan?' I said, 'I do,' then he gave me a wink and said, 'That's good.'"

Mesmerized by this account, Jennifer had stopped writing minutes earlier. "And he never contacted you again?"

"Never," Genifer answered. "Reading your article, I thought he might have died shortly after leaving the hospital. Some freak accident of fate."

"From what I know about the people he associated with, I doubt his death was an accident at all." Jennifer pulled out her phone. "Can you stay a few more minutes?"

"I can."

"Great. I have to make a quick call," Jennifer said, standing. "I'll be right over there. This should only take a minute."

"Okay," Genifer replied, unsure why the reporter was being so secretive. "I'll be here."

Before she'd reached the spot she had indicated, Jennifer had Detective Speers on the line. "Are you still at Met?"

"I'm heading to the front doors now," Speers said, out of breath. "Ken from security and I watched the camera footage. We saw Jimmy Hughes place a patch on the old woman's back while she was in the O.R. waiting area."

"Are you kidding me?" Jennifer cried out.

"Dr. Singh examined the body and confirmed that there had been some type of sticky pad on Mrs. Klemens' skin, which was probably disposed of by an O.R. or I.C.U. nurse in all the confusion," Speers replied seriously. "She's going to run some tests on that area to determine what, if any, poison or sedative residue evidence was left behind."

"That's almost as crazy as my news," Jennifer said, teasing her co-investigator.

Detective Speers stopped at the front security desk, where Maryanne was giving him an expectant look. "And what's that, Miss Malone?"

"I know who tried to kill Helga *the first time* at her home."

***

Jennifer returned to the patio table where Genifer appeared to be preparing to leave. "Sorry about that. I had to pass along your identification of the man in the overcoat to a detective who's working on Helga's case."

"The police are already involved?" Genifer asked, thinking her information alone would be the spark to light an investigation. She felt tears forming in her eyes again. "I should have come forward sooner. I was afraid for my family. When I saw that this horrible man was dead, I figured it was safe to talk." Pausing, she lifted her head to meet Jennifer's eyes. "We are safe now, right?"

Jennifer didn't want to frighten Genifer further with the possibility The Men had several thugs behind Henrik Dekker and Jimmy Hughes. "You did the right thing by calling me, Genifer, whether it was a couple of days ago or today. Your information is very important, trust me." Genifer relaxed a little. "If you still have time, I'd like to make some notes about what you told me earlier."

"My meeting isn't for ninety minutes," Genifer replied, as she took off her light jacket to reveal a tattoo on her right forearm. Noticing that Jennifer was trying to read it, she said, "It says, *Be the change you wish to see in this world*. I guess today's the day I put my faith in the proverb I found in a fortune cookie last year."

Jennifer laughed as she opened her notebook. "I had one that read, *There's no better time than the present.* Let's see if both our fortunes are really true."

***

An hour later, a relieved Genifer departed for her meeting with a clear head. The dread she'd been carrying since finding Helga was gone. Jennifer assured her the police were investigating Helga's death based on a lot of other factors, which she couldn't share.

Jennifer checked over her notes and dutifully called Mitch at the office to update him.

"Has this woman talked to anyone else?" he asked, excitement in his voice.

"Only Yours Truly," Jennifer bragged. "I gave Detective Speers her phone number, so she can expect a call from him."

"An exclusive about a murder no one knew happened. This will be huge, Malone!" Mitch said.

"I expect a raise," Jennifer replied, "and a parking spot in the office garage. Parking ten blocks away each day is kind of unnecessary, don't you agree?"

"You deliver me this story and I'll get you that spot."

"If you don't, there's going to be trouble. Anyway, I'm off to clear up the one nagging detail that's bothered me from the start."

"The flower delivery?"

"You got it. From there I'll swing by the cop shop and see if Jimmy has confessed his sins to Detective Speers."

"Okay, but don't be long," Mitch warned. "I'm clearing the top fold of tomorrow's edition for this and need you to fill in the space with words."

"Aye aye, Captain," Jennifer said, getting into her car. "I'll be there shortly. At this stage I can't see the significance a dozen yellow carnations could have played in Helga's death, but as you know, I tend to be thorough."

"Oh, I know," Mitch said. "And don't forget to ask flower lady about the shooting next door."

"It's on the tip of my tongue now," Jennifer confirmed. "Do you have the name of her neighbour?"

Mitch took a piece of paper from his desk. "The last name is Johnston and her first name is Trillia. Can that be right?"

THIRTY NINE

On the way to Elaine Stanton's house, Jennifer reflected on the craziness of the morning's still unfolding events: Dr. Richmond being M.I.A. and thankfully no longer performing Helga's autopsy; Jimmy Hughes in voluntary custody waiting to assist the police in solving a fake theft problem at the hospital; Detective

Speers and Security Ken reviewing the camera footage of Helga's final moments alive; Dr. Singh's confirmation that a patch or foreign substance had been applied to Helga's skin, likely accelerating her demise; and finally, Genifer Grant identifying John Doe #2 as Henrik Dekker, the third member of The Men to be connected to Helga.

How did this insanity start with a short story about John Doe #1, who still isn't identified? Jennifer wondered, parking in front of 162 Lemon Tree Street, a small bungalow that had garden beds full of flowers. She didn't see any carnations, with the only yellow represented being the colour of a late 1980's Camaro in the driveway. "Good times ahead," she said, getting out of her car and walking to the porch door.

Unclear if the doorbell had worked, Jennifer knocked, which elicited the rabid barking of a dog from within. Moments later, the door opened.

"Can I help you?" a woman in her late thirties with brown shoulder-length hair asked.

"I hope so," Jennifer responded, holding out her business card. "My name is Jennifer Malone from *The Daily Telegraph* newspaper. Would you happen to be Elaine Stanton?"

"I am. Is this about the shooting?" Elaine examined the card.

"Yes and no. I do want to discuss the incident last night," Jennifer replied, glancing over to 160 Lemon Tree Street, which was a mirror image of this house. "But first I have some questions about an unrelated topic. Do you have a few minutes?"

"Sure, come on in and enjoy the air conditioning," Elaine said, stepping back to allow Jennifer inside. "And don't mind Milo, he's all bark and no bite," she said of a shaggy black Shih Tzu in a doggie bed in the corner.

The combination living room/kitchen made the area appear bigger than Jennifer had thought outside. Noticing how clean and well-organized everything in sight was, from the coffee table, to bookshelves, entertainment unit and the counters, Jennifer was impressed. "I wish my apartment was this neat."

Elaine smiled. "I used to work as a housekeeper at Metropolitan Hospital years ago, and I guess the saying, 'there's a place for everything and everything in its place' rubbed off on me." She gestured to the kitchen table. "Is here okay to talk?"

"That would be perfect," Jennifer said, taking a seat and getting her notebook out of her purse.

"Would you like a cold beverage?"

"No, thanks," Jennifer answered.

Elaine sat across from Jennifer. "So, what's this about?"

"It's funny you brought up working at Met. You're still there, right?" Jennifer began.

Elaine hesitated with her answer. "I'm in the kitchen now."

Jennifer almost asked if she knew Jimmy, but didn't.

"Does this have to do with my work at the hospital? If it does, I'd like my union rep present," Elaine said, sounding defensive.

"Not at all," Jennifer said, trying to smooth over the misunderstanding. *I wonder whom Jimmy may have contacted before going to the police station,* Jennifer thought uneasily. *Stay focused. The flowers! Unrelated to Jimmy!* "What I'm here about relates only to a hospital gift shop purchase you made on Sunday. A dozen yellow carnations? Do you remember buying those for a patient?" Jennifer held back revealing Helga's name until she absolutely had to do so.

"For Helga?"

And there it is!

"Yes, that's her," Jennifer confirmed. "I believe you wrote out a card with them."

Elaine couldn't understand why a newspaper reporter was in her house talking about some hospital flowers, but figured she'd paid cash and had nothing to hide. "I did. It was, *All the best, Helga!*"

Jennifer flipped through pages of her notebook. "Did you add, *See you soon?*"

"I think so," Elaine said.

"What did you mean by that? Were you and Helga friends?"

For Jennifer, this was the moment of truth. A simple answer like, 'She was a family friend. My mom knew her,' or 'I used to live in Greenheart Station,' or 'We met at a craft show and started to talk.' Anything basic would be satisfactory. *I have my exclusive to write,* Jennifer was thinking absentmindedly. This flower delivery probably wouldn't make the story in any case. *"Why is that important?"* Mitch had said. *"Patients get flowers all the time."*

"You should ask Trillia that," Elaine said, jolting Jennifer out of her daydream-like state.

"Excuse me? Trillia? As in Trillia Johnson, your next door neighbour?"

"The one in the same," a female voice answered from a back hallway. Jennifer and Elaine looked up as Trillia walked into the room. "I'm Trillia Johnson. Why are you asking about the flowers I had Elaine buy?"

Jennifer stared at the tall, skinny bleached-blonde woman with enormous breasts, who appeared to be very distrustful. "You ordered the dozen yellow carnations?"

Trillia was not pleased that anything associated with Jake Wagner was being investigated. "Why are you asking?"

"I'll be honest with you, Trillia," Jennifer lied. "As a favour to the patient's family, I was asked to locate Elaine and thank her. They were wondering how Elaine knew Helga, that's all. Now you're telling me you sent that lovely bouquet. I want to give credit where credit is due."

Anger instantly flashed across Trillia's face and she yelled, "Get away from the table, Elaine, and call 911!"

At first Elaine was confused. "What's going on?"

Trillia ignored the question, instead asking one of Jennifer. "So you're working for Helga's family?"

What have I got myself into here? Jennifer said to herself, frightened by the turn of events. *I never want to see another yellow carnation in my life.* Remembering what Dr. Singh had told her earlier, Jennifer said, "Yes ... for a woman — a distant cousin of Helga's. I have her name written here somewhere," Jennifer said, sorting through her notebook, stalling for time.

"You're lying!" Trillia shouted, grabbing a heavy bookend off a shelf, causing the books to slide against each other at an angle. "Jake ordered those flowers for his aunt! There was nobody else involved."

Jake? A new connection to Helga? Dare I pray it's Jake Wagner?

"Trillia's boyfriend asked her to get the flowers, but I was the one who delivered them to Helga's room," Elaine spoke courageously, feeding off her friend's rage.

"Ex-boyfriend," Trillia corrected Elaine. "It doesn't matter, though, because this woman is here to kill me."

"What?" Jennifer and Elaine said in unison, both bewildered by the accusation.

Singling Jennifer out with her free hand, Trillia said, "She is probably Jake's new girlfriend and he sent her to kill me, like he sent that asshole last night to my house."

Jennifer remained seated, stupefied by the chain of revelations playing out in front of her. She recalled speaking to a pastor at a crime scene and he explained the meaning of life as follows: "There are moments in every person's life," he had begun, "when the heavenly skies open up and a ray of sunshine shines down so brightly as to change one's world in an instant. This could be the acceptance of a marriage proposal, the news of a pregnancy, the sudden loss of a loved one, winning the lottery or losing a job. In every case, the individual knows that from that split second forward, their lives have been altered forever."

This is my time, Jennifer surmised. *Every choice I've ever made as a journalist has come to this. Now if only I can survive it.*

Jennifer looked at Elaine. "Please do as Trillia wants and call 911. Ask that a Detective Speers come to the house right away."

"Don't!" Trillia screamed at Elaine. "It's a trick of some kind."

Jennifer stayed focused on Elaine. "Tell the operator Jennifer Malone from *The Daily Telegraph* newspaper barged in uninvited and won't leave. Feel free to add that you think I planned the attack on Trillia last night, and give both addresses."

Elaine was again frightened. "Why would Jake send a thug to hurt you, Trillia? Did he break up with you or did you break it off with him?" As she said this she realized it was irreverent who had ended the relationship. "He's a travelling salesman. How hard could it be for him to find another woman in a town far away from here and just move on with his life? Or is that what happened?"

Jennifer was watching Trillia, who resembled a deer in the headlights. *Jake is no travelling salesman.* "I don't know anything about this Jake person, Trillia. Maybe he's from Helga's in-laws' side and they haven't met yet. Families are funny that way. My father told me he had a shifty cousin twice removed—once forcibly." Jennifer waited for the women to get the joke, although neither did. *Tough crowd.*

The comedy may not have registered, but Jennifer could see some areas of Trillia's stern face relax. "I didn't consider that," Trillia said, lowering the bookend to her hip.

Sensing her opportunity, Jennifer pounced. "Trillia, are you telling me convicted murderer Jake Wagner is your ex-boyfriend and he asked you to send Helga Klemens flowers at the hospital?"

I can't be any clearer than that, can I? Jennifer thought. *The moment of truth arrives . . . now.*

The verbal combination figuratively dazed Trillia, who was unable to move or speak. And like a wayward punch that inadvertently knocks out the referee in a boxing match, Elaine was also left spellbound, but not speechless.

"That monster who killed his wife?" she asked Trillia, whose entire body shook for an instant. "The one from that TV trial? He's your dreamy boyfriend? What is wrong with you?"

I didn't see that coming, Jennifer admitted to herself, moving her head side to side to watch the match unfold.

Trillia returned the heavy bookend to the shelf and wandered to the couch to sit, mumbling, "I wasn't thinking. I was lonely."

Been there, done that, Jennifer thought.

"Trillia!" Elaine cried out as she went to the couch to comfort her friend. "Why didn't you tell me? You don't need to be dating murderers to be happy."

Note to self: Relate that dating gem to Cassie for her Ms. Love column, Jennifer thought. She continued to be enthralled at the sight of the two grown sorority sisters hugging each other, as if finally confronting the fact that the popular quarterback was nailing the head cheerleader. While in college Jennifer had witnessed such a scene, finding it pathetic then and even more so today, when one considered the jerk boyfriend had arranged to have the pompom queen killed in cold blood as she begged for her life. Realizing that her two questions to Trillia had, in principle, been answered in the affirmative, it was time to bitch slap these two losers back to reality.

"Trillia," Jennifer said in a strong clear voice as she stood from the kitchen table and positioned herself closer to the front door. "How do you know your attacker was sent by Jake? For reasons too complicated to get into, I need to know the answer before another innocent woman is attacked," Jennifer said, feeling that some melodrama of her own was fitting.

Trillia looked up, her mascara running like the saddest clown on the planet, and replied in a unexpectedly steady tone, "He told me."

"What did he say?" Elaine wanted to know, taking over the reporter role.

The horror of the attack poured into Trillia's mind: the appearance of a man on the porch; the confrontation; the threats; the counter attack; the duct tape; the police; the shooting. Like a victim of abuse, she'd buried most of the actual conversation she'd had. Now confronted to bring it out into the light, she did so in a burst of tears and horror.

"I asked him, 'Did Jake send you here?' and he laughed at me, going, 'Ding, ding, ding – winner, winner, chicken dinner!'"

"Okay ... and did he say anything else or mention any other people?" Jennifer asked, hoping Dr. Richmond or Jimmy or Henrik might have made a virtual visit to the scare party.

"He didn't — the man who attacked me, Colin somebody — but the man on the telephone did," Trillia said.

The hits keep on coming. "What man and what phone call?"

"After I'd tied him up with duct tape, this Colin's cell phone started to vibrate and I answered it, but didn't say a word. So like a second later, this young guy says, 'Stop foolin' around. Clive wants an update and he's already called me three times!'"

"And what did you say?" Elaine pleaded.

"Nothing," Trillia answered. "I hung up."

"Clive?" Jennifer asked, concluding it had to be Clive Hill from The Men. "Had you ever heard that name before?"

Trillia turned her full attention to Jennifer, who had taken a step toward her. There was something in the woman's manner that gave the indication she was trying to help. "I don't know anyone named Clive."

"What about the caller? Did you recognize his voice?" Jennifer followed up.

"No, but the caller I.D. came up as James–"

"Hughes?" Jennifer finished Trillia's sentence.

Astonished, Trillia replied, "Yes, that was it."

Jennifer reached for her cell phone and called Detective Speers. "Do you still have James Hughes in custody?" she asked, feeling lightheaded by the time he picked up.

"I'm about to go in and talk to him," Speers answered. "Apparently, some expensive lawyer from Vincent Palanovich's office is on his way here too. For a lowly housekeeper, this Jimmy character knows people in high places."

"Don't go in yet," Jennifer implored. "You first need to contact the officers from a shooting last night at 160 Lemon Tree Street, and go through the attacker's cell phone."

"You've got my full attention, Miss Malone."

"Before he was killed he received a phone call from James Hughes — at least that was the name associated with the number on the caller I.D."

"And where did you get this information?"

"From Trillia Johnson, the brave woman who was attacked and answered the phone. I'm with her ... as you should be in twenty minutes. Come to the front door of her neighbour's house at 162 Lemon Tree Street and I'll let you in."

"Anything else?"

"Did I mention that Jimmy brought up the name Clive Hill during his brief phone chat?"

***

As they waited for Detective Speers, Jennifer spoke with Trillia and, by extension, Elaine. Aside from the whacked-out doomed love relationship angle, the most intriguing aspect of the interview for Jennifer was Elaine's changed attitude. She'd gone from the initial correct *How could you date a murderer?* outrage, to the more wounded incorrect *I don't know if we can still be friends, Trillia, because you didn't tell me the truth,* outlook on life.

This is why I have no close girlfriends, Jennifer thought.

When the knock on the front door occurred, Jennifer answered it, finding Detective Speers and the police supervisor from the previous evening on the porch.

"What — no flowers or chocolate?" Jennifer asked with a smile. "Usually when I reveal this much to a man, it's after a costly dinner and a few drinks."

Both officers smiled widely.

"I'll check my expense account when I get back to the station and give you a call. How does that sound?" Detective Speers said, as they were led to the living room, where Trillia and Elaine remained on the couch.

"It sounds fabulous," Jennifer said, reaching for her purse. "I'll let you four get acquainted. I think I have enough to write the first draft of my story."

"Write all you want," Detective Speers told Jennifer, "remembering everything at the hospital is still off the record."

"Duly noted. Don't worry, I'll be getting a more detailed update from you later today," Jennifer said, heading for the door. Turning to Trillia and Elaine she said, "Thank you for your assistance. Sorry my visit started on such a bad note. With these two distinguished gentlemen, though, it's going to end on a high note for everyone ... except for Jimmy and Clive."

The group smiled at the comment, except for Trillia, who was lost in her own thoughts. She was the one who was sorry for threatening Jennifer with that bookend. She was the one who started the whole mess with her lovelorn messages to a convicted murderer. Once Jennifer explained how the carnation delivery fit into Helga's timeline at the hospital — *How could I have been so stupid not to connect the name of Jake's aunt to Kaye Wagner's grandmother?* — she was depressed that she'd likely caused the woman a great deal of emotional pain as she waited for her hip surgery.

Watching Jennifer reach for the front door handle, a new round of emotions swept over her involving Jake, Kaye and Helga.

"Jennifer," Trillia said abruptly, stopping the reporter in her tracks. "The attacker told me one other thing about Jake that didn't make sense. He was trying to calm me down and said, 'If it eases your mind any, he wasn't going to kill you like he did his wife and brother.' Do you know what that could mean? Did Jake murder his brother too? I didn't know he had a brother. They never mentioned one during the trial."

In another moment of clarity, Jennifer knew Jake Wagner had a brother and where he was hiding out: the Met Hospital morgue.

Hello, John Doe #1.

Jennifer made her way to the kitchen table where she sat to watch the lawmen interview Trillia, and her soon-to-be-former best friend, Elaine. Knowing Mitch would be nearly bald from tearing his hair out waiting for an update, Jennifer sent him a quick message in the style of an old time telegram:

> Mitch. Stop. Clear paper's top fold for next three days. Stop. Inform web geeks of upcoming internet breakage possibilities. Stop. Five little words. Stop. Pulitzer Prize for Investigative Reporting. Stop. Can't stop smiling. Stop.

FORTY

THURSDAY

As with any wild animal that finds itself cornered, James (Jimmy) Hughes had two options: take the rap for his involvement in killing Helga Klemens, Henrik Dekker and Benny Wagner, or sing like a prized canary. He also didn't need Detective Speers to state the obvious that Clive Hill and Dr. Martin Richmond would turn on him to save their own skins.

"Let's talk," Jimmy said calmly, after being confronted with the hospital video evidence and caller I.D. information from Colin's cell phone.

In short order, Clive Hill was arrested at Davey's Den, around the same time Dr. Richmond was attempting to board a private plane wearing a fake moustache. Inside his carry-on bag and taped to his body were stacks of cash totalling $50,000. As the police put him into a waiting cruiser, Dr. Richmond was heard saying, "My lawyer is Vincent Palanovich and I'll be back here at the airport in a few hours!" Contacted later in the day, Vincent Palanovich stated that he'd never met Dr. Richmond and didn't know anyone by the name of James Hughes. "I can confirm that I've been retained by Clive Hill, an outstanding entrepreneur with deep ties to the community, to vigorously fight the ludicrous charges laid against him by the city police. In addition, we're considering libel action against Jennifer Malone of *The Daily Telegraph* newspaper for slander and defamation of character, for her misrepresentation of Clive Hill's business dealings and his character in a recent series of articles."

"Ha — the paper's lawyers will love to hear that," Jennifer said, watching the news conference in Mitch's office.

"Don't worry about them," Mitch said with a wide smile. "Vincent just gave us hundreds of thousands of dollars of free publicity that'll help curb any legal costs – not that he has a leg to stand on."

With the enthusiasm of a pack of wolves thrown fresh meat, the *Justice For All*'s panel continued its wall-to-wall reporting, covering the arrests and Jennifer's role in solving three murders.

"Have you decided when you're going to appear on one of their shows?" Mitch asked, as a commercial for erectile dysfunction popped up on the screen.

"So far, I am only scheduled as a guest on *The Nation Today* Monday morning," Jennifer replied with a shrug. "My old friend, Susan Donallee, is cutting her vacation short to interview me."

"Isn't that special," Mitch laughed. "She's a bigger media whore than the amateurs on this station. They look like recent graduates of an internet-based school of journalism."

"They do appear to be wet behind the ears," Jennifer commented. "As for your assessment of Susan ... if you dropped the 'media' part you'd also be correct, if memory serves."

Mitch laughed again. "Isn't she on her third husband?"

"That isn't the problem. It's being caught with other women's husbands that's at the core of her relationship issues."

Mitch shifted in his chair. "Speaking of relationships ... Cassie told me you have an upcoming date with a paramedic named Patrick."

"One, Cassie has a big mouth," Jennifer said. "And two, he's just a guy. I already had to cancel one date because of this *Met vs. Men* story. I think I'll always be married to my job first and foremost."

Mitch got up and walked to the door. Looking out into the bullpen he noted that the entire staff was congregated near a TV switched to the *Justice For All* channel. He quietly closed the door and took a seat next to Jennifer on the couch.

"I'm going to impart this wisdom to you only once, Jennifer, so listen carefully," Mitch began, getting her full attention. "This career will bleed you dry before you know you're cut. The newspaper business is like a runaway train. A great story like this one," he said, pointing to the television screen, "careens down the tracks at a speed too fast to safely make the turn up ahead at the edge of a cliff. The feeling of exhilaration, the motion of the train, the level of danger is omnipresent, and it's a sensation few experience in their lives. But you've been on this ride before and came out the other side in one piece ... only to climb aboard the next crazy train, as soon as the ink dries on your latest story."

"Are you firing me, Mitch, or is this your attempt to save my soul from the evils of my chosen career field?"

"The board upstairs would fire me before they'd let you go," Mitch replied.

"So what you're trying to say is that the job shouldn't be my whole life?"

"Yes. From experience, it's not worth it," Mitch admitted. "At this point in your career, you can basically write your own ticket in this industry. What you did as a reporter in the past week ranks with Woodward and Bernstein's two years' worth of reporting to bring down Nixon. You're that good, Malone. Trust me on this. And as much as I'd hate to see you leave, my fatherly advice is that when this hoopla is over go on vacation. Take this Patrick guy, if he can get the time off, and decide what you want to do with the rest of your life, instead of this job deciding it for you."

Jennifer didn't know how to reply, only saying, "Thanks, 'Dad,'" as she leaned against Mitch's shoulder.

They watched another half hour of rehashed *The Murder At Met* coverage before Mitch said he had work to do. "Do I have everything I need for tomorrow's edition?"

"Almost," Jennifer said, standing and stretching her arms above her head. "I'll send a new piece after Helga's funeral."

"I forgot about that."

"I wish it were a conventional funeral for Helga's sake, but when *Justice For All* offered to pay the expenses and broadcast it live, her distant relatives jumped at the opportunity – either to avoid the cost or seek their fifteen minutes of fame," Jennifer said sombrely. "Thankfully, Helga's neighbour Glenn persuaded the TV people to stay away from the church for the visitation period, to only show the actual service, and not the internment service at the cemetery. From what I heard from Detective Speers, the Greenheart Station Police will be out in full force ensuring the mourners won't be harassed in any way during the services."

"As it should be," Mitch agreed. "Send me what you've got by 10:00."

"I will," Jennifer replied, walking to her desk to grab her purse.

On the big screen TV, pictures of Helga were being shown; wedding shots, birthday parties, as a young woman, as a new mother. With the family's permission, the images were released to the media by Glenn. "Helga Klemens was one of the finest women I've ever met and these photographs are how she should be remembered," he stated with tears in his eyes.

While waiting for the elevator doors to open, a new male reporter Jennifer had met once in passing, asked, "How do you like your new parking spot in the garage?"

"It might be the best perk I've ever had as a reporter," she stated with a wide smile, entering the elevator. "That and getting paid for doing something I love to do. What more could a girl want?"

***

Jennifer was thankful for how peaceful it felt inside Helga's church, in spite of the circus outside on the streets. In a brilliant move, Glenn had organized Greenheart Station senior citizens to serve as gatekeepers, ensuring that only residents and known friends of Helga gained entry, much to the media's dismay. In fact, besides two TV camera operators, Jennifer, and a reporter named Ron from the local paper, were the sole journalists admitted inside. Glenn had arranged to have them sit in his usual back pew, alongside Luke and Maryanne, the other invited guests.

"How are you two doing?" Jennifer asked, knowing they'd become overnight press darlings. She had continuously updated them on what was going to be printed, but this was their first time together in several days.

"We're on leave from the hospital," Luke said, "orders of the CEO."

"And we're getting paid," Maryanne added. "Plus, I've got job offers from five news organizations."

"I hope you're going to take Mitch's offer and work with me," Jennifer responded, excited by the prospect of shaping a fresh mind into an award winning reporter.

"That's a no brainer, although I admit I do like the attention."

"And what about you, Luke?"

"Maryanne can have the spotlight. I'm just enjoying the time off and reading a lot of books these days," Luke answered.

Glenn arrived and sat next to Jennifer. "Hi, Jennifer. Hi, Ron," he said to the reporters. "Thank you for coming."

"It's our pleasure," Ron said, moving his camera bag to the floor to give them more room on the pew.

The organist started to play and the minister walked up the aisle, trailed by two men guiding Helga's casket, with Genifer Grant keeping step behind them. As they made their way to the front of the church, Jennifer remarked to Glenn, "I wasn't sure if Genifer would come."

Glenn continued to look forward, a grin on his lips. "She has a very special message to give today."

Jennifer had never witnessed a funeral service held in a church. Any she'd gone to were performed inside a funeral home. Due to the number of expected attendees, she guessed a bigger venue was required.

The minister opened the service by reading an appropriate passage from Psalm 34.

"The Lord is close to the broken hearted and saves those who are crushed in spirit. The righteous person may have many troubles, but the Lord delivers him from them all." He paused and then went on, *"He protects all his bones, not one of them will be broken. Evil will slay the wicked; the foes of the righteous will be condemned."*

Tears fell down the weary faces of many in attendance as the minister proclaimed how Helga's passing would not only affect their lives, but also those who'd never have the opportunity to meet her in the future. After the singing of Helga's favourite hymn, it was Genifer Grant's turn to stand at the podium.

Clearly emotional, Genifer clutched a handful of tissue in one hand, as she opened a small book with her other.

"What is that?" Jennifer asked Glenn, thinking the unfamiliar book had some kind of religious connection.

"Helga's travel diary," he replied softly. "I found it when I was looking for her phone book. Genifer wanted to read a passage from it and the family approved ... with my urging, of course."

There was an expression of pure joy and love on the old man's face as Genifer began to speak.

"For most of you here, Helga was always a good friend or reliable coworker or devoted church goer. From talking to many of you, I've learned from a tender age right through to her golden years, Helga was an outspoken, devoted woman, but also a loving wife, mother and grandmother." Genifer stopped and looked out over the crowd to find Glenn in the back row. "As well as a great neighbour."

Jennifer gently held Glenn's hand in hers, which he lightly squeezed.

"What you might not be aware of is that Helga was an explorer, travelling to the far reaches of the world to experience cultures so different from ours here in little Greenheart Station." Genifer saw several people smile and nod their heads. "Thankfully, for those who didn't accompany her on these excursions, she left behind a travelogue that detailed the sights, sounds, smells and adventures from every trip." Genifer held up the book in her hand. "I would like to read for you an excerpt from a trip Helga took a few years ago. I believe it'll give us a better appreciation of who this wonderful woman was and where she came from."

Genifer repositioned the book on the pulpit and began to read in a softer tone, as she attempted to channel Helga's emotions.

Visiting the City of Linares in the south of Spain is like stepping back in time. Its wonderful atmosphere and Old World values is embodied in the shops I entered, and within the hearts of every resident I encountered during a brief stopover enroute to Madrid. In a picture shop, I saw a framed photo that spoke to me, as if it had been waiting for me; a long-lost friend, again found. The salesman told me the local photographer was a young man named Miguel Ángel Avi García, who took lovely, moving images of landscapes from all around the province. "Why does this one picture intrigue you, Señora?" He then pointed to similar striking photographs by the same artist. "I can't quite explain, but this chair with three legs reminds me of one owned by my family," I answered him. "You see, when I was ten years old my parents sent my older brother and me from our home in Berlin, Germany to North America. They wanted to protect us from the coming war. Both my mother and father were caught up in violent demonstrations and died shortly afterwards, or so we were led to believe. My brother, who was sixteen, returned to avenge their deaths for the Fatherland, leaving me alone in a new world, living with other lost children in an orphanage, to fight for myself every step of the way." The salesman looked closer at the framed photo. "So, this chair with its ripped backing represents … what?" I could tell he was totally mystified by my story. "Not the chair — the missing leg. That's what caught my eye. The one thing not present is the most significant part of the picture, because it symbolizes me. The other legs are stand-ins for my parents and brother who decided to weather the elements of a changing world, while I was away making a life for myself." I remember taking a step closer to the frame, to admire the detail of the cloth upholstery flapping in an unseen wind through the desolate forest behind it. "Where was this taken?" I asked. "Just outside of the city where they used to mine lead and silver. The chair is sitting on the edge of a mineral washery that closed in 1969," came the answer. "Are there any mines still in operation?" The man said, "No, the entire area is deserted." The chair continued to fascinate me. "Why on earth would someone place a chair in the middle of nowhere to disintegrate over time like that?" The salesman said, "Maybe the chair hasn't been discarded. Maybe it's waiting for some handyman to see its beauty and replace the missing leg, making it whole." It was then I realized why the photo had so impacted my soul: After years of feeling abandoned, I now believed that upon my death I would be reunited with my parents and my brother, and yes, we would be whole once again.

Genifer stopped and gently closed Helga's travelogue. Glancing at the pastor, she said, "I hope your heavenly handyman has granted Helga and her loved ones to sit at His table to get reacquainted after all these years."

"I'm positive He has, Genifer," the pastor responded, standing and giving her a hug. Turning her toward the gathered mourners, he said, "Can I get an Amen?"

And the church was filled with the unified sound of that single word, which was a cue for the organist to start playing.

The following half hour was a simple celebration of Helga's life and how God's love touches everyone. As the pastor concluded the service, Jennifer squeezed Glenn's hand and whispered, "Helga's in every smile and tear shed here today, and she's thanking you from above for such a beautiful farewell, my old friend. No one is ever going to forget this service."

Glenn flashed his humble smile. "I think I did too well. I'm not sure how my kids can top this send-off. Can you promise me that you'll see they at least try, Jennifer?"

"I'll do my best," Jennifer replied, "but that's years from now, right?" she asked, as they stood to watch Helga's casket pass into the church's vestibule.

"Yes, many years from now, that's the plan!" Glenn said happily.

Glenn stepped into the aisle to follow Helga's casket outside, where he helped place it into the hearse.

From the church steps, Jennifer watched Glenn and longed for the love and respect he'd shown for Helga time and again. Seeing Luke and Maryanne exit the church hand in hand did nothing to sidetrack her thoughts.

Could Patrick be my Glenn or Luke? she imagined optimistically. *A girl can dream.*

EPILOGUE

MONDAY

Jennifer went from her successful *The Nation Today* appearance back to the *Telegraph* offices, where she received a standing ovation from her colleagues when she stepped out of the elevator.

"Great interview!"

"You were fabulous!"

"The camera and Susan Donallee love you!"

Jennifer was enjoying the ongoing accolades when Mitch stepped out of his office and said, "Did you hear they arrested Clive Hill's right-hand man — John whatshisname — the accountant?"

"For what?" Jennifer replied, continuing to her desk, blowing kisses to her fans like she was a star on the red carpet.

"They're saying some false tax filing for The Men organization, but I'm guessing that's only the beginning of his problems," Mitch concluded. "Funny thing is his wife, Beth, was interviewed and she said that nothing at Davey's Den will change. Quote: 'It'll be business as usual now that I'm in charge.' Unquote."

"She's the one who served dinner to Luke and me. Wow — talk about breaking the glass ceiling. You go, girl!" Jennifer said with a laugh. "I don't plan on being in the same space as her ever again, just sayin'. Assign it to Rich Simpson. I owe him one."

"I'll check his schedule," Mitch said. "He might be too valuable to *our* organization to send him into danger like that." He appraised the reporters still milling about. "Hey, Newbie!" The young man who'd asked Jennifer about her parking spot looked over to the editor.

"Me?" he asked eagerly.

"Yes, you. Little Miss Rock Star Reporter here needs some additional information from the recently self-appointed boss down at Davey's Den. Can you handle that?"

"Ah ... right away, Mr. Carson," he stammered, nabbing a sports jacket off the back of his desk chair.

"Slow down and sit down," Mitch ordered. "Malone will give you the details when she's good and ready."

Jennifer held up both hands, indicating she'd be with him in ten minutes. This made him smile from ear to ear.

Until Maryanne comes on board, Skippy, you're my project, she thought.

"Can you tap out a blurb about your NCN interview for the website guys?" Mitch asked Jennifer.

"I'm a blogger now?"

"You're a writer. Be thankful you have a job," he said with a grin. "Feel free to mention how tanned the host looked against the white backdrop." Mitch turned and re-entered his office without saying another word — his way of getting her back for the numerous times she'd rudely hung up on him.

Entertained by Mitch's antics, Jennifer sat at her desk and opened a blank document on her computer. "Where to begin?" she said to herself, deciding to title the piece, "When Print Meets TV." As she typed the byline her phone rang. "Jennifer Malone's desk. How can I direct your call?"

"Am I speaking to Jennifer Malone, the reporter?"

The young woman's voice did sound familiar. "I suppose it would depend on who I'm talking with," Jennifer answered, taking out her notebook.

"I saw your appearance on TV a little while ago," the woman answered, not stating her identity. "I love your writing and can't believe you solved those murders on your own."

"Thank you for the compliments, but I don't really have time to chat."

"I'm sorry," the woman apologized. "The reason I'm calling is that I'd like you to interview me."

Jennifer was getting annoyed, yet maintained a professional tone. "Again, I'm still working on the story that's getting all the publicity these days ... and have a few others that need my attention. Why don't I transfer you to—"

"I'm confused."

Yes, you are.

"I thought that I was one of the stories you were working on," the caller continued. "At least that's the impression you gave our mutual friend last week."

Stymied, Jennifer asked, "What's our mutual friend's name?"

"Carlton. He's the doorman here at The Bella Vista Hotel & Spa," the woman replied. "My name is Becky Mayville and I'd like to give you an exclusive interview about my relationship with Councilman Roger Tilley. Do you have time to hear my story or should I call Mark Orr at *The Star* to see if he's not so busy."

Jennifer began to laugh. "It's an honour to talk with you, Becky. As for Mark Orr ... he's a hack who works at *The Star* because *The Daily Telegraph* has high standards for its reporters. Trust me, you've got the right girl on the right day at the right time."

"I thought so."

"I could be out there at 11:00. How's that?" Jennifer inquired, already packing her notebook in her purse and closing off the computer page.

"Carlton will bring you up."

"All right then. See you shortly."

Jennifer walked into Mitch's office. "FYI – the blog piece is on hold. I've got a lead on Hot Beckster's whereabouts and need to check it out."

"Are you joking?" Mitch asked. "My heart can't take much more excitement!"

"I promise I'll update you in a few hours, Mitch," Jennifer said, exiting the office. She stopped and faced her boss. "By chance do the bean counters authorize expenses like seaweed body wraps, hot rock massages, facials and manicures?"

Mitch's face went blank. "How would I know?"

"I guess you wouldn't, would you. It's a girlie thing. I'll ask Cassie." Jennifer gave Mitch a wave.

"You're going for a massage?" Mitch cried out in disbelief, following Jennifer into the hallway.

"Only after the seaweed wrap detoxifies and purifies my skin," Jennifer called to him, opting to take the stairs instead of waiting for the elevator. "Don't worry, Mitch, I know what I'm doing."

"Malone, get back here!" Mitch demanded, as the stairwell door shut. Glancing quickly at the assembled staff, he noticed the new reporter with his hand in the air. "This isn't a classroom. What is it?"

"Jennifer ... I mean, Miss Malone, left," the nervous reporter replied, "without talking to me about my assignment. Is she coming back soon?"

"Your guess is as good as mine. Stay there and don't move until she decides to grace us with her presence again." Mitch entered his office and closed his door. "Honestly, that woman is trying to kill me."

***

Before exiting the parking garage, Jennifer returned a call from Patrick she'd missed while at the television station earlier. "Did I look and sound all right? I swear the woman who put on my foundation to reduce glare from the studio lights used a putty knife."

"You looked and sounded fantastic," Patrick said. "Are you heading into the office?"

"No," Jennifer said, "I was there for five minutes and am now heading to a ritzy hotel way out in Chester Hills for an interview."

"Oh … okay," Patrick said, sounding disappointed by this news. "So … are you calling to reschedule our date tonight? I can cancel our reservations at Fetta Trattoria, if you have to work. It's no big deal."

Jennifer was certain if she rescheduled it would be a big deal. The scope and magnitude of the *Murder At The Met* story had already overridden any social plans they might have made, and to his credit, Patrick completely understood this part of her life. Plus, they had spoken on the phone over the weekend, as Jennifer needed to talk to anyone outside of the newspaper as a way to de-stress. Big stories or breaking news would always have that effect on her personal life, yet Jennifer knew even the smallest stories often took precedent when it came to her relationships. The Becky Mayville/Councilman Tilley story would be a monster, but she wasn't going to let it interfere with her date.

I can do this, she thought, remembering Mitch's life coaching advice. "No, we're on for tonight," she said, feeling better already.

"Excellent," Patrick said enthusiastically. "I'll meet you there at seven thirty."

"Perfect," she replied. The brief silence that followed gave Jennifer's mind time to switch into its normal cynical mode to override what she was feeling in her heart. "What's your opinion of The Beatles?" she asked, unable to help herself.

The dead air felt like an eternity to Jennifer.

Just answer the question, Patrick!

"I'm more of a Bruce Springsteen and The E Street Band fan, but I guess The Beatles are pretty good too."

Pretty good too? Pretty good too?

"So ... to clarify, you do like The Beatles?"

"Really? Who doesn't like The Beatles?"

A smile bigger than the one she wore listening to Trillia describe her obsession with a convicted murderer spread across Jennifer's lips. "I know, right?" she replied. "See you soon and don't be late."

Patrick knew he had passed some kind of test and said, "Never for you, Jennifer."

Jennifer closed her eyes and inhaled the dry parking garage air, imagining she was on a beach watching the waves with Patrick in a bathing suit walking to her with a drink in each hand.

I could get used to that, she thought.

She started her car and heard Paul McCartney belting out *Can't Buy Me Love*, which caused her to break out in another grin. Driving into the mid-morning sunshine, she was glad she'd added a half-hour travel gap to get to the hotel, as cars were lined up for blocks due to road construction. She attempted to bypass the mess via other side streets, only to find that everyone else had the same idea. As she inched along each congested route, Jennifer realized how tired she was due to the early TV call time. Figuring caffeine might help with the drive and the subsequent meeting with Hot Beckster, she stopped at a convenience store for a cup of coffee. *Yawning may not go over too well during this interview.*

Returning to her car a few minutes later with the song *Ticket To Ride* bopping in her head, Jennifer's cell phone began to ring. She placed her coffee cup on the roof and looked at the caller I.D. display that showed an unfamiliar number. Hoping it was Patrick calling back on a coworker's phone, she answered it.

"Jennifer Malone here."

"Hey, Jennifer," a man's voice greeted her as if they were old high school friends. "My name is Steve Cassidy. I'm a private investigator, working on a case I hope you can help me solve. Do you have a minute to talk?"

THE END

Author's Note

Every story has its own unique beginning and *Abandoned* is no different.

During a random internet search six years ago, I stumbled across the stunning front cover picture – "Chair With Three Legs" – and saved it for future use, not having a clue where it may lead. For some reason, the image stayed with me for four more years. I did a little research and discovered the photographer, Miguel Ángel Avi García, lived in Spain. I contacted him and he agreed to allow me to use the picture for a novel I had yet to write.

With the cover now established my next task was to come up with a great story for reporter Jennifer Malone to investigate. This was proving to be a challenging assignment until one day the idea was presented to me while working as a patient transporter at a metropolitan hospital. For full details, you need only to read Chapter One of this book, focusing on the discussion between Luke the transporter and a senior citizen named Helga. Their interaction recreates one I had with another elderly patient, (who thankfully didn't suffer the same fate as poor Helga). I remember walking out of the O.R. waiting room thinking, "Don't let them kill me," would make an excellent opening line for a mystery novel. The rest of the story awaits in *Abandoned*.

I hope you enjoy this novel as much as I did writing it.

All the best!

John Schlarbaum
November 2017

Discussion Questions:

1. What is the significance of the title, *Abandoned*?

2. The author is male – do you feel he did a good job portraying a female main character?

3. Surprising plot turns often throw the readers' theories into disarray. What plot turn did that for you in this novel?

4. Was this truly a mystery or can the reader figure it out early on? Can an easily figured out mystery still be engaging and entertaining?

5. Was the ending satisfying? Did it seem like the culmination of clues laid out or did it come as a surprise?

6. What in the story stuck with you?

7. What characters did you love or hate?

8. Aside from the Helga hospital investigation, did you enjoy the other overlapping stories Jennifer was working on (i.e. the Becky Mayville scandal and John Does)?

9. Did you find Helga's funeral chapter a fitting conclusion to her / Glenn / Genifer's storyline?

10. If you found yourself in a similar situation as Genifer, what would you do? Who would you talk to? Have you ever experienced such a situation?

11. If you found yourself in a similar situation as Luke, what would you do? Who would you talk to?

12. While investigating, Jennifer often tells little white lies or holds back information from her interviewees and coworkers. Do you think she ever went over the line ethically trying to get answers to her questions?

13. How do you feel about Trillia's relationship with Jake Wagner? Did your attitude toward her change as her storyline unfolded?

14. How did you feel about Elaine's reaction to finding out that her best friend had kept a secret and outright lied to her? Do you think they'll remain friends? Have you had to deal with a similar situation with anyone in your life?

15. The author has worked as a patient transporter, as well as a private investigator. Did the information gathering scenes in the newspaper offices and events in the hospital feel authentic?

16. What is your opinion of The Beatles?

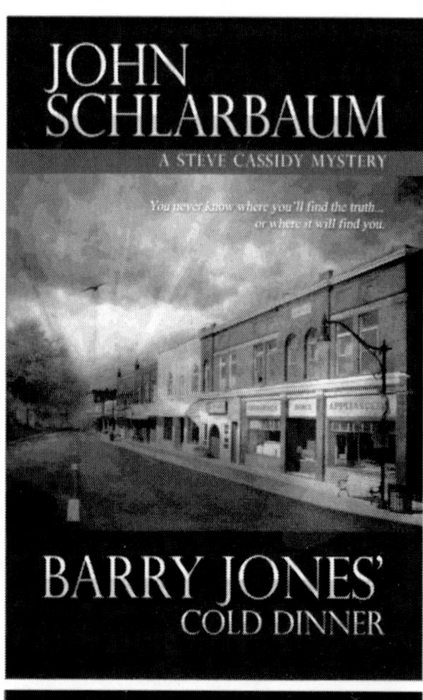

Also available in eBook.

For more information visit: **www.scannerpublishing.com**

Do you have a question, comment or review?

Contact the author!

"Author John Schlarbaum"

@jsmysterywriter

Email: john@scannerpublishing.com